the
iceweaver

Other books by Margaret Lawrence

Hearts and Bones
Blood Red Roses
The Burning Bride

. the iceweaver

MARGARET LAWRENCE

Perennial

An Imprint of HarperCollins*Publishers*

A hardcover edition of this book was published in 2000 by William Morrow, an imprint of HarperCollins Publishers.

First Perennial edition published 2001.

Designed by Kellan Peck

The Library of Congress has catalogued the hardcover edition as follows:

Lawrence, Margaret (Margaret K.)
    The iceweaver / Margaret Lawrence.— 1st ed.
        p.cm.
    ISBN 0-380-97621-8
        I. Title.

    PS3562.A9133 I28 2000
    813'.54—dc21   99-058661

ISBN 0-380-79613-9 (pbk.)

01 02 03 04 05 JT/RRD 10 9 8 7 6 5 4 3 2 1

Tell me about yourself now, simply, one thing at a time.
Who are you? Where do you come from? What parents? What place?
What manner of ship did you sail in? Why did the sailors abandon
  you here?

Homer, The Odyssey, *Book I, ll. 197–99*

. the
iceweaver

I

the bay of spirits

The sun is setting pale ivory, like the faces of old faded women. She watches it through webs of ice on the twigs of a quince bush in the garden, noting the minutiae of cloud-drift, the ragged flight of certain birds. On a broken bench with the paws of a lion she sits very still—a solitary girl not yet thirty, a little mad from her losses, caged since birth in reverberate silence.

A heroine from an old tale in which the blank pages speak loudest. A stone lady mourning her dead.

Her body begins to sway back and forth on the bench, moving to the memory of some secret vibrance that passes over her in waves, like the wind over meadow grass. It lives in the sheer fabric of pale skin pulled tight between her thin, straight nose and the cheekbones that rise, winglike, towards her temples. In the small bones of her back that align themselves in a perfect right angle with the stone slab where she sits. In the delicate soles of her feet. Naked in summer, these vulnerable instruments hear not only music but fire, distant laughter, the footfalls of animals, the approach of summer storms.

She will never feel music again. All afternoon, she has been taking her leave of such small, keen, human pleasures, and this is the last of them. When it is gone, she will have purged herself of the future.

To be free of the past is another matter. She is thinking now of a certain night when she danced, a mathematical sequence of steps her father taught her in childhood, as he taught her to pick out simple tunes on the spinet—the purest kind of music, to which the ear is superfluous. As she moved to these geometries, the pale blue silk of her gown stroked the skin of her shoulders and her body gave up a soft scent of herbs from the cornflour powder she wore. The fragrance of dancing, that is how she remembers it. Rosemary. Lemon balm. Monarda leaves, crushed. They were kept in a small bag of fine lace buried deep in the powder box, to perfume without trace.

It is how she conceives of the rest of her life. To walk through the world without footsteps. To live by geometry, giving nothing away, requiring nothing. To dissolve like the fragrance of powder or soap.

She does not bother to wash now, does not own a comb for her hair, which is the color of sumac leaves after an early frost. When she is hungry enough to remember her body, she steals a few potatoes from an unguarded root cellar or an egg to drink raw, straight out of the shell. She is a talented thief, but the scraps are scant use to her. She is almost breastless, thin as a twist of rope.

She has other warrens to hide in, but only this derelict house at the edge of the wide lake sustains her. Where looters have ripped the old boards apart looking for treasure, certain angles of house wall expose the elegant bones of neoclassical structure, a perfect dream of balance in whose ruin she finds rest. In the sloping garden, the stump of a column stands tangled in creeper, at its pediment three marble fingers of startling purity, the hand long since crumbled away.

Along this cove bedded in balsam fir and black spruce and maples, she has stumbled upon an older world oddly at peace with its failures. There is nothing between God and her scorn but the dark fold of Lion's Tooth to the eastward, already huddled in fog.

There are three mountains above the Bay of Spirits. Lion's

Tooth. Old Dog. White Lady. Except for these three and the frozen plain of the wooded lake at the foot of the blackened house, the universe is hollow as a cracked cup.

It is six days past the beginning of January, the year 1809.

The soldiers patrolling for smugglers and embargo breakers are nearly out of sight now, specks of gaudy blue and red and buff fading away to the north, where the lake touches Canada. A half-mile up the cove, at the dead end of the Albany turnpike, a dozen dry-docked flatboats make humps like stranded whales under twenty inches of snow. No one can go west now; until the breakup of ice in mid-April, they can do no more than dream of it. Even the tavern road from the smug little town is quiet.

Aside from the exile, the dark man leading a pack mule, and a lamed grey mare, there are no ghosts on the lake.

The daylight is going, a candlewick drowning in tallow. The girl straightens her back, pulls her boots free of the layers of snow-sodden skirts, and goes to kneel beside her dead at the edge of the lake. She has hauled the body here and kept it almost a fortnight in the deep cold of the abandoned mansion, unable to surrender it. For a moment, she bends over to press her face against the cold woolen patches of the old quilt it is wrapped in, making the tying-knots scratch her as she did in her childhood.

But there is no human scent left in it now, and no memory, only the sour smell of lye from the homemade soap she stole to wash the graveclothes. She ties a long strap to the leather thongs binding the wrappings, winds the end four or five times round her arm, takes up the ax she has stolen, and drags her mother's body out onto the lake.

The man sees her emerge from the fog more than a mile away and takes her for an animal crossing the ice. With the burden behind her, she moves clumsily, waddling like a black bear and hunched down to the weight of what she drags. Where she stops, a wedge of pearlescent light cuts the clouds and slants suddenly onto her, and for a moment she is spectral, something he remembers from medicine dreams in the long months during which he was traded like a talisman from village to village in the vast western country.

Then he sees her let go of the burden and move her arms up and down, warming herself. She is not a dream after all, she is suddenly human and brittle, a little absurd. She is not the faithless

English wife, Hester, that he left here. She is not even, God help her, a black bear.

John Frayne laughs softly at himself, and the long raw scar down his cheekbone shoots pain behind his eyes. For a moment it blinds him and he growls under his breath, his fingers knotted in the mane of the grey. In the palms of his hands there are holes, some time healed, as though nails have been driven into them and then pulled out again.

He does not often remember precisely how he came by these wounds, who inflicted them. For a long time in the west, he believed himself dead. He lay naked, discarded in the hollow of a bank of wild plum beside a creek, a great gouge from some blade in his chest. Bees buzzed among the plum blossoms, stinging him at random till his body was swollen, hard and tight as the shell of a locust. The trees were a cage his wounds would not let him escape—the new-set globes of green fruit, the sharp spikes along the branches. Heavy syrup scent of the blossoms, honey and licorice and cassis, perhaps coriander, the air liquid with it, bearing him up. His mind was stripped clean of itself, wandering backwards, bleeding away.

Then hands touched him, lifted him, coaxed his bee-stung eyelids open. Tribesmen dressed for some festival, brightly painted, small bits of silver metal twisted in the fringes of their shirts and jingling as they walked. Osage. Maha. Mandan. Ponca. Pawnee, with their faces painted black. Some other tribe, never known to the palterings of history. There were no maps of their countries; for months he had drifted unchallenged from one to the other— writing, sketching, thinking, trading now and then for beaver pelts, observing and mapping the landscape. Wherever he was, it was not yet America; perhaps it would never be, perhaps it would always remain unpossessable. Freed by this cleansing thought, he had invented the world as he found it, collecting roots and wildflowers and the stems of certain grasses, to which he gave names as he chose.

Devil's pitchfork. Heartsburden. Spirit grass.

An old man with no eyes who leaned on a shepherd's crook tied with owls' feathers bent near to Frayne's battered body, rubbing the leaves of this strange grass on his left breast, his forehead, his lips. The heart, the brain, the voice. The houses of the soul. It was a holy plant, to anoint him for the journey of death. The fine blades were hairy and tasted of mint, like cold water.

They laid a piece of white bone against his lips, and he kissed it, an icon. An eagle's feather to give wings to his soul. The claw of a bear to give strength for the passage.

Someone was playing a cedarwood flute. The tune might have been Egyptian, Greek, Turkish, even Celtic. He had fallen from the sky into some other universe, some other, more gracious millennium.

Of what tribe are you? the old man said. What are you called?

His eyelids had been stitched down and dyed crimson, long streaks of paint like black tears down his cheeks. His mouth was broad and soft, and his hands moved gently across Frayne's body.

Is it true you are pale, like the moon?

The blind man spoke the hand language common to tribesmen, and beside him a young boy waited to interpret John Frayne's reply into words. But he could not answer. The wounds in his palms and his chest had been stanched with spiderwebs and bound in plantain leaves, then both wrists tied down at his sides for safekeeping. There were leaves on his face, too, where the flesh had been sliced to the bone.

I have enemies, he said in useless English. Devils. He could not have said who these enemies were, nor did he fear them. He had surrendered even his fear.

The tribesmen carried him to a broad valley and lowered him into cool water to take down the swelling from the bee stings. There was a current moving through it, waking the surface of his skin and making his sleeping penis rise, hopeful and cruel. The water seeped into his wounds and made him liquid, tidal, so that the essence of him seemed to flow into the world. A woman came to him, wading naked into the water, and gave him her breast to suckle. He had had no food in many days, and her milk was rich, tasting faintly of fruit.

I killed my father, he told her. It was a truth that had driven John Frayne since the age of four, inciting many failures, many small deaths and hopeless escapes from circumstances that might, in time, have absolved him in his own eyes. I killed my father, he said again to the woman. I will defile you.

But she did not take her milk away. Four times a day he was fed so. They put him into a hollowed-out cottonwood log, like a coffin, and floated him downstream as they travelled, shading him with a deerskin stretched tight over withes. At night the wise man sat beside him, telling stories in his own language, a thin murmur like the trickle of water from rocks. Frayne's hands grew well enough to use, still awkward but capable of simple responses, and slowly he learned how to speak with them fluently. The sweet-limbed young boy was always there, always speaking between them with his soft, girlish voice, passing the strange words to the old man like nourishing food from his mouth.

Sometimes Frayne could see long lines of fire snaking far away in the blank prairie darkness, as though many stars had crashed down and were burning away. Light was holy to this nation. At night they pulled back the deerskin covering to let the moon find him and he lay naked and helpless, his fair skin reflecting the cool bluish glow. They had never seen white skin before, and one by one they came to look down at him, touching him gently. Someone stroked his sex alive and two women collected his semen in a leather cup.

Saku, they called him, their name for the sun.

Are you a god? the old man asked.

I have many wounds, Frayne replied.

The soft hands danced and tangled above him, weaving invisible threads. That is nothing. Gods also bleed.

He was far to the west, a high, flat country of deep grasses. In his mind, he calculated the days, choosing the month and the date at random. Without paper or quill or the use of his hands, he kept journals, reread old stories he knew by memory or reshaped as he told them, wrote letters by speaking them aloud.

The fifteenth week of my godhood. Autumn approaches. A flock of great white cranes follows the river beside us. Because I am also white, the people believe the birds are good spirits I have summoned to bless them. The strange cries of these birds rack my heart before dawn.

Now came Odysseus, royal Laertes' son, man of guile and tested
    courage,
Back to his own house, tangled in rags and begging cast-off crusts
    to eat,
His nakedness too poor to claim in his own great name his wife
    and son,
Nor the cypress-vaulted halls of his father, the wide cloak of
    sea-purple,
Nor the fine-woven tunic of scarlet that was hid away for him
    at home.

To Hester, my wife. I am rich now, as you wanted. I have money in New Orleans, with a madman called Carrington, at the address I wrote you. If I live, I shall come home. Kiss my son in my name.

The lake ice is almost three feet thick at its deepest, but the wild girl's ax is very sharp—not really an ax at all, but an adze, meant for hacking the bark from cut logs. Still leading the mare and the pack mule behind him, John Frayne at first thinks the heavy blows are gunfire. In the blink of an eye, he drops to the snow-covered ice and begins to pull more snow over him, eating it, drinking it, hiding his long body with it, covering his thick black hair to make it white. His breath comes in sharp stabs and his eyes stream in the damp cold. Suddenly he is a little boy again in an Iroquois village, hiding from Patriot soldiers with his Loyalist mother and sisters. He is choking on black-powder smoke, the volleys of musket-fire almost drowned by the screaming of horses and women and old men, and of children now almost thirty years dead.

Frayne's whole body jolts on the ice. I, I am to blame. "Mother!" he cries out, hands clawing for the skirt of her gown. "Elizabeth!"

When he looks down, his hands are full of snow; he falls back onto the ice, staring up at the darkening sky and the distant blackened shell of his father's house silhouetted against it. The roof has fallen in on the east wing and only the central chimney is standing. Here and there a strip of old sodden French wallpaper flaps in the wind, a rag of lace curtain hangs limp. After eight years of wandering, John Frayne has come home at last. But why?

His mother is married again, to a drunken innkeeper just outside Montreal, and his sisters are settled in England. Wherever his wife Hester may be, she is surely not sleeping alone. No, it is only the boy he has any hope of reclaiming. If anyone can reconcile John Frayne to his ghosts, it must be Timothy, his son.

★　　★　　★

He can no longer see the girl's shape in the dusk and the rising night-fog, but the great blows of the adze do not falter. Frayne can feel them in the old wound on his face, jarring the nerves alive. He puts up his hand, expecting to feel fresh blood, but finds as usual only the scar that refuses to heal and harden, the heavy growth of brown-black beard that fails to disguise him from himself.

The mule's ears are back and its eyes roll, and the mare with the lame forefoot jitters. "Now, old Pewter," John says, and lays his face against her nose, letting her smell his warm breath, that he is not afraid anymore. "All right, my old love. All right, my girl."

He has cut himself an eight-foot spruce pole, and he holds it out before him like a blind man's cane in the thickening fog, sweeping a path through the snow and tapping the frozen surface to listen for the resonant twang of sound ice underneath. Even in deep winter, old ice can go rotten. The fear is not drowning, it is falling and freezing; if he breaks through and goes down, he will live no more than two or three minutes in such cold.

Suddenly the heavy blows stop and a wind springs up. Frayne feels the air buckle, the weather changing, growing colder. Once he defined himself by books and maps, by philosophy, poetry, science, the charts of old sailors and travellers. Now he lives by his senses—smelling moisture in the air, the sharp scent of spruce almost as heavy as summer, bearing down on his skin with a weight that means snow. He pulls up the hood of his striped blanket coat and takes a thick cloak of buffalo hide from the mule's pack to tie round him. Glimpsing the shoreline, he makes for the cover of a grove of balsam fir.

The wind drifts the fog away, and swirls it in devils, lifting up snow that stings his eyes and makes them ache. He rubs them, uncertain. This was always a place of spirits. His few boyhood playmates would not drink from the lake nor swim in it for fear of them, and against the lowering sky, the figure of the lone girl seems almost transparent when he glimpses her again. A child, he thinks. A child's ghost. His father's huge laughter roars in his ears as he holds two-year-old Frayne spluttering and terrified under the surface.

I baptize thee in the name of the father, and of the son, and of the holy ghosts.

She has swept off the snow with branches of fir and made a wound in the ice, a hole such as men make for fishing in winter, only bigger, two feet or more across—almost a cavern. Beside it, a small fire burns. Working carefully, she lays on more boughs until the pitch blooms up, tall flames eating the fog, the air scoured clean with the incense of winter.

There is a muffled shape near the hole, rocks tied to it by leather thongs. Since his father, Jack Frayne has seen many dead, and something of each of them lingers to encumber the living. A sense of the griefless neutrality of prisoners clings to this girl. A long debt like his own, that can never be paid.

"Who is it?" he calls out to her, thinking instantly of Tim. Once again, it seems he has fallen into some alien country. He wants allies, someone to speak his own language. "Who has died?" he demands, a desperate edge on his voice.

But she does not reply, does not notice the small avalanche of snow his shout brings down from the fir boughs. She is too near to her dead for her senses to serve her as they would have done before. There is no other sound but the soughing of wind in the evergreen branches above Frayne's head and the crack of the burning sap. Kneeling at the head of the corpse, the girl slips her two hands under its shoulders and slides it toward the hole.

Then she halts. Her body crumples and her fists pound the muffled shape till it leaps up and falls back again, over and over, slamming her rage into what is left of her mother—the breast, the belly, the thighs. How dare you leave me cheat me break me delude me? How dare you force the world and this body upon me and then escape yourself?

But aloud, she is mute. Her mouth gapes wide, her eyes staring into the fog as she strikes cruelly, down and down. Breaking some

old bond. Forging another so strong it will take her along with
the dead. At last she makes a shrill sound, a long, metallic wail
that might be the scream of some breaking machine.

"Annnhhhh-ahhhhhhhhhhhhh!"

Frayne steps out onto the ice, but the girl's cry stops suddenly,
as though it is cut by a knife. The body slides into the dense black
water with a hollow splash and for a moment he thinks she will
follow it. Her own slender body curves above the jagged cave of
ice, swaying gently back and forth, back and forth in a last dancing
rhythm, her dark-red hair falling in wretched tangles over her face
in the firelight. A wide mouth. A thin, chiselled nose, a little longer
than need be. Deep eyes that look colorless in the glow of the
fire. In full daylight, perhaps amber, bronze, russet. A plain creature, ragged, too thin for her bones.

The man's clenched fists open, the long fingers spread wide,
the pierced palms exposed. He feels something break in his mind,
some resistance to living. I wanted my mouth on your skin, he
will tell her later. The bend of your throat when you looked up
and saw the men coming. Not to fuck you. I didn't want that.
To drink up your spirit. To save what was left of my own.

There are four men, all unemployed until spring, all too drunk to care much for anything but the burning in their bellies. They have spent the afternoon in Schoolcraft's tavern at the bend of the turnpike; there are six taverns in New Forge, New York, one for every thirty-five freemen. Winters are long here; you can drink, pray, or fuck, and a few whores come and go at Schoolcraft's, to keep the freight-wagon drivers happy, and to service the travellers who come in on the big twelve-seater sleigh that runs back and forth from the market town of Cayuna with packages and mail.

Respectable men do their drinking much closer to town. The Philosophical Society meets at Tom Lashaway's, in the assembly rooms upstairs where the Episcopalians still hold service on Sundays. The Federalist Club gathers twice a month at the Dog and Lantern next door to Aldrich's General Mercantile, and so do the Masons. The Library Guild—appropriately enough—meets at George Book's, across from the Young Men's Academy.

But Schoolcraft's is far enough out of sight of the town to be tempting. A few renegade Methodists sneak in when their wives aren't looking, a few schoolboys and apprentices come to try their half-fledged wings. No townswomen ever drink there. Slaves and Indians are not allowed to drink at all, but it is said Tucker Schoolcraft would sell liquor to the bats in his barn if they gave him cash-in-hand.

"There, by God," cries a scrawny man with a red felt cap, hearing the girl's shrill cry as they break from the woods and catch sight of the broad curve of the snowy lake. "That's her, all right!"

"I don't hump no crazy bitches," grumbles a lump of dough

with stubby legs under it, reeling along with the rest. "Zeke Root caught her thieving his old woman's wash off the line, said she bit him clear through to the bone to get away."

"What I got in mind for her ain't got no bone." The third man sniggers, stops to piss beside a yellow birch. His name is Guido, said as though it were Guide-Oh.

But the fat man, Royall, only shudders. "I don't care. I don't like that damn lake. I don't like them goddamn Indian spooks."

"Shut your mouth!" orders the fourth man.

Except to issue commands, he does not talk to the others. He has drunk just as much as they, but he is not their companion. He nerves himself sometimes with liquor, but he drinks it alone in the woods, and never for pleasure. It is a punishment to him, like sleeping with women. His face is square and blunt-featured and stubborn, and his large dark eyes devour the horizon, picking out landmarks from the fog. His name is Benet, and he carries the net.

It is eight feet square, made of knotted hemp rope, tarred black and very heavy. Sometimes they haul it between boats to drag the lake for suicides and lost children, sometimes use it to catch scavenging bears and renegade dogs. Today, though, they are out for more interesting game.

Jacob Benet—Catcher Benet, they call him—gives a signal and they break into a dogtrot, each taking a corner of the net, swinging it out so the rising wind helps to spread it, then running to catch up to it, then swinging again. In spite of the drink, they move fast on the snowy lake, now and then hitting a stretch of bare ice and sliding, their boots squeaking as the hobnails cut their paths. The fat man stumbles, is dragged by the others, rights himself. Benet is blank-faced, quick. The little man with the red cap almost flies.

The girl is down on all fours near the hole, her attention still upon the dead. Her palms rest flat on the ice and she feels the drumming of the men's boots before Frayne can reach her or warn her. She looks up, her head turned, the dark bulk of Old Dog like an ink blot spreading on the sky beyond. White Lady watching, the last light on her shoulder.

"Now!" cries Catcher Benet, and the heavy net crashes down

on the girl. It falls round her slight shape like the cage of Frayne's plum thicket, a fate she was born for. She struggles hard—kicking, biting, her long hair tangled in the ropes. Her thin hands drag at the hempen cage till the fingers bleed and the nails pull away and break.

Something glints at her side, some weapon she is trying to get hold of. But she cannot. The big man grabs her, net and all, drags her backwards, falls with her onto the ice. Then all but Benet are on top of her. She can smell the drink, a cheap rum punch they call Kill-Devil. The stink of boiled cabbage and liver-and-onions on their breath. Of old rancid lard on Guido's hair.

The roads are full of ruts and they have swarmed out of one. She dreams the faces of their women and sees her own face as she will be in a year, perhaps two, if she is lucky. Blank. Sullen. Abandoned by God.

Through the net, their hands find her, pull up her skirts to the waist. Her legs and hips are bare, the dark triangle visible between them, the flat moon of her belly above. She kicks hard, twisting sideways, but they hold her down, spraddle-legged on the swept snow.

Benet abstracts himself, turning his back on what happens, his grizzled brown hair blown loose from the old-fashioned black ribbon that ties it at his nape. He is seven-and-forty, almost an old man, and he has seen such things often before. When they have finished, he will believe that nothing of significance has been taken from the girl, nothing she could not easily spare. The same will be true if they kill her.

But the liquor makes the blood slam at Benet's temples like an animal wild to get out, and his eyes are drawn back and back to her thin face, to the paleness of her bared skin. Does he want her himself? If so, he will not confront the truth of it. He braces himself, tries to focus on the shapes of the mountains, the scent of the pine smoke. I am not here. I am travelling somewhere, a clean place where nothing human lives.

The heavy net weighs down the girl's face and her shoulders and breasts, and the fat man clutches her hair through the net to keep her quiet. Still she makes no sound but the deep, crooked gasp of her breathing. The pounding of her bootheels on the ice. They have not the courage to hit her. Instead they curse her, command her to stop kicking, to offer a tacit compliance.

She has given herself before, out of curiosity or sadness, to one or two eager boys she can scarcely remember. At the time, in her school days, she had been altogether alone, surrounded by strangers in an old, sullen country, and night after night she had dreamed in her narrow dormitory bed of the light, warm touch of a human hand—on her arm, her shoulder, the top of her head. Hope of a human equivalence deluded her, that she might somehow be loved like other women, normal women who could hear love and speak it.

But she will not be made to collaborate this time. She kicks and flails, but the men hold her legs down, pegging her onto the ice like the skin of an animal.

A slight jab and it is done, an unremarkable process. If it hurts her, she gives them no sign of it. Her body lies still as the dead, the narrow hips lifeless under the little man's acrobatics. His name is Caleb, and as he mounts her, he shouts it over and over into her ear.

"Caleb, goddamn you, say Caleb! Say it, say my name! Calebcalebcaleb!"

There are many days, even months, when she does not think of herself by a name, but it comes to her now in the sharp-edged buzz by which her mother's voice used to reach her. Jennet. I am JennetJennetJennet. IamIamIam.

She is utterly silent. Tearless and ascetic, she fights the reflexes of her own body, refusing him the power he craves, a glimpse of the pain that rears hard and dark inside her. She stares up at him, eyes wide open and mouth clenched shut. "Goddamn you," he growls between his teeth. "Say stop. Say no!"

His eyes are pink-rimmed like a rabbit's and when they meet hers, his sex inside her spools out seed only briefly, then wilts, withdraws of its own accord. Feeling foolish in front of the others,

Caleb shoves himself in her again and she bites down hard on her lower lip so that it bleeds and the blood dribbles onto her chin.

"How much she bring, you figure?" says Guido, unbuttoning the flap of his own breeches to take his turn.

"Two shilling a month, maybe." Caleb looks down at her, spits into the hole in the ice. "*She* ain't worth much. County won't pay no more than two for *her* keep."

"Chrissake, be quick," says the fat man, Royall. "I don't like this place!"

"Hell, she'll bring more'n two shilling," Guido insists. "Nobody wants to keep a wild bitch like that on the cheap. Nossir, I aim to bid four. If you take her for less, you're damn fools."

When they have brought her into New Forge, the girl will be auctioned off by the county poormaster, along with a handful of others—widows, simpletons, cripples, old paupers not sound in their wits. Whoever bids lowest will be paid that amount every month for as long as he feeds her and puts clothes on her back. What else he does with her is his affair.

Guido hunches above her as Frayne runs full tilt on the ice towards them, the long spruce pole in his hands striking out in both directions like a pair of oars through deep water. Running jars his healed wounds, makes him feel that great vents are opening through which his reason is escaping.

"EEEeeeeee-yaaahhhhhh!"

As he breaks through into the clearing, his buffalo cloak flapping straight out behind him, his cry is as shrill as the girl's above her dead. The hood has slipped back and his hair is flying loose, long almost to his waist, very black and tied with a clutch of feathers. His black beard is clotted with frost, and snow blows in a nimbus from his shoulders, his arms. It seems he sheds light as he runs.

"Spooks!" cries the fat man, and lets go of the girl just before the end of the spruce pole smashes into him. Royall falls with a thump and a whine, blood gushing from his nose. Caleb and Guido grab at their breeches, goggle-eyed, and the girl rolls sideways, the net still tangling her arms. Frayne's ice pole catches Caleb in the groin, exactly where it was aimed, and he runs, groaning and whimpering and furious, the others stumbling after, the nails of their boots scuttling like rats' claws over the ice.

Only Jacob Benet is left. Immovable. Stolid and brown and hard. If he were an animal, he might be a badger, not dangerous unless he has something important to lose. Frayne stops short, lights the end of the pole in the coals of the fire.

It flares up with a liquid hiss just short of Benet's chin, but the Catcher does not flinch. "What's your business here?" he asks calmly.

The long burning pole slashes from side to side, leaving trails of sweet-smelling pitch smoke that hang like hieroglyphs in the moist air. Frayne glances in the direction the men have gone.

"I'm a spook. I've come gathering souls."

Benet only nods. "I'm bound to take her in. She's a thief."

"What's she stolen? Diamonds? Rubies?" Frayne's eyes narrow, puzzling. "You didn't come to screw her, you're not like the rest of them. What's she to you?"

"Poormaster's due here tomorrow to hold vendue. I serve on the town board, I'm the catcher. Make up the quarterly roll of paupers and orphans to be wards of the county, bring 'em in to the vendue. Old folk. Loonies." He looks Frayne up and down. "Tramps."

"Get away," says John Frayne in a voice so still the wind almost eats it. "She's paid high enough. Jesus Christ. Let her be."

For a long moment, Benet stares at this dragon-slaying ghost, at the strange light blue eyes and the shock of dark hair and the scars. At the girl still writhing to free herself.

" 'Spect she'll keep," he says, and stumps away toward the town.

★   ★   ★

The girl's skirts are still caught up in the heavy net, her half-naked body shaking with fury, with the cold and the shock and the lost sense of herself. The fire is almost burned out now, a thin sliver of moon rising above the trees to the east. I never saw clear till I looked at your body, Frayne will tell her. The little wings of your hipbones, like birds' wings, like the cheekbones of saints.

He drops the spruce pole and takes a step in her direction. Something flashes in her hand. She has found her weapon at last, a stubby blade with a handle. Too thin for a skinning knife. An old snapped-off sword with a fancy silver quillon and a wolf's-head grip. She hacks at the tarred ropes with it, but she cannot cut through them.

"How did you come by that sword?" he says.

Eyes lowered, he reaches one hand to pull down her skirts, to blunt the edge of what he is feeling. The section of rope she is chopping gives way and her blade strikes hard at his forearm, slashing the blanket coat and the woolen shirt underneath. Blood spurts from it, soaking the coat sleeve, more mess than damage, and what pain there is will come later. It is too cold now to feel.

The girl sloughs off the net like an old skin and steps away to stand staring at the blood on his sleeve. She is thinking how her mother once moved through a candlelit room with a man's severed arm in her apron. How her hands wore birth blood like a pair of silk gloves.

Frayne is talking again, a distant buzzing that irritates the girl. She stares, trying to capture the shapes of the words she cannot hear. "Who was it you sank in the lake?" he says. "I saw you hit him. Why did you hate him so? Was he your husband? Is that his sword?"

Him. Him. The ring she wears has deceived him, a thin band of gold with a red stone that gleams in the near-dark. Till now she has forgotten it and she stares down at it, puzzled, as though it has just now appeared there, fallen like John Frayne from the sky.

"I said nothing to that pack," he persists. "But you must tell me, I'm owed that. I left a wife and a son in the town yonder, and this house was my father's, it could be they've been living here. Who was it you sank?"

The girl cares enough to catch only a fragment of what he is saying. Hate. Husband. Sank. Him.

"Can't you hear me?" he says. "Answer me. Listen."

But she watches his face instead, memorizing its landscape. How the dark brows curve slightly up at the ends, stopping just short of his temples. How his skin is fine and almost too fair for a dark-haired man, deeply sun-browned but fading around the base of his throat, in the deep eye sockets, returning him to a kind of belated boyishness. How his odd blue eyes look aslant at her body, then look quickly away when she meets them.

She is shaking all over, her teeth chattering, but when she turns abruptly and walks away from him, she moves with a perfect society posture, like the girls he knew in London a lifetime ago, like the St. Louis and New Orleans ladies. They had got it from French governesses and dancing masters and mamas out to catch them rich husbands. Straight-shouldered, narrow-assed, back like a ramrod. Breasts laced tight and spilling out over low-cut muslin dresses, high-waisted, so sheer you can fancy the shadowy cleft of their legs as they move.

Suddenly Frayne laughs, his father's huge laugh that cannot be resisted. "Where the hell did you learn how to walk without moving your arse?" he shouts after the girl. His laugh hangs in the air and she hears something of it, some distant resonance that stops her in her tracks, makes her turn and look at him.

"So you *can* hear." His eyes lock her to him for a moment. "Stay with me, then," he says softly. "Sleep. Talk. Mend yourself."

His gentleness seems to frighten her more than his boldness and he thinks she will break and run. But standing there at the edge of the spruce grove, she makes a cup of her two hands and taps them against her left shoulder, her heartbeat.

John Frayne's breath catches. It is the Indian hand language he learned as a child in the Iroquois villages where the outcast Loyalists found their only shelter on this continent. But those snug log houses set in acres of apple orchards are ashes and cold stones now, all the war stories silent. The only Indians hereabouts lie wasted at the bottom of the lake.

Who is this girl, then, and where has she learned how to talk with the fingers? Who has taught her to walk like a lady and scratch like a mountain cat?

Arm still bleeding a little, Frayne cups his pierced hands and makes the sign in reply. Friend, it means. Equal.

For another long moment she watches, but John Frayne looks away, to the shattered walls of his father's house, the home he has travelled through alien countries to come to. When he looks up again, she is gone.

Certain collisions of passionless stars have created a world, within that world the encounters of seeds, of animals, of human creatures, resulting in birth or in death. Whether these collisions occurred by design of some universal protean force known as god, by pure chance, by honest mistake, or by cunning betrayal, is a matter of complete irrelevance to the daily continuation of man's life. To remind yourself of this will make you equally calm in the faces of the most overpowering love and the deepest treachery. It will not inform you which of them is which.

—John Stephen Frayne, Meditations on the *Meditations* of Marcus Aurelius

Unable to move without bleeding, robbed even of language, Frayne lay many weeks in the cottonwood boat as it wove in and out of the streams to the westward. Each day, as a discipline of mind, he forced himself to abandon the use of one of his senses in order to heighten the others. He learned to distinguish the sounds and flavors of the nameless women who fed him, who lay beside him in cold nights to warm him. One wore the grey hide of an antelope and even blindfolded he knew its soft, felted whisper. When his lips brushed the skin of another's arm, she gave off a taste of licorice. It came from a certain root used for cooking and healing, a species of wild anise, and in his mind, he sketched the plant carefully, its fernlike leaves and its small abortive blossoms and its great bulging root.

He lived by the rustle of willow branches as the boat moved between them, by the drift of windborne seeds across his face and the scramble of insects in darkness, of small animals through the high grass, shrews and ground squirrels and field mice and voles.

Sometimes there was thunder that shook the water and the earth and made the leaves of the willows tremble. In the distance, he could make out a darkness that seemed to move, to flow like a river in flood across the flat grassland. Buffalo, they said, and he heard the nervous screaming of horses, the monotone singing that was this nation's form of prayer. For days and nights, he found himself alone in the camp with women, with old men. When the hunters returned, he was given a piece of the roasted hump, chewed to a paste and mixed in a gourd bowl with wild cherries. It was said that the spittle of women carried a virtue, that it brought balance of mind and good luck.

The blind man sat always beside him, rubbing three smooth

white stones back and forth in his hands. Like all white things, they were holy. The old magician gently lifted off the oiled leaves and stroked the holes in Frayne's palms with the stones.

Who did this damage? Some brother-god? Why were you cast out?

From envy. From greed. I don't remember.

The gods are cunning. They have many twists and turns, but they love what they torture. That is how they teach men to be gods.

Sometimes at night, the blind man dazzled the people with tricks, and it gave him great power. He could summon up a blackbird from an old water-skin. He could swallow an arrow, shaft and all. His body painted with white clay, he could lay red-hot coals on his skin and not be burned.

Frayne could, of course, think of rational explanations for these wizardries. The blackbird was made of deerskin and feathers, a hand puppet the old man produced from his warshirt and waggled convincingly. The arrow had a shaft like a telescope. You gripped the head in your teeth and pushed the hollow shaft closed, so that only the fletching stuck out. The white clay had insulating properties.

He knew he would one day be called upon to make magic himself, to preserve his position as a god among them. But he had only words and the maps he had come west to make, maps as yet undrawn that spread themselves in his mind while he lay healing. Great whitened bluffs that caved away into a wide, shallow river, sometimes taking with them huge trees, boulders, hapless men. Hills like the sand dunes of a desert, but covered with dry, reddish grass, dipping down into shadowed valleys that rolled away into infinity. A sky so vast no instrument would compass it, a sky from which the earth dropped every night into deep sudden darkness.

These he translated into mathematical estimates, into miles and acres and the angles and curves of gradients. The undrawn maps lay in his mind like precious cargo; they were his comfort, and he drew them like blinds across memories too harsh to endure. Whether he would ever set these mind-maps down with a pen, he had not the faintest notion. They were his secret magic, and he would not offer them to any man except in desperation.

But when the gash on his face had healed enough to make speaking less painful, he began to tell the people stories, his low voice weaving in and out of the dark like the boy's cedarwood flute. Young men danced to the tune of his speech in the moonlight, their eyes closed and their naked limbs rubbed with sweetgrass oil that smelled of new-mown hay.

Voha, he said, invoking the sky. E-hani, our father in heaven, they replied. We believe what we do not understand.

I lived in a fine house long ago, when I was a boy, Frayne began. Three years old, perhaps four or five. Age has never had meaning to me. The past is always present and words live forever. I can remember the faces of old men now dead who bent over my cradle, the shape of certain shadows cast on the nursery wall—by bottles of unguent, by terrestrial and celestial globes, by the thin nose of my mother, by a pair of scissors I believed was a bird.

One particular day I sat cross-legged on the grass in a garden with banks of blue and white and purple and yellow flowers. Pansies, they called them, my father had sent for the seeds from England. My nurse—a kind and intelligent old woman of repellent appearance—played a board game called Purchase with me. There were small wooden pieces painted red and white, and I was greedy to keep them and wept when she took them away one by one. I can still feel the shape and the weight of each piece in my hand, and I did not understand how it could cause me such pain to be robbed of a thing that was only wood and paint. Like the gods, I was greedy. I wanted eternal success. I believed that the loss of these small things would erase me from the universe, that without them I would disappear.

This I had from my father, a quirk of blood and seed.

He wept when they came in the war and said they would take his house away. Having bribed someone at the English court, he had come by a grant of worthless land from the king and built on it a miniature castle, in what was then deep, inaccessible forest. My father drew up the plans of a gentleman's house that would have suited perfectly the landscape and climate of Kent, where his family had come from, or even of France. Naturally, he took no thought for the great weight of snow on flat roofs, the crashing of tree branches in storms against domes of glass. He made beauty. Ceremony. Stone and fine wood. Walls painted with pictures of gardens and trees and ships under sail. Through high glass windows, he gathered the inheritance of centuries to him and believed he possessed it.

I loved him far more than I have ever loved God.

My father was a joker, a trickster, always laughing. A huge man with many appetites. For wine for food for women for land. It was more than greed. He loved whatever he ate drank fucked owned. He gave himself to it, a truer definition, he said, than religion, philosophy, politics, or marital fidelity—which my mother most wisely did not demand of him. Nor, for that matter, did he ever demand it of her.

When he knew he would lose, that they would call him a traitor and drive him out and seize his land and his house, he began to hide things away. Silver teapots. Statues. Boxes of books. He had many hiding places, it gave him pleasure inventing them. Building trick boxes. Secret panels in wainscoting. Tiny invisible drawers sawn out of great trees in our woods and put back again, the bark stuck on with a glue boiled from hides.

There were raiding parties everywhere from both sides, they would invade houses at random demanding betrayals. Where are the Tories? Where are the rebel bastards? Some of the raiders had no politics, they were just thugs out for what they could steal and smuggle and sell. People invented imaginary targets to keep them happy. A man with greasy yellow hair and pop eyes who lives half a mile beyond the foot of Old Dog Mountain, go there and get him. A man with a limp in the cabin at the head of Black Lake, take him instead. An old crone. A hunchbacked dwarf. A pirate. One by one, farms and villages were burnt, vicious attack and more vicious reprisal, like a Renaissance feud between rival princelings, or a holy war in which God fights for both sides at once. Lies floated in the air like contagion, absurd accusations. I heard so-and-so drink the health of the king. I heard he named his son George Washington. I heard he's a spy for one side or the other, whichever you like.

At last the lies could not be distinguished. My father himself had been courted by both sides and accused by both, but he cared little for politics. He could not have said whether he was Patriot or Tory, and in the end, it was not of importance. All truth was invented. All falsehoods were true.

I heard he has a vast treasure hidden away, they said of him. A payment for treason, for spying. Gold. Silver, whole bars of it. At the head of Lake Paschal, at the Bay of Spirits, the manor house there. Captain Frayne's castle.

It was I who invented this story. A small bookish boy being taunted by bullies, defending himself with wild tales. My father is richer stronger smarter. Possessed of huge untold wealth. At last, passed from boy to boy, from child to father, the lie grew immense and overwhelming. I said nothing. I began to believe it myself.

My lie became a universal delusion; with it, I let evil come into the world. My father died of it as surely as though I had poisoned him, poisoned the whole universe and brought it crashing down into chaos and war. Again and again they invaded him, questioning, searching the house and the garden, dragging his books out and burning them. Demanding a truth that had never existed. Violated day after day, his mind wandered and grew vague and disappeared at the last into hiding.

I found him hanged one day from a tree in the garden, an oak some three hundred years old by the girth of its stem. He had chosen it carefully, a limb strong enough to support his huge weight without cracking. He did not wish to be saved by mischance.

On the night of this story, the blind wizard left at Frayne's side in the cottonwood boat a fine quilled deerskin pouch containing certain hoarded books of his father's he had brought west with him, certain loose pages written in his own odd, knotted handwriting, which his enemies had stolen along with some beaver skins and a horse. Finding them useless, they had thrown the old books aside and a small boy of the tribe, gone out to the deep grass to relieve himself, had stumbled upon them. So the collision of passionless stars had begun to return John Frayne, by honest mistake or by cunning betrayal, to the ruin from which he had come.

At the mouth of a granite cave where the spruce grove thickens into forest rising up to the base of Lion's Tooth, the lone girl squats on her heels in the darkness on the night of Frayne's arrival at the Bay of Spirits, striking sparks with a flint onto damp pine-needle straw. It catches, dies, sparks again, catches, burns steady. On this small fire, in a stolen vessel thick with rust, she heats water from the spring at the edge of the grove. It runs under a thin layer of ice which she breaks away with the stump of old sword, letting the water run through her two hands like a funnel.

The spring water is very clear, very cold. It is said to be poisoned by traces of arsenate run down from the mountain, but she is certain this is slander. She drinks from it eagerly, sure that even if it is poison, it will do her some good.

When the water in the rusty pot is the next thing to boiling, she strips off every stitch of the clothes men have soiled and steps out bum-naked onto the snow. It is deeply cold now, perhaps ten degrees above zero. She lifts the vessel over her head and lets the hot water fall onto her neck and breasts and shoulders, at first a thin stream, then a strong pour, until steam rises from all along her clean body. It hangs in the cold air for a moment, a used soul that abandons her. Then it condenses and freezes, tiny drops spitting down, leaving pits in the snow.

II

a bird in the house

The crippled Frenchman Leclerc first heard of the wild girl he calls Sparrow nearly a year before Frayne's return, while he was turning the rungs of a cheap wooden chair in the factory at Germantown, across the lake from the old house on Spirit Bay.

Marius Leclerc had been officially dead since the Battle of Austerlitz in the cold winter of 1805, when he had deserted Napoleon's army. Nothing drew him back to his village in Normandy, and he had come out of France with no particular purpose in mind, other than leaving one place and perhaps arriving alive at another. While the wound in his foot healed an inch at a time, he wandered through the frayed borderlands of several countries, working at odd jobs among strangers, until he felt that he bore the ravaged map of Europe in his bones.

When he found himself at last in America, someone said to him, you are free here. Here all men are equal. The rich do not own you. It came as a terrible blow, as though a cannonball had struck him.

Twenty years ago, when the wind of revolution reached his village, Leclerc had been a young man of thirty-two, and had gone to the barricades with his friends to fight for the noble cause of freedom. But what came of it was scarcely noble. Like a pack of playing cards from which the king and queen are discarded, the knaves rose to eminence, while at the bottom of the deck the cards with no faces were played out one by one in obscurity, just as always. Different men rode in the fine carriages that drove by on the high road to Paris, but the dust still tasted the same.

In the year of Austerlitz, there was an emperor in France again, and Leclerc found himself an old man of forty-seven, childless and womanless, his only relatives two drunken brothers—partners in a small cartmaker's shop—who jeered at his frugal and celibate habits while they ran him head-over-heels into bankruptcy. To escape them, he enlisted in the Grand Army of Napoleon, sending all his meager pay to his creditors as a matter of honor. A fortnight before that terrible battle that was to make him a deserter in his own eyes and a dead hero on the rolls of his country, the last of his debts was paid. Marius felt he was clean now, and ready to die.

As it turned out, of course, he was not, and the fact continued to puzzle him. What had made him save himself at the last minute? Perhaps it was only that—like an opium addict—having once dreamed of freedom, Leclerc could not deny himself the chance to dream again. You are free here, you are any man's equal. Go where you like. Do as you choose.

When he heard these words in Boston and again in New York and Philadelphia, hope swelled in him, and the nagging certainty that, given freedom, he must know how God willed him to use it. For weeks he waited in silence, studying the faces of men on the street, of their servants, their whores, their women and children. He did not pray; after many battles, conscious prayer seemed absurd. His blood prayed in silence. As he walked, his bones murmured to God. I need a garden to tend. I need shoes to polish. I need to bake a loaf of good bread with brown crust.

When at last God sent him a sign, it took the form of a notice of employment in a Philadelphia paper. Wanted to hire. A man of good will for the making of chairs.

★   ★   ★

What people in America called a factory was even smaller than in Normandy. Germantown was a raw, muddy village of immigrant craftsmen, mostly Bavarians and Schwabs and East Prussians, some Swedes, a few Russians and Poles. There was a glassblower, a harness maker, a wiredrawer, a cobbler and saddler, a factory in which women and girls braided straw hats. The workshop of Franz Zimmer's chair factory was a large barnlike structure in the yard of a sleepy farm where geese honked and hustled. Most of the carpenters were apprentices of sixteen or eighteen—cousins, nephews, brothers-in-law just come over from Europe. With these callow, good-natured boys, Leclerc grew fat on kraut and dumplings at Zimmer's generous table. He slept with the boys in the loft, snoring heavily on narrow pallets of straw spread with Frau Zimmer's clean quilts.

On Sundays, he went dutifully to the Lutheran church with them, to have the remnants of lust scoured out of him because it pleased the old German. As a young boy, Leclerc had meant to enter the priesthood, but he had not been to confession in almost twenty years, and—until he encountered the girl in the ruins of Bay House—he believed the intoxication of such intense devotion had left him entirely.

The young apprentices laughed at his sober piety during the glum three-hour services, they thought of nothing but girls and they teased him continually. Frenchie, they called him. Don't feel so bad, Frenchie. If we get us some women, we'll save an old one for you.

They were too young to fear monsters and they didn't hold Napoleon against him. When he cried out in the night, they found extra quilts and covered him to keep him warm.

Don't be sad, Frenchie. Don't sorrow. We'll catch you the wild girl that lives by the lake.

Leclerc was fifty-two now, with a paunch from the dumplings and little round spectacles that never stayed on his nose. His mouse-brown hair was greying, visibly thinning, and age spots had begun to appear on the soft white skin of his forearms. He no longer saw his own face when he looked in the mirror; he saw a clock, its hands spinning faster and faster. Surely it was not too late, he thought. But he did not mean only women, as the apprentices thought he did; Marius Leclerc ached for a real sense of purpose, for something to which he might devote himself completely. All his life he had walked the paths that others set down for him. He had worked for his father till the old man was crushed by a cart, and then for his grieving old mother, to keep her in some modest comfort. Then it was the turn of those sots, his brothers, and their gambling and women, and in all that time Marius could not remember making any conscious choice.

Now it seemed God had at last granted him freedom, and choice was its burden. Surely, surely *le bon Dieu* intended some human use for him, something beyond the making of plain wooden chairs.

But no tongue of flame appears above him, and Marius hangs the mirror with its face to the wall and limps onward. His hands grow skillful at shaping the sweet-smelling boards of aged walnut and maple, at turning rungs on the lathe and chipping out patterns of wheatsheaf and grapevine along the backs. Zimmer pays him a decent wage, but the money means nothing. Leclerc treasures the ability of his eyelids to open and close, the faint warmth of sawdust when it clings to his damp skin, the comforting movement of his chest as his breath enters his body and leaves it. Alive. Alive. To this rhythm, he walks, dragging his bad leg behind him. Shaves. Puzzles out the future.

To what purpose do I take in the air and breathe it out again? Of what use the dry whirring of brains?

In the wake of Napoleon's armies, he had seen people hanged by their heels from church steeples, as though they were bells. Children drinking the blood of dead horses, in towns where the wells had been fouled by human corpses. Once a whole village buried alive in a landslide brought about by the firing of cannon. When they dug down, the survivors uncovered entire rooms intact— old women with their knitting, a man at a card table with a game of patience laid out before him. A small white dog, who appeared to be sniffing a pot on the hearth.

Even now, when Leclerc wakes under the clean quilts, he can smell battle-death all around him, a smothering sweetness with a dry edge that cuts into his eyes, his nose. Creeping out of his bed, he limps from one of the sleeping apprentices to another, watching their bodies to see if they breathe, if they show any visible wounds.

Awake in the dark, his bones begin to pray again. Give me a loaf. Give me a garden. Give me a child.

"Who is this wild girl you talk about?" he asks the boys cautiously. "What's her name, then?"

"Nobody knows," they say, smirking and digging their elbows into one another's ribs, certain they know what he wants with her.

Marius blushes. "She does not talk?"

"Some say she does," one boy insists, with a cackle. "Old lady Grünewald heard her. She hollered Shitface, and then ran away!"

"But she won't say her own name," says another. "If a witch says her name, she'll go straight up in smoke."

"I don't believe in witches." Marius frowns. "Has she no parents? No husband? Where does she live?"

"The old haunted house," they tell him, making goggle-eyed faces. "They say a pirate owned it, a Britisher, and he left buried treasure. He comes back to guard it, and if you go there, he takes off your head."

Leclerc only smiles, but early that spring he begins to spend all his Sunday afternoons at the Bay of Spirits. Entering through a broken-out wall in what once was the library, he climbs over gaps in the ripped-up flooring, looking for traces of the unknown girl. For many months, he finds nothing. There are still a few crumpled and water-soaked books left behind by the fire and the looters, and he gathers them carefully. They are in languages he cannot read—Latin, Greek, German, Italian. Walter Scott he might manage, but the English the village priest taught him is too poor to read Milton. Only one book is in French, the *Essais* of Michel de Montaigne.

He does not take it away from the house; already he thinks of the place as the wild girl's home, and Marius is no thief. He brings a hammer and nails and makes a small shelf instead, where the old carved mantel has been hacked in half. There he arranges the seven precious books by size, by the faded colors of their leather covers, which he feeds with neat's-foot-oil to restore them. What *philosophe* lived here? What powdered ladies leaned down from the gallery, to the tinkling notes of a harpsichord, a violin, a flute?

At home, he had left behind him a cheap old fiddle, which no doubt the brothers and their slattern wives had used for kindling wood by now. I must have music, he thinks, and his bones begin to demand it of God, growing more and more greedy. Give me Bach. Give me Mozart. Give me a violin, a cello, a flute.

Noticing the fineness of the walnut floorboards, he begins to repair them, laying them carefully over the joists and nailing them back into place, mending the broken ends with new boards which he buys from the sawmill in New Forge. Oiling and rubbing in waxes until there is one square yard of the floor upon which the past dances and the dead ladies smile.

Each time he returns to the place, he limps through all the rooms that can still be reached, hoping for a glimpse of the girl. One wing has been burned almost to the ground and some of the floors in the bedchambers upstairs drop away without warning, a sheer fall of thirty feet to the garden beneath. Bats nest there. Once he disturbs a roosting owl that flies at him squawking. The girl is somewhere nearby, Marius is sure of it. She will not show herself yet, but he is a patient man.

As early spring turns into summer, he stays downstairs, giving the birds the freedom of the upper rooms. He begins to read the French essays, but he finds that crucial pages have been torn out at random, leaving phrases that hang like the breakaway rooms overhead. A great shame if. The imprisoned boy was. I found by chance a.

Of these fragments—which seem to feed his mind more than

the pages on which whole paragraphs are clearly legible—Leclerc tries to construct what will serve for some meaning, but it always eludes him. Eight or nine months have gone by, but still the wild girl does not appear. Perhaps she is only a guardian spirit here, like Marius and all the dead.

In the crotch of an old oak at the back of the tumbledown spring-house, the girl Jennet perches every seventh day through that summer to watch him. Sometimes Leclerc stays late, weeding the overgrown garden by moonlight, sitting very still on the uppermost terrace while opossums, raccoons, now and then a black bear and her cub come to forage. He observes these innocents without apparent fear, and does not try to approach them or tame them. Once the sow bear waddles over to sniff at his feet, then bumbles away again. A kit fox jumps onto his bent back and stands there, barking to summon the moon.

From her room at school in Scotland, the girl had been able to see in the distant garden the white marble head of a man—some statesman or ancient Roman hero. A certain bird with spots of blue on its wings often roosted there, and at twilight a black-and-white tomcat leaped lightly from a stone wall below and stood like a mountaineer on top of the statue, surveying his domain. As season gave way to season, the vacant stone eyes took on varying expressions—weeping with spring rain, masked with autumn leaves, bandaged with snow. The deepest sorrow had emptied that face and unmade it, leaving it cool and passionless, clean even of kindness and the fear of life and death.

She longs now for such perfect neutrality—to be nothing, hate nothing, to require neither resistance nor submission.

At the school, she had more than enough of men's efforts to enforce a petty submission upon her, they dirtied her more than any casual fucking. A ruffled lace cap for her hair, to be put on before inspection each morning. A facial expression as insipid as porridge, the eyes always modestly lowered. Having proved herself unable to blush, Jennet was slapped in the face and shown the red welt in the mirror. There now, miss. That's what it looks like on a proper young lady. Caught running like a hoyden one day across a heather-purpled hillside that soiled her best stockings, she was forced to stand motionless on a table in the refectory from luncheon till well after teatime.

Through this day-long ordeal, the young masters came and went in the room, finding excuses to glance at her, forcing her for fear of more punishment not to meet their eyes. Even the gentle one whose hands had stroked her breasts and whose lips had spelled out on her thigh the terrible lie, I love you, came to stare and smirk and walk away with his friends.

I will be a stone, she thought. If I love anything, I will love only stone. She slipped out of the dormitory that night to the garden where the Roman statue stood, cool and perfect and unloving, needful of no one. Unbreakable. She put her arms round the pure white marble, and when she woke in the damp, grey light of the Scottish morning, her arms were around it still.

Leclerc has become the girl's statue now. Like the old ruined house, he calms the wild panic that rises in her unpredictably, at terrible moments when she is certain she will drown in the speaking world. From the tree where she sits like the guardian tomcat, she sees Marius one night as her mother grows sicker and the summer nears autumn; he is gathering ripe pears in the orchard, laying them carefully into a basket with a hole in the bottom through which the moonlight shines. Barefoot, a straw hat on his balding head and his shirtsleeves rolled up, he sits down on the lion's-paw bench, peels one of the fruits and eats it, laughing at himself in the darkness and swiping at the juice that runs down his double chin.

The moon swims through the garden, turning the tapestry of wild fern to a Sargasso Sea. Over the hunched shape of the Frenchman, it breaks like a tide, a new skin of lambent water that washes all his foolishness from him.

This is how you recover a life, she thinks. Waiting by moonlight. Eating ripe fruit. Walking in the footprints of animals. Jennet is no longer sure she wants to recover her life, that she has ever possessed one. No one knows her entirely, not even her dying mother, who remembers a dream of a child and wants only to keep it alive now, to keep it somehow inside her, with her, even after she dies. But the sight of Leclerc takes away Jennet's despair and leaves her clean and calm. A good, quiet man, she thinks, like my father. A raw tenderness in him, reaching out like tree branches into the air.

As she watches, Marius picks up the broken fingers from the foot of the column in the garden, and tries to fit them to his own.

Then, two months before John Frayne's return, the mellow autumn turns to a foggy November. An army is massing at the Canadian border, and old Zimmer's apprentices are eager to volunteer, to march off and attack the British fort at the head of the lake. Teach the Redcoats a lesson, that is the cry now. Bonaparte is riding roughshod over Europe and Nelson's navy is bleeding, starving, depleted; he stops neutral ships to kidnap Yankee seamen and press them into the service of England. The myth of American independence is one King George can no longer afford to indulge.

In the west, in Indiana and Ohio and along the Missouri, British agents—at least, so it is said—stir up trouble with the Indians, provoking terrible battles to secure trading rights for their fur companies. England needs money to provision its ships and its armies, and the Louisiana Purchase is a prize ripe for the plucking. Spies for both sides are everywhere in the western country, the British spies—it is rumored—mostly Tories driven north thirty-five years ago, during the Revolution, and only lately returned, men with grudges and dubious loyalties and friends in all the wrong places.

Thomas Jefferson writhes, fumes, writes letters of protest, sends out spies of his own. For fear of a war he cannot win, an embargo has been placed upon trade outside American borders for more than two years now. Zimmer's chairs are piled high in his storehouse and cannot be hauled the eight or nine miles up to Canada, they must wait for wagons going east or west. Ships rot in Boston harbor. In the cities there are bread lines, soup kitchens, epidemics, intermittent riots. Freedom is dying of peace.

But Jefferson's term of office will end soon and he will not run again, he is a man of his word and he swears that once he leaves Washington City, he will never set foot there again. They call him a French-lover, an immoralist, a weakling besotted with good living and women. The old men are all out of favor now. The aristocrat Adams paces and grumbles at Braintree, and worries about his daughter's impossible marriage. Thomas Paine's books are burned; he is a pauper, a drunk, an atheist devil who, like Socrates before him, corrupts the minds of the young.

All this washes over Marius Leclerc like a dream, like moon-skin. He has seen it before, the taunts, the sneers, the suspicions—all the lunatic contrivances that pile up into war.

But the Frenchman is free now from the consequences of history. He can think of nothing but the girl. The seven books. The square yard of sound, polished boards. The violin.

One November Sunday afternoon just before freeze-up, when the lake water is almost black with cold and the skeins of Canada geese have thinned to a few straggling flocks flying southward, Leclerc enters Bay House with his usual reverence and is startled to find an old cloak tumbled on the few restored floorboards of the library. Blood, he thinks at once. The blood I have shed in the war has pursued me!

But as usual, he has jumped to a foolish conclusion, aided by hazard and circumstance. His spectacles have fallen from his nose accidentally, and without them, the faded old cloak is the brownish color of old blood that has dried.

Recovering himself, Marius picks it up. A heavy woolen cloak of an old-fashioned style, burned in one or two places as though it has hung too close to the fire while drying. The hem heavy with mud and leaves, raspberry burrs and weeds stuck here and there in the matted fibers.

Hearing a faint sound overhead like the scurry of mice, he looks up and sees the girl, balanced on the third step from the top of the ruinous stair. Jennet stands very still for a moment, her wide red-brown eyes fixed upon him, meeting his own, and her hair Medusa-like, tangled and snarled and without any cap or bonnet. Her dress is made of homespun, but it has been carefully cut in the fashionable high-waisted style of the Empire, the skirt kilted up now with a broad leather belt, her bare legs showing unashamed beneath it.

Jennet had been sitting all that day with her mother, Hannah, who was dying a mile away in the cabin of a free black woman, an old doctress called Aunt Hope. For the sake of the sick, it was kept very hot in the cabin, and heavy old quilts were hung over the window and doorway to keep out the light, which was thought to contain harmful vapours. The hearthfire and the smoke it gave off seemed to sour the air in the place, and the girl felt sick herself, dizzy from the nearness of death.

Go away, her mother said. I don't need you here.

Hannah was of another time and place, cleaner, harder, less brittle. Since her husband's death, she had kept the girl close to her, living by her skill and her wit and wandering gradually westward in the hope of hearing some word of her sons, Robbie and Charlie— whether they had been taken for sailors or soldiers, whether they had died in the west.

But here at New Forge, it had ended. Her old horse had died and she had nothing to trade for another. Jennet herself had had money once, a legacy from the aunt who had paid for her schooling, but it had all gone west with the boys, on the promise they would settle and send for the women. It was hard to find work at first, for Hannah was not known here and trusted, but she would not let the girl go as a servant for fear of what might befall her because of her deafness. She trudged out in all weathers for a few paltry shillings, growing poorer and poorer in the will to survive.

But now dying had made Hannah herself again, very strong-willed and vivid. It seemed to the girl she was burning away. I don't need you, she said again. Get up and go into the air.

Though she looked very young, Jennet was past the age when most girls hoped for marriage. She was not even certain what the word meant; like most abstractions, it annoyed her. What she was now, she would always be. Had always been, from her conception.

But her mother was right; this small space was not enough, any more than the chairs were enough for Leclerc. I need to run, she thought. I need wind on my face. She put on the old cloak and went into the dooryard, the ancient black woman padding softly beside her. Aunt Hope's eyes were very bright and she wore a white cap made out of the leg of an old knitted stocking. Her skin was the color of charcoal, and crumpled, like paper after it is burnt.

What ails? Jennet said in her odd, toneless voice. She had known more words once, but they had begun to slip away when her mother fell ill, and seldom formed themselves into sentences now. The production of sounds, too, grew more difficult. She said less and less, and her voice grated in her throat as though she ground the words out between millstones.

Aunt Hope shrugged. Belly's swole up some, she said. Maybe worms. Maybe got her a lump.

You bleed her?

Nope. I ain't much inclined to go a-bleeding my sick folk. Aim to poultice her. Make her puke some, see what she brings up.

Will she die?

Not soon, my honey. She ain't the kind to go easy. The old woman laughed. She's like me, your old mama. Got to pay out her ticket first, 'fore she can go.

There was a doctor in New Forge and an old Swede in Germantown who knew something of bleeding and blistering. But there was no money, and Aunt Hope did not demand it. Winter be here pretty soon, she said. You bring me in some dry firewood, girl. Look me out a loaf of maple sugar, I got me a terrible sweet tooth.

The twelve other blacks in New Forge were slaves, and lived all together in little cabins at the end of the town nearest the cranberry bog. There was a high fence around the cabins, and they locked the gate from the outside at night. But the girl was not used to slaves, she did not understand the meaning of that word, either, and thought it must be something like marriage.

To most people, though, slavery was natural enough. New York was not the same as New England; it had always been a feudal society in which great men owned almost all of the land and rented it out by the year. Except for the lack of free will in the bargain, slavery did not seem so much different from indenture. And most of the poor had long since resigned any will of their own.

Aunt Hope Pomfrey was the only free black in all Talbot County. She was an aberration, a freak of nature. How she had come to be free, nobody was certain, but it was clear that she meant to stay that way. If anyone tried to cause her commotion, she took after them with an iron roasting spit, hollering cuss words in a language of her own. She had a little cow no bigger than a billy goat, and hens and a half-dozen guinea fowl, and more than thirty stray cats that she fed and made up names for, and from whom, at the rise of the new moon, she drew blood for curing old Mrs. Hawley's shingles. People called her a witch and one time the Methodist preacher damned her soul from the pulpit, which made her cackle with delight for nine days running.

But when a man or a wandering woman had no money and not much chance of living without it, they sent him or her to Aunt Hope.

Through the autumn, as her mother grew sicker and sicker, the girl had cut firewood from dead trees in the forest and hauled it up to Aunt Hope's cabin, dragging a canvas sling along the path. Jennet was very strong and knew many things that lay dormant in her mind and her muscles until they were wanted. When she had to, she worked like a man.

Once the firewood was cut, the girl ventured into New Forge. In Aldrich's mercantile store she saw a sign printed broad, with a carpenter's pencil: Best Maple Sugar, two farthings a loaf. No one was certain which money was real, so that some called it by the old English names and some by the new Yankee ones; there were dollars and pounds and shillings and pennies and farthings, but few people had any of them in real coin. Some towns printed coins on stiff paper and cut them out in little circles and used them to trade with, like small boys playing storekeeper. But most people haggled and bartered for whatever they needed, just as they always had.

The girl, though, had no money and nothing to trade with, and the sign asking for farthings seemed so foolish it made her want to laugh. Jennet slipped two of the crumbly, honey-brown loaves into the soft leather bag she wore round her waist whenever she went out stealing, and before Herod Aldrich looked up from his ledgers, both the girl and the sugar were gone.

Where did you come by it? Hannah said sharply. Her dark eyes looked up from the pallet, small blue lights glinting in them from the dance of the hearthfire. Even dying, she missed nothing, evaded no moral dilemma. Answer me, miss. Did you steal it?

The girl nodded. She could steal, all right, she had done it since childhood as a way of getting her own back on the hearing world. But she had never been able to lie.

Aunt Hope was gorging her sweet tooth blissfully, pleased enough with her bargain. But the dying woman did not give up her control of the girl. Have I not taught you better than thieving? she said. Would your father not weep to see you do such things?

Two words came clear to the girl. Father. Weep. Tears gathered in her eyes, but did not fall. I love you, she said, measuring the spaces between the words so as not to run them all together.

I-one-two. Love-one-two. You.

Hannah drew her down where she lay and Jennet curled against her as she had done in the featherbed at home in her childhood. At sixty-one, Hannah Josselyn had already lived almost ten years longer than any woman she knew. Three years before, her husband, Daniel, the girl's father, had met an ironic end, a jest of God upon them. She had borne six children in the course of her life, but so far as she knew, only this girl was still living.

Yet Hannah did not feel old in her mind. To die was a waste of herself and she resented God for it. All her life she had fought against waste.

Go now, Jennet. Go into the air and find something alive. But don't steal it, she said with a smile.

The first living thing the girl sees is Marius Leclerc, the dead Frenchman. In France, he is now a famous personage who has given his life, it is said, at the Emperor Napoleon's side. The emperor, who had been at the time some fifteen miles away from the battlefield, watching safely from a hilltop, claims to remember the death very well.

"I'm sorry," Leclerc says to the girl as she looks down at him from the top of the stairs. He is not certain why, but he has said it again and again all his life, long before his desertion from the army. It is not a sense of guilt like John Frayne's so much as a sense of his own incompletion, a certain knowledge that something was gone from him at birth that God has not yet put back. "I am sorry," he says again, and wipes his mouth with the back of his hand.

Jennet stares. As usual, she has come to Bay House to touch the books. Like Marius, she seldom reads anything from the pages, but the damp, musty scent of the paper makes her think of Daniel, her father, who long ago taught her to read from old books. She likes holding them in her hands, savoring the weight of them, the stolid, blocky forms, which have the same griefless neutrality as the statue. The paper is very thin and she can feel the shapes of the words as they lie on the pages. Serene. Indifferent. Not requiring to be loved.

But today she has no time for books. Her bold stare makes the shabby Frenchman even more shy than usual, and he takes off his glasses again and begins to polish them on the tail of his coat.

"Bird," she says, a hoarse murmur. She crosses her two hands in front of her, making the shapes of wings, flapping them. "Poor-one-two. Bird."

★   ★   ★

At the head of the curved stair, which is missing its banister, there are three doors on each side of the hall. To the east, where the windows once faced towards the town, most of one wall is burned away and the floors are unsafe. But except for a few missing panes of imperfect glass and the tumbledown fireplaces that no longer connect to a chimney, the rooms that face northwest towards Lake Paschal are whole.

Even before the girl pulls open the sagging old door, Marius can hear the sound of wings beating against glass, against walls. Stopping for a moment, a few breaths of stunned silence. Then beating again.

It is a desolate noise, like a sword in the brain. Yet it is gallant. Determined, like a small boy who climbs again and again up a tree from which he is certain to fall.

A bird in the house means death. Leclerc's old mother had a hundred such omens. A bird in the house. An umbrella opened indoors. A candle not snuffed before daylight.

The girl slips into the room and he limps inside with her. There is an old wooden horse on wheels tossed aside in one corner. A faded globe of the world, the countries painted on vellum stretched thin over a wooden ball, a second globe with a map of the constellations. A few wooden stools and a bench, very low to the floor, as though a family of gnomes might have lived here. It is a children's room, a nursery and schoolroom. The bench is a desk, with a hole in it for holding an inkpot, three names carved into the wood with a penknife.

Emma. Elizabeth. John Stephen. This last name is repeated in several ebullient variations. Johnny. Jack. Jackie. John.

Above them, the bird soars, rebounds from the wreath of plaster ladies on the ceiling. Sinks to the floor. Rises, flies into a wall on which someone once stencilled a border of roses, now faded to an absurd shade of blue-green.

It is a young sparrow, small, very frightened. Blown in by some storm and unable to free itself. "Poor child," murmurs Marius, and holds out an arm. "Poor bird." But the bird does not perch; it flies at him, fierce, as though this entrapment is his fault. Comes at his eyes, his spectacles. At his broad, solemn face which is running with tears.

In the end, it is Jennet who acts on the creature's behalf. She picks up the miniature desk by one end and smashes it against the windowpanes, and they crash down in musical slivers—onto the floor, down into the overgrown garden. Surprised by the noise, the bird sinks to the floor for a moment, its small body hunched together, its head drooping.

Marius lowers his arms from his face, and the girl scoops up the sparrow, her hands cupped carefully round it. She throws it out of the empty window, and for a moment it plummets, suicidal, mourning itself as it falls. Then the wings open of their own accord, as though by no effort of the bird. A current of air catches it by chance, and it is gone into the woods.

The girl turns to Leclerc. Lays a finger on his forehead where the bird's claw has caught it. "Sorry," she says in her strange voice. There is something in it of the beating of wings.

In December the snows came, and Marius took them for a sign from God. He did not go again to Bay House, for now it was three hours' agonizing walk around the lakeshore. Before freeze-up, he had crossed quickly by rowboat, but he would not hobble across the lake on the ice, it struck terror into him.

At Austerlitz, Bonaparte's artillery had pounded into the head-long Russian retreat across a frozen lake. Fire the cannon, came the order. Send them all down. The whine and thump of the balls, the simultaneous sound of ice cracking underneath them. The rational universe giving way in a barrage of confusion. In some holes, three or four men fell through together, their bodies stuck for a split second like a crowd in a doorway, barrels of guns, the blades of sabres like branches, piercing the air. Marius could not forget these men. I used to know how to skate, his friend Cruchot had said as they ran, and was drowned an instant after. The losses that morning were said to be thirty thousand, perhaps forty, perhaps fifty.

Since that day, ice had been a horror in the mind of Marius Leclerc. If each man's hell is unique to his uttermost terror, Leclerc's is the cracking of ice underfoot.

But in January, on the day after John Frayne's return, the little Frenchman had no choice but to cross the ice of Lake Paschal. He was sent to New Forge by old Zimmer to buy five pounds of finishing nails for the chairs, and to limp all the way around by the shoreline would take him too long. The old man would rant and rave at him, the apprentices would jab one another and accuse him of having a woman in town.

Marius reached Aldrich's store that morning shivering with fear and desperately scant of breath, beads of sweat freezing on his brow and his upper lip. There was a dark man in the shop, a long, slender man who looked strong but who bore an odd fragility about him. Something tenuous, as though he might suddenly fade out of sight. He wore a beaded necklace and buckskin breeches and Indian leggings, and a plain homespun shirt belted with a braided thong of rawhide; he glanced up when the Frenchman entered, then looked away again. He was being measured for a suit of gentleman's clothes, and now and then his blue eyes clamped shut and he tossed his head in faint irritation, a wild thing enduring the biting of flies.

Herod Aldrich, the storekeeper, was gruff and disinclined to put men at their ease; he owned almost all the land between here and White Lady, and this power made him grudge small tasks. He seldom waited on customers now.

But something about this woodsman with the terrible scars made Aldrich shoo away his assistant, Mrs. Fanning. "Not seemly, ma'am," he mumbled, although she had measured countless other men for mail-order suits. "Leave him to me."

Fifteen years ago, by a series of wily maneuvers—all perfectly legal—Herod Aldrich had come by the royal patent that was seized from John Frayne's family in the name of the new Patriot government; there had been no town then to speak of, only a handful of farmers, a few aging trappers and potash-makers. Aldrich induced a joiner to come, and a cooper—Jacob Benet, it was, Catcher Benet—a bricklayer, even a printer and bookbinder. As though the place were Boston or Philadelphia, Herod laid out thirty acres into neat little city lots, every house with the same amount of ground, and on them he built wooden cottages, all alike, and all to be leased but not purchased. He had the town council pass rules against the keeping of hens and livestock, and there were no fields, either; no one was to grow his own wheat for flour, nor his own flax for spinning. If you wanted salt pork or pickled eggs or new gloves or cloth for a gown, you bought it at Aldrich's store and ran up a bill, and then another.

Older women resisted, they bought wool and flax from neighboring farmers and kept to their self-sufficient work. But the young ones began to turn their spinning wheels over to the children for playthings; first Aldrich made them need to buy and then he made them prefer to. Chinese rugs. Cloth from the bolt, printed muslins and calicoes brought in from Europe. Franklin stoves to set into their parlor hearths, with a pipe up the chimney. Whale-oil lamps that gave a blinding light, brighter than a dozen candles. Astral lamps, they called them. Brighter than stars.

As yet, very few could afford them, but that made them matter even more. The printed calicoes had a papery texture, faded easily, and wore out quickly. You could not cook on the stoves, and they dried the air and made the boards of tables crack and the rungs fall out of chairs. The lamps sweated out oil and had to be perched on a thick pad of rags. For months, when the whalers were still at sea and oil could not be come by, they sat dark and useless.

But they were new, and to complain of their defects was to grumble at the future, at progress. A world was slowly being born in which the only inalienable freedom was the freedom to buy.

It *had* been, that is, until Thomas Jefferson's embargo brought trade to a standstill. War was the remedy, that's what the Federalists said, the surest way to get the country back to the serious business of buying and selling. What they meant was that power lived in money, and in a country in which blood was no guarantee of position, it had to be bought or done without.

Herod Aldrich had no intention of doing without it. He had always meant to rise in the Federalist party, the party of gentlemen; the son of a Connecticut pork butcher, he had built his whole life around becoming at last a gentleman among gentlemen, and he had labored for years to cultivate all the right acquaintances to get himself nominated for the Senate in a few more years. But gentlemen's party or not, Aldrich could not support this war of theirs—how could he? Why, it would almost certainly be fought along the border with Canada, right on his very doorstep; his land was threatened, his town, his people. The dilemma made him nervous and angry, and just now Herod Aldrich took it out on John Frayne.

"How will you pay for all this, may I ask?" he said sharply, looking the strange frontiersman up and down.

Leclerc, sifting his fingers through the nails in open kegs lined up on a bench near the window, bit his lower lip and frowned, insulted on behalf of the dark man. Few men liked the storekeeper, and Marius was no exception. At home in Normandy, he had known a man of the same sort, a merchant named Casoudal, who owned several vineyards and almost twelve thousand acres of rich farmland, and thought of nothing but money. When the Revolution came, Casoudal had put on the red cap and marched about with a musket on his shoulder like a peasant, his eye carefully fixed on the property of the old Comte de Cornoillier, a helpless invalid who lived alone with his old-maid niece. Having insinuated himself onto the local Committee of Public Safety, Casoudal had the old man arrested and his property seized. By that time, every village had its guillotine, and the Cornoilliers died on an absurd contrivance improvised from an old doorframe, a rope, a crosscut saw with the teeth filed smooth, and some crates that stank of fish.

"How will you pay, sir?" the storekeeper repeated, tapping his pencil on the counter. "I must have some assurance."

Frayne looked around at him, as though Aldrich were a speck in the distance. Last night, his first night in his father's house, he had cut off his long hair with a skinning knife, so that it fell now in a soft, ragged fringe around his face. As he hacked with the blade, he could feel the west slipping away from him. When he had finished, when his hair was cut short, he took from his pack the three white stones the Indian wise man had given him. Putting one of them into his mouth, he tried to extract from it the flavor of certain streams in the west, steeped in cottonwood leaf and the fine sprouts of willow. It was to him the flavor of survival. But he could not taste it here.

Poking about in his mother's ruined kitchen, he found an earthenware cup, very old, with small fissures all over its surface. There was a pattern on it of blue leaves that curled back upon themselves, and they put him in mind of the cottonwood leaves. The chimney that served that part of the house was still whole, and—using the cup to hold soap—he built a fire and shaved himself, stripping away all disguise from the purplish-red scar. It ran in a curve from his left temple, down his cheekbone to the flare of his chin, the skin puckered slightly so that the corner of his mouth, pulled tight to the left, seemed always to verge on a lopsided smile.

"I'll need ten dollars on account," insisted the storekeeper.

A plain coat cost eight shillings, but it was an expensive—to Aldrich's mind, a presumptuous—outfit this backwoods monkey had ordered, deep green wool with black velvet facings to the coat, and cream-colored nankeen breeches in the new pantaloon style. He had bespoke a pair of boots, too, Hessian boots of tooled Spanish leather. A grey silk cravat. A gold stickpin. A pocket watch. A fine cambric shirt with high starched points to the collar. A silk-and-beaver hat in the newest London style, black, with a half-high crown. A dark grey woolen greatcoat with a double cape.

Not the clothes of a dandy, it was true. But certainly those of a gentleman. The word was irksome to Aldrich when applied to such a fellow, and the irritation deepened when Frayne smiled and bent to unfasten a scrip at his waist. There was a detached grace to his motions, to the subtle changes of his expression, the slight hunch of his shoulders.

He laid down a Spanish gold piece on Aldrich's counter, worth a hundred dollars. There was no paper money just now, and if you had coin, it was French, English, Spanish, Russian. But for two years, ever since the embargo, no foreign gold had entered the country by trade. Misers had it. Smugglers sometimes had it, and so did those in the pay of foreign governments.

"Gold coin? We seldom see such in these parts." Aldrich cleared his throat nervously.

John Frayne smiled. "I've come lately from the west, and in New Orleans, Spanish gold is still common enough currency. Clip it, if you like. You'll find it's genuine."

The storekeeper accepted the gold piece with a bow. If God

had any voice on the earth, He rattled like a coin. "Will you be wanting to bespeak a corset, sir? Breeches these days are terrible tight."

Frayne laughed softly. "No corsets," he replied in his low, even voice. "But I think this gaudy coin ought to buy me an answer or two."

Herod Aldrich had a longish nose with a slight hook on the end, and his face was a broad, white oval, flushed by the heat of the stove in the small room. Above him, strings of tin cups rattled in the draft from the damper, and bushel baskets thumped softly on their nails, as though they were breathing. Who are you? What mask are you wearing? Can I afford to refuse you? Am I richer than you?

Herod Aldrich glanced down at the scars on Frayne's palms, where a second coin—this one silver—had appeared as if by magic. The storekeeper inclined his head slightly. "At your service, sir."

"How did the old house at the head of the lake come to burn?" Frayne includes everyone in the room in his question, even the dowdy Frenchman still bumbling about at the counter.

"There was a bad storm some three years since," replies Aldrich. "Lightning struck one of the chimneys. But it wasn't much loss, even then."

"Who owns it now?"

"The land is mine, sir. I hold the government's patent to everything this side of White Lady. The foxes and owls and the tramps from the freight boats more or less own the house." Aldrich ventures a smile and a shrug.

"How much will you take for it? What's left of the house, and the garden and orchard. The old sugar bush and the meadow before it. I make it about twenty-five acres."

"I don't sell land, sir, that's well known hereabouts. I only rent it." Herod Aldrich speaks coldly, without any inflection, as men speak to their slaves.

John's blue eyes narrow. When he looks at the storekeeper,

something passes through his mind like a cobweb he has walked through. I know your back, how it leans with a secret wind, first one way, then another. I remember the shape of you in a window, in a doorway, silhouetted, perhaps, on a hilltop. Hester's voice comes with this opaque memory, on the night Frayne came home without warning and glimpsed a man leaving their cottage. Found the stains of unknown seed on the bedclothes.

I don't love him, Hester said with a shrug. But I don't love you, either. Bedding's a practical business. When you're hungry, you eat.

Frayne shrugs the image and the voice away for the present. Since the west, his memory cannot be relied upon except in random knife-thrusts, he can never be certain how much he remembers and how much he invents. Besides, Bay House is his son's legacy, and Tim is what matters now.

"Well, sir," he says. "I don't rent land, or houses. I mean to repair the old place and set improvements afoot, and it makes no sense unless I own it. Come along, Mr. Aldrich. You surely have no use for such a ruin, you will sell it me. Sixty dollars, cash-in-hand."

"I fear we cannot do business," replies Aldrich, narrow-mouthed.

"A hundred, then."

It is an excellent offer, and the storekeeper knows it. Cleared farm land sells for a dollar and a half the acre now, and this strange fellow has almost tripled the usual price. Aldrich had paid only fifty cents for it himself, and his supply of cash is at a low ebb just now, like everyone else's.

But something about this graceful man in the buckskins itches Herod Aldrich, pricks his need for control. Besides, Bay House has a meaning to him beyond the ordinary, just as it does to John Frayne. "I will rent you the land for fourteen cents the acre per annum," he says. "It's a fair market rate. Take it or leave it. I've no wish at present to sell anything that's mine."

Frayne smiles his lopsided smile. "Well, well, we shall see. But one more question, if you please."

A slight deferential bow from the storekeeper. His clothing is twenty-five years out of date—buckled knee breeches, a broad-tailed coat, and a tricorne hat when he walks down the streets he calls *my streets*. When he attempts high-toned formalities with his political cronies, he is jerky and awkward, as though somebody moves him by wires. At twenty-three, barely able to read, Herod Aldrich, still clad in the leather jerkin and bleached homespun apron of a butcher's apprentice, scraped together three dollars to join a subscription library. The first book he borrowed was entitled *The Gentleman's Compendium of Comportment for All Social Encounters*.

But the present encounter is most certainly not to be found in its pages. "Question?" Aldrich says, and then glances away again, shamefaced and huffing, ashamed of his lack of polish. "Ask what you will. I'm sure we've nothing to hide in my town. Eh, Mrs. Fanning?"

The lady clerk abandons her bolts of lace and bobs him a curtsy. "We ain't a town for secrets, sir. No, indeed."

"Excellent." John includes them all in the question. "Does anyone here know a woman called Hester Frayne? She sometimes called herself by her maiden name, Sheldon. A plain woman, capable. Brown-haired."

"What do you want with her?" Aldrich says, glancing around the room as though Hester might be hiding in one of the corners.

"She's my wife," Frayne says. "Or she was when I left for the Missouri country. My boy's with her, he'd be ten now—or nearly. Timothy Frayne."

The eyes of the draughts-players open wider, and a woman buying calico rushes out smirking. For a long moment, nobody speaks. Something dark and ancient has entered the room, watching with eyes of saurian indifference.

But only Leclerc seems to see it. He stumbles in a rush to the counter, stepping hastily between Frayne and Aldrich as though they are two boats about to collide in a fog. "I also have—I—I wish—" he stammers. "I wish to— To buy a violin!"

One of the checkers-players sniggers and slaps his knee, and the atmosphere relaxes.

"I—I have seen a young woman in the woods," the Frenchman goes on, blushing bright crimson. He can feel himself panting, as though he has run half a mile over the ice a second time. "Can—can you tell me where she lives? I mean—I mean— No harm. I—I wish to give her—a violin. Other things. Shoes. Combs. I wish—"

Bemused, John Frayne breaks off to listen, but Herod Aldrich is still hard-eyed and says nothing. Mrs. Harriet Fanning, rolling up a bolt of blue ribbon, sniffs into her lace-edged handkerchief and stifles a laugh. Marius does not mention the house at the Bay of Spirits, nor the books, nor the newly-laid boards, nor the bird.

"Do you perhaps know this girl's name, madame?" he asks the woman at the ribbon counter. "Can you tell where her family lives? I saw her once in the autumn, but since then . . ."

His voice trails away, awkward and foolish. The middle-aged clerk, Mrs. Fanning, puts her nose in the air, the two bunches of looped braids that stick out of her lace cap quivering, making the pink satin ribbons dance. "She's a tramp and a lunatic, that one. And no better than she should be, I warrant. Such creatures don't have names. Or if they do, it's as well not to know them."

Leclerc looks up at the smug face of the woman, like one of Franz Zimmer's dumplings, with two currants for eyes. "No, no, madame. She does not speak many words. But if she proves to be the same person I know, she is called Fauvette," he replies without blinking. "Fauvette D'Hiver."

Sparrow, it means. Winter sparrow. As soon as he speaks the name it begins to seem that he has not invented it but recalled it, drawn it out of a past that has just returned to him after many years. In his village there had been a woman called Nanon Barriat, an aging widow his brothers had urged him to marry. She's as scrawny as a sparrow, Jules told him, but what warm-blooded woman would want you? Besides, said Leon with a laugh, a bony old sparrow will suit you as well as another.

Frayne's voice draws Leclerc out of his reverie. "Is it the girl with the dark, reddish hair?" he says. "You say she speaks sometimes, then?"

Leclerc blushes. "Yes, monsieur. Believe me, I wish only to be of service to her. She is no tramp, but a—a lady, a gentleman's daughter. I am a friend of—of her father. I knew him in— In Paris."

He has never been to Paris. But nobody questions his story; such coincidences happen every day with these *émigré* Frenchmen. Hundreds have come since the Terror, but even here the mad logic of war seems to pursue them. They stumble upon abandoned loves, betrayed friends, estranged children. A week ago in a scoop-hollow village on the Albany turnpike, the ex–Duc de Revailles, who was driving a freight wagon full of turnips, met his old enemy the ex–Comte de la Moines, and was killed in a duel on the spot.

"That house by the lake," Hetty Fanning lisps, glancing over at Frayne, then at Aldrich. "Old wreck of a place, used to be a regular nest full of Tories. People get up to all manner of things there, so they say. And as to that wife of yours, Hester, if you take my advice—"

A sudden noise from the street interrupts her. It is a strange cry, high and shrill, and it ebbs and flows in deep gasps. John Frayne pushes the storekeeper aside and is out of the door in two long strides, but Marius does not need to go out to look. His absurd, chubby body slides down the front of Aldrich's counter until he is hunched beside the barrels of salt fish like a bird that is trapped between walls.

"Annnnhhhh-ahhhhhh!"

The girl Jennet is wearing her mother's old cloak, which falls open as she walks. Her hands have been tied in front of her and a leash fastened to them, attached to the harness of a brown pony who plods along quietly. So slow is his pace that she is not dragged, even though her ankles are fastened together and she can take only shuffling steps, like the cripple Leclerc.

Jacob Benet walks beside the pony, patting it now and then to keep it steady in spite of the noise of her cries. He is a man of little imagination and therefore of little feeling for women, they have no reality to him. But it does not make him cruel or stupid. Tree stumps still stand here and there in Broad Street, some of them waist-high, girdled with ax cuts and left to rot slowly away, and Catcher Benet leads her carefully around them in a zigzag path toward Tom Lashaway's tavern. The poormaster's covered box-sleigh is tethered there, and one or two light cutters, their horses steaming and snuffling in the cold. This is the day on which vendue is held, on which disputed wills are set to probate and orphans put up for indenture and poor folk auctioned for the price of their keep.

"Annnnhhhhh-ahhhhhhh!"

With every step, the girl howls. The wall of cold buckles and cracks with the sound and gives way on both sides of her. Frayne moves closer, parallel to her, catching the new, clean scent of her. She has washed the fool's seed off her, he thinks.

A second rope net somewhat smaller than the other falls down over her body like a birdcage, lashed tight around her upper thighs so that she is able to walk or be pulled, but not to fight or to run. It is the sort used to transport slaves to the sale barns. Yesterday, once the first knot was cut in the dusk at the edge of the lake, Jennet had thought herself free of such cages, but now she knows the greatest truth of living. There is more than one net in the world.

Frayne's voice is quiet, something in it of command. "Loose that thing from her. Untie her feet."

"Nay. She'll run, and I'll have another day's work catching her."

"She won't. I'll see to it."

Benet laughs softly. "When this one runs, nobody stops her."

Frayne looks down at the girl's feet, which are short and square in the worn boots. When she moves, she stamps them up and down as if she might stamp open the earth and disappear into it. He remembers the sound of them, kicking the ice under the weight of the men.

But it is only her face he can think of now. I have seen your picture in many churches, he will tell her later. A disillusioned virgin, holding god in your arms.

Where is Jennet now? Where is her mind, her memory, her passion?

She is thinking of a night when the sun did not set, that strange light of the Scottish summer that can soften rocks. A man lay down with her, the first who had touched her, the young teacher she trusted whose slender body in that light turned to gold in her arms. She cannot remember his name nor his face, she has blotted them out. But a word that he taught her comes now to find her, heavier, tighter than any cage of rope.

"Lost," she says aloud in the hoarse, half-strangled voice. "Awst."

Still at her elbow, Frayne cups his hands together and makes the sign for friend, but she cannot see him. She is blinded by the net, the leash, the blank wall of the world. He reaches through the squares of tar-blackened rope and grips her arm, and the girl looks at his pierced hand as though it has grown from her, a sprout of her bone. He clenches his left fist in front of him, then lets his right fist graze it, a glancing blow like a heartbeat. Courage, he says aloud, and she reads the word from the shape of his mouth.

Courage. It is the same in French. From the storekeeper's doorway, Leclerc, too, reads the word on Frayne's lips and shudders. At Austerlitz, he heard officers shout it from the shoreline to men who were already drowned.

"Take off that net," Frayne says again.

Catcher Benet stops, turns to study him. "Who is it that asks?"

"I do. John Stephen Frayne."

"Frayne," Benet says like an echo.

Without more discussion, the net is removed.

Mrs. Lydia Monk. Widow and aged pauper, sixty-four years of age. Seamstress, plain cook, washerwoman, spinster, all household work.

Gabriel Hines. Aged pauper, seventy-two years of age. Farmer. Able to lay stone, perform simple carpentry, and tend cattle. Has own tools. Vision imperfect.

Noah Gould. Orphan pauper and simpleton, about fourteen years of age. Illiterate. Tame and tractable, but liable to mischief.

Unknown Female. Madwoman and pauper, aged about twenty-five years. Deaf and mute.

So Benet writes them down in his log book, in a thick, awkward hand.

The four wards of the county stand in a row beneath a tarnished brass chandelier whose expensive wax candles are not lighted this morning. Spiders have built webs between them, the sheer strands drifting in nameless currents of air, and dust wraps the age-softened wax in a heavy, felted jacket.

Wax is for gentlemen, the girl's mother used to say. Twice a year, they went to the chandler's shop to buy long, straight, hard wax candles and set them in two silver candlesticks in her father's small study, where—unable to sleep—Daniel Josselyn pored over the shipyard account books far into the night. The books added up to failure, to the end of his last possibility. The silver candlesticks, a last gift from a loved aunt, were sold to buy a cow.

Aging and insomniac on his weather-scourged island, he burned tallow-dips stuck in a cracked earthenware cup. When he died, it was sudden and brave, and for that she is grateful.

But of all Jennet's losses, her father's remains the keenest, his love for her the most amazing. For Daniel's sake, she has kept the old cup with its pattern of curling blue leaves in her small sack of treasures, and set it out where Frayne found it, by the hearth of the house she now thinks of as hers. Dip me some candles, my Flower. Bring me back the light.

The high-ceilinged assembly room above Lashaway's tavern is dim, long shafts of bronze winter light slashing down and turning the poormaster's wig a peculiar rusty shade, like overbrewed tea. His name is not important. He is a foolish old man in a petty position, and he fancies the wig lends him dignity. He is, of course, wrong.

There is a huge old hearth, but a fire is built in it only for the annual dance they call the Federal Ball, which will not come until mid-February. Today it is very cold in the big room, Benet's breath steaming as he stands by the poormaster's table.

"Pauper the first, step forward!" cries the clerk.

He takes Mrs. Lydia Monk by the arm and leads her to the center aisle, between two benches of bidders. They are mostly farmers whose wives want unpaid household labor—someone to scour pots, stoke ovens, empty the slop jars from under the beds.

One or two people bid, and Mrs. Monk goes to a bird-beaked old woman in a coal-scuttle bonnet who collects the first month's county fee from Benet and hurries her new servant away. Next comes the simpleton, the boy Noah, who goes to a ropespinner from Germantown, to be indentured as an apprentice. The spinner is a decent enough fellow; Leclerc, sitting at the back of the room, knows him slightly and is glad for the boy.

Herod Aldrich, who seldom attends vendues unless his property is at issue, is also present; like the Frenchman, he has followed them here from the mercantile store. He takes a seat on the end of a bench at the back of the room and those who sit near him can hear his fists pound down, down, down on the wooden seat at his sides.

But Aldrich does not bid for the old fellow, Gabriel Hines, who is troubled with cataracts—nor does anyone else. If no one can be found to take them, paupers are sent to the county poorhouse in Cayuna, on the other side of the Divide.

The old man stares down at his folded hands, bleak and shamed. The poorhouse is a byword, a thing all old folk dread more than dying. When at last it confronts them, some take their own lives or disappear into the forest, to be found starved to death in the spring.

Frayne steps quietly up to where Gabriel is standing. "I remember a man who came to my father's house to build bookshelves," he says in a low murmur that only the old man can hear. "A tough-minded Yankee with an arm like a tree trunk and a kindness for little boys. He put me up on his shoulder and set me high on the topmost shelf and let me watch him at his work. Fine work it was, too. As I remember it, he sang while he labored. How did it go, now? 'There was a jolly miller once, lived on the River Dee . . .'"

"God save me! Why, I can scarce believe it!" The old man's failing eyes open wide, but he keeps his voice lowered. Gabe Hines is tall, perhaps six feet four or five, with broad shoulders and skin as smooth and unlined as a boy's. "That's gone thirty years now! It's not— Can it be— Are you not Master Jackie?"

"I am. I was."

"But what the devil are you doing here, sir? How do you come to be in the court? And your mother, where is she? And Miss Emma and Miss Lizzie?"

Frayne does not answer, he only gives a squeeze to the old fellow's arm and turns back to the poormaster. "I am satisfied, sir. I will take Master Hines, and glad to have him."

"Well, I'm blasted." The official scratches his head, setting his wig askew. Puts a pinch of snuff inside his lower lip, so that he looks even more like a monkey. "Very well. How much do you ask a month for his keep, then? Must make a bid to the county like the rest, you know. Keep to procedure."

"Very well. I ask nothing a month." John glances at the wild girl as though he has never seen her before, as though he has not already begun to live in her proud, secret spirit. "For the young lady, too," he says. "I'll take on her keep, but I want no fee from the county."

"Lady, is it? Humpf!" The poormaster looks John up and down, from his moccasined feet to the scar on his face. "And how do you propose to feed the pair of them? You'll be guardian, you know, and if they do any crime, it's your doing too, in the eyes of the law!"

"If they do any murders, you may come and stretch me, and welcome to it. Anything else, I will pay for with this." John Frayne unfastens his scrip and dumps it out on the table. Coins of all nations fall out, bounce onto the floor and roll away into cracks. Some of the farmer boys run after them, chasing them under benches and table legs. "Will that serve you for earnest, that I'm good for their keep?"

The poormaster huffs and puffs. "You're an impudent ape, sir! You come prancing into this court without so much as a how-d'ye-do—"

"This is a vendue, not a court, and I've shown you the color of my coin." Frayne steps closer to the table and lowers his voice. "I have offered to keep two of your paupers at no cost to the county, sir. By the law you must give them to me. If you fancy a bribe, we can see to that later, in private. Come now, what do you say?"

"You ain't even resident here!"

"I am now. I've been on the Missouri some years, but I was born here and my father is buried here. I mean to take up his place and work it."

"Well, hem— I'll make no fuss over old Hines, you may have him and welcome. But, by gad, I'm a man and a Christian, you know. What do you want with the girl? Hey? Man alone, used to savages! What do you want with her?"

"She's said to be stone-deaf, mad, and a thief into the bargain. Is there anyone else willing to keep her for nothing?" Frayne turns to the sparse crowd on the benches. "You there, the man with the red cap! What'll you bid for her? You were eager enough to have her yesterday at a bargain, out there on the ice."

The poormaster looks at the silent girl. Benet stares up at the dust on the candles. Caleb and his two friends slouch and duck their heads, and the official says nothing to them. "I can't just give her away to be used for a drab, sir," he says to Frayne. "Have you a wife and a respectable household she may serve?"

"I have a wife. Hester Frayne is her name, or perhaps Hester Sheldon. Does any here know her? Does any know of my son, John Timothy Frayne?"

Again the names fall like heavy blows. At the back of the room, Herod Aldrich rises to leave, his pasty face flushed and his fists bulging out in his pockets. He is older than he looks, more afraid than he looks, and more alone.

The poormaster lets out a whoop. "By gad, I thought I should know you—though you've turned yourself out like a savage! But those blue eyes are the clinker—you're Captain Frayne's son, all right, the old Tory's whelp!" He slaps the desk and explodes into laughter. "Take your mad girl, in that case, and welcome to what use you can make of her. Ha, ha! 'Strewth, you'll lie cold indeed, I warrant, if you wait for that wife of yours to warm your bed again!" His small pink eyes turn gleefully to Benet. "Eh, Jacob? What say you to that?"

Frayne's voice is steady and quiet, and his hands work at untying the leash around the girl's waist. "Do you mean to say Hester is dead, then? God rest her soul." It is, he thinks grimly, more than she would wish him in return. "But my son," he says. "What has become of my—"

"She's not dead," says Jacob Benet. Sometimes he has wished her so, and himself with her. "Hester is my wife these five years," he continues in his slow, deliberate voice. It has a grain in it, like oak or black ash, deep-running and concentric. "If you care to take Hester back, you may have her," he says. "But as for your boy, Tim's my own son now, and you'd best leave him be. He knows you for a scoundrel and a villain, and he will not so much as speak your name." Benet smiles, an odd, brittle smile, like the curve of ice at the edge of a bucket. "Best take that net of mine yourself, Mr. Frayne," he says quietly. "You'll have need of it, I promise you, for the boy'll never come to you unless he's dragged."

John Frayne's body seems for a moment to sway, almost to hover in the air. Suddenly he remembers with terrifying clarity how the blood spattered into his eyes when they drove the nails into his palms, holding them down onto a fine mahogany table. Where it was, in what tent or mud lodge or cabin or St. Louis mansion, he cannot yet remember. Only voices come back at odd moments, all asking the same question. Whose are you? Who sent you? Who tells the price of your soul?

The answer is always the same. "My son," he says softly. "My Tim."

His fingers grip Jennet's arm, then let go. She might run away now easily enough, and for a moment Leclerc, on his knees gathering up the spilled coins from under the benches, is certain she will try.

But she is very still, like the Roman statue. Within herself Jennet has a second pair of secret eyes that devour the world even when she appears to be unaware of it. Maybe this is what death is like—to see and not be seen, to live and not seem to live. When her mother heard no birth-cries, she at first believed she had borne a dead child. Perhaps, the girl thinks, she was right.

"Go if you like," Frayne's mouth says. Jennet lays the palm of her hand lightly across it and he says it again, letting her feel the shapes of the words. "You know where I will be. Go if you like, and come back when you need to. You are free." He laughs, low, like a growl. "But don't steal any more, or they'll lock us both away."

For a moment she hesitates, and her hand lingers on his mouth, the pressure of fingertips very slight on the terrible scar alongside it, like a current of air on the raw skin. She draws in the scent of him, blended of tobacco and homemade soap and seasoned leather, and the clean, cold wool of his shirt. She is aware of the Frenchman on his knees in the back of the room, of a certain nerve in her left eyelid that jumps for no reason, of the metallic flavor of fear in her mouth. She waits for a moment more, uncertain of what is beginning, of whether she wants anything to begin.

Then her back straightens. Frayne holds out a hand and she takes it, stepping with small, neat, stamping paces beside him. Slips her arm through the crook of his elbow like a lady on promenade in the park.

"Home now," she says, and Leclerc, his spectacles dangling from their ribbon and his hands overflowing with money, thinks unaccountably of birds.

III

lot's wife

Do the white gods take wives, Saku? the old Indian magus once asked Frayne.

When he was well enough to ride, they gave him a white mule with a beaded bridle and took him to be seen by any who had strife or sickness among them, or whose lodges were threatened with war. By the time summer turned into autumn they had travelled many miles together, he and the blind man and the gentle young boy, visiting village after village of the people so that his presence might absolve them. *The people*, they called themselves, as if there were no other. Still, there were many clans among them, Owls and Foxes and Bears and Horses and Ravens, and feuds sometimes arose over marriage portions or the claims of a warrior to brave deeds. All these they brought before the wise man and his tame white god as they moved about the high, grassy plains under a sky in which even the clouds seemed to lose all direction.

Yet Frayne continued to map this vast emptiness without ink or paper. In his mind he could have moved through it backwards, directed any stranger to a particular spring of pure water, to a grove of cottonwood under which certain health-giving plants grew. With his eye he estimated distances, the subtle rises and falls of topography, the approximate boundaries of various tribes. Three miles from Black Willow Creek to the Fountain Rocks. Ground rises to the northward at an angle of four degrees climbing to seven. Otoe village ten miles to the east.

In summer the people lived in skin houses, circular tents that could be struck and hauled from place to place, wherever the hunting was best. They were traders, and men came from other tribes, from the Crow and Assiniboin and the Cheyenne and Cree, and sometimes even the Lakota, the great Sioux who were everyone's enemy. They traded hides and horses and guns, and bought corn and squash from the people, but whenever they came, Frayne was hidden away and a watch was set over him, for fear they might steal him.

Wounded Face, the women called him. Our Father, Saku of Many Wounds.

In the Wild Goose Moon, at the breaking of the new winter, with snow spitting dry from the northwest, the three wanderers rode into a village of the peaceable Fox clan, a wide circle of round earth lodges in which some of the old men and women remained year-round, tending gardens of corn and squash and burying the harvest in deep pits lined with dried grasses to keep them through the frozen months. It was a good place, settled and kind and domestic, and as Frayne sat in the dank warmth of the lodges, watching the women bend and stoop and squat at their cooking, it made him think of Hester, of the way her skirts grazed the coals and were always singed black at the fold of the hem.

I had a wife, he told them. A woman with grey eyes, like a wolf. I had a blue-eyed son.

The villagers were gathered that night in a great lodge where the ceremonies of manhood and courage took place, where purified women were welcomed back to the tribe after childbirth and the dead were blessed before their long journey. A campfire burned in the center and the smoke of it rose in a column, to escape through a hole in the roof where the radiating beams came together like spokes in a wheel. The walls were hung with story-pictures painted on deerskin that told the clan's history winter by winter, and below these, on benches draped with the soft skins of buffalo and fox and ermine and bear, the silent men sat with their dark-eyed women, while dogs snuffled for bones at the fire and children came up one by one to touch the white skin of Frayne's chest.

His hair had grown long now, and some of the maidens were sent to tie feathers and bells in it as an offering to the gods. Two of them held back, afraid to approach him, but the third stepped up boldly. She was very young, no more than seventeen or eighteen, with long, fine limbs like the boughs of a willow, and strange, almond-shaped eyes that laughed in the firelight. Her waist-long hair was plaited and looped up at her neck, and she had painted the part with a narrow line of scarlet. In each of her ears she wore three loops of red-and-white beads, and her gown was made of fringed antelope skin, tanned to the color of a pigeon's breast.

Her dark eyes danced across Frayne's features, sorting them, approving of this one, disapproving of that. But when she got to his beard, which had not been shaven all summer, the girl could not take her eyes from it.

Gods grow hair in funny places, she said with a giggle. When she laughed, red glass beads on the fringes of her sleeve made a music like harness bells. She fastened an eagle feather into his black beard and tugged at it.

Christ! he cried out. She had opened the scar on his cheek and a few drops of watery blood ran down from it.

The lodge fell suddenly silent and the girl gasped and put her hand across her mouth. Someone pulled her away, but she freed herself and stood proud and alone, her eyes still on Frayne's countenance. He wiped off the blood with the back of his hand, his pale eyes following her movements through lowered lashes. Stepping near him again, she bent down and picked up a stick from the firewood and handed it to him.

I am foolish, she said. Saku will punish me now.

Frayne took the stick from her. What is it? he asked the boy, who was always beside him. What does she want of me?

She has wronged you. She begs to be beaten.

The tribesmen sat silent, watching and judging. It was expected of him and he knew he might lose their respect if he did not beat the girl. Gods, after all, must be able to punish.

What is her name? he asked.

She is Tacha. Deer Woman. A silly, stuck-up girl, she thinks too much of herself, that's what the others say. It's high time she was beaten.

Has she no husband to beat her?

Nah! No one will take her as first wife. Second wife is as good as she hopes for, her father is poor, he has no horses to give with her. She will be servant to first wife, and bear servant-children.

Frayne threw the beating-stick into the fire, took the proud girl by the hand and settled her beside him. Then he turned to the old man, the magician, who was called the Prophet. Do gods marry for love? he asked.

The blind man smiled. He drew a deep breath, as though he were drawing the girl into him by the fragrance of grass-oil and dried elderflowers that clung to her. When he breathed out again, the crimson eyelids seemed to crumple.

Gods are gods, Saku. It does not keep them from being damn fools.

I took a wife for love, but she could not love me, Frayne said as the boy began to dance and the old man took up the flute. Someone was beating a skin drum in the background and one by one the others rose to the dance, the rhythm mounting and falling with the story.

My wife was a girl when I met her, and I was very little older. Her people were farmers, but her father was dead and her mother and aunts kept her strictly, and drove away all her suitors out of jealousy. Power was all that concerned them, to impose their will on the universe. They could not bear the thought that Hester would survive them, that she would marry and have children and the land would pass into the hands of strangers to whom the will of the mother and the aunts meant nothing. Little by little, they sold off the property and spent most of the money, determined to leave Hester nothing. That was how I came to meet her. I was hired to survey the farm for sale and make a map of it—so much woodland, so much pasture, so many high fields, so many water meadows.

In what country, Saku?

A green country, called England. A very beautiful country, very old and full of spirits. But I did not belong to it. I was carried there as a young child.

Ah, gods may be captives, then?

Am I not a captive here?

The old man smiled. To escape was impossible. To be freed was unlikely. Since Frayne's appearance among them, the Prophet had consolidated much power among the clans on the strength of the white god's friendship. It was said that, for the good of his people, the old magician had poisoned many in the past who disrupted the tribe by resisting his wisdom.

Many gods and many men are in exile, and I was one such, Frayne went on. The surface of my mind knew nothing but England, but the dark of me remembered another place. I remembered my father's fine house and his gardens and the lake and the mountains. I belonged there, if I belonged anywhere. It was where my sins began, and I could not forget the great fir trees and the statues in the garden and the way the house lay, looking north to the far country my father told me of, where ice never melted, and bears were the color of snow.

Bad ghosts live in the north, muttered the Prophet. This father was foolish. A house should face east, where the light is new and clean.

Perhaps. But I could not forget it, Frayne continued, and I swore to earn it back one day, so that a son of mine might claim it. I had an uncle in London, my father's brother. He grudged me every farthing, but he paid for my schooling and apprenticed me to learn mapmaking from an old master in Yorkshire. I repaid him to the last penny. I was a master surveyor at twenty-one, and the prosperous farm in Devon where my wife Hester grew up was my first job, once I was free to grasp life on my own.

I saw her first as she stood in a high meadow looking down at the sea, with the wind blowing her skirts. Her bonnet blew off and Hester ran to catch it, and I wondered years later if she had left it untied for that very reason, to give her an excuse to come near me. She was laughing, and her hair had fallen loose as she ran, and her face glowed with the wind and the salt air. She seemed to me very beautiful, guileless and sweet. An innocence that might cleanse me. I stood still by my surveyor's instrument, watching her through it and knowing she would come to me. She was almost upon me when she saw me—or so I believed at the time.

What can you spy through that glass of yours? she said. Her hair was light brown, almost silver with the sunlight upon it, and it fell across her eyes and her mouth like a mask, to keep me from seeing her clear.

Come and look, I said, and I turned the lens to face the ocean.

Oh, see! There's a ship far out, Hester said with her eye to the instrument. I wish I was aboard it. I wonder where it's bound.

And where should you like to be bound for? I asked her. The Indies? Madagascar? Madeira?

For wherever you are going, she said, and reached out for my hand. I should like to go there with you.

I came to think later that she would have said the same to any man she had met in that place, to any man over whom the aunts and the mother had no power. Hester turned round and gazed at me deeply, and her eyes were the color of November ocean, as though it rose cold in her like a winter tide and filled her. I do not think she had seen me at all.

But I could not stop wanting her, and I truly believed that I loved her. What does any man know of loving at twenty? In a month we were married, and we went out to Canada, almost penniless, for her mother denied her any dower. I think Hester tried hard to love me too at first, and I cannot say now what prevented her. Something I did without knowing it. Something I was or was not—as I say, she had never really seen me. I was often away marking boundaries and she was too much alone and the country was cold and the work was hard for her, and if ever God had taken notice of us, He seemed to have blinded His eye. By night, I heard her weeping, and when I spoke to her or touched her, she would turn away and deny me even the giving of what little comfort I could. At last we had a son, and he lived and was beautiful in my eyes, but she hated me for loving him, as though every thought I gave to him was stolen from her.

One day I came home from the town and found her out in the wind, on a high place, looking out through my instrument. What do you spy through that lens of yours? I asked her. I wanted to go back where we began and start over again, to erase the pain in her that made an ache in me.

No more ships, she said. I see no ships at all.

And so she betrayed you at last with some other, some enemy? asked the Prophet.

We came back to my father's country, to the house they had taken from him. I thought she might learn my dreams from it and come to know me, even though it was no longer mine. But it only grew worse for her, she hated my memories and envied them, and she began to punish me for them, and torment me to make me jealous.

She wished to live in your soul and possess it, said the Prophet. Some are put into the world without souls of their own.

Hester said many times that she had taken a lover, Frayne said slowly. She taunted me with it. At first, I thought it was only a story she made up to hurt me, because she had lost hope, and pride along with it. But time made the story come true, for one night I came home late from my work and found that a man had been with her. I saw him, a shape in the shadows like something the wind had blown in and left there. I could not even hate him, so insubstantial he seemed. He was a ghost, and so long as I stayed with her, so were Hester and I.

But did you not demand his name of her? You might have killed him and had back your honor.

No honor worth keeping can be had back by killing. Besides, cause me pain though it did, what the man took was Hester's own. She had taken it away from me long before—if she ever gave it at all.

Mihewi, Sun Woman. The sun is great but it is not faithful.

It is covered with dark for the deeds of our enemies to come secret upon us. It draws away into cold and sends ice to the rivers. If you had punished this woman, you might have forgiven her, Saku.

I did forgive, Frayne said softly. I do. But Hester didn't want my forgiveness. It was only my absence she wanted, and I gave it her. I left her alone, and my boy with her. Christ. How could I have kept him, young as he was then, barely weaned? To lose a child tears the heart. But to waste it, to become a stranger to it—

John Frayne fell silent. The dancers stopped and the flutes ceased to play, and the girl Tacha, who still sat with her small hand in his own, was weeping silently, as women of the far tribes weep, without tears, but bleeding from the root. She lifted his hand to her face and kissed the nail holes.

In granting this woman her freedom, you enslaved yourself to her forever, said the Prophet at last. The gods are wise to be jealous of granting such freedom.

His hands moved in his lap and a field mouse appeared in them, trapped in his fingers and struggling. He let it run up the sleeve of his tunic, then snatched it again and snapped its neck and cast it into the fire.

Freedom walks in many disguises, and many evil things are mistaken for it. Once it is given, it may unloose a thousand plagues upon those who have begged it. But no god is strong enough to take it back again.

To be a man with two wives is to follow in the footsteps of Abraham, Isaac, and Jacob. To be a woman with two husbands is to be an acre of property disputed that will grow to a burdensome waste. Worse still, it is to be a spy in two camps, with no hope of reward from either. and the bane of regret concerning both.

—Hannah Trevor, later Josselyn, *Journal of the Year 1784*

"You told me Frayne was dead!" cried Jacob Benet, bursting into his wife's kitchen once the vendue was over.

Hester raked out some coals onto the hearth and set a spider over them for the venison gravy. "Never," she said.

"But you let me believe so! I'd not have wed you if I thought you had a husband living!" Benet sank down on the settle by the fire and stared at her. "After this I'll be a laughingstock. Aldrich will have nothing to do with me now."

Hester bit her lip to keep from laughing. "Oh, he'll be glad enough to keep friends with you. Who else would scratch his backside as you have?"

"Well, and what if I have?" Jacob's dark eyes narrowed to slits in the square, sun-browned face. Her taunts had grown wilder of late, but he would not be provoked into using her harshly. "I mean to get forward in this town and this county," he said, "and that's how things work. If you don't know as much, then it's high time you learned. I make no doubt Aldrich'll be governor one day, or sit in the Senate."

"And what will you be then? Will he make you ratcatcher?"

Hester spoke with some justice, and he knew it. Nothing had ever been definitely promised him, and little had been given. Oh, there had been a series of lackluster local posts—the unsavory task of poormaster's catcher the most recent—but you had to pass tests if you meant to be trusted and rewarded. That was it, you must take the long view of things, and in that view nothing mattered but money. If you had it, you had freedom, and you could sit out the lean times in comfort. Had Aldrich himself not begun as a poor man?

Trust nothing but money, that was Jacob's motto, as it had been

Herod Aldrich's. The great money-men were kings in their own domains—Judge Phillotson, the chief justice; Bartram Hargrave, who ruled Cayuna and most of the county adjoining, and would run for the Senate in two years; Senator Shackleton, the great landlord of Albany, who had just been reelected; and Aldrich, of course.

That power used him Jacob knew, that he served it at the price of his pride and his common sense and his power of choice. But, he told himself, he would take all those intangibles back, once he came into his own and had money, and power of his own along with it.

Did it never occur to him that Herod Aldrich and Shackleton and the rest were his natural enemies, who would never allow him such power lest it challenge their own? Perhaps, at the wolf-hour just before dawn, when he lay sleepless in the bitter cold bedroom, hearing Hester's shallow, dangerous breathing beside him.

But by daylight, all Jacob's wild hope came back again, the delusion even stronger than ever. This was still America, after all, a man could do anything here. Besides, Aldrich's party had recovered enough seats in the Congress to give the new president a run for his money. Since the election, Jacob felt he was dancing on the edge of some great possibility.

"There's war brewing, woman," he told Hester. "Right here, up on the Lakes, and we're close to the heart of it. They'll likely march up into Canada soon, maybe sail up to Fort Regent. That means more troops, and troops means rations and rum. It means gunpowder. Think, can't you? What do you keep 'em in? How do you carry them?"

"Barrels." Hester's grey eyes closed for a moment. It was the kind of dream she might have expected of Jacob. A fat contract for barrels.

"Aye," he said proudly. "I'm a damn fine cooper, I make the best kegs and pails and hogsheads between here and Pittsburgh, well known for it. I've got a shopyard piled high with them and no place to sell them." He paused for breath and wiped his lips with his kerchief. "Er, not since the Canada trade ain't lawful, that is."

It was true that the embargo had been hard on business at first. But the yard of the coopering shop across from the house was not always piled high with unsalable barrels. Hester had noticed that the work picked up abruptly, till the pile of finished barrels grew great. Then the journeyman, Topas Logan, would hitch up the ox on the same Thursday at the end of each month and drive off about nightfall with a sledgeload of new kegs and barrels and buckets and churns covered over with canvas. Sometimes Topas would go alone, and other times he and Jacob would be gone for a day and a night. Now and then they would come back with a fine piece of beefsteak for the table or a painted toy soldier for Tim, and money would be flush for a while.

After one such time, Hester went into Aldrich's store to buy a new washboard and found a half-dozen other women there, buying rat traps and fire tongs and lengths of calico, till old Hetty Fanning was near run off her feet making change.

"They'd a good run this week, eh, my dear?" said Topas Logan's round little wife with a nudge at Hester's elbow.

"Run?" she said vaguely. "What run?"

"Why, up the border." Bess Logan peered at her, puzzled. "The smuggling, my dear. You know. Border-running. Up to Fort Regent. It's the only place around here with money to spend."

Hester seldom thought of where money came from; it was either there, or it wasn't. She only stared. "Smuggling?"

The women looked at one another and smiled. "*Ach,* that ain't nothing," said Frieda Tolberg, the glassblower's wife from Germantown. "They got to pass them laws, I guess, but they don't mean nothing, them trade laws. To sell them *Englisch* a little glass and a few barrels and some of these here nice yard goods of Aldrich's—well, I guess that don't hurt Mr. Thomas Jefferson none. Ha, ha! I ain't good friends with Nelson, nor Napoleon neither. How about you, Minnie?"

"*Ach, ja,* sure. He sent me a new hat for Christmas!"

"Just like Josephine's, I bet!"

Hester stood silent, their laughter washing over her. She didn't mind Jacob's breaking the law, laws meant nothing in the process of living. But like Frayne on the night he caught sight of her lover's disappearing shape, Hester had glimpsed a world of manipulation and maneuver she had not known existed, and a side of Jacob she might one day use against him, if need be. She stood silent, storing her weapon away.

"Poor Hester!" said one of the women, looking over at her blank, sober face. "Ha, ha! I bet she's the only one left in three counties that don't know how us common folk lives hereabouts!"

But she was mistaken, for there was one other. The boy with two fathers, John Timothy Frayne.

"Where do you go to sell the barrels, Dada?" he had asked Benet once.

Tim spoke very little as a rule, and almost never asked questions. He was a silent, intent child who treasured the natural world in peculiar, secretive ways. It was the boy's greatest pleasure to step out alone into the dark, cold dooryard, his eyes closed, his feet measuring distances as a dog does, or a fox—by the subtle changes of temperature, of aroma, of resilience to sound. He had inherited Frayne's secret geographies; here is a chopping block, he would say to himself, and his knee would bump against it. Here is a grind-wheel for sharpening knives. The sounds of names, too, he savored, though he read poorly and knew almost nothing of books. Granite. Maple. Witch hazel. Chickadee. Jacob was not verbal, he was silent and abashed in the company of talkers, and the boy offered his own silence as a bond between them. When he spoke up to question a point in particular, it was seldom out of mere curiosity.

"Where do you go to sell the barrels?" he asked Jacob again.

"Why—to Cayuna."

"But Thad Lumley says the road's snowed shut that way."

"It was." Jacob glanced at Topas, who was taking his noon meal with them. Then he tore a biscuit apart as though it had done him some harm, and began to slather it with the morning's churning of butter. "They— They broke the toll road open now. Dragged it clear."

"Have they no decent cooper in Cayuna?" Hester asked with a sly smile. "How is it they need so many barrels from you?"

Topas stared sheepishly down at his plate and Jacob grabbed for the apple conserve, scowling over at Hester. "They— They ship barrels and staves and such out to Pittsburgh," he said thickly. "They've a good contract there with an outfitter. Sutler needs all he can get just now."

Tim was silent for a time, fiddling with a biscuit on his plate. He did not look at his mother, his whole concentration on Jacob, on the sense of his own detested separateness. I am not his son. No matter how much I hate Frayne, no matter if I kill him someday, I will always be his, and not Jacob's.

"But, Dada," he said, pronouncing the fond name with great deliberation. "Cayuna's away east of here and Pittsburgh's west. And why must you always go by night?"

Jacob threw down his spoon and the stew in his shallow, earthenware plate slopped out onto the table. "For the love of God, be quiet, boy, can't you, and let a man eat!"

That had been almost a year ago, and Hester had never said the word "smuggler" aloud to her son or her husband. It was the one taunt she had never yet struck him with. She was saving it up, and her use for it came on the day of the vendue, the day she learned of Frayne's return.

Benet felt her watching him from the hearth, and returned to their quarrel, the problem of what to do about Hester's leftover husband. "This business with Frayne is ill-come-by," he snapped. "I must keep in Aldrich's good books now especially, even you must see that. There'll be army and navy supply contracts letting any day now, as soon as the old fool leaves office."

It was how people spoke of Thomas Jefferson these days—the old fool. War would begin, the embargo would end at last, and there would be rich political plunder, once they had held the grand Federal Ball in February. On that night, state senators and their ladies, county judges, and even a congressman or two would arrive in fine sleighs and cutters at Tom Lashaway's inn, to dance and drink and then trade out favors and contracts over midnight supper at Aldrich's mansion.

Jacob Benet had meant to be there somehow, at that elegant supper. Poor men with no education had risen to power before, Herod Aldrich was one of them. But there was scant hope of an invitation now.

"If I'm ruined, it's your fault," he growled at Hester.

"Do they let army contracts to smugglers, then?" she said. "Or is it only fools they can't abide?"

She turned out half a dozen new brown loaves onto the table, her head aching her fiercely. The bedroom and parlor were always cold, but the heat in the kitchen grew stifling when you laid on enough wood for baking. The pine smoke made her eyes water, and she opened the kitchen door and leaned on it, letting the cold wind bite her alive again.

"I may be a smuggler," he cried. "Who in this town isn't, I'd like to know? But I'm no fool!" Hester thought he would lay hands on her at last, she had secretly hoped for it, for she knew it would shame him to strike her. But Jacob was not such a man. "You deceived me," he panted. "You said you were widowed!"

"You deceived yourself," she said in her smothered voice. "You loved the boy well enough from the first, you'd have done anything to get *him*. How do you think he would fancy you if he knew you were sneaking out smuggling? Shall I not tell him? He might find John a welcome enough father, after all."

"You mustn't speak of it! Not to him! You must promise!"

She smiled. "No, no, you couldn't bear that, could you? You couldn't bear that he should see you as you are."

Jacob shook himself like an animal dazed by torchlight. "Promise! You must not tell the boy, you mustn't shame me before him!"

Hester's body bent almost double, as though she were going into labor.

"The boy. The boy. You never once cared for me, did you? You never wanted me at all."

Catcher Benet turned away from her eyes. "I— I wanted what other men want! I wanted a decent wife! A kind home with children in it! I still do!"

Hester wiped her hands on her apron. Since her marriage to him, she had grown thinner and harder, her fair, freckled skin stretched sheer across the high forehead, her large grey-brown eyes shining like pewter out of the perfect oval of her face. Her teeth were bad and there was a streak of grey in her brown hair, but at thirty-three, she was still a woman to be looked at, perhaps even pursued.

That fact should have given her hope of a future that contained something like loving, but it did not. She had thrown hope away with John Frayne.

After Tim's birth, when they were still on the farm in Upper Canada, she had prayed there would be no more children and had done what she could to make sure of it. Some women were enriched by childbearing, but it had made Hester feel small, as though the baby took away her existence and made her nothing. For months afterward, she had done little but weep, and Frayne's gentleness only worsened it and made her resent him.

Then he let her alone, thinking solitude might heal her, and she resented that even more. She focussed all her anger at him, filled her whole soul with it, wanted nothing so much as to hurt him. He was like a madness that had come upon her, a great burden she could no longer bear to carry, and she wanted only her old sense of wholeness, the freedom of her mind. At last, when they had come to New Forge and it was plain there was no other way to make him abandon her, Hester Frayne took a lover to drive John away. Even now, she flattered herself he had left out of jealousy.

As it turned out, "lover" was scarcely the word for the man she took up with, the man who had been her weapon against Frayne. If Hester had cherished any hope of enduring tenderness there, she was sadly mistaken. He grew sullen and cold, and soon abandoned all use of her.

She was left with only the boy whose existence had brought about all of her troubles. Hester did her duty by her son, but some part of her could not love him, and his prescient silence, the intelligent tilt of his head, dismayed her and set her off balance, as though another great weight had been laid on her. When she felt it would certainly crush her, she wed Catcher Benet.

"What will you do with me?" she says, without turning to face Jacob.

He does not answer her, he only shivers. "Shut that door. The fire's dying."

Hester pauses for one more long moment, drinking the cold into the mask of her face, pulling it deep, deep inside her. Then she does as she is told and returns to her cooking. Jacob must not be pushed past forgiving her.

"What will you do with me?" she says again. "Now I'm another man's wife."

She smiles, that almost imperceptible lift of the corners of her mouth that so aggravates him. It is how she registers contempt.

"I ought to send you back to Frayne, by God," he mutters. "It's what you deserve."

"John will never have me back now, he's too proud."

"Aye, I expect you fouled his bed, didn't you, same as you've likely done mine?" Jacob Benet sits hunched before the fire, his fists clenched and held out before him as though he is shackled. "Slut," he says, and spits into the fire.

It is not true. She has been faithful to Jacob, but Hester does not trouble to say so just now. She is elsewhere, a high place like the corner of her mother's farmland back in Devon, where you can look across silver-green distances to where the sea lies gleaming, breathing deep like a lover. There are no doors to be closed there, and the air is light and cool. It is the place she first saw Frayne.

"I knew John was coming home," she says softly. "I saw him in dreams, with a pack on his back, like a peddler."

On the high cool plateau of her mind, she has begun to want him back again, or someone like him, to crave some delicate touch on her skin. Jacob's hands are like paws, square and stumpy, with layers of callus as rough and sharp as claws.

He laughs. "Oh, Frayne's no peddler, that I promise you. Peddlers don't throw down a hundred pound in coin and walk away without a whistle."

"A hundred pound? He's rich, then?"

"Aye, damn his eyes."

Hester bites her lower lip. "He wrote to me once, but the letter was two years old when it came to me, and I never had another. I thought he must surely be dead."

"From the look of him, somebody's done their best to finish him. I wish to God they had."

"Ah, then he is much altered," she says softly. "Still, I should like to see him again."

She reaches up a hand and lets it stroke back a lock of her hair that has escaped from her cap, pretending the fingers are Frayne's. When she washes herself in the shallow copper pan by the hearth, she sometimes imagines she is washing his fingerprints from her. But next morning, they are back again, aching like wounds.

"Well, you won't see him. Understand?" Jacob gets up from the settle and takes her by the shoulders and shakes her until she drops the ladle with which she has begun to baste a joint on the spit. It is the nearest he has ever come to hitting her. "If you shame me, if you try to take the boy and go back to him, I'll kill you. And Frayne, too," he says.

But it is only bluster. Hard as he is, Jacob is not a killing man. He has had to say something to fright her, to give him his manhood back. Nothing about him is simple, and even his anger is tainted with love.

"Ah, there now." His grip eases on Hester's shoulders and he lets his heavy hand lie on her breast almost kindly. "No need thinking of Jack Frayne, my girl. He didn't want you and the boy eight years back, and he don't want you now. He'd only run off again, like before."

"He didn't run off. I *made* him go. It was my doing."

"But you said—"

"I was angry. I was so angry in my heart."

"Did he beat you? Misuse you?"

"He did nothing. I was angry, that's all. It comes over a woman sometimes." She stares down at Jacob's hand on her bosom. "You men may come and go as you please. But once a woman is wed, she is snared forever. It rankles, Jacob. It rubs raw, like that net of yours."

He takes his hand away. "I don't—understand you," he says.

"No." Hester's eyes close. "Never mind."

Jacob stares into the fire. "Frayne may not care to have the boy back, it may all blow over. He's come for the old man's property, that's plain. Them old Tory land grants Aldrich bought up after the war." And the treasure, Benet thinks, almost laughing at the thought of it. He has heard the talk of Captain Frayne's gold, as they all have, it is like an old fairy tale, but he could almost believe it. Money has a heartbeat that death does not stifle.

"Where'd Frayne get all this money from that he's throwing about?" Jacob says. "Where was he when he sent you the letter?"

"New Orleans, I think. It was read out to me, you know I've no learning, and I never kept the paper. Anyway, John's as good as a stranger to me now."

"I think you must talk to him and find out what you can of him. Where he's been. Who he's been with."

"But you said I was never to see him!"

"No, you are right, you must not." Catcher Benet begins to pace back and forth before the fire, his boots scraping the sand on the floor. "But I must think on it, how it ought to be managed. He's a twister, that's plain enough. I must know how to deal with him. I must!"

"John was ever a plainspoken man, Jacob. He's clever and bookish, but I never knew him vengeful nor deceitful."

"Then why did he call himself Sheldon when he come here nine years back? Don't sound so plainspoken to me! Sounds like a trickster and a liar and God knows what else!"

"It was I that made him take my father's name and not call

himself Frayne. I was afraid they would come in the night and drive us out, some still hate the Tories so bad hereabouts, and the English even worse." The country lilt of Devon is still in Hester's voice as she goes on, looking up at him, wistful, almost tender. Jacob stops pacing and looks at her. "You remember, my dear," she says. "It was my name when you met me. Mrs. Sheldon. My mother's wedded name."

He is softened by this gentleness in her. But it has betrayed him too often, it comes when it serves her and vanishes in an instant. "Aye, you told me the truth of it before we wed," he says gruffly. "I'll give you that."

Hester's pewter-grey eyes seek the shadow of the spinning corner. "I trusted you from the first, Jacob. I had nobody else."

It was all she had told him when they met. I have no man anymore. I'm poor and alone and the boy needs a father. Had he asked her if Frayne were dead or alive then? Had he said, what's become of your husband? Why? Why had he not?

Hester's voice is a murmur now, to which he scarcely listens. Some is lies and some truth, but Jacob cannot bring himself to separate one from the other. Her words wash over him and dissolve in the air.

"They were building the turnpike," she is saying, "and John found work there, surveying, laying grades and what not. He went west when the road was finished, he'd a letter from some old friend of his father's in New Orleans, offering work."

"Was he English, this friend? What was Frayne to do for him?"

"I don't know. Surveying, I imagine. Property. John said he'd come back when the job was done, he left us most all of the turnpike money." She shrugs, an odd movement of her shoulders, as if she is trying to shake off a weight from her body. "It wasn't much. I manage as well as I can. Only there's never enough."

"Did you— Did you love him, then?" "Love" is a word Benet seldom uses, and the asking has not come easy.

Hester thinks again of the high meadow in Devon, of the distant, breathing sea, like Frayne's breast that smelled of bruised grass when she lay against him. "I was a girl," she says dully. "Girls love without thinking."

"Did he—love you? Did he love Tim?"

"I don't know," she whispers. "How should I know such a thing?"

It seems to Jacob as though she is mourning, and his anger at her wandering husband rises again and sears him. *If I had had such a son, I should never have left him. If I had been able to love, I should never have stopped.*

"Hester," he says kindly, "you must let him go now and not think of him anymore. I'll see to everything, there's no need to be afraid. Besides, Frayne's bought himself a woman from the poormaster, that wild girl I caught by the lake. The mad girl, you remember? She'll serve him well enough."

"Where are they?" Hester says quietly. "Where will they live?"

"At the old house. Bay House. They say he means to buy it back."

"To live in it with her," she murmurs. "To shame me, because I might've been mistress there."

"No fear of them staying long at the Bay, girl. Aldrich won't sell it."

"He will sell. In the end, he will sell."

Hester stares into the hearthfire, watching the ash-ghosts rise and disappear up the flue. *So my days will be now,* she thinks, and the old sick panic seizes her that she remembers so well from her girlhood, the terror that nothing will change, that she will end like her sour old aunts, each assigned to a task and a corner. The spinning aunt, Jessie. The carding aunt, Ada. The churning aunt, Hagar. One by one they grew old and died and disappeared, leaving only their tasks to burden other women.

So I shall be. Like a flake of white ash in the backdraft. Like a bug in a box.

She draws closer to Jacob, slips her hands inside the leather jerkin he wears. He is thick at the middle, built like a ramrod. Through his calico shirt, she can feel the muscles of his broad back tense across his shoulders.

"Love me," she says. "Please, Jacob, out of kindness. Please."

She presses her mouth against his, slides her tongue into it, feels his hands ease down her back till they clutch helplessly at her buttocks. His sex is hard now, she can feel it through her gown and her petticoats where she offers her hips to him.

"I don't want Frayne or anyone," she says, and for that flickering moment it is true enough. "I want you. If only you could love me a little. . . ."

"Christ, I do," he moans, his face hidden in the curve of her neck, and she takes his hand and leads him into the ice-cold little bedroom. She has not yet made up the bed, the curtains are parted and you can still see how their bodies have lain all the night, separate, in two small hollows of the featherbed with a ridge like a stone wall between them.

Jacob stares at the bed and at Hester's hand that leads him towards it. "Ah, you torture me," he whispers. "It's no use, and you know it."

"No, no," she whispers. "There's always a use in loving. Even when it hurts."

She takes off her gown and begins to unlace her stays so that her breasts fall free, for she knows he loves the sight and the touch of them, because they are tender and fragile like the fine things in rich men's houses, like delicate porcelain cups and fine crystal that sings out when you touch a fork to it. Having no knowledge of such things, he longs to own them, though he has no use for them and secretly fears them. It is the same with her body.

Hester goes to where he is standing and pulls his face down against her breasts. "I love you, Jacob," she says. "I thought John was dead years ago. I would never deceive you. I would do anything for your sake."

Jacob Benet does not quite believe her, but he feels her cold hands inside his shirt, stroking his chest and his belly. He can hear ice cracking on the panes of the single small window, a branch of the maple tree scraping against it. "Steady, now, steady!" he hears a man's deep voice say in the shopyard. It is Topas Logan, the hired man at the cooper's shop, yoking the ox to the sledge to load up more barrels from the great seasoning pile in the yard. They are darkened by weather and water-soaked, and even empty, the weight of the greatest crashing down on a man's leg will smash the bone beyond repair.

If I were a printer or a joiner or a farmer, I might have been happier, thinks Jacob. But these great, cruel barrels hold scant pride in the making. He can hear the low rumble they make as Topas rolls them up onto the sledge, like winter thunder that never ends in rain.

"Give me a child," Hester murmurs, beginning to unfasten his breeches, "and then let us leave here. You are my husband now, nobody else. I want a child of yours."

It is his body she needs, his touch to convince her of her own existence. Jacob will not take her for need or for pleasure, and a child is the last thing she wants. But the hope of it will make him tender and willing.

"No!" He pushes her away, and the look on his face is a dagger. "You know I cannot!" he rasps. "I've done my duty in that way this five year, and nothing's come of it!"

"Because you take no pleasure in me. You make it only a duty."

"Pleasure makes a sin of it!"

"Oh yes." She smiles her acid smile. "Because I take pleasure and you don't, my pleasure is a sin and your coldness a virtue."

"Decent women ought not enjoy such things! It's not natural!"

"Who told you so? Deacon Aldrich? King Herod?" She laughs aloud, bending her head back. "Look at me! Touch me! Do you think women are made out of wood?"

Hester's legs will not hold her up any longer and, bare-breasted, she sinks down onto the cold floor. There are patches of ice on it where frost falls from the unplastered rafters.

"Christ, Benet," she says in a hoarse whisper. "Why did you marry me? Was it only for Timmy? Or did you think I could turn you into flesh and blood?"

He throws a quilt at her. "Cover yourself, for God's sake! You— you look like a whore!"

"Call me what names you please," she says. "You know they aren't true."

He stumbles to the washstand and bends over the basin to vomit. "I loved you," he gasps. "On the night we was married— you know I did!"

"Love, you say?" she spits out at him. "I remember some fumbling. Was that what it was?"

Jacob staggers out of the room and Hester hears the kitchen door crash and then his deep voice, barking orders at Topas. He will go to Schoolcraft's now, and buy a jug and go up to Old Dog and drink by himself, till he almost forgets what she has said to him, what he has not said to her. When it is late enough, dark enough, when the barrels are well on their way up to Canada, he will come home and she will hear his heavy boots stamp up the loft ladder to kiss Tim good night, and before long the bed will sway and creak as his body sinks into the goosefeather mattress. All night she will lie awake, listening to his breathing beside her, smelling the salt, sweat, animal spoor of him. Smelling his fear of her body.

At last, near morning, he will turn to her, nerved and tense and facing her like a danger he dare not be afraid of, enduring his body's brief use of her as a man might bear the cutting out of a cancer or the cauterizing of a wound.

Then the basin, the sour smell of his vomit. The door closing behind him.

Now she sits abandoned on the cold floor of the small, unpainted bedroom. She has neither jealousy left her, nor greed, nor hope, nor passion, and she can neither go back nor go forward. A strange woman stares down at her from the mirror tilted awkwardly above the washstand. Hester looks down at her naked breasts and crosses her hands over them. How pale they are, almost white in the dim little room. She laughs softly at the sight of them.

Salt, she says. I have turned into salt.

IV

three children sliding

A leather bucket of water, cold and clear. A triumph.

Until today, the pilgrims at Bay House have drunk only lake water, pulled up through the hole the wild girl hacked in the ice on the day of Frayne's return. It is pure enough, but the taste of death is in it, and besides, it takes a brownish color from the needles and cones that fall into it along the shore. "I remember the drinking water here," John says to old Gabriel Hines. "So cold in the summer it made your nose and your front teeth ache. Different from England or Canada. Different from anywhere."

He must have that perfect water back again, and they spend two days cleaning out frozen leaves and ice—and a family of field mice—from the old springhouse, till the tiny stream bubbles up at last and flows free. It is the same underground stream the girl washed in, but it breaks to the surface here at the edge of the grove of balsam fir to the east of the house.

For the drainpipe, they work in turns to auger out the heart of an oak log, straight and hard and not inclined to rot quickly. The gouges and bits and frows are all Gabriel's, and most of the knowledge. They have hauled out new timbers on a stoneboat pulled by Sally, Frayne's pack mule, and with these they brace up the springhouse walls and build gable trusses for a new roof. They mix mortar and lay new bits of wall where the old ones have crumbled.

Gabriel's eyes are blue-grey, webbed by cataracts, so that they make John Frayne think of the face of White Lady with the long, steep falls of Pearl River slipping down across her like a veil of ice. The old man is almost a giant, so tall that unless he is sitting down, Frayne has to look up at him, and this submission John finds salutary and cleansing, somehow comforting. Gabe's hands are broad and strong, like his back, and they are never idle, so full of knowledge and instinct that it has turned into part of his body, like a secret tendon or a nameless bone. When he sits by the fire in the kitchen—as yet the only really habitable room of the place— he whittles small objects out of various hardwoods he searches out in the forest. A whistle in the shape of a bear. Four hickory plates, as perfectly round as if he had cut them from patterns. A set of cherrywood spoons. A fine comb of green ash for the girl.

"Here, now," Frayne says, and gently separates a few strands from the chaotic reddish-brown bramblebush that is her hair. The wooden teeth catch and pull, and she jumps up from the joint stool by the fire and gives a strange cry, as though he has cut off her ear. She turns on him, fierce-eyed and animal, mouth open and teeth gleaming.

John drops the comb onto the hearthstone. "I did not mean to hurt you," he says. He doesn't shout at her as most people do at the deaf, and he knows by instinct the purpose of her solemn-eyed stare. He has begun to speak very clearly and carefully, using few contractions and forming the sounds with the front of his mouth, so she can follow them. "Are you hurt? I am sorry. Sit down."

Jennet relaxes, but she doesn't sit down. She smiles, the non-committal smile that lives mostly in her eyes and with which she greets everything except open attack. His steady patience infuriates her; she wants him to shout back, to threaten her—to give her some excuse to run away so that she may choose of her own will to stay with him. Otherwise she is still a prisoner, still caught in Benet's net. She takes a strand of Frayne's thick black hair between her thumb and forefinger and fondles it, and for a split of a second he thinks she will speak.

"Say it," he coaxes her. "Speak the words."

"Poor mite," says the old man, wiping a tear from the veiled eyes.

But pity is no more use to Jennet than combs and whistles. If she spoke, it would be to ask them the hardest of questions. Why am I here now? What am I worth to you? Not even the anger of equals?

Suddenly she yanks on Frayne's hair so hard she makes him yelp, and the lock comes away in her hand, a smear of blood on the root. "Crazy bitch!" Frayne rubs his head and swears in three languages.

"Are you hurt?" she says and makes a sound that can only be meant for a laugh. "Sorry." Sahr-we.

"By Harry!" cries Gabriel. "She's talking!"

John sees the girl with her hand to her mouth and her thin shoulders shaking, and he starts to laugh, too, and Gabriel with him, until at last they bend double and stamp their feet and dance and howl with delight till they roll on the floor. They are the first words Jennet has said since the day in the poormaster's court. They are a sense of humor, a razor-honed wit, a battling self-regard she has kept hidden away. Perhaps more important, they are a test of John Frayne, and he seems to have passed it. They are friends now, and she has chosen to stay.

That night, making his usual round of the place before sleeping, he finds her under the broken glass dome of the entry hall in the moonlight, hacking at her filthy hair with an old rusty scissors.

"No!" He grabs her wrist and takes them away from her, throws them into the farthest corner he can find. She backs away and stares at him, her eyes glinting gold in the darkness, her breath like a curtain of smoke in the cold and her fingers flexed, the uncut nails at the ready.

"Not that," he says, feeling the physical surge of her fear. "I don't want that."

It is a lie, of course; he wants her badly, to touch her thin, cold body, so slight the moonlight seems almost to pass through her bones. But he steps away from her, letting her watch him.

"How old are you?" he says quietly. "How old must you be to have hair the color of burnt wine? I want to see your hair falling down long and sweet."

All next day, Frayne tramps through the forest looking for an elusive meadow he remembers from childhood, where stiff broomgrass grew thick. He digs under the snow and comes home with a sodden, frozen armful, which he dries by the fire and binds into an Indian hairbrush, a mikahe, the grass stems folded double and the fold wrapped with a thong to make a handle. From his pack, he unearths some trade-goods ribbon of a bright scarlet and weaves it into the handle, then ties on a fancy of owl feathers to please her.

"I had a wife in the west," he tells the girl that night. "A woman of one of the nations there. Tacha, they called her. Deer Woman. I loved her, though I thought I was dead and loved nothing. I gave her such a brush for her hair."

But the deaf girl refuses to use it. Except for the tumbledown roof under which they all sleep, she accepts nothing the two men offer, so far not even food. At mealtimes she slips out of the house and is not seen again for some hours. Once Frayne catches sight of her at the top of a slope, the old red cloak wrapped tight around her. She slides down the snowy hill on her backside, leaning sideways to keep from colliding with trees, her mouth open and tears streaming from her eyes as she rolls in the snow.

Life is still in her, he thinks. She will come back from this grief.

Another time he finds her sitting crosslegged beside the burial hole in the ice. Every day the lake and the bitter cold try to seal it shut again, and every day she goes out and hacks it open; it is her channel to her old lost self, and her only escape, should she need it. She sits still and tearless, looking down at it, frail as a cut-paper silhouette. John lays a hand on her shoulder and she turns her face up to him.

"Who was this dead man?" he says. "Did you love him or hate him?"

*   *   *

Though she says nothing of importance out loud, in her mind the girl Jennet holds long conversations with these three men, with John Frayne and old Gabriel and Leclerc, the lame Frenchman. In her thoughts they are one, and all ask the same questions. But it is Frayne to whom her mind always replies.

Did you love him or hate him? Your husband, I mean. Did you kill him?

Men assume only other men are worth mourning or murdering.

Do you love me or hate me? I would settle for either. To be something, to be part of the scheme of you.

You want me to say I adore you, that the sight of you cancels out grief?

You watch me, I know you do. When I eat. When I work. I feel your eyes on me, trying to read me as a bear takes the measure of a cave before winter. Is it wide enough? Warm enough? Will it leave me a means of escape?

To watch implies no particular attachment. Yesterday I watched a family of rats moving house from the barn to the privy.

Don't drive me away with potshots. I'm trying to love you.

I don't want love. I don't want anything. Except maybe a cat.

Dogs are better, you can train them to protect you.

I don't want what is trainable. I don't care for protection. I had a cat once that I loved. I haven't touched that softness for years now, not since my great-aunt Sibylla sent me away to school. The softness is all a deception, a mask. A cat is hard and strong in itself. You can't know it or own it. You can't teach it tricks.

I heard once there was only one school in the world that taught deaf-mutes to speak. In Scotland, was it? Yes, Scotland. Was that it? Can you write English? Who taught you the Indian signs? Can you read? What are you good at? What else do you know?

I won't do tricks anymore. My mother is dead. I am not who I was, now that she is no more on the earth. I am nothing now. I have to grow myself over again, to belong to myself and to nobody else.

How old are you? Twenty? Twenty-five? You look young,

but I think you are older. What is the name your mother called you? I wish I had known you as a child, before anything hurt you.

You are dark in your spirit. Are you in pain? Do the scars on your body ache you in secret? You have holes like Jesus in your hands.

Hunched there on the snow-clouded lake, John Frayne bent low, his mouth a foot before hers. You want to die, don't you? To go under the ice. You hardly seemed afraid when that weasel fucked you, you didn't cry or show pain. You killed part of yourself to keep it from him. You are mourning it now, but be careful. Grief is like poison. If you take too much, if you swallow it too deep inside you, it begins to taste better than food.

They call her Sparrow. Frayne knows French and he remembers the name Leclerc had for her. But Fauvette is too fancy, too much like a storybook lady.

"Tell me your real name," he says over and over. "You can talk when you want to. Talk, damn you. Tell me who you are."

He holds her hand to his mouth and repeats his demand; she seems to know words by her memory of their sizes and shapes, by the motions of lips and tongue and the suspiration that creates them.

"Name," he says again. When there seems no other way, he falls back on the sign-talk. Question, say his long fingers. You? Call?

But she will not tell him. She picks up his pierced hand and lays it flat against her mouth and he can feel her lips move. They purse slightly, as though they are kissing him. But he knows this is no mere kiss, and no answer; it is a lesson. She is teaching him how it feels to be her.

Sparrow's breath strikes his palm, a faint click of tongue against teeth, and his mind ranges over the English sounds. Buh. Chuh. Djuh. Her mouth widens, opens slightly, the lips flattened onto his palm. Then a strange, grunting noise, the tongue flat on the roof of her mouth and trying to escape. Finally, a staccato explosion of breath. Tuh. Duh. Puh.

This finished, she does not let go of his hand. Her tongue searches the place where the nail pierced him and he can feel her warmth enter him, the saving spittle of women with magical powers. It is not desire that moves her, it is something else, something more. He is not a man to her now, and perhaps he will never be. If Leclerc is her statue, John Frayne is a wound she needs to heal.

Her eyes are closed with concentration and her face is pale, the wild, filthy hair damp with sweat and clinging close to her forehead. Frayne, who has been used for more than two years as a holy object, cannot abide it from her. He takes his hand away and goes out to walk in the cold, where he is free to be only a man.

They have been nearly a fortnight at Bay House. At first the whole town was talking and Herod Aldrich called them squatters, but he has done nothing and already the talk has begun to die away, persuaded by Frayne's money. They seem to have passed beyond danger; they are castaways washed up here together. Everything done in this place is a ceremony, and they all feel it, They comport themselves with the sober innocence of children trying to master unknown tasks.

There is no sign of Hester or Benet, and Frayne makes no move yet to claim back his son. He must think, but he is still too raw from the west, too defenseless. Like Ulysses when he stepped naked from the thicket and clasped the knees of the king's daughter, he needs to grow back the amphibian skin of civilization. He works, eats, snuffs the candle and waits for the sound of Sparrow's stamping feet as she prowls the upstairs rooms, for Gabriel's soft mumbling as he sleeps by the kitchen fire. No one disturbs them, and they begin to contrive something that feels like a life.

Some days Sparrow goes off before daylight and does not return until well after dark, with Frayne's leather scrip full of something she will not show nor share. He does not follow her, does not ask if she is thieving again, and the old man listens, whittles, watches their shadows through his slowly closing eyes. So long as Gabriel has work to do, he can see well enough with his hands.

"What shall we do for a roof, sir?" he says to Frayne as they finish the last of the springhouse walls.

"Why do you always call me sir?"

"You're my master. You feed me and keep me."

"If I had a dog, I would not be its master. Call me John. Or Jack."

This last comes from Frayne unexpectedly, and he gasps, amazed at himself. No one has ever called him Jack except his father.

Gabriel nods, a soft smile on his broad lips. "And the girl, Jack? A different sort of thing to master her, eh?"

"You old rogue!" Can it be that Frayne is blushing under his scars? "I can't even get her to wash that wretched, dirty hair. I suppose you know it's full of lice? Besides, have you seen me lay a hand on her?"

Gabriel's dim eyes seem almost to sparkle. "Why, Jack. I can't see if you've got hands on you at all, let alone where you put 'em."

"Huh!" Frayne begins to rive shingles from a block of green ash with a maul and frow. "Have you no family left, Gabriel? No sons?"

"Me and missus had but the one. Name of Edwin."

"Where is he, then? Why does he not help you? Surely, if he knew of your troubles—"

"Ned were took by the sea," the old man says, laying in a careful line of mortar under the stone lintel and smoothing it with a giant finger. "Rowed up the lake one day, a-fishing for bluefish, and he never come back."

Frayne's blue eyes narrow. "What do you mean, the sea took him? We are nowhere near the sea."

Gabriel picks up another trowel of mortar. "Lake gives onto a river. British fort there, Fort Regent. River gives onto a great lake. That lake gives onto the St. Lawrence. And from there to the sea is naught but a whisker."

"So he was pressed, then? Taken for a British sailor?"

"We'd a letter from Halifax. Patrol from the fort took him up, said he'd strayed 'cross the boundary in his boat. Borders and bounds be terrible hard to see in water, John."

"Have they taken many by force from these parts?"

"Two or three of the Germans from over the lake. Four from Cayuna. Besides Ned, there be none that I know of from New

Forge, only one slave that run off to the British for the sake of his freedom."

John stops, begins to work the sharpening stone on the blade of the frow. "So they may be shot for a spy, or else go to sea to fight Boney." His eyes close as he waits for an answer.

But he knows it already. To live is to walk a narrow rope whose ends are jerked by the blind contentions of power to which any simple man is an irrelevance. Put one foot before the other. Pretend the rope is not jerking. When you tangle and fall, all the guilt will be yours.

"Aye," Gabe says. "Our side don't take 'em by force, but it takes, all the same. They got up a company for the Ohio country two or three year ago, to man the forts there. All boys, they was. Half of 'em drunk for the first time in their lives. Not many like to come back from there, neither."

Frayne looks away, for a moment unable to be with Gabriel or with anyone. What shadow is it that drives him deep into himself at such moments? Fighting the urge to delve for an answer, the old man reaches out a hand for him, groping as though for support. Finds John's shoulder. Holds it hard.

A long silence, the grinding of stone against blade. The smash of the maul on the frow again. The sharp crack of splitting wood.

"What of your own son?" Gabriel says after they have worked together for almost an hour more. "Will you not claim him from Benet?"

"I don't know how, Gabe." Silence again. "I haven't come home to tear the boy into pieces, like the women who came unto Solomon. What sort of man is this Jacob Benet? I've seen little of him, and what I've seen I didn't much like, I can tell you."

Gabriel shrugs. "Catcher Benet? Oh, he's not a bad fellow. Hard when need be. Stubborn. Inward-turning, if you see what I mean. Mostly does what he's bid, like most men." He squints into the webbed sunshine, probing gently, trying to find John and bring him clear. "Will you take back your missus from him?"

"No."

"But you've a right to her under the law! If a man go to sea and leave his woman and she marry again with his body unfound and unburied, his right is prior if he comes back alive after all.''

"I came back for the boy, not for Hester."

"That's rapped out mighty sudden, sir."

"God damn it, Gabe! Don't call me sir!"

They settle in to work again. The small roof of the springhouse is finished and Gabriel stops to light his pipe when Frayne's soft, level voice comes. "Where does this Benet live?"

" 'Cross the lane from his coopering shop. End of Green Street, next door to the smithy. Will you go and see the boy, then?"

"Maybe."

"No need to fear him."

"I don't fear him!"

"Oh, aye. 'Course not."

Another long space, in which Frayne splits more shingles, stacks them, pulls another log between the brace-dogs. "Is your Ned living, Gabe?"

"Killed two year since. Battle of Denmark." Gabriel probes again, this time reaching deep. "Sons don't keep forever, Jack."

A last silence. "I'll go tomorrow then."

Frayne is away from Bay House all the next morning. He has never hunted a small boy before, and he finds it requires a covert, some pretext that will bring him near enough to Benet's shop to catch a glimpse of Tim without being spotted by Hester, whom he is not yet prepared to confront. The mare, Pewter, gives him his excuse; she still favors her forefoot, and a smith is almost as good as a surgeon. It is just past ten o'clock when John leads her into the yard of Dutch Schiller's smithy, next door to the cooper's shop.

The smith is a big old Pennsylvania German with a shock of white hair and a jaw bulging with tobacco, the juice of which he spits out at random, causing his customers to duck and dodge with some dexterity. At the moment, he is painting a Conestoga wagon, slapping on the bright blue paint westward travellers favor.

Laying down the brush, he looks John up and down, from his shaggy black mane to his Indian moccasins. "Want to buy a wagon? New wheels. I make a good price for you." He spits again and grins. "*Na,* you don't look like no farmer. *Was ist denn los mit dem Pferdchen?* That mare you got needs a new pair of shoes."

As Dutch begins to pry off Pewter's ruined shoes, Frayne finds a bench just inside the open doors of the stable. His eyes are fixed on the yard of the cooper's shop a few hundred paces to the east, and on the small house across the road they call Green Street, which ends abruptly in a half-cleared woods of oak and birch just beyond. A red ox, a newly-felled oak still hitched to his yoke by a drag-chain, steams and stamps near a stack of cut barrel staves left out for aging, and the blows of an ax can be heard from the woods.

The house is overhung by a huge old lightning-scarred sugar

maple, and in its lower branches someone has built a magnificent treehouse. It is carefully and handsomely designed, a broad hexagonal platform of planed and mitered boards with half-high walls of red-stemmed osier, woven in and out between posts that support a sound thatch of tied and weighted straw. A sturdy ladder leads up to it, twisting and turning from crotch to crotch as the tree spreads and rises. It is a labor of love and of thought, and no ten-year-old boy could ever have built it. It can only be Benet's work.

So then. Tim is loved. Catcher or not, Benet is a good father to him, and Frayne cannot help being both glad and sorry. How much easier it would have been to come back and rescue his son from a bully who beat him, to take him up like the old man and the girl, who had nowhere else to go.

"Whoa-ha, Red!" cries a voice, and Frayne feels his heart jerk inside him as Tim lopes suddenly into sight along the path from the cutting. "Steady, Old Red," the boy says, and begins to unfasten the chain from the ox, laying his head on the broad, warm flank as he works, and making his cheek stroke it up and down, up and down, till the big creature rolls his eyes with pleasure.

"Bring us back the haul-chain, Tim!" cries a man's voice from the woods. "And then set to work on them buckets for old Pinckney, will you? Look sharp, son, it's cold in these woods, and I've three more to fell today."

"Be right there, Dada," shouts the boy. "Almost done!"

The nerves in the scar on his face scream at John Frayne, as if someone has struck him. Tim has Hester's coloring, the thick, light-brown hair that spills out under the blue-and-white knitted cap, and the spattering of freckles over the cheeks. He looks up from his work and stares away toward the house, and John glimpses the Frayne eyes, that strange transparent blue you cannot look away from. He has the Frayne stature, too. Tall for his age and well-muscled, built for climbing and coasting and riding.

Something seizes Frayne, sharp as the claw of the iron hook on the log chain. This I made. This I put into the world. Whether eight years of absence have lost him any right to the name of father is a point of no importance. It is the boy who claims *him,* not the other way round.

Still, to thrust back into Tim's life again, to uproot him and reclaim him like a forgotten parcel, even to come to him as a stranger and say, I am your father, not this man who has raised you and loved you. Split your heart in two and give me the half of it.

I cannot, Frayne thinks, and once again his whole body convulses. I cannot ever have you back again.

In spite of the cold and the packed snow, the sun is bright and warm in the yard. Tim runs into the woods with the log chain and when he returns, he brings out from the workroom the task Benet has assigned him—a half-finished bucket of oak staves, lashed together with a hoop of hickory wood. A knife blade gleams in the sun as he bends over his work, cutting a buttonhole end in the thin split of hickory to lock it into the second hoop that will finish the bucket, his body still and intent, his hands moving with lightness and grace and the sober conviction of an artisan. When he works at some familiar task, Tim's mind races, leaping the wall of Benet's tense little kingdom of work and sleep and work and sleep. By now he knows, of course, all about Jacob's border-running; denied answers at home, he has found them from the sons of other fathers who disappear to the northward and come back flush with money. Sometimes he slips out in the dark and climbs up to the treehouse to see the smugglers' torches far off on the lakeshore, but not only for the boyish romance of what is illegal and dangerous. It is how the lights speak against the darkness. Come to me. I am here. I am waiting.

Do they draw Jacob, too?

"A sap pail, isn't it?" Frayne strolls so easily into the snowy yard that the boy jumps when he speaks and almost ruins the carefully-shaped tab that fits into the hole he has cut in the hickory split. "Not so long now till sugaring, I guess."

Tim looks up, tongue poised between his teeth and head on one side. His eye is caught by John's leggings and moccasins, by the necklace of blue beads and the long blanket coat. The town boys talk of this, too, and since the day of the vendue Tim has had to endure more than a few taunts. Frayne, Frayne, snow and rain, Tory bastard's home again. Father and son, father and son, one for all or two for one?

"Couple of months yet till sugaring," the boy says mildly, watching John slantwise, through a crack in the world, his heart pounding. "Sap won't start running till near March," he says. "Cold's deep this year."

His memories of Frayne flicker and dance around him, and although he has tried for five years now, since Hester's remarriage, Tim cannot altogether replace them with Jacob. A large hand over his small one on the reins of a wheezing old pony. Arms that tossed him high in the air and caught him again, and fell with him into a huge pile of dry leaves. Sycamore, Timmy. Smell how sweet they are, like maple sugar. Say the word, son. Sycamore. A baby in a homespun gown and a dark-haired man crouching in long summer grass with his arms spread wide and his eyes like a torch in the scintillant dusk. I am here. Come to me. I am waiting.

"What's your name, son?" John says casually. He has an intense pleasure in pronouncing the word.

"Tim." The boy's blue eyes narrow. He is too old for his age, he sees too much and draws too many conclusions. "John Timothy Benet." He emphasizes the last name, glances up to observe Frayne's reaction. "But I don't much take to the John part." Another pause. "It was my real pa's name." He looks Frayne in the eye. "I hate him, he run off when I was two."

At ten years old, there is no extenuation. John changes the subject, deluding himself that the boy does not know him. "Are you the cooper's apprentice, Tim? Because I'm in need of—of a churn. Not too big—I've a horse at the Dutchman's, over yonder, but she's lame and I can't put much weight on her. Oh, and a small barrel for wood ash. To make lye for the soap, you know."

Timothy draws a deep breath, relieved, more than willing to

deceive himself, too. Perhaps the man is only a farmer then, one of a thousand who set out for the west and found that money didn't grow on trees there either. Only passing time while his horse is being shod.

"I'll look them things out for you from the storeroom," the boy says, "but I can't write down the money proper, I ain't learned how to cipher. Dada's yonder, cutting trees for staves, and Ma's gone off someplace." He frowns again. "She can't read anyhow."

Frayne looks down at the split of hickory that will hoop the rim of the sap bucket. "That's neat work. Easy to spoil wood when it's that thin."

"Not when it's been soaked enough. See how soft it is?"

"You like coopering, don't you? Better than school?"

Tim stares down at his boots and kicks a lump of snow into slush. "Schoolmaster won't have me no more."

"Why not?"

"Brained him with a coal-scuttle."

John chuckles. "I once hit a schoolmaster with a walking stick. Mine had thrashed me. What did yours do?"

"Smacked my hand with a poker. Broke my knuckle—that one there, see how it sticks up funny? Next time I brained him first. I'd be apprenticed by now, but Dada says ten's too young for it." He grins. "I'd rather go to sea, anyhow, and fight Boney."

Tim goes into the shop and returns with a neatly-made little churn and the barrel Frayne has asked for. John pays him and writes down the amount himself in a homemade account book with hand-ruled lines, which the boy puts carefully away. All the while he can feel Timothy watching him, still unsatisfied, still considering every movement as evidence. From the wood lot, the blows of the ax have fallen silent. Frayne knows he can risk only a few moments more without colliding with Benet.

"You're a good boy, Tim," he says. "Your Dada must be proud of you. That's a fine treehouse he made you."

"We made it together, it's a beaut, ain't it?" The boy's eyes sparkle and he laughs, Hester's secret, unsettling laugh. If he knows who John is, he forgets for a moment. But it doesn't last long. "Mister," he says all of a sudden, "you been west, ain't you?"

Frayne looks at himself and smiles. "As you see."

"My real pa went west when he run off from us."

"It's a big place. Men get lost there. They don't mean to. But they do."

The boy waits a moment, taking aim. His eyes meet Frayne's and become them, an identity they both know without speaking. I am you. I am your only hope and all your sins.

"I thought my pa was dead," Timothy says carefully, his voice like a knife blade. "I prayed for it all the time when I was little. I don't think I believe in God anymore, and I don't pray." He glances away and then back again, sudden as the slash of a knife blade. "But I still wish him dead, every night of my life."

That night, Sparrow returns with something slung over her shoulder that rattles as she walks. It is a string of dried apples, and they feast for the first time, all three pilgrims together, baking the fruit on the embers in an old iron spider John unearths from the cellar. He finds more every day that time and the looters have left them—pots and kettles, rusty garden tools, leftover sections of wainscot and panelling. Where he can, he replaces the damage, but it is as though the old house has been left him like a puzzle with some pieces that fit, and certain crucial ones—window glass, plaster, sound flooring, shingles—still missing. This hit-or-miss chaos they share with several families of mice and a raccoon who comes and goes from the Captain's old billiard room.

But tonight Bay House is a home again. The rich scents of apples, of rabbit stew with wild onions, and of Gabriel's pipe smoke fill the kitchen. After supper, John takes out of his pack the cedarwood flute with which he courted Tacha, his Indian wife, and begins to play an old song he remembers from childhood. Its sound is strange, the melody transposed to another scale, another universe. Something of the music reaches Sparrow and her foot taps in time with his own, and old Gabriel sings out in a deep, robust baritone, ignoring the strangeness.

Three children sliding on the ice, all on a summer's day,
As it fell out, they all fell in, the rest they ran away.
Oh, had these children been at school, or sliding on dry ground,
'Twas ten to one they had been safe, and never thus been drowned.

"I remember your father, John. How he sang." The old man laughs. "When he let loose on Awake, My Soul, why, confound me, the Devil himself come to and sung along!" Gabe's smooth face grows sober, the milky eyes searching for Sparrow's slim shape by the hearth. "Can the dear child hear us, John, do you think?"

"Don't know. She hears the flute, or some part of it. She hears shouting, loud noises. Sometimes birdsong, I think, if it's shrill. Jays. Redbirds. Can you see her at all, Gabe?"

"Somewhat. Like a fire through a fog."

"I think she hears pretty much as you see. Have you never heard bells in a fog?"

"Oh, aye. Draws a man hither. But he don't know just where. Jack?"

"Gabriel?"

"Don't she draw you?"

Frayne doesn't answer; he takes up his flute and plays another children's song.

On the green carpet here we stand,
I'll take my true love by the hand.
I'll choose the one that I love best,
Before I lay me down to rest.

"Is Sparrow handsome, John?"

"Not very. All skin and bones. Big eyes. Mouth too big for her face." Frayne considers her critically. "And her ears stick out some."

"Jack?"

"Yes?"

"There's a danger in her. She's a puzzle a man could get lost in. There's a danger in this place of yours, too. Best you know it."

Frayne laughs. "Spooks, you mean?"

"Nay, don't scoff at the dead. But they do say your father left treasure buried hereabouts. That you know where it is, and that's what you come back for. I heard talk when we went to Griff's Mill for the lumber."

"Treasure?"

"Aye. Gold, they say."

That long-ago lie has come stalking Frayne. My father is richer than yours. He has millions of pounds sterling. He has a whole trunkful of gold. Once a lie comes into the world, the blind magician once told him, it never leaves till the teller is dead. Perhaps it will be so, after all, and Tim's prayers will be answered.

John covers his eyes with his hands for a moment, his head bent very low. "Christ," he whispers. "Make it stop."

"They watch us, Jack," the old man says softly. "Guido and Royall and that other one, Caleb, he's a right bastard. They'll do anything for a penny."

"I know. I saw the damn fool's red cap in the woods, it's as good as a beacon. And Benet? Is he watching us, too?"

"If he does, you won't see him. He's a loner, is Catcher. What he does, he don't do for money, exactly. It's hard to put a name to it. But he's hitched himself up to Herod Aldrich's wagon, and just or unjust, this is Aldrich's land now. I reckon he'll claim whatever's buried on it."

"He seems in no hurry. I've paid him no rent and taken no lease here."

"Oh, he'll play you out a bit, I warrant, like a fish on a line. See what you dig up here, before he sends his bailiffs to turn us all out."

"Come along, Gabe. Aldrich isn't foolish enough to believe these treasure stories. He's a businessman. He's waiting till I up the ante on my offer, nothing more."

The old man shakes his head, the pipe smoke drifting like a cloud around him. "Scoff if you like, Jack, but them stories of Tory treasure be true enough. Back in Seventy-nine, Mother and me hid our pewter in a cave at the foot of Old Dog to keep it from raiders, and when we went back for it after the war, there was boxes and trunks and all manner of things hid away there. Nobody knows better than you that the Tories wasn't allowed to take nothing with 'em. I reckon most hoped to come back and claim their own."

"Mmm. Grandmother's dishes and Aunt Sukey's mildewed quilts. Old bedframes and cradles. Now that you talk of it, I do remember my mother packing up her second-best china teapot and hiding it somewhere. Will that do you for treasure?"

"Well, well. Mock if it pleases you." Gabriel pauses, chews on his pipe stem. "What'll you do if Aldrich won't sell you the place?"

"All I want is the house and the grounds, and Aldrich will sell if I wait him out."

A long pause. Frayne thinks the old man is dozing. Then the voice comes to find him; like all the old, Gabriel speaks from a very great distance, uncertain of his path. He reels out the words like the filament of a spiderweb, convinced beyond fact of some eventual connection. Let me reach you. I am here.

"Your father was a decent man," he says. "As I remember."

"Don't know about decent. He was strong enough not to welch on his sins. But human enough to commit them."

"They say he took his own life, before the raiders could get him." The old man draws heavily on his pipe, his eyes open wide in the ebb and flow of the firelight. "It's a thing you think of, when you're my age. Take it by the throat and shake yourself free, 'stead of waiting for God and the rot in your bones to finish you." Another pause. "Them people you've been with—did they believe in God?"

"Many gods. Some kind, some sly, some bitter cruel."

"Jack?"

"What now, Gabe?"

"Did you see your boy today? When you bought the churn?"

"You're too damn smart for an old codger."

"I'd like having a boy about the place."

"I saw him. He's fond of Benet, and he's well-treated. That's all there is, for now. Maybe it's all there'll ever be, I can't say yet."

"Never mind, then. I'm glad you come home, Jack. 'Tis good to have somebody back from the old days."

"Thanks, Gabe."

"But, Jack? If ever you should go out a-hunting that treasure of old Sandy's—"

"What about it?"

"Keep your back to a tree."

The two men sleep by the fire at night, but Sparrow sleeps cold and wherever she chooses, moving her pallet of old quilts and blankets from room to room. Frayne buys candles and sticks one in the earthenware cup for her to light her way to bed, but she leaves it behind in the kitchen. Every night, candle in hand and soft-footed in his Indian moccasins, he moves through the house to find her, to see whether she risks frostbite, whether she lies too near some weakened timber, some section of crumbling wall he has not yet shored up. Sometimes he finds her on the landing of the great staircase, beneath the faded mural of ladies and gentleman strolling under weeping willow trees, but for the most part she seems to prefer the old library, where the square of polished floorboards gleams in the cold moonlight. Frayne spies the books Leclerc has arranged on their shelf, takes down a copy of Homer.

The girl lies on her side, her head on her arm and her body curled under the blankets. She watches him like a dozing cat through its third eyelid. Measures his movements, the care with which he steps across the floor. He squats down and lets his fingers drift over the smooth boards Leclerc has restored. Then he begins to read, his voice rising and falling, reaching her dimly like the notes of the flute or the movement of wind against her skin.

Many cities he glimpsed and learned the turn of many alien minds.
Many trials he weathered, heartsick on the breast of the sea.

This is the reason Jennet sleeps at a distance, to make him come to her, to feel along her back the faint vibration his feet make on the floorboards, to hear the low burr of his voice that scrapes like a brush at her muffled eardrums. Every night for fourteen nights she has lain in these cold rooms waiting for him to appear, his shadow in the light of her father's candle. With the light on his face, she can read the shapes of his words as he speaks.

> *Here trees are always in the season of fruiting,*
> *Pomegranates and golden pears and red apples,*
> *Honey-sweet figs and olives, dark and smooth and ripe,*
> *And the bearing of these ancient trees will continue forever,*
> *It will never flag nor fail nor die.*

Because of the cold, because of the ache in Frayne's eyes, she does not undress at night. Like a queen in a fairy tale, she lies with her father's broken officer's sword beside her, the silver pommel in the shape of a wolf's head gleaming in the liquid candlelight. Why, after the men on the lake, does she take such care in defense of her honor? Are the scraps that remain more precious, having been gathered so carefully over these last days and pieced back together? She can feel herself being restored like the floorboards, each loss slowly measured and replaced, the dry heartwood fed with healing oils.

Or is it the man himself, John Stephen Frayne, against whom she defends herself? Is it some primal fear that he will take more than her body and leave her nothing of her soul at all?

> *So we stood there together, the living and the dead*
> *Exchanging the heartsick stories of unwilling travellers,*
> *Deep in old private griefs, the tears flooding our faces*

He does not need the book to read. What he does not remember, he invents, submitting himself to the tale, to the climb and drop of the rhythm. The king returning in rags. The queen beset by thugs. The abandoned son.

At last he stops and lies down at arm's length from the girl, flat on his back on a patch of unrestored flooring, the candle between them. His pierced hands lie outstretched and palm upward, waiting to be filled. "You are safe here," he says, and she copies the shape of the word with her own mouth. Safe.

She kneels above him for a moment, the flame of the candle below her, almost touching the frayed hem of her sleeve. The old sword slips away into shadow, but the girl herself is a blade in the dim light, bright and sharp.

"Be still. I want sleep," she says in her mechanical singsong. I want to step on a bridge I can trust.

Sparrow lies down beside him, her body pressed against his back and her mouth on his neck at the fringe of his hair, tasting the faint leftover salt of his laborer's sweat, her arm resting on the curve of his hip. Her breath is quick and sharp, like her footsteps, the rhythm of her fear of him, of her grief that comes and goes and comes again. Tonight she has put herself into his hands; if he moves, if he turns towards her or tries to hold on to her, she will break and disappear.

Frayne knows this and he lies very still, obeying her orders. Only his voice moves, swaying like candledance. I had a wife in the west who died singing. The skin of her arms was the color of maplewood, but elsewhere it was different, blended of many shades. Fawn and butternut and strong tea mixed with milk. I could draw you a map of her body, all the colors filled in and perfect. I had a wife who died singing, and when she was dead, I could not leave her. I carry her bones on my back.

At last the girl slept. Her weight grew heavy and relaxed against him, her breath deeper and steadier, each inhalation longer and the spaces between precise and regular, as though she were breathing by the tick of a clock. Frayne slept, too, a deep sleep such as he had not known since he left the tribesmen.

Sometime in darkness, he woke suddenly to find Sparrow gone. The candle in its earthenware cup was gone from the floor, but the moon was very bright through the broken dome of the hallway. A snow had fallen in the night, the light, dry January snow of the mountains drifting in through the jagged glass, like hard grains of rice that slipped from his body in a small avalanche as he stood up, and crunched under his feet as he walked.

There was a sound in the house he had not heard before and yet seemed to remember, a heavy, rhythmical banging, muffled by distance. Like a loose shutter banging in the wind, except that there were no shutters left and no wind was blowing. There was only the dry snow, hissing against the walls and sifting in through the missing siding boards.

Thump. Thump-ump. Thump-ump. Thump-ump.

There was a definite rhythm to it. Tentative at first, but then steady and certain, like someone who has not danced in years trying the steps and then finding them, beginning to enjoy it and giving himself up to the music.

Thump-ump. Thump-ump. Thump-ump.

Following the sound, he who prided himself on his memory entered a part of the house whose geography he could hardly remember. It was built out beyond the main living quarters, a hallway lined with cupboards and shelves and narrow doorways. Some were open and led suddenly outside through smashed walls and mazes of fallen timbers. But from one doorway, a wedge of light cut through the cold darkness.

Thump-ump. Thump-ump. Thump-ump.

The sound came from a long, squat, slope-ceilinged room with a great ruined hearth at one end. Looters had carried the stones away to build hearths of their own, and the slate roof, too, was almost gone. Frayne remembered it now, how his father had sent for slates from Boston for this part of the house, because here the danger of fire was greatest. The hearthfire always burned here, where the kettles of washing were boiled and strung up on swinging poles to dry. Where herbs were hung in great bunches— lavender and rosemary and thyme and sweet basil and marjoram. And strings of braided onions and dried rings of apple and pumpkin and pear. Where yarns were dyed and soap boiled and candles dipped. John's two sisters, Emma and Elizabeth, had disappeared through this door every morning to learn spinning and weaving and fancy sewing from Mrs. Datchet, their mother's housekeeper, and if fathers and brothers invaded, they were soon turned off with a flea in their ear.

The workroom, they called it. The women's room. The weaver's room.

The rafters now are bare and black and they smell of fire even in this cold. At the far end, where the shadow is deepest, Sparrow sits on the bench of an old loom, her feet moving the treadles. Thump-ump. Thump-ump. There are four treadles and sixteen harnesses, the heddles inside them made of fine twisted wire with an eye in the middle. Through this the warp passes, the heddles lifting and falling back as the girl moves her feet, making an invisible pattern of ice.

Some woman took shelter here, some weaver-woman fallen back on her skills. She warped the loom and began a pattern, and the old threads are still stretched on the bed. Ice hangs from them, tiny droplets like crystal that ring when the girl lifts the harnesses. Icicles drip from the heddle horses, and from the beater and the cloth beam and the lams and the warp beam. Ice coats the treadles and the bench, and for a moment the girl Jennet herself seems to be made out of ice, with grains of dry snow on her hair and her shoulders, where it sifts through the burnt-away beams.

She has set the candle on the corner post and the snow sizzles as it strikes the flame, which burns steady, blue at the center, dancing with every stamp of the iceweaver's feet.

The weft thread is rotted away from the roller and trails down like a cobweb, and still she weaves, the rhythm of the treadles steadier and more confident. The drops of ice break free and fall with a tinkling sound like a music box as the harnesses move back and forth, back and forth. More of the old threads break, but she does not notice. The invisible pattern of her mind grows and changes and reappears. Thump-ump. Thump-ump. Thump-ump.

"What is it, Jack? I heard a great clatter." Old Gabriel comes feeling his way down the hall, finds Frayne's shoulder, clasps it. "Is it Sparrow? What's the trouble? What's she doing?"

"Could you fix up a loom, Gabriel?"

"Loom? Oh, aye. So that's what it is. Well, I think so, if you lend a hand to it. I built one once for the missus, and the pattern is easy to compass. It's getting the parts to fit proper."

"Have we beams enough to mend this part of the roof for her?"

She must have a room, John thinks. A sound roof. A warm fire. A door to lock or leave open. A bed to herself.

"I'd say there's plenty of beams," the old man replies, making quick calculations. "Have to shingle it, though, there's no chance of replacing them slates, not with a war coming on."

"And some stones for the chimney. And mortar."

"John?"

"What is it?"

"Is there light in the room? Can you see her?"

"Through a fog, Gabe."

"Then tell me. Is she beautiful now?"

All that night Jennet weaves the ice. Hannah taught her the skill, the salvation of women by stitching and weaving the scraps, the loose threads of the world. Her feet on the treadles, her hands working the beater stick connect her to the force of this mother, who could piece anything together and heal it. They are three loose threads here, she and John and old Gabriel. But so far they do not make a pattern, or if they do, it still melts away like the ice.

The candle gutters, and Frayne and the old man fall asleep to the thump and recoil of the treadle. After sunrise, when there is barely enough light to see, the girl slips from the bench and pads up the rickety stairs. From her hiding place in the old children's schoolroom, she takes a piece of paper and a stolen penny pencil, then sits down crosslegged on the floor, at the low desk where Frayne's name and his sisters' are carved.

Dearest Hannah, she writes—the only name by which she knows her mother. All her life she will write such letters to her dead, sitting alone in lamplight or moonlight at battered tables where all the tenses merge.

Dearest Hannah. There is a man with holes in his hands, an exile, a man my father would have loved. He is kind to me, but he is lost in himself and lost in the world. I love you. I forgive you for dying. Forgive me for letting you die.

She folds this paper away in one of the books from the Frenchman's shelf, the copy of Milton's poems. Then she takes a second sheet, upon which she writes only a few words.

When he wakes, Frayne finds this page laid in his palm and holds it up to the morning light to read it.

Jennet Sparrow, she has written. *Your friend.*

On the following Sunday afternoon, Leclerc came stumping around the lakeshore to visit, and found two hens and a gaudy rooster parading the garden and Frayne in the kitchen, washing Sparrow's hair.

They had found an old copper wash boiler and the girl knelt beside it in her worn old shift, her neck bared and her head bent down and her eyes squeezed shut as John poured warm water over the terrible tangles.

I used to do this for my mother and my sisters, he was telling her.

Though her eyes were shut and she could not read the words, he knew that some part of the steady sound he made found her and soothed her, and in her presence he began to tell stories, to make magic of truth as he had at the campfires of the wandering nation that had saved him, speaking a language of rhythm and silence that did not depend on the meanings of words.

Leclerc stood as though he had been bewitched, letting the man's ageless voice wash over him. The accent was indefinable, touched with upper-class England, with Cockney London, even sometimes with France. There was a tinge of some other language, too, something that might have been Arabic or Hindi. A sound of deserts and wind and the wearing away of great rocks.

My sisters had always had maids, the voice said, but when the rebels drove us out and took everything from us, those days were over. As a little boy in England, I took an odd pleasure in learning how to be poor. I cleaned gentlemen's boots for a penny. I cadged apples and sold them from a tray hung round my neck. At home, I drew the girls' baths and washed their hair like a servant, and they let me do it. But they could never forgive me. Even after my uncle had educated me and passed me off as a gentleman, I was never their brother again.

In spite of this loss, Frayne was smiling. He still loved the ritual, the care with which he tested the temperature of the water to make sure it would not scald her, letting his hands stroke the surface, then plunging them in like a pair of swimmers. He mixed the soft homemade soap he had bought with the filthy, snarled sections of Jennet's wet hair and worked it in with his fingertips, gently, feeling the nerves of her scalp waken and thrill. He rinsed, soaped again, mixed a last rinse with vinegar to lend shine.

For a long time Leclerc stood silent in the doorway, listening to the magical rise and fall of the low voice and watching the ceremony of Jennet's renewal with bashful, half-closed eyes. With what grace he attends her, he thought sadly, like a priest. I should be sure to make the water too hot. To spill soap in her eyes. I am a fool. A clumsy fool.

"Your—your money, monsieur," he mumbled at last. "From the floor. From the tavern, where the court was. I gathered up what was left."

A small cloth bag of coins clutched in one hand, he stepped into the steamy kitchen. As his eyes took in the girl in her shift and the dark man with his sleeves rolled up to the elbows, he began to back out again. He knocked over a stool and ran into a makeshift rack where two pairs of wet stockings and a petticoat were drying.

Frayne had noticed the Frenchman's presence for some moments, but said nothing. Now he stood up from the washtub, his hands dripping suds on the floor.

"Tell me," he said with a grin. "Did you really order the fiddle?"

"Order what?"

"The violin. This is the backwoods, *mon ami*. Here we call it a fiddle. Did you order it, or did Aldrich and that dragoness clerk of his send you packing?"

Leclerc had nowhere to look but the floor. "Ah. I have not played in many years, monsieur, and one loses the skill of it. To play Bach here, or Mozart . . ." His voice trailed away, then gathered strength and made a new assault. "The— The boys where I work, the apprentices—they assured me you were still living here in the house. I gathered up your money, but you left before I could return it."

He set the bag of coins on the table Gabriel had made from two sawhorses and a wide plank of pine. There was no proper settle by the fire as yet, but there were benches pulled up to the table, so that the three of them could sit down together. There was room for a fourth, but something in the arrangement of the scant, makeshift furniture, the rolled sleeping pallets in the corner, made Marius feel he could not be wholeheartedly welcome. Already a history had grown up between them of which he knew nothing. No doubt they had also moved the books from his shelf.

"I have no wish to disturb you," he said, as Frayne poured a last rinse over Jennet's hair. "I shall go. I shall not come again. Tell her— Tell her—"

"Tell her yourself." John gave the girl an old homespun shirt for a towel, and she stood up from the washtub, her hair swathed like a Hindu. He laughed. "They say turbans are quite the rage now with the ladies in London and Paris. All she lacks is a few feathers to stick in it."

"I— I must not stay longer, sir," mumbled Leclerc. "I must go."

"Sit down, man. Have a smoke." Frayne handed him Gabriel's long-stemmed clay pipe from the mantel. "Don't be bashful, we won't eat you. Have you never seen a woman peeled to her shift before?"

Marius took the pipe and sat looking at it. "If I am truthful, I must admit I have not. Or—at least, only by chance." He looked up. "I will take no offense if you laugh at me."

Frayne did not laugh. His pale blue eyes studied the Frenchman's chubby face. "You're welcome here, monsieur," he said softly. "Will you do me the favor to tell me your name?"

The round face was suffused by a blush. "I am called Marius

Leclerc. From Rocqueville, in Normandy. Not far from Rouen. You know France?"

"Only by proxy. New Orleans. St. Louis. Montreal." Jennet sat down by the fire and John began to separate the wet, tangled strands of her hair with Gabriel's comb. "Was it you that polished the boards in the library?" he asked.

Marius smiled, a broad smile that lit his foolish face and made it seem confident and serene, almost handsome. "Ah, they are fine boards, are they not? A beautiful grain. I cut them and laid them myself."

From the back of the house came the sound of sawing and hammering. "You made a good job of it, they're well-fitted," said Frayne. "I don't suppose— We need the skills of a real cabinet-maker and joiner. Chiefly a new pole for a loom, a roller-bar to hang the heddles from. That's the job in hand now, but it needs a lathe and a man who can use one. And there are other things, too. Wainscoting. A few bits of furniture to go on with. It's a great deal to ask. But I'd pay you, of course."

"No, no, monsieur! It would be nothing, I work every day with a lathe and my master is a kindhearted old German, he won't object! Ask me anything! I have found—" Here he paused, still uncertain of Frayne. Already there were many stories about him among the apprentices. "I have found great peace in this house," Leclerc said at last. "After I left the war, I could not discover any reason for living, for how one ought to begin to . . . to . . ."

His voice drifted off again. This dark fellow was plainly a man of decision, of action. How could he understand what had made Leclerc run away and play dead, what kept him becalmed here?

As Frayne's fingers moved through her hair, Jennet watched the little Frenchman's face, reading his words, the emotions that moved across him like cloud-wash over the sky. "Begin," she echoed.

"Ah! You have got her to speak again!"

"She reads lips. When she wants to." John picked up the grass brush, the mikahe, and began to stroke Sparrow's hair with it. "Otherwise we get by with twiddling our fingers. She is Jennet—

she won't tell me the rest yet. That's Gabe Hines back there in the workroom, making a row with the hammer. I'm John." He looked up suddenly, spearing Leclerc with a gaze. "What war did you leave, friend?"

"I—I—left in— In a manner of speaking. One may leave a war, but the war may have other ideas. I was wounded at Austerlitz."

"Where's that? Germany?"

"Why, it's a village in Austria, monsieur. You have not heard of it? Napoleon's army wiped Austerlitz from the face of the earth." The Frenchman looked down, overcome with shame, but unable to resist Frayne's magnetic stillness, the smooth rhythm of the brush that rose and fell on the girl's damp hair. "I was one of that army," he said. "I was wounded in the foot by a fragment of shell, and as I lay on the surgeon's table in the dressing station, I heard them sharpening a saw to cut off my leg. It did not seem rational, Monsieur Jean. To give a leg for the sake of a foot."

"Ah. They are paid by the piece, you see. A leg brings them more than a foot."

Leclerc glanced up at him. "You have been in the army, then?"

"I know how bastards think."

Frayne's concentration seemed entirely centered on Jennet. Her hair was drying in the warmth of the fire, and the brush brought the color up, a dark red-brown like old brandy, with a high glint of gold.

"I crept down from the table," Marius went on, "and hid myself in a heap of dead men the orderlies were carrying out to the burial carts. There were Austrians, French, many Russians. Poor decent fellows. At night we could hear them in their camp, as the Russian priests prayed and sang over them. As I lay there waiting among their dead bodies, I heard cheering outside. 'Vive l'Empereur!' Bonaparte came often to the hospital tents after battles, to view the wounded. I heard the surgeons lead him to where we were lying. 'Ah, see there. The wretch with the bad foot is dead,' one of them said, and poked me in the ribs with his boot. 'Ha, ha! He's cheated us of six francs for that leg of his.' Through my eyelashes, I saw the emperor above me, sipping at a glass of Madeira. 'A fine chap,' he said, and his adjutant pinned a medal on my tunic. They wrote down my name as a hero. I read it in the newspapers, it went out in all the dispatches."

He heard Frayne make a low sound, like an animal's growl. "Well, then. So you are a true hero."

"I? I ran away from the fighting. They loaded me onto the dead cart with the others and when no one was looking, I jumped off and crept away and hid myself." He had told no one of this before. The words seemed to come of themselves, in some other voice than his own. "When my foot was enough healed," he went on, "I made for the coast and shipped on a merchantman. I was two years at sea, and then I came here. I'm a traitor and a coward, sir, not a hero!"

"To walk away from the ill-usage of powerful fools is the truest test of a hero."

Leclerc smiled ruefully. "Ah. You know the *Essais* de Montaigne. You are clever, monsieur. And most kind."

"But the argument doesn't convince you. I see it in your face."

"I have not yet—made amends to myself." The Frenchman looked down at his stubby fingers; no wonder there was no music in them now. "But tell me. How is it you had not heard of Austerlitz?" he asked Frayne. "It is more than three years. Surely all the world knows of it by now."

"There were other wars where I've been," Frayne said. He laid down the mikahe and ran his hand across the long, smooth fall of Jennet's hair. "See? She is beautiful, is she not?"

"Ah," whispered Leclerc. *"Ma fauvette."*

The girl stood up and looked wide-eyed from one of the men to the other. "Wars," she said, and marched away.

On the street corners of Rome, there were men who sold snow from the mountains for cooling the wine at great men's tables. They had clear water flowing along small aqueducts through the cellars, in which they kept live fish for guests to catch with their hands, as a boy tickles trout. These fish were then prepared to their tastes at the table, with many rare sauces and delightful spices. Great men, it is said, also had fools to entertain them at table. The fish, for their part, may be presumed to have seen little distinction between the one and the other. Thus is defined the difference between dinner and diner, between catcher and caught. It is seldom a pleasure, believe me, for a simple fish to have dined with great fools.

—John Stephen Frayne, Essay on the *Essais* de Montaigne

There are seventeen fir trees in the grove at the edge of the lake, and once Leclerc has gone back to Germantown with a promise to help mend Jennet's loom, Frayne goes out to watch the last of the light fall through the long, soldierly trunks of these trees. Under one of them—though he cannot remember which one—his father lies buried.

Eyes seem to watch him from somewhere. Ghosts, he thinks. Treasure-hunters. For my sake, put your back against a tree.

Why did they hurt your hands? says the girl's voice behind him. When he turns to her, he sees Jennet has brought a pierced-tin lantern with a candle inside it, so the light will fall on his words. Why did they cut you?

They said I was a spy.

I don't know that word. What does it mean?

Somebody who is caught in the middle. Somebody with knowledge one side wants to use against the other and is willing to pay for.

Is that a bad thing?

It depends on what use they make of you. A spy in himself is nothing. As a human being, he doesn't exist. What he wants doesn't matter.

What did you know?

Not much. The names of rivers. Of mountain ranges. The places where plants grew, where certain animals grazed and wintered. The names of nations, tribes of men. I made maps of their countries.

I like maps.

So do I.

★ ★ ★

Frayne's memory has come back to him in the past week like the falling of leaves from a tree, exposing little by little the stark truth of bare branches. If he had to assign it a place, he would say that this memory lives in a small room, a miniature copy of a great man's St. Louis parlor. Outside is a riverbank, a single rutted lane down which blanketed Indians trudge with their loads of beaver and otter and marten skins.

It is a trading post on the Missouri, the last post of civilization, built by a man with old Captain Frayne's delusions of grandeur, but without his eye for balance and his taste for irony. The room is gaudy and flash, and it smells of wet weeds from the moss-chinked walls, and of the muddy, roiling river at the foot of the bluff. There is a damask sofa, shipped up by flatboat from New Orleans. A silver tea service. A crystal decanter of wine. A mahogany table.

Where did you find him? asks their owner.

A long, chiselled face burned brown by the weather. Black eyes that seem to bore inward, deep into the skull that holds them. A Spanish accent, a Creole. A velvet coat and a silk cravat. A gold earring. A voice like thorns under the skin.

He was up beyond the Villages. Making maps.

This one is sloppy with liquor and, like most *engagés*—the hired hands of the fur trade—he stinks of castoreum from the sex gland of the beaver, the bait they use to set the traps. The Villages are the Mandan villages, mud huts far to the northward, where the Indians sometimes are born with blue eyes and fair hair. It is the point at which the river turns west, and beyond it the fur lands are vast and untapped. Power is latent in every tree, every animal, every acre. America is a bone to be chewed.

Whose are you, *amigo*? For whom do you make these maps?

Frayne has a rope around his neck and another between his legs. The drunken *engagé* pulls the second one tight, so that his feet are lifted perhaps two inches from the polished black walnut floorboards. A tantalizing distance. His toes grope for it, almost touching. The rope saws at his sex, and he wonders how they will cut him. He has seen men in the west without ears, without noses, without penises, without scalps. Men with their hamstring tendons cut, able only to hobble and crawl.

The rope eases and they let him down. Who owns you? Who pays you to map out this country? British? French? Are you one of Fronval's men, from St. Louis? Are you John Jacob Astor's?

New fur companies are forming every day now, since Lewis and Clark have returned, and three nations want the key to the west that will give them an edge in the war that is coming. They all have their bully-boys; it is how the world has always divided itself—into those who make and those who take, and are taken from in their turn. Meriwether Lewis travels with the expedition journals under his blanket and a bodyguard beside him. He is pursued everywhere, obsessed with the need for protection, with the treasure he carries on paper and in memory. Others have died with their minds full of geography. Frayne will not be the first.

For God's sake, he says, I'm only a trader. I trade skins, just like you do.

Traders carry beads and tin cups and trinkets, says the Spaniard, who belongs to no country but greed. Traders don't carry books and pencils and paper for maps.

I tell you I came out from St. Louis to make my fortune with a party of trappers, but I lost my way! I was trained a surveyor. It's an old habit to mark things and measure boundaries. I don't work for anyone. Let me go.

He is lying and they know it. They are brutes, but not idiots.

For whom do you mark them, these boundaries? For the British, no?

Don't be stupid. I'm not British.

You read British books, we found some of them. You talk like a British.

I lived there as a boy, that's all. The king owed my mother a pension, but she never got it. You think that makes me a king-lover?

I think it makes you poor enough to spy for his money. Or anyone else's.

I'm from York State, I tell you. I don't spy for anyone.

Ah! A man named Frayne owned most of upper York State once. He was a Tory. An English. I heard they had hanged him. He was your father, eh? Your uncle?

I don't know him. I'm nobody's son.

They torture him most of a grey afternoon, while the Spaniard reads aloud from a page of Frayne's journals.

In the Shining Mountains. On the east side of the valley, five peaks shaped like convex lenses, the color of ash.

He is stripped bare-ass naked and arched like a bow, backwards over the table, his sex hard and risen. Now they will cut me, he thinks. But he is wrong.

Between the two northernmost peaks, a pass, very high and cold, but lacking snow at this season. Saddle boiled and eaten this day.

Something buries itself in his groin, hard, bitter, like a cannon-ball. The butt of a rifle. Whose are you? Where are the rest of your papers, your maps? You may as well tell us.

I ride bareback and walk much of the way over sharp stones which seem to me volcanic. Last boots worn through. Made six pair moccasins from elk hide.

I'm nobody's. I never was. Jesus Christ save me. Save my soul.

Beaver here very rich. Two forks of the Green River meet one-half mile beyond a grove of cedar. Indians watchful but friendly. Game scarce at this season. Mink and marten abound, but no deer.

He's English, goddamn him. He's a spy for the Bay.

They think he works for the British fur company, the Hudson's Bay Company. HBC, they have already begun to call it. Here Before Christ.

Use the knife, says the Spaniard.

Frayne expects the searing pain of castration and his legs kick like the girl's on the ice. But it comes elsewhere. A sense of cold along his cheek, dragging in a long ragged curve to his chin. Blood runs down onto the table beside him, and he wonders if they have cut his throat.

If you confess, we won't hang you.

Christ. You bastard. I told you. I'm not a spy. God Jesus Mary Christ.

Very well then. The hands.

He thinks they will chop off his hands, but instead they use large nails, meant for spiking timbers together, or the hulls of sailing ships. When they go through his palms, they shatter the boards of the mahogany table, and as the wood splits Frayne thinks his bones are cracking. Confess, you damn English bastard. Who owns you? Give us your maps.

For a moment, perhaps for an hour, he faints. As he wakes, they are pulling the nails out. His eyes open and he stares up at the long, sardonic face and sorrowing eyes of the Creole, whose hand is stroking Frayne's cock.

Vuélvele. Turn him over.

This wound is the deepest. He lies with his face in his own blood as the Spaniard takes him with practiced skill, with boredom, with a soft moan of sad satisfaction. When Frayne begins to vomit, the grating pain lessens and there is only the feeling of terrible cold. When they grab his arms to turn him over again, he cannot feel that he has hands, he thinks they have fallen off and run down with the blood and the vomit. He stares at what is attached to the ends of his arms, puzzled, as if they belong to someone else. Is this what they did to my father? The Spaniard is sipping wine from a cut-glass goblet, and wiping his mouth with Flemish lace.

They load Frayne onto a mule, his slashed face banging its flank, his arms flapping, hands pouring out blood like wine from the Spaniard's decanter. After a time, the blood stops. Now it is gone, he thinks. I have used it all up.

He is wrong. They spill him off the mule and finish him by sticking a skinning knife into his chest. Then the plum thicket. The bees. The breast-milk.

In the darkening grove of seventeen perfect fir trees, Frayne's body is trembling wildly, like a puppet being shaken apart by a mad puppetmaster. The girl Jennet takes one of his arms and puts it around the trunk of a tree, then does the same with the other arm. She leans against him, so that he is pressed between her warmth and the supple strength of the tree. He can feel both of them lean in the wind that is rising, feel the sway of their sap, the saving rhythm of root and trunk and branch. To Jacob Benet, Catcher Benet, who is watching from the slope of Old Dog just above them, they appear in the wavering light of the old pierced-tin lantern to be a single thing—the man the girl the tree.

For the first time in his life, John Frayne is crying, and his tears are tree bark, they are scented with pine. He sobs a long time in the darkness, but at last he is quiet.

Why tell me this? Jennet says in his ear. She has grown fond of it. A good ear, flat to his head, the lobe not too long. Why give me your war?

He turns to let her read him, his eyes two dark smudges. So you would know me. That we are equals. That not only women are used.

You came home to die. Didn't you?

I don't know. I suppose so. If nothing is left.

All of a sudden Jennet reaches for him, pulls him against her, and his face finds the small hollow of her neck where her heart beats, strong, like the thump of the loom. Her clean hair smells of the vinegar rinse. They stand so for a long time, as the light through the snow-burdened trees grows dim and the sun drops like an India rubber ball behind the dark bulk of White Lady. At last Frayne moves away, but only far enough for her to see his face by the light of her lantern. His arms lie along hers, his fingertips in the warm crook of her elbow.

Did you ever fall in love? she says.

He laughs softly. A silly phrase she has learned from her reading, from an old-fashioned novel. I don't fall anymore. I go slower.

I love the Frenchman.

He's too old for you.

That's why I love him. I don't have to fuck him.

Ladies don't use such words, Jennet. They don't speak of such things.

Why not? What other word is there?

Why— I—don't know. Tumble. But ladies don't say that, either.

She claps her hand over her mouth and her shoulders shake with silent laughter. Tumble? Babies tumble. People who fall down by accident. Tell me another word. A ladies' word.

Lie with. Sleep with.

Pooh. Lie with is tell lies together. Sleep is sleep. It's not fuck. Do one's conjugal duty.

What's con—con—con—

Never mind. Love, then. Make love.

That's silly. How can you make love? Love either is, or it isn't.

Jennet? Who taught you what fuck is?

A master at school. Dead now. Lung fever. Long time ago.

Did he give you the ring?

Hannah's. Her wedding ring. I took it when she died.

Hannah?

Mother. You ask too many questions.

Your mother? Ah, so that's who you sank in the lake. Did she die here, at Bay House? Did she string you the loom? Did she teach you to weave?

Yes. No. Yes.

And who taught you the Indian-sign? Whose sword is it you carry?

Tell me about your wife. Tell me about Hester.

Who told you her name? Did Gabe tell you?

You did. When they sold me. You said her name then.

I didn't think you were listening.

People never think I know things. Would I make a good spy? Is it better than thieving?

Not much. Jennet? The master at school. Did you fall in love with him? Or just fuck him?

You talk too much. If you're going to talk, then read from the book again.

He has no book here, but he needs none. His low voice begins
its song as the last light falls through the trees.

A god came out of the sea and the air and advised me,
You must set up a great loom in the royal hall of Odysseus,
The threads stretching out to infinity, the weaving gossamer fine,
For the shroud of a king must not ravel and tear.

Frayne?
Yes, Jennet?
Would you like to fuck me?
No, Jennet.
Liar.
I'd like to love you. I'm not as cynical as you.
What's sin—sin—
Cynical. Hard-hearted.
Pooh. I don't want you anyway. You're too old. Bad as the
Frenchman.
I thought you said he was good?

If he is truly Odysseus, home from the wars to find me,
There is a sweet mystery by which I shall know him,
More deeply, more simply, than before he was lost to all hope.

Jennet?
What?
Where did you get those fool chickens?
They followed me home. John Frayne?
Now what?
I don't love the Frenchman. But I don't want to love you
either. I don't want to love anything yet.
I know.
It was a lie about the chickens. I stole them.
I know that, too. I paid for them yesterday, when I went to
the village. You're going to get me in trouble if you don't stop
this thieving.

What kind of trouble?

I could lose you. They could take you away.

Then I won't steal anymore.

Thank you. That's a comfort.

The eggs are nice, though. They're good for Gabriel, he likes them.

Why, yes, Jennet. I expect he does.

V

the ape with an eye of gold

In early February, a fortnight before the Federal Ball, the three friends and the Frenchman Leclerc were in an open field to the west of the house gathering rocks to repair the chimney of the workroom, when Frayne remembered the first of his father's hiding places.

Before the war they had grazed sheep in that meadow; it was good for little else. Such flat land as there was in this mountainous country had been scraped level by glaciers, and when they melted they had left boulders and rocks behind them at random. A farmer might cut down the trees to clear a field to the plough, but even after that was done, he still had to cope with the rocks. For every one you dug up and set into a wall or a chimney, three more seemed to jump out of the earth.

Halfway across the meadow there stood a very dark granite boulder, almost as high as Frayne's head and shaped like the prow of a ship. Letting the others go on without him, he passed this rock once, then circled back to it, navigating around it like a sailor who remembers some danger his charts do not mention—a buried shoal, a whirlpool, a riptide. Round and round it he went, arms folded, brows knitted and blue eyes fixed on the ground.

★   ★   ★

More than thirty years have passed since the day he came here
with his father, and no matter how hard he searches for the whole
shape of that day, Frayne remembers it only in blindingly vivid
fragments. It is a pastoral painting that someone has glued onto
wood and cut up into irregular pieces, so that only slashes of color
and light can be seen here and there, surreal segments of what
once had been peaceful and whole. As always, time confounds
him. There is no future and he cannot separate present from past.

The jingle of coins in a pocket. The smell of his father's
tobacco. The raucous cries of a pair of blue jays giving hell to the
housekeeper's cat.

A small, black-haired boy in his first pair of breeches. Until
this spring, his fourth birthday, he had worn gowns and been that
neutral thing, child. Now he is boy. He has legs now, in fine
white woolen stockings, and feet in shiny new boots. The sight of
them, exposed as they are, still surprises him, and he looks down
at them and laughs with delight.

Jackie? What are you up to? Trot along, boy, don't lag like
poor old Blunt.

The foul-tempered old steward trails behind at a dog-trot, mut-
tering to himself as he always does. Botheration. Confound me.
Damn foolish. Plague take 'em all.

A fool of a dog with one brown ear sniffs and snuffles, its bark
shrill and excited. Digging under the edge of the rock with its
forepaws, making a tunnel. Then suddenly the dog disappears and
only its barking is with them, muffled and far away.

And Frayne's huge father, Alexander Frayne. Captain Sandy,
whose shoulders are almost three feet broad. The little boy Jackie
fits both feet into one of his father's muddy bootprints, laughs,
jumps up and lands in a puddle, making splashes of mud all along
his white stockings. A fine rain is beginning to fall. It softens the
folds of the mountains and pushes them down like the housekeeper's pleating-iron laying folds in a ruffle.

Ha, ha! Blunt, you old rogue, bend your back now! I can't
crack it, sir, it's too hard. Nonsense, hold the chisel and give me
the hammer. Tie that rawhide tighter, man. Keep out the weather.

No damn good if the water seeps in it. Lift, Blunt! Lift! Bear down on that crowbar!

Our treasure. The Ship Rock will guard it. Remember it, boy. Mark it down on your map.

But I have no map, Papa.

Make one now, Jack. There is no better map than the mind.

"John Frayne!" Jennet's strange voice rasped through the damp, cold air and jarred him out of his memories. "Come and help!"

Gabe was leading the mule with the stoneboat behind it—a low, curved sledge that slipped easily over the snow-packed ground—as Leclerc and the girl pried up usable rocks from the ice with a shovel and a long-handled crowbar. Wearing a pair of the old man's breeches, her skirts tucked up to her waist and Frayne's buffalo cloak tied around her, she shoved with all her might, even hung on to the bar and jumped up and down on it, while the Frenchman heaved on the shovel. But her slight weight would not budge the ice that held one especially stubborn rock.

"Frayne!" she shouted again. "Damn you!"

Gabriel laughed. "That's what you get for making her talk, John."

Marius Leclerc looked up from his work. As always, his attention had been focused upon Jennet, but Frayne, too, was a puzzle. There was at times in the blue eyes a certain brilliance that made Leclerc nervous around him, a dance of light that gave him a look of displacement, as though he were here in disguise. Well, well, thought the Frenchman as he took off his spectacles and mopped his face with a red-checked kerchief. Perhaps it is only amusement. Why should he not be amused at a fellow like me?

It was his commonplace answer for all mysteries, including the fickle will of God: I am ridiculous. I am unlovable. I am of no special use in the world.

From under his long, light-brown lashes, Marius looked across at the girl, still jumping up and down on the end of the crowbar, her hair in two braids, a few shorter strands falling loose and damp across her forehead, her wide mouth slightly parted.

"Why do you stay here, Jeanette?" he asked her. She did not reply and he touched her to make her look at his mouth. Then he said it again. "Why do you stay here? With—with Monsieur Frayne."

She stared at him. "He owns me. The court said."

"Pah! Nothing owns you. Besides, he lets you go off on your own and you always come back here. Why? Do you love him?"

"I don't. Want to."

"I don't believe you! What is he to you? What do you see in him?"

Jennet made a soft sound in her throat. "They tortured him. Is that the word for it? Torture." Tor. Tchur.

"Ah. The scars." Leclerc was watching Frayne circle the Ship Rock. "Why? What had he done?"

"Why did they mean to cut off your leg? For money. Why else do men do things?"

He was abashed now; he had not thought she had heard when he told Frayne the story of Austerlitz. "But this does not tie you to him," he insisted, "whatever others have done to him! You feel pity and mistake it for love! You do not think clearly!"

Jennet shrugged, a small jerk of the shoulder, a tilt of her head. "Part of me died," she said. "I had to have someplace for the rest of me. This is as good as anywhere else." She looked up at him and smiled. "Do the dead think clearly, I wonder? Yes. Yes, I'm sure they do."

"Give me that shovel, *ami*."

Frayne strode over and took what he wanted; then he went back to the Ship Rock, still circling it warily as though some *djinn* might come out in a cloud of black smoke if he touched it. He poked at the great hulk of striated granite, banged at it with the shovel. Finally he knelt on the ground and scraped away the snow that had drifted against it on the northernmost side.

Something about the angle at which it sloped downward was familiar. John held some of the snow in his hand till it melted, then tasted it and spat something out. Next he ran his hand along the surface of the rock about ten inches above the ground, selected a spot a few inches lower and struck hard with the rod.

A piece gave way, a flake of gray-black rock which seemed to open the fissure that Frayne had been feeling. There was a kind of seam in the rock. Where the dark surface had chipped away, a narrow line of greyish-white mortar showed clearly. Sandy Frayne and his old servant had broken out a large chunk of the Ship Rock on that long-ago day, dug a hiding place under it, then replaced it with mortar to hold it firm. To begin with, the seam had no doubt been darkened with boot polish or with lampblack, and time and weather had blended it into an almost invisible surface.

"What is it, Jack?" Gabriel peered down at the broken-out rock.

"One of my father's tricks, I think. Have you a hammer and a chisel ax, Gabe? We'll have to chip out the rest of this mortar."

The old man went to rummage among his tools in the leather bag the mule carried, and the girl knelt down beside John. Leclerc stood aside from them, watching, his breath making a harsh growl in his chest.

Jennet laid her hand on Frayne's arm. "What?" she said, peering at the raw seam in the rock.

"A hiding place," Frayne told her carefully. "My father left it for me."

"Money." Muh. Nee. She said the word in two halves, each half wrapped in scorn.

"It might be," he replied, glancing at her sidewise.

Jennet's face assumed once again the neutrality of grief that had begun in the last few days to leave it. "You only stay here for his secrets," she said coldly. "For his gold."

Frayne was a taker, then, a snatcher and grabber, like the young master at school, like the men on the ice, like her own brothers. She had begun to be lured back to living, but now she withdrew again, wanting to touch taste smell no one but herself. From the day of her birth, God had never tired of playing such tricks on her, putting things in her path she might love or become, and then snatching them away by death or disillusion. Now that he had found his treasure, John Frayne would go, too.

"I hate you all," she said to him. But this time she withheld her voice from him. She made the Indian sign with her fists. "I hate your father, too."

John's blue eyes flared. "Had your own father no secrets? And your mother, what secrets did she leave you? Why did Hannah come here to die?"

To explain would have been to let him deeper inside her, and Jennet would not. What a fool she had been. She got up from his side and walked away toward the woods, and Leclerc limped a few paces after her.

"She doesn't want us, Frenchman," said John Frayne quietly. "Let her go. Buy yourself a nice fiddle instead."

Leclerc turned on him, voiceless, his round face drained of blood and his fists clenched. His mind had settled upon Jennet that first day on the staircase, and by now he often caught himself imagining the most minute of her actions—how she must wake from sleep in the morning, raising one arm above her head and stretching her slender fingers to cast shadows on the sunlit wall. How her breath made a white veil before her in the cold, into which she arose as one walks into spiderwebs in the autumn.

I love her, he thought, but the words spoken in his own voice would have seemed ridiculous. At fifty-two, he had never yet made successful love to a woman. When he approached them, when he fumbled with laces and buttons and laid his chubby, eager hands on their smooth bodies, their imagined laughter caved him in upon himself and he stumbled away as a wolf goes off to die.

In a world satisfied with the joining of atoms adrift in the universe, Leclerc's bones still prayed aloud for purpose, for a love that offered connection but demanded no possession and passed no judgments upon him. He ached for a single deed that might complete him in his own eyes, and make him whole.

Give me a harvest to gather, his mind chanted in secret. Give me a hearthstone to sweep. Give me something to die for.

Marius shuddered in the cold and turned his eyes away from the girl as her slim, dark shape climbed slowly up the hill and disappeared among the trees at the foot of Lion's Tooth. Gabe came back with the tools and stood squinting after her. "Is that our Jennet I heard stamping the snow up the hill? Where's she bound for?"

Frayne glanced at the Frenchman. "Who knows?" he said. "Off to steal us an ox."

With Gabriel working the chisel and Frayne and Leclerc wielding the hammer by turns, the mortar began to give way inch by inch. The stone cap was loose from the main part of the rock, but it remained frozen down at the bottom. "Stand away," the old man said. "Just you aim me at the right place."

After four or five great blows of his hammer at its base, the chunk of rock fell away. On the back, it had been worked nearly smooth with a stonecutter's chisel, so that no space underneath need be wasted. Frayne hauled it out of the way and looked down into a deep, narrow gash in the earth, carefully lined with oilskins and dry straw. Lying flat on the snowy ground, he reached down into the hiding place and felt for its contents. Something lumpy and hard and heavy, wrapped in rawhide and dipped in wax. "I can feel it," he said, "but it's stuck down tight with the frost."

"Let me try," said the old man. "My arm is some longer."

So it was. In another ten minutes, the hide-covered package lay on the ground at the foot of the Ship Rock. There was an angular bulge at either end and something that rattled when you shook it, and a sober kind of weight that made it seem portentous. "We'll have to cut this waxed skin away," Frayne said.

"Not here, Jack." There was an urgency in Gabriel's deep voice. "This place is too open."

John laughed softly. "You still think Aldrich is watching us, do you?"

"Don't count your money by candlelight in a room with a window, my old pa used to say." Gabriel's milky eyes were cold as granite. "You bring that poke of old Sandy's on into the kitchen and see to it there."

This time Frayne didn't argue. He and Leclerc began to work the false front of the rock as well as they could into place again, until—with a packing of snow at the base—it presented more or less the same face to the world that it had for the last thirty years. They went back to their work and said no more of the hide-wrapped package that lay on the stoneboat.

At last they had enough stones for the chimney, and the light was almost gone. Frayne straightened his back and took hold of the mule's bridle. From the woods just above them, where the spruce-covered slopes rose to meet the foot of Lion's Tooth, something flickered in the gathering darkness. It was not the glint of setting sun on a spyglass or on the polished bore of a rifle; in the west, he had formed the habit of scanning the countryside for such telltale signs of an enemy.

This was different. He waited, said nothing to the others. In a moment he saw it again, and this time there was no mistaking it. It was fire, more than the brief spark struck to light a pipe or a campfire. It could only be a torch flaring, at some distance from where he had seen it the first time. Two men, he thought, sending signals. The lights moved, left to right, then up and down, like a question and answer.

Sparrow had not come back to the meadow. No smoke rose from the kitchen chimney of Bay House. When the torch flared next, it was no more than half a mile from the path she had taken through the woods.

Frayne tried to shake it off. Hunters, perhaps. A few old deer-stalkers still worked these woods for hides and furs in the winter. Perhaps somebody off cutting firewood. A party of young folks gone sledding and stayed too late. But he could not persuade him-self out of the nervous prickle along his backbone.

He was almost beyond earshot by the time the others noticed him, pausing only to snatch up his weapons—Gabriel's crowbar and Benet's rope net, which still lay in a heap at the edge of the meadow. In all his time in wild country, John had never killed a man, never inflicted a wound except for the killing of game. The old man's voice boomed after him. "Jack! Where are you bound, boy?"

"The girl," Frayne shouted, and loped away up the slope and into the blackening trees.

If they hurt her again, I will kill them all.

He carries no light to betray him. He slips through the dark, pausing only to improvise a pair of snowshoes from hoops of willow tied with the rawhide lacings of his leggings.

The net is almost too heavy for one man, but Frayne learned on the prairies how to carry great weights without strain over many miles, how to balance his body against the rise and fall of terrain, against wind and temperature, against the terror vast spaces inflict on the mind.

See with the roaring in your secret ear, the Prophet told him as they sat by the fires. Scent the wind through your fingers. Here is an amulet, the eye-socket bone of a marten, to give you vision and skill.

Voha, Frayne murmurs, and kisses the bone to invoke this precious sentience. He reaches deeper into his pack and lays his hand for a moment on a small bundle wrapped in rawhide. Bends low above it, singing under his breath. Bright air and soft winds walk with her. Sweeten her journey where I cannot travel. Nathea, great country of the peaceful dead.

The bundle contains a bone of his Indian wife's middle finger, a fragment of one of her thigh bones, and a long, silken lock of her hair. "Walk with Sparrow," he prays to her. "Keep her from harm."

In his smoke-darkened buckskins, John is nearly invisible as he lopes through the trees, riding the surface of the snow and skirting eastward, rising up as the slopes of Lion's Tooth climb on grayish-pink granite scarp, moving always towards where he first saw the torches, south and east of the house.

There is a half-moon rising, tipped downward to spill out bad weather in a day or two, and it shows him a trampled path in the sunken snow. It was not made by snowshoes. There is a long double track like sledge runners, and many booted footprints, most of them made so recently that the edges of snow have not yet sunk in upon themselves. An hour ago, perhaps two.

Frayne bends down as the tribesmen taught him, studying the snow, smelling it, tasting it with the tip of his tongue. The boot prints are not Jennet's. By moonlight, he can make out five different sets, perhaps six, all men's boots, four pair of them hobnailed like those of Caleb and his friends. They do not circle as hunters will; they know where they are bound, and they go with a purpose.

Not to watch me dig for treasure, he thinks. Not to come for me.

The path is older than his presence here, cut out of the birch-fringed spruce woods while he was still in the west, the dead fern and bracken tramped down by many months' usage and the snowy track dragged smooth and hard to make it easier for a heavy sledge to travel here. It is pulled by an ox, but his are the only animal tracks to be seen. Frayne skirts the edge of the trail, crawling a few yards now and then to put the snow at eye level, but there is no sign of deer or porcupine or opossum or weasel, no scent of bobcat piss on the clumps of birch that gleam white in the moonlight.

Wild animals desert a place such as this for two reasons: the scarcity of food or the overwhelming terror of a dominant predator's scent. Men have been coming back and forth on this trail for some time now, leaving the essence of fear in their footprints.

Using the iron crowbar to help him, John climbs higher, so that he is above a point where the path forks. The tracks of the sledge take the lower fork, and so do most of the bootprints. Behind him, to the east, the candles are lighted for supper in the boxy frame houses of New Forge. He can see the great dark jagged hulk of Bay House below him, the smoke of old Gabriel's

hearthfire hanging pale in the damp air. To the northward, the
frozen lake is gray-white, inscrutable, crowded with ghosts.

Then far away to the north a dim light flares, bobs from side
to side, goes out. Nearer by, a mile or two up the shoreline,
another torch kindles, then another. They move out onto the ice
and someone waves them in odd geometrical patterns—triangles,
circles, then triangles again. Not soldiers, they do not signal so.

From the flank of Lion's Tooth, the torch Frayne saw from
the meadow flares again, then another a half-mile nearer the lake,
then another—somewhere near the wagon road from Schoolcraft's
tavern. The lights on the lake are quenched suddenly. They have
confirmed his message. A wolf howls, then another and another,
moving down the shore of the lake like an echo. The lights are
swallowed by dark, and except for the glimmer of ice and the
creak of great branches, the forest is blank and still.

"Oh where have you been, Billy Boy, Billy Boy, oh where
have you been, charming Billy?"

An hour after the last torch, a lone man comes down the track
singing softly, a tin lantern rattling as he walks and shedding a
meager wedge of candlelight onto the path. A husky fellow,
shaggy-haired and lightly stooped in the shoulders, not young,
ordinary.

"I have been to court a wife, she's the joy of my life— What
the— Jesus Holy Christ!"

The heavy net drops easily over the singer and he is caught
like a rabbit, facedown in the snow. Frayne jumps down lightly
and straddles his captive's broad back, the iron crowbar pushed
tight across the nape of his neck.

"I can't breathe!" the man sobs. He is blinded and muted
by snow.

"Who are you?" John demands. "What're you up to out
here?"

"Don't kill me! I'm Topas Logan. For God's sake, man, don't
break my neck!"

"Answer my questions, then, that's all I want of you. Who's
sending the signals down yonder? Who's driving the ox and the

sledge that passed by here? You leave sign a two-year-old could read."

"I can't tell you names! I swore an oath, we all did! We're border-runners, that's all, we haul potash up over the border in barrels and sell it in Canada."

"And whisky? And rum? And Lancaster rifles?"

"If they'll fit in the barrels—but it ain't often we come by such. We do no harm by it." A pause. "Who the hell are you, anyway? Army? Excise?"

Frayne keeps the bar across the man's neck, but he holds it loosely. "So, then. The lights mean it's not safe to move your cargo up the lake tonight. A night patrol out, is that it? I hear there's the better part of a Pennsylvania division massed just this side of Fort Regent. Artillery and foot, and two companies of light horse. Is that where the rifles come from, some willing quartermaster? How many cannon have they?"

"Who the hell are you?" For a long moment Benet's journeyman is silent, his face still in the snow. When he speaks again, Logan's voice is thick with a fear of more than Frayne's crowbar. "I'll say no more. Kill me or else let me go! I'm a married man with three young ones. I want no part of your war, nor your spying."

"It's not my war. But I mean to live through it." Frayne removes the crowbar, lays a hand on the thick-muscled shoulder. "Get up," he says gently.

Topas shakes off the net and sits rubbing his neck. For a moment the small circle of flickering candlelight falls on Frayne's face. "Sweet Jesus!" whispers the journeyman. "Who sliced you?"

The scar has broken open again with the strain of the night's work. Blood seeps from it and trickles down John's cheek and chin, soaking the hooded collar of his blanket coat. He puts up his hand and feels it, wipes the hand on his breeches.

"Not one of ours done that, surely," Topas says. "We're not brigands. Unless Caleb— I wouldn't put much past that one."

"It wasn't Caleb. But who's your master? Herod Aldrich?"

Topas laughs nervously. "Master? Where the hell have you been, man? This is America. It's every roadrat for himself."

"If you're caught trading rifles, it's treason. Is Jacob Benet one of you?" John said. "Is that how you come by the barrels?"

"Him? He's an old Bible-beater, I should know, I work in his coopering shop. Thou shalt not steal, that's his watchword. Shalt not smuggle."

Again the tense laughter; he is lying, and Frayne knows it. "Shalt not covet thy neighbor's wife?" he says.

"Oh, aye. Ha, ha. That, too."

"He coveted mine."

"Ah." Topas Logan drew in a breath. "Then you'd be—"

"Benet's wife's husband. You may give him my greetings. From his son's other father, Jack Frayne."

Jacob Benet needs no telling. On the escarpment above them, in a shelter of pine boughs, his badger-body hunches, waiting. This is his work now. His life is dedicated to the watching of Frayne, to the fear of Frayne's presence, to the tracing of Frayne's every motive and move.

And yet he does not hate the man. Because he has almost no knowledge of himself beyond the body that houses him, Jacob Benet has no sense of the selfhood of others, of what heals them and breaks them and makes them complete. Frayne is a threat, that is all that matters to Catcher. He has come to take Timothy away.

If Benet has wanted a modest success, if he has tangled himself in the net of favors and services and scant rewards that Herod Aldrich holds out, it is not for his own sake, not from greed or self-interest. It is for Tim, for the boy, to make him proud. Only with Tim has he ever been fully himself. Of all creatures on earth, only the boy has ever created in Jacob the secret warmth his mind tells him must be loving, like the miraculous heat that keeps birds alive under the snow.

"Dada?"

Going into the house for his dinner the previous day, Benet heard Tim's voice from above, in the treehouse. "Best come down and eat, boy," he said. "Smells like venison pie."

"You come up first." Timothy's freckled face looked down at him over the wicker half-walls, his blue eyes liquid. "I got something to tell you."

Jacob climbed up the ladder, his short, sturdy legs in their corduroy breeches making a whooshing sound. He jumped lightly over the wicker and crouched down beside the boy. "What is it?" he said. Tim might almost have been crying, but Benet could not imagine such a thing as tears. "What's up?" he said. "Why are you hiding?"

"He was here. My—my father."

The boy had never used that word in connection with John Frayne before, and Jacob's eyes grew small and hard and seemed to retreat into his skull. "Was he, now? When?"

"This morning. He was here once before, near a month ago, only I never told you."

"Why not?"

"Scared to." Tim stared down at his hands in their bright green mittens. "Scared you'd take after him. Maybe kill him."

"Would you like me to kill him?"

"They'd hang you! He ain't worth your little finger, let alone your neck! Promise you won't, Dada!"

Warmth flooded over Benet. "All right. Then I won't kill him," he said. "I promise."

"He talked to me some the first time he came. Didn't say who he was, but I knew him. Ma told me things. How he had a way of looking through you, like he was seeing your bones. How he talked fancy. Schooled, you know." He said nothing of his own memories, of the man with his arms spread wide in the dusk. "Today he didn't say nothing," he told Jacob. "Just come into the yard."

"Did he see you? Did he try to lay hands on you?"

"I was in the shop, watching out the window. He didn't knock on the house door, nor nothing. Ma was inside baking, with the kitchen door propped open. You know how she does."

"Did he speak to her? Go into the house?" Jacob's face was glazed and set; if you touched him, he would break into shards.

"Never said nothing. Just climbed up here, in the treehouse. After a while he climbed down and walked away again." The boy swiped at his eyes with his sleeve. "This is our place! I don't want him here! I hate him!"

It was not true, of course. Oh, he longed for the simple refuge of it, a way to calm the wild surge of his confusion. But hate required a stupidity of which Tim was not capable. In his mind, John Frayne sang to him. *In Scarlet Town, where I was born, there was a fair maid dwelling.*

"I hate him!" the boy sobbed. "If he dares speak to me again, I'll kill him!"

By some instinct to tenderness he had never known he possessed, Jacob drew Timmy against him and held him, so close he could feel through his palm the throb of the heart under layers of clothing. "No need to hate him," he said. "No use in it."

I must do something, Jacob thought. I cannot let him be wounded so. I cannot give up my boy, my son. My life.

"Why don't he leave us alone? Why don't he go back where he come from?" Tim's arms were locked around him, small and strong and full of possibilities. "Promise I won't have to go with him. Make him go," he murmured through tears. "Make him go away and never come back."

"He will go away." Benet's lips brushed the thick soft brown hair. "I swear he will."

What might living be like if he could touch Hester so, hold her as he does Timmy? What a universe of closed doors might creak open for Catcher Benet? But only one woman has ever penetrated the selfless mask of his disengagement, and he does not think of her as woman. She, his mind calls her. The wild girl. The mad thing by the lake.

From his lookout in the woods, he has seen the girl they call Sparrow pass back and forth to the cave at the foot of Lion's Tooth. Sometimes he draws very close to the path, hidden only by thickets of scrub cedar, and once he puts out his hand and lets the muddy hem of her skirt brush against it. Feeling something unnatural around her—in the damp wind, in the absence of squirrels, in the puddle-ice that is shattered where a boot three times bigger than her own has stepped into it—Jennet stops in her tracks,

and Benet can hear her breathing quicken, feel the slightness of
her that drifts a little in the wind. He remembers the paleness of
her skin that day on the frozen lake and longs to see it again,
the thin, fragile legs that could almost be snapped with a pair of
strong hands.

Standing still on the path, she shudders slightly. Is she also
remembering that day, how the men came down upon her from
nowhere? Can she still smell the rancid grease on Guido's hair? Or
has Frayne's body already erased them from memory? Jacob's mind
has come alive these last weeks, an understanding that lived in him
like a sleeping bear for forty-seven years has at last begun to
awaken, thrusting him into deep and terrible chasms. His eyes
close for a moment, seeing her and Frayne together, the joining
of their bodies.

She goes on and he follows her up the slope where the trees
grow dense and the little spring trickles out into them, frozen on
the surface but still flowing under five or six inches of ice. It is
very dark here, the spruce boughs grown almost together overhead,
the snow deep and pure except for the path she has trodden.
Moving aside the door she has woven of branches, Jennet goes
into the cave.

It is the name he has heard Frayne and the old man call her
lately. Jennet. Jacob's lips form it soundlessly, trying to compass
her selfhood, the separate thing in her that is woman, set like a
jewel in a fine polished ring. Jennet, he says. But there is nobody there.

He waits a long time in the woods, until the wild girl comes
out of the cave again. She goes back down the path, and when
he can see her brownish-red cloak far enough below him to be
certain she will not turn back again, Catcher Benet goes into the
cave.

At the front, it is very narrow, scarcely wide enough for two
people to lie down side by side. But beyond this constricted neck,
the cave broadens out like a funnel, and there is a crevice in the
granite roof through which you can see the sky; it is just the right
size to let smoke escape, and he finds the remains of a campfire.

On a ledge, she has set the stumps of one or two tallow candles and some paper spills, and he squats down to strike sparks from his own flint-and-steel till one catches the paper.

It is a slow business and takes almost three-quarters of an hour. Time means nothing to Benet now. He tells himself he must see what is here, he must take an inventory of the wild girl, to know how Frayne values her, whether she is enough to turn him aside from taking Tim.

But it is for himself that Jacob stays. When the candle is lighted, he finds a stone room, swept clean with pine boughs and hung with bunches of herbs. Ledges of stone upon which, at random, she has laid out her treasures, her simple ornaments. An old shell or two, cleaned and polished, brought from somewhere where there is ocean. A blue jay's feather, striped with black and white at the tip. A painted wooden box full of papers Benet cannot read for the unsteady writing. A string of old brass uniform buttons from a militia regiment in Massachusetts. A pair of carding paddles for cleaning wool before it is spun. A glass goblet, the stem twisted and the foot an expensive amethyst color, the bowl slightly cracked. A bundle of old quilts and another, a bundle of clothing.

This he unwraps. Finds there a silk gown, cut low at the neck, ice-blue and still handsome, but once very fine, with white roses worked in silver on the skirt. A piece of cream-colored lace, a veil or a shawl, with a small, reworked tear in the corner. Blue satin slippers with heels made for dancing. A set of stays with a white silk cover of faded embroidery. A fine cambric petticoat tucked along the hem, and a camisole to match.

After that day, he comes again and again to the cave when she leaves it. Marks down in his mind what is still there, what is missing. Little by little, she is taking her life to Bay House—the box of papers, most of the bunches of herbs, all but two of the quilts, the old goblet. At last only the fine clothes are left, the final self she is not yet willing to give.

This is what women are. The ceremonial shreds that they gather, that keep their souls living.

Jacob snuffs out the candle and lies down on the cold floor of the cave and holds the silk gown against him, stroking its softness with thick, roughened fingers. So Frayne must hold her, he thinks. So his hands must touch her. So they must have touched Hester.

There is a sweet, piercing fragrance that clings to the dress, they have wrapped up a bundle of lavender with it, a few stems braided with ribbon and tied. A tussy-mussy, the women call it, a nonsensical thing. He slips it into the breast of his shirt, to leave scent there.

"Hester," he whispers with his mouth on the soft silk. "My heart will crack."

Jennet Sparrow does not go to the cave on the night of the treasure. Instead, she has gone visiting the black doctress, Aunt Hope.

The new name and the house on Lake Paschal have changed the girl, that is plain. Layers of pain are growing together inside her, making a new thing she is not yet sure of. She has come here to test it. To sit by the fire where Hannah's pallet lay for so many long weeks. To see if the ghosts will rise up and claim her.

"My father," she says, summoning him in her hoarse, measured voice.

"Lord bless him," Aunt Hope intones. "Bless his name."

"Daniel Josselyn." She pronounces it as he taught her. Joss-Ellen.

"Daniel, Lord. Daniel 'mongst the lions."

"He had one true friend besides me and my mother and brothers. An old woman, Sibylla. Aunt Sibylla. She had eyes like a blackbird and after my second brother, Charlie, was born, she took me to live with her. She was an old spinster who longed for a daughter, and I was her toy-child. She bought me silk dresses and bonnets and sent me to school to be a lady and learn talking."

"Praise be the favor of heaven! Praise be the angel of mercy!"

"My mother pined for me, and I for her. Is there such a word? Pined."

"Yes, Lord! Pined clear away."

"Hannah pined. We were one thing, and with her, I never needed to talk. But she wanted me to be anyone's equal. I couldn't see any use in learning, any way I could use it in the world as it was. But she thought as my father did, that if I knew enough and was proud enough, I would one day come through."

"No slaves in heaven, honey. Only free souls there."

"Daniel was rich and poor and rich and poor again. But he was always the same. A true thing. He liked poor men best, and so did my mother. All his family hated us. When we had no other place left, we went back to England for a time, and his brother set the dogs on us."

"Lord, Lord. Ain't no home in this world for the just."

"After he died, my father came back to me sometimes. To tell me things. I could see his hands move in the air before me, his two fingers that were missing. Tie your bootlace, Jenny, you'll trip and break your neck. Poetry is of graver importance than history. Clean your teeth properly with a flannel cloth before you sleep."

The girl's voice is exhausted, and she falls silent again, knitting away at a sock with four needles made of fine wire and a ball of soft black yarn spun of combings from cats' fur.

Aunt Hope's cabin is warm and dark, and overwhelmed with cats of all ages and colors. They climb up the loft ladder and perch on the rafters and sleep in heaps of tabby and ginger and black by the hearth, white chins in the air and paws tangled around one another for comfort. Now and then one of them wakes, puts its nose to the pounded dirt floor. Its tail starts to lash and its forepaws flatten, the back legs in an athlete's crouch. The cat—this time a big grey tabby—launches himself into a dark corner.

A brief scuffle. Around the room two dozen pairs of opalescent eyes snap open, watching the hunt. If the big tabby fails, he will be shamed before them. He will have to fight one after another of the toms to prove himself worthy of the hearth again. His eyes in this light are a transparent blue, like John Frayne's.

"Here Puss, here Joshua," croons Aunt Hope, and the big striped tom comes to her and lays a mouse on the hearthstone at her feet. He settles down to the task of demolishing it, purring happily, with his flank rubbing Jennet's boot.

"I seen that blue-eye man of yours." Aunt Hope looks slant-wise at the girl. "Out in the woods, three days ago. Maybe four. You say that man's name for me, Jenny."

"No." She scoops up a half-grown fall kitten and holds him to her face. "Shu," she murmurs. "Shu-puss."

"Hunh! I know plants can make a man plenty sick, if so be he's got it comin'. You tell Aunt Hope how he use you, my sweet lamb."

"He doesn't use me."

"What, girl, never?"

"No."

"What he want with you then?"

Jennet puts down the kitten and takes up the knitting again, working the stitches off the needle so fast that three or four slip off and make runs in the fabric. "What heals faces?" she says at last. "He has a wound."

"Hmm. Hold a hot iron against it, burn it shut."

"No! That would hurt him!"

"Ha! You don't like that, huh?" Hope laughs and the crumpled black paper that is her face crumples tighter. "I know you. If he was a hurtin' man, you'd hurt him back quick enough."

Jennet brushes all this away like a bothersome fly. "What else? Comfrey root?"

"Lord, yes. Comfrey heal most anything. 'Less the blood be poison." The tiny old woman gets up and begins to pace before the fire, shooing cats out of her way with a basswood stick. "Let me see now. Let me figure. Pennyroyal. Burnet root in a poultice. I give you pennyroyal already. Got me plenty burnet to spare, and some comfrey." Aunt Hope shakes her head. "Your mama, she had more cures than me. She had her a whole book of cures, I remember, all wrote up fine. What you done with that book?"

"I took it to Bay House. Hid it."

"You fond of secrets, ain't you?"

It was what made Jennet steal, not need nor the greed for things. Because it was secret and skillful and nobody controlled it but her. "Yes," she says.

"Well, you look that book out, girl. Let your mama talk to you. Spirits talk with most almighty voices to them that does listen. You read some in her cure book, she sure tell you what be best."

Aunt Hope crouches down by Jennet's side and the wide brown eyes set in whites shot with tiny red veins gaze up into the girl's. "He the reason you got your hair all fixed pretty?"

"Comfrey," the girl says, scribing her memory. "Burnet. Pennyroyal. Yes."

It was very late when Jennet left the old black woman's cabin, and the kitten was with her, wrapped up warm in a sling of old wool and tied close to her breast under Hannah's threadbare cloak. When she cleared Aunt Hope's orchard and turned onto the path to the lakeshore, she ran straight into Frayne.

"Where the hell have you been?" he said angrily. But it was too dark for her to hear him. "Come on." He grabbed her by the wrist and pulled her back through the gnarled pear and apple trees till he saw the small light of the cabin. "So you've got friends after all, have you?" He turned her to face him and put her palm over his mouth to let her feel the shapes of the words. "Who lives there?" he demanded.

"Friend," she echoed.

"Man? Lover?"

"Pooh."

"What the— Pooh?" He looked down at her face in the moonlight and began to laugh, his broad shoulders shaking. "What the deuce kind of word is that? Pooh?"

"Teach me then."

"Bosh. Piffle. Nonsense."

"Pooh is better."

"Ah, Sparrow." Suddenly he drew her slight body against him, lifted her up so his mouth touched her face, so she might hear with her fine, pale, cold cheek. "I'm so sorry," he murmured. "I wasn't kind. I acted like the back half of a jackass."

"Yes," she said. "Jackass."

Something squirmed fiercely between them, and terror-stricken meows issued from under the cloak.

"So you've stolen us a cat now?" he teased.

"Down," she commanded, and he let her go free. When the cat had been pacified, Jennet reached up a hand and felt where the blood and collected matter of the old wound were still seeping down Frayne's cheek. She laid her palm lightly over his lips. "What have you done?" she said. "Who hurt you?"

"Nobody. A branch caught me, that's all. I came looking for you, I was worried. Then, when I saw you flouncing along like the dickens just now, I got angry."

He said nothing of the smugglers. They did not matter, so long as Jennet was here. The army didn't matter, either. There was always a war brewing somewhere.

"Jackass," she said again.

"That's right. You bring out the jackass in me. Who lives in that house yonder?"

"Jealous jackass!"

"Jennet? Are we friends again?"

"Maybe." The girl's eyes had a wicked gleam in the darkness. "Say sorry again."

Frayne's Indian wife, Tacha, would not have understood what it meant to be asked for forgiveness. If he hurt her feelings, she rolled up her blanket and went to pass some days in the women's lodge, where no men were allowed. To be hurt in the spirit made you unclean as no wound could. It was like menses or childbirth, and could only be healed by the purification of sisterhood. In the women's lodge, an old granny past bleeding in body or soul set tasks for the others, taught them to weave on a strap loom; to stitch fine buckskin into pouches, war shirts, wedding clothes; to embroider trade beads and quills in patterns passed along from one to the other on painted skins.

As they sewed, the women sang. Earth is a woman. We are her firstborn, men are the green fruit, we are the tree.

Sometimes this process of restoration took a day, sometimes a week or a month. When it was over, Frayne would wake from sleep in the night to find Tacha beside him, her body tensed like a bowstring, the long brown limbs scented with pine smoke, the rich droop of the small breasts as she hovered above him. "I am clean, Saku," she would say, and lie waiting for the touch of his strange, white-god's hands upon her. "I have taken back my self."

Now, in the snowy woods above the Bay of Spirits, Frayne slips those same hands inside Jennet's cloak, lets them lie quietly on the breast of her gown where the kitten is sleeping. He can feel the heart of her beating, how the breath rises in her, then slips easily away again. His hands do not offer to rouse her; they are still in this refuge, like the cat that draws peace from her body. Tacha will forgive him this quiet touching. It is all he wants, all he needs now. To live in Jennet like the warm lodge of women.

"I am sorry," he says. "For what has left you here grieving. For the net. For the ice, what they did to you there. But don't trust me too much. Trust the Frenchman, he's innocent, nothing stains him. Christ. I wish I were—incorruptible. Like you." His hands retreat again and he shakes himself to be free of regretting. "Enough! Let's go find us a fire, and I'll grovel as long as you like."

"What's grovel?"

"Kiss your pretty backside. Beg your pardon."

"Ladies have backsides?"

He laughs. "No, I don't expect they do."

When they arrived, Captain Sandy's treasure was safe on the table, and both Leclerc and the old man were asleep in the kitchen, the Frenchman with Frayne's rifle cradled in his arms. The better part of Napoleon's army could have tramped past and taken the famous "gold" with it, and he'd have slept straight through the invasion, thought John with a laugh. He put a blanket over Gabriel, while Jennet fed scraps to the cat and stirred up the hearthfire under a haunch of venison still warm on the spit.

Frayne went out to the springhouse for a bucket of water and when he returned, she had gone. He went to look for her at the half-repaired loom, but the workroom was dark and empty. At last he heard her rummaging about above-stairs and thought she had gone off to bed in one of the rooms there. But a few minutes later Jennet was back, a small bunch of dried herbs in each hand which she began to tear into shreds and put into an old butter crock. She swung out the pot hook with practiced ease and tipped in some hot water from the heavy iron kettle, just enough to wet the torn leaves and make them steep into a vile-smelling, ugly, green juice.

"That tea smells like wet weeds in a muckhole," said Frayne.

"Lie down," she commanded. "Let me wash off the blood."

"It's all right, my bird. It'll heal in a day or two. It drains a bit now and then, but it closes at last, and—"

"I'm not much like a bird. My father used to call me Flower, because flowers don't need any words."

"A gentle father." He smiled. "I wouldn't call you a flower, exactly. Well. Maybe a nettle."

"Blast you." She shoved at his chest with an arm that was nothing like a daffodil. "Lie down, I said."

John did as he was told, and Jennet knelt down at his side with the basin of steeped herbs. Using her fingertips, she dipped a clean rag into the foul concoction, wrung it out just enough so that it wouldn't drip, and laid it onto the opened wound.

"Goddammit, that's hot!"

"Good."

"What is this, penance? I said I was sorry I snapped at you!"

"How long since they hurt you?"

"Two years. Almost three."

"It should've healed in a fortnight."

By the light of the candle in her father's old cup, she bent over him, her hands moving back and forth, soaking the poultice and wringing it, laying it on again. Frayne watched her, fascinated.

"Who taught you this?" he said. "This doctoring and healing?"

"Hannah. Mother. I don't know so much as she did. Almost nothing."

"How did she die?"

"A growth in her belly." She took up John's hands and turned them palm-upwards. "What other hurts are there?"

"They don't break and bleed anymore. They're fine. Tell me more about Hannah. Did she die here, at Bay House?"

"No. I brought her here after. She died where you found me tonight."

"The cabin? Did you live there together?"

"No. An old woman. A healer, her place. After Hannah died, I brought her here. I needed time alone with her. To remember how we were before."

"Before what?"

"Nothing. Be quiet. Lie still."

"Before what?"

"Before—things began to end."

"And your father. Is he living? Where is he?"

"Dead."

"Tell me."

"We lived in Maine, on an island, and a ship ran aground on

the rocks. He went out with the boat hook to help them. He was old and the sea was too much for him. He didn't come back."

"Is that why you put Hannah into the water?"

"I thought she might find him."

"But this isn't the ocean."

"Fire is fire. Water is water."

"Yes. Maybe you're right."

Frayne lay still for a time, watching her body bend and move in the firelight, listening to the soft, intermittent murmurs of the sleepers and the crackle of the fire. "When you say 'father' your voice is like music," he told her at last. "Tell me why you love him so."

"I can't. Not yet. Let me see where they hurt you last."

She slipped her hands into the band of his breeches and pulled his shirt up, so that the old knife wound in his chest could be seen. It was long healed now, the scar a narrow, brownish track just below his left nipple.

Jennet's hair fell across it like a shadow and he felt her hands move over his chest, barely touching him. Brushing his shoulders and neck. Stroking the palms of his hands, then the backs, then each finger. Slowly, the touch so light that it might have been sunlight or mist, or snow falling onto him.

What this delicate probing touch had to do with the healing, Jennet could not have told him. As a child, she had gone with her mother to birthings and deathwatches, and always there was this careful swaying dance of the hands above the damaged body. The low song of the bones drawing fear from the dying, drawing pain from the sick and laboring and into herself like a vessel, letting it pass away through the fingertips, into the air and the darkness and the roaring of wind down the chimney.

Where did you learn this? she had asked her mother. It was after Aunt Sibylla was dead and Jennet had come back a lady from the school in Scotland, when the lighthouse her father kept on Breakers Isle at the northernmost corner of Maine seemed an exile to her, not a refuge as it did to her parents.

Daniel loved the sea, and he was happy tending the great

whale-oil light and the floundering shipyard that was meant to repair their shattered fortunes—though not even Sibylla's inheritance had been able, in the end, to do that. As for Hannah, she went out almost every day in her dory, rowing from one tiny Maine island to another, tending her women and old folk, trading for what she could not make or grow at home. "Come with me, Flower," she would say. "Like the old days."

And so the girl went, much too splendid in her high-waisted sprigged muslin gown and her pleated silk bonnet and parasol. By the end of the night's labor, she was splattered with birth blood, overcome with amazement as Hannah wrestled and swore and bullied a child into life. As a little girl, Jennet had glimpsed it, but now it was different; it entered her body and ached there.

Where did you learn this? she said.

As women learn. From my mother. From her mother. From Aunt Julia. You remember Aunt Julia?

Teach me, the girl said, and little by little her school-self, her lady-self, was abandoned.

But she had not learned enough before it was too late, and it had not prepared her for what would come later. Her father's sudden loss. The long search west for her wandering brothers, through Hampshire and Vermont and York State, growing poorer and poorer, earning their living by change-work and midwifery. Then the slow decline of her mother. The furious, wild contest with death.

In the kitchen of Bay House, Jennet is crying, silent tears streaming down her face where she kneels beside Frayne. The strange, hard, moaning sound she makes in her grief, like the grinding of rocks, like the thump and return of the loom. Looking down at him, studying the planes of his body. Learning the map of his hands, the dunes and oases and the subterranean streams that feed him, all the places of his soul she will never be part of.

"What is it?" says Leclerc, waking suddenly. "What's the matter?"

"She's mourning," Frayne replies softly. He reaches up a tentative hand and touches her wet cheekbone, then withdraws it. To offer her comfort would be to diminish her. Perhaps someday she will come to him. *I am clean now. I have taken back my self.*

"Do you love her, monsieur?" Leclerc's hands are balled into fists in his pockets.

"Christ, man," John whispers. "Don't you?"

Jennet grows slowly aware of the low, irregular buzz she knows is conversation. She wipes her eyes and pulls down Frayne's shirt, but he takes her hand and holds it against his mouth for a moment. She thinks he means to give her the shape of some word or other, but his lips do not move on her palm. There is only the warm dampness of his breath, the faint pull of his mouth against her skin.

At last he lets her go and Jennet returns to the poulticing. Gabriel wakes and pours out cider into the hard leather mugs they call blackjacks. "What did you find in the woods, Jack?" he asks.

"Border-runners. Nothing to do with us."

"It is late, *mes amis*," says Leclerc, getting up from the bench. "I must go."

What is between Frayne and the girl has grown stronger, deeper since the afternoon, and it angers the Frenchman, makes him ashamed of himself for his foolish urge to love what will never love him back.

"Stay a bit," says John's voice from under the poultice. "Have some supper with us."

"Shall I unwrap the treasure?" asks Gabriel.

"Yes. Why not?"

Let me tell you a story about treasure, Frayne said. As the compress of herbs sent its warmth into his body, he lay watching the shadows of the girl and the old man and the stumpy little Frenchman where they fell on the wall, his low voice weaving around them like the warp of the moonlight that came in through the patched-up, bottleglass window.

My father was like a king of the old days. Once he was dead, his power over my mother and sisters seemed to end, but for me, it grew greater. This story is his, and it is told in his words. I remember them all, I could write a whole book in his fashion. In my mind, he has never died. He has seen all my sins and my failures, and I have heard him laughing. I hear him now.

Some centuries ago, a man of honor and probity built a fortress in the wilderness, a simple tower that rose up from a barren plain. Armies marched over the wasteland from time to time, one bully chasing another, and farmers and villagers came to the tower for shelter. None was ever turned away. None was asked to pay tribute, nor to pray to any god but his own. So kind was this lord that it was said he possessed a heart of pure gold.

In time, musicians and poets came, too, and he sheltered them gladly, for they were most vulnerable of all to the ravages of war. Painters came and drew murals on the walls and ceilings, pictures of fruit and flowers and dancing women, their breasts so soft that men stroked them and wept when they learned they were plaster and paint.

At last came a maker of statues, a sculptor who had travelled far and witnessed much. He had been on crusade to Byzantium and Jerusalem, and on the plains of Damascus he had seen the corpses of five thousand infidels slit open for the gold and jewels they were believed to have swallowed. When he reached the safe tower, he was mad. The lord sat by his bedside many nights, sponging his forehead with cool water while the court musicians played on psalteries and dulcimers, till at last the mad sculptor awoke.

What can I do to heal you? the lord asked, thinking the madness had almost left him. They say you have a heart of gold, the sculptor said. The lord laughed. I am no better than any other man. The hearts of even the commonest men may be golden. The sculptor smiled a crooked smile. And have you any real gold?

A single nugget only, the lord replied. A curiosity, given me by a traveller. It holds down the papers on my writing table. I have no other use for it here.

You say you wish to heal me, said the sculptor. Very well then. Give me a block of stone, a hammer and chisel, and your nugget of gold. Then leave me alone and do not disturb me for a hundred days.

For many weeks, the sounds of the sculptor's labor could be heard in the chamber. Then late one night he called for wine, and terrible noises came from the stair that led down to the courtyard. In the morning, the lord was awakened by a terrified shriek. He ran to his chamber window and looked down into the garden.

The sculptor had brought down his statue and stood it there in the courtyard to be admired—an ape with one blind eye and a nugget of gold for the other. It was an ugly creature with long dangling arms and drooping, womanish breasts, and its private parts swollen with lust. Beside the ape, among a planting of flowers, the body of the sculptor hung from the branch of a tree.

Surely there were two golden eyes to begin with, one man said as they cut the sculptor down. Only a fool would make a one-eyed statue. Ah, certainly! Someone has stolen one of the gold nuggets and killed the poor wretch to get it, said another. Whoever finds it will be rich! Search the chapel! cried one lord. Search the grooms' quarters! cried another. Those lords would steal their mother's teeth, muttered one of the grooms.

Next day there was a battle in the courtyard, and when it was over five lords and twenty grooms lay dead. On the walls of the great hall, the painted ladies wept. The one-eyed ape stared out at the carnage, and in the great lord's chapel, the body of the mad sculptor was heard to laugh out loud.

Bury them both in the plain, said the lord of the tower. Lay that accursed sculptor in the arms of his ape, and let the earth cover them, gold eye and all. Do it by night, and set no mark over the grave.

After some weeks, the king sent his messengers. My gracious king claims the ape with the eye of gold as his tribute, they said. Give it up, or all in this place will die. There is no gold, cried the lord. You will find nothing but bones and a piece of stone. The mad devil asked for one golden nugget and I gave it him, but even that has been stolen. He loosed a plague upon us. See there!

The meadow looked as though moles had been working in it. Tunnel after tunnel crossed it, all converging at the spot where the sculptor lay buried in the arms of the ape. The king's men dug up the blind statue and just as the lord said, the one golden eye was missing. You have stolen the gold yourself, said the king to the lord. Give it up to me now, or all in this place will be killed. I have no gold, sir, said the poor lord. You must find mercy in your heart and spare us.

Burn the tower, commanded the king. Kill this fool and when he is dead, bring his heart to me. In the space of a few hours, the safe tower was ashes, the poets and musicians all put to the sword and the painted ladies turned to smoke that drifted away westward with a soft sound like moaning. The king was at supper when they brought in the lord's heart on a salver. Take off the cover, he commanded, and let me see.

As they lifted the cover, a strange laugh was heard that shook the king's tent and opened great cracks in the plain. Horses fell into them screaming, and the knights and ladies ran wailing. The king's arms seemed to grow longer and his breasts drooped and grew womanish and his private parts bulged. I am blind! he cried. I have no eyes! Help me, for God's sake! Show mercy from the goodness of your hearts!

The world is as you would have it, said the voice of the sculptor. You shall have what you ask for. Take it up and make eyes of it. The last good heart lies there.

The king's fingers groped blindly. On the salver before him lay a nugget of pure gold.

"Did the sculptor hang himself?" asked old Gabriel softly.

"Of course."

"Like your father?"

"Oh yes," Frayne replied. "It was part of the trick."

"And the tower?" Leclerc asked him.

"Home," Jennet said, and they all fell silent in the clean-scoured warmth of the room.

The bleeding from the cut on Frayne's face had stopped when the girl took off the last of the poultices. He got up from the hearth now, and the four stood together around the scrubbed-pine plank table. Gabriel had cut open the thongs that bound the package containing Captain Sandy's treasure, and the Frenchman had scraped off the wax very carefully, in case what lay inside might be inadvertently damaged.

"What do you wish for?" said John Frayne.

The old man looked up and smiled faintly, his webbed eyes almost white in the light of the candle. "Something I can see clear with my fingers. Something useful, but with a fine simple shape to it. Ah, I have it! A good sap bucket—the old-fashioned kind—for sugaring off in the spring!"

John laughed. "You, Frenchman? Don't tell me. A fiddle? A mouth-harp? A pipe organ?"

Leclerc's round face was suffused with a blush. "A good bottle of French wine, monsieur. I should enjoy that. And perhaps some music to go with it."

"I can't promise the wine, but the music you shall have now, and welcome." Frayne took out the Indian flute from his pack and sat down on the bench by the fire. "And you, Jenny?" he said. She did not look up and he touched her hand to draw her eye to him. "My late, great papa's granting wishes this evening. Come, let's hear yours."

Jennet bent and scooped up the kitten and held it to her face, so that it hid her mouth and nose and only the magical dark-amber eyes and the reddish-brown brows and the cheekbones like those in the paintings of saints could be seen. She looked at John through the drift of soft fur. *You have delivered me. You have parted the sea and let me walk like an Israelite, dry-footed from Pharaoh.*

"A cow," she told him thoughtfully. "Cats like milk. And a quern to grind wheat and make flour. And a warming stone to sleep with, because my feet get cold. And some thread for the loom." She waited for a moment. "And Robbie. I'd like Robert to come."

Frayne bent nearer. "Who's Robert?"

"Brother."

"Where is he?"

Jennet sniffed. "Too many questions," she said.

"You may ask her till Doomsday, John, but you'll not get it out of her now till the time's right," Gabe said with a laugh.

What he says is true. They are remaking chaos among them, each fragment of past or present crucial to the possible order that lies beyond them, perhaps forever unreachable. Time and space, the arrangement of atoms, are everything. The true shape of things may never emerge, or, coming too soon or too late, may shatter them all like a dream.

The girl slipped her hand into Frayne's, only the fingertips touching. "Now *you* wish," she commanded. "What you want most in the world."

I want you, John thought. To become you. But he did not say it aloud. His blue eyes flickered shut. "My son," he said at last. "I want Tim."

The treasure of Captain Frayne contained the following: a parcel of books wrapped in oilskin—*The Diary of Samuel Pepys*, *The Winter's Tale* by William Shakespeare, *The Canterbury Tales*, and one or two others; a paper of fine English needles, some wools, and a small frame for embroidery; and a wooden child's toy, called a hammersmith. It consisted of two sticks upon which were fastened the painted figures of two wooden men with an anvil between them. One was dressed as a farmer and one as a merchant; their arms were outstretched and each man held a hammer.

When you pulled on the handles evenly and in turn, each man struck the anvil with his hammer. But if you did not, if your touch was not sure and your hand was not steady, the bent shape of one man did not rise before the hammer of the other came down upon it.

A scrap of brittle, yellowed paper was wrapped around one of the handles, a verse written upon it in a hand that John knew at once to be that of his father, Alexander Frayne.

Here you may see Fair Liberty,
How bright she shines upon us.
But are we now the hammered,
Or the thing that hammers on us?

VI

currants

It is very late on the night of the treasure when Leclerc pulls his old flop-brimmed hat down over his ears, ties a muffler around it, and steps out into the country of stars. In the garden of Bay House he pauses, looking up at strange constellations he can no longer be sure of. The cold has eaten the fog from the lake and it lies white and still, the darkness rising up from it like a perfect ebony column whose top brushes what looks like the Great Bear. Around it, the other stars swim in a great sieve of cold moonlight, denying identity, denying place. The universe conspires to deceive him. Perhaps it is not the Great Bear. Perhaps the girl's name is neither Sparrow nor Jennet. Perhaps the old man only feigns his bad eyesight and Frayne's scars wash away when he bathes. Perhaps Napoleon is right, and the fine fellow with the wounded foot is really dead, after all.

There is a squeaking sound of Sparrow's bootheels on the snowy path from the kitchen, and her hand lays itself on the Frenchman's arm. The music of John Frayne's cedarwood flute filters out through the chinks in the kitchen wall, a strange tuneless weaving.

"I want to dance," Jennet says. As always, her voice is mechanical; she might be talking to the garden bench or the broken statue. But she spreads her cloak gracefully and drops Leclerc a curtsy in the elegant manner he has observed in her at odd moments. "Dance with me, Marius."

It is the first time she has used his Christian name, and it unnerves him. "I can't, *ma belle*," he stammers. "My foot."

But Jennet cannot see his mouth move and so does not heed his objections. She takes his hands and leads him, and they separate, circle, turn. Their dance has nothing to do with the flute music. It comes from the girl's mind, and as it passes into Leclerc's bones he forgets his lame foot and the ice and the stars. For so long as the dance lasts, he gives himself up to her, and when she ends it, when she lets go of his hands, he stands bereft, arms dangling limp at his sides, head bowed in the darkness.

She steps close to him and lays her head on his shoulder. His eyes flicker shut and in a moment he feels her take off his spectacles. Her lips brush his eyelids, first the left, then the right. She reaches up her two thin hands, the fingers faintly webbed where they join at the palm. Prehistoric, he thinks. A creature of old life that is born by mischance into a world that no longer remembers her, that cannot afford to acknowledge her instinctive rightness.

In her presence Leclerc is desperately mortal, and every cell in his body is dying and being reborn. He has taken her inside him, but he does not yet know what she is to him, what to do with her, that beyond her there may be whole continents of love to explore with women he has passed in a mist and never seen.

But Jennet knows. She puts his spectacles back on his nose and laughs softly, her hand in his own.

"I am God's fool," he says to himself.

"Come tomorrow," she tells him. "I will steal us a bottle of wine."

Frayne and the old man are asleep by the fire and it is long after midnight when Jennet picks up the stub of candle and goes up the stairs to the schoolroom. She takes from her hiding place behind a half-rotten section of wainscot a treasure of her own, just as precious as anything Captain Frayne might have left here. It is the painted wooden box Benet saw in the cave at the foot of the mountain, very old, the faded artwork in egg tempera depicting a branch of ripe cherries the odd brownish-red of the girl's hair, and that of her father's.

The box was Hannah's; it has a lock, but no key, the hasp long ago broken.

Inside is a bundle of papers, cheap pages marked off in lines with a pen and stitched into sections with bootmaker's thread. In some of the margins there are grids, weavers' drafts of odd patterns called Star of the Forest or Cross and Sword. These names are inscribed in Hannah's nervous handwriting, and are marked *For My Daughter's Loom.* It was her plan for Jennet's survival in case no man would have her in marriage, a skill that would always bring enough to live upon. How could she have known that soon all but the poorest in settled country would scorn to wear home-spun, that looms would begin to stand idle and the weaver-women go begging?

But the old trades moved west with the country. In the backs of the bright blue Conestoga wagons that creaked out on the turnpike bound for Ohio and Kentucky and Indiana and Missouri, there were still spinning wheels and looms enough, and the women who used them.

And that, too, was Hannah's plan, as it had once been Daniel's. West, Jennet. We'll go west, where Robbie and Charlie have gone. West with the country. Somewhere we'll come upon them. Somewhere the jumble of living will make up its pattern again, and grow whole.

As the girl turns the pages of the old journals, she can hear that voice clearly; they are filled with Hannah's old-fashioned diction, her acerbic practicality, her unflagging labor, her ambivalent hope. *Am owed six shilling for assisting this night at Mrs. Tilman's delivery on Switchback Island, God knows when I shall ever be paid. Our old Daisy being dry, traded three new loaves and a pork pie to Abijah Bidewell at Gaines Head for the milk of one cow for a fortnight. Dipped five dozen of candles this morning. The winter is long and Husband reads late of an evening. God send the wicks do not smoke.*

There are twenty-four of these journals, the last still blank. The girl's fingertips brush the pages, feeling the dry, wavy shape of the paper, the rough scratches of the quill pen that almost tears through to the back of each sheet. But not quite. The pressure applied to each letter is exact, and the homemade ink does not blot or smear, though its color changes slightly with the seasons—the deep red of berries in summer, the brownish-green of walnut shells in autumn, the red-brown of butternut shells in winter and spring. When Jennet bends her face to the page, she catches a faint scent of lemon balm and rosemary and lavender, the fragrance of Hannah.

To cure a running sore. Scraped bone mixed with stiptic, laid on with the beaten yolk of an egg and let dry to seal the wound. To heal lameness, a salve of sweet clover and camphor in good white goose grease.

She turns page after page till she finds these receipts, and writes out a list with her stolen pencil on the back page of the last, empty journal. Scraped bone. Camphor. Stiptic. Sweet clover. Goose grease. The yolk of an egg.

When she is finished, she tears off that page and takes another. *The Journal of Jennet Sparrow,* she writes. But the name no longer satisfies her. In the beginning, it was a cloak of invisibility, but it is not enough for her now. *Jennet Trevor,* she writes. It is her oldest name, her bastard name, from before her true father could marry her mother. *Jennet Josselyn.* In spite of her love for Daniel, his name, too, sits unsteadily upon her. It is still his, and has never quite become hers, nor even Hannah's.

"Tell me the name of your Indian wife again," she said one day to Frayne.

"Tacha. It means deer."

Even now that they spoke often to each other, they were never quite certain of reaching one another by mere speech. He made horns on his forehead with his fingers. "Deer," he said again, making sure she could see him.

"But what was her other name? Her last name?"

"She didn't have one. My people don't, they only have clans."

"They had clans in Scotland when I lived there. Do the Indian men wear skirts, too?"

"So your school *was* in Scotland! But you don't speak with their accent. How long did you live there? Did your mother go with you?"

"Don't change the subject. You call them your people?"

He shrugged. "For a time, I was valued there."

I value you, she wanted to say to him. I am your people now. But she did not. "Tell me about clans," she said.

"I had no clan. They considered me a sort of—of teacher, and such men belong to all clans. Tacha came of the clan they called Foxes. Her father was called Mato. That means bear, because his mother dreamed of a bear on the night he was born. But he was still a Fox. Our daughter was Uma. Butternut, that means. If she had lived, she would have been a Fox, too."

"You had a daughter?"

She knew of the son he longed for and the wife he refused to claim, but somehow this Indian wife and daughter made him more real to her, steadier and more comprehensible, more like Daniel. Jennet's thin face seemed transparent where she stood in the cold sunlight that came in through the rafters of the workroom. She felt as though roots had begun to grow out of her body and reach for him.

Frayne was up on a ladder, talking as he fitted a new piece into one of the beams. He looked down at her, his blue eyes dark with pain. "Our girl lived only four days," he said. "Tacha— Tacha died later."

"Of the borning?"

"The women said not. They said she died of the child's dying. And other things. Troubles. War." He was silent for a moment, trying to compass the way he might tell her. "Indians have no sense of the future, they live in the present. Every moment is eternal. If there is joy or physical pleasure, it's pure and perfect because they can't conceive of its ending. But if you lock them in a windowless room, they think it's a tomb and stop breathing. When grief comes, they see no end to that, either. When they grieve, they stop living." He paused, his hand reaching down to touch her hair. "I think you are like that. Or you were, when we came here."

"Uma," Jennet whispered. Her hand found John's ankle and gripped it, and her body leaned towards him, her cheek against his deerskin legging. Life takes refuge in the feet, her mother had once said to her. When it slips away elsewhere, you can still find it strong there.

Frayne returned to the work, but Jennet could feel through her body how the life in him had grown tense and determined, braced against his memories, against the windowless room, against the hole in the ice.

"What's your surname, Jennet?" he asked her, looking down so she could read him. "I'm not fool enough to think it's really Sparrow."

"Surname?"

"Second name. Father's name."

"Josselyn. But that's past." She drew away from him. "The Indians are sensible. I don't think women should have more than one name. My father's name is his own and his father's, and his father's before him. A whole string of Englishmen with houses and property and history. They have nothing to do with me now."

"But you loved him. Take his name for the sake of your loving."

"You loved Tacha. Did you buy her a spinning wheel and call her Mrs. Frayne?"

He laughed. "Dearest Jennet. You are aptly titled, and if I were to marry you—which I admit is about as likely as that I should marry the Empress of China—I wouldn't change a syllable of that mad name of yours."

She frowned. "What's wrong with my name?"

"Don't you know what jennet means?" Frayne's blue eyes sparkled now with pure mischief. "It's what you call a lady mule."

*   *   *

The Journal of Jennet, she writes on the blank page her mother has left for her. I *am not a bird or a flower. I am not a mule. I am not Aunt Sibylla. I am not my mother.*

I will not hide myself in some man's name. Besides, John Frayne has had too many wives already. He is secret and says I must not trust him a minute. But when he sleeps by me, he is steady and sweet, and he asks nothing of me. A man does not lie in his sleep.

She puts the journal away in its box again, then goes down to the unfinished workroom. Frayne wakes to the sound of the loom treadles thumping, and slips through the dark house to watch her. The worst holes in roof and wall have been patched, but there is still no fire and the loom is not yet whole. Ice still dances on the rotten old warp threads and hangs from the cloth beam and glitters on the heddles. The candle is almost guttered, making only a faint glow that shows him Jennet's face as she works. It is full of purpose now, all the numbness of pain washed away from it.

Frayne takes pleasure in merely watching her think, the concentration on her face, the intelligent curve of her brow. She imagines the perfect weft as she imagined the steps of the dance she performed in the snow with Leclerc. John had spied on them shamelessly, touched by their sweetness, the reticent movements of their bodies. As he had when he first saw her, he felt something rise in him, a tenderness for living that made the nerves thrill along his backbone. An irrational need for a future, for an end to the past and a limit to the eternal present in which guilt is the only constant.

I wanted to treasure you, he would tell her on the first night they lay together as lovers. I wanted to touch every pore of your skin, all the secret places and blemishes, to leave myself like a clean envelope around you, like one of my father's safe hiding places.

But I am not clean. You must not think so. You must take me with all my sins, if you take me at all. Someday I will tell you. But Christ. Not yet.

The loom clatters on and he feels himself begin to shake. He needs liquor or opium, something to numb his mind and his want of her, and his fear of the wanting. But he has nothing. Still shaking, he creeps back to the kitchen and lies down, pulls the buffalo robe over him. Slowly the shaking abates and he lies quiet, trying to dream back the rocking of the cottonwood boat in the water, to hear again the voice of the old magus that lulled him to sleep like a child.

Instead, it is Jennet's crisp bootheels he hears as they come tapping along the back hallway. There is a gust of cold air as she opens the door and comes in, and he feigns sleep, watching her through half-closed lashes while she brushes her hair with the mikahe and plaits it into two braids. At last she slips under the robe where he lies and he feels the weight of her body against his back as usual, her arm across him and her hand in the hollow under his rib cage.

"Shu, shu," she says. "Be still now. I love you."

For a moment, Frayne cannot be sure he is breathing. Except for his wife's stolen bones, it is more than two years since he has been with a woman. The Monk, they called him at the inn in St. Louis. Frayne the Monk, who's too good to lie with a whore.

"Don't wake him," says the girl's voice behind him. "I love you, but be still now."

Then Frayne feels the kitten's needle-claws against his back and hears it begin to purr. The cat. It's the cat she loves, not me. Jackass, he thinks, and bites his tongue to keep from laughing at himself.

From wherever the dead stand when they draw near to watch over the living, Tacha and his father are laughing, too.

He is up very early next morning, mixing mortar and laying the new stones to the chimney of the workroom, when he hears Sparrow's bootheels in the hall.

"You walk like a squad of infantry on parade," he says.

She frowns. "I want some of your money."

"You mean there's something you can't steal?"

"I won't steal anymore, I'm through with that. I told you, I don't lie. But if we stay here the rest of the winter, we need things. Flour. Salt pork. Sugar. Tea. Lard. Some pickles and dried pumpkin and apples and beans. Good white beef tallow, and ashes for lye. A big kettle for boiling soap and making candles. A bolt of plain cloth, unbleached muslin will do well enough. And some stout thread for mending." She smiles. "A spinning wheel, a big one, a walking wheel, that's what I want most. And some wool."

He laughs. "You never cease to amaze me. Weaving. Dancing. Doctoring. Don't tell me you know how to spin?"

"Of course. I didn't grow up a spoiled brat of a boy, like you did. I know gardening, too. We could buy seeds in the spring, there's an old kitchen garden next to the orchard."

"Make a list of what you want, then. Can you write, too?" He had tried long ago to teach Hester, but she had never learned the skill of it.

"Yes. I've already made a list. Oh, and a bed-screw and some new rope. There are bedframes upstairs, but the ropes are all rotten. We could bring one of them down to the kitchen for Gabriel. He works so hard and he's too old to be sleeping on floors, his bones ache him. I can sew a husk mattress, but the ropes would want tightening to hold it. You need a bed-screw for that."

Frayne nods. "And what else?"

"Some medicines. I've written out the names."

He climbs down from the ladder and studies her. "You're very thin. Is the medicine for you?"

She tosses her head and her long braids bounce. "Never mind, then. I'll have to steal it after all. People you steal from don't ask questions that are none of their business."

"Give me the list, you little mule."

She hands it over, a full half-page written in large, squarish letters. Camphor. Stiptic. Scraped horn. Goose grease. A bottle of wine.

"And a cow?" he says. "Does this say 'cow'?"

"Yes. You bought a churn, but not a cow. And if we had our own geese, we could pluck them in the spring and make a feather-bed. Husks are all right for a while, but feathers are best. And some sheep, for the wool. Then we won't need to buy cloth anymore. When the loom's finished, I can make you shirts, I know how to cut them. And I want to warp a coverlet for Gabriel, for the bed." She stops, breathless and flushed with excitement. "Frayne?"

"Yes, dearest?"

Jennet looks away from him. He has begun to use soft words to her and it frightens her. "Will we really stay here?" she says. "I wish it was spring. Will we be here by the spring?"

"I'll put it on the list," he says. "I promise."

"And John?"

"You've never called me that before."

"If you make such a fuss, I won't call you anything."

He laughs, his face turned away from her. Can she hear him if she does not see his lips move? Surely not. And yet sometimes he wonders.

"I love your hard spirit, Jennet Sparrow," he says to the ceiling. "I love your scratchy voice and your loud boots and your practical greed and your storehouse of talents. I love the dark of you, that is even gentle when it bites."

There is a long silence, and he begins to believe she has heard him. He feels her fingers brush his leg again and lie there, no more than an instant. "Go and find your son," she says, and goes stamping out.

It was almost noon when John Frayne arrived at Herod Aldrich's store in the center of New Forge. He handed Jennet's list across the counter to the uppity lady clerk, Mrs. Fanning, who looked it over through a pair of gold-rimmed spectacles. "Wine?" she said, peering at Frayne and launching a disapproving sniff from her cavernous nose. "This says 'bottle of wine.' Mr. Aldrich is a Methodist, he don't hold with wine."

John smiled. "I cleave to the Scriptures, ma'am. Jesus was *not* a Methodist, and I still require a bottle of wine."

A youngish man in a brown wool coaching cloak and a tall beaver hat with a dent in it had been eavesdropping shamelessly. "By gad, sir," he said, "that's a good one! Must remember that one the next time King Herod chides me for taking a drop in season!"

Hetty Fanning's iron curls seemed to stiffen a bit under the frills of her cap and she turned a baleful eye on the young man, who began to whistle, nonchalantly and quite out of tune.

"She'll have writ down every word, sir," he murmured to Frayne with a wink. "Aldrich'll have it in his pocket by nightfall." He grinned. "Oh, well, confound the pair of 'em, eh? Coach'll be in soon and I'm for a bit of high living in Albany."

The dapper young fellow retreated to a bench by the window, where one or two other passengers were waiting for the sleigh-coach that would take them to Cayuna, and then over the Divide to the east. A soldier—a sergeant in the buff trousers and fitted blue blouse of the New York militia—came in at the door, and from outside, men's voices and the rattle of harness could be heard.

"If you want bottled spirits, mister," said Hetty Fanning with a twitch, "you'd best try the Dog and Lantern. And that fancy suit you bespoke come in yesterday. Sam? Drat the boy! Here now

Sam, fetch that box from the back and take it out to the grey horse! This man's leaving! Soon as he's *paid*."

His eyes on the sergeant, Frayne fingered a reel of blue satin ribbon. "I'll have this as well, if you please. And some hairpins. And a string of those buttons, the mother-of-pearl ones. And that warming pan. And a bolt of that stuff there. The cream-color."

Hetty stared. "Why, that's fine lawn, mister, it's five shilling a yard."

"I'll have it. And that bolt of lace. Oh, and that bonnet on the stand there."

With a disapproving snort, she bustled away, her starched apron crackling and the hiked-up bosom of her stylish gown heaving with distemper. Frayne drifted around the crowded, overheated shop, toying with washboards and kidskin gloves and birch brooms, till at last he was near enough to the door to see what had gathered a crowd there.

The sergeant had brought in a mounted patrol of six, one or two grizzled veterans and the rest boys of eighteen or nineteen, shivering in spite of their cloaks and half-strangled by the chin straps of their plumed and visored shakos. All but one had dismounted and lounged around the doorway of the Dog and Lantern; the man still on horseback had two civilians under guard, shackled together and led by a long chain. They slumped onto the ground, exhausted, their faces bleeding where branches had scratched them.

One was unknown to John, a young farmer with lank blond hair and a soft-brimmed brown hat. The other was Topas Logan, Jacob Benet's journeyman, the man Frayne had questioned in the woods. A woman with a grey shawl over her head crouched down at his side, her narrow face frightened and her eyes glazed and distant.

Several men had gathered in the street, drifting out from the inns and the apothecary's shop and the chandler's. A half-dozen young boys with sticks for guns were marching and drilling on the split-log sidewalk outside the Academy, and somebody had painted a sign and hung it up over the doorway, where it flapped foolishly. Long live Freedom. Death to Spies and Traytors.

A snowball flew out of the air and struck one of the soldiers, knocking his shako off. "Why don't you drive out them British from up the fort, 'stead of meddling with decent men down here?" shouted a red-faced fellow with his hair in a queue. "Cowards!" cried a woman. "You go tell Mr. Jefferson to try living without a penny to his name, and see if *he* starves before he'll smuggle!"

For two or three minutes, the snowballs flew thick and fast. "Pre*sent!*" cried the man on the horse, who was taking the worst of it. The soldiers drew up in a line and put their rifles to their shoulders, and the snowball fight came to an abrupt end. The crowd began to drift away and the boys resumed their drilling, but Topas Logan's wife Bess would not move from his side.

"Here, Tim!" Logan called out, and Frayne saw the boy come out of the shadowy doorway of the chandler's shop and crouch down beside the shackled smugglers.

"Colonel's had these borderers in his sights for a month or more," the sergeant was saying. He looked out at the prisoners and shook his head, his eyes lowered. "Too bad, I call it. Always the little fish you get hold of."

"Smuggling's how the poor live in these backwater border counties, Sergeant Ferris," said one of the men waiting for the sleigh-coach. "We are too far off to trade with the east and the south. Unless we take Canada into the union, it will always be so on this side of the mountains."

Ferris helped himself to a long whip of licorice from a jar on the counter. "What were they carrying?" the young dandy asked him. "What was in the barrels?"

The sergeant's eyes sparkled. "What's your name, sir?"

"Why, Will Slocum. Lawyer Slocum."

"Did I *say* barrels, Lawyer Will Slocum?"

The young man blinked, but he recovered himself quickly. "What *did* they use, then? Coffins? Butter churns?"

Everyone but Sergeant Ferris laughed. "As to cargo," he said, "there was nothing to earn 'em worse than a few weeks in jail and a flogging. We chased the cart out onto the lake, though, and the damn fool ox broke through and went down."

"Somebody'll miss that poor beast," muttered one of the men by the stove, "next time his young ones go cold for the hauling of a load of cordwood."

"Who leads 'em, that's what I'd like to know." The sergeant frowned, studying Frayne's odd appearance, the necklace of blue beads and hawks' bells, the scars. "That old house by the bay, now. I seen lights there in the night, and smoke coming out the chimney. Fine place for a smuggler's den. Who lives there, I wonder?"

Frayne stood very straight, his blue eyes fixed on the sergeant's brown ones. "I live at Bay House, as I reckon you already know. Bring your men there and search it. We have nothing to hide."

Ferris turned on him. "And who might you be, mister?"

"My name is John Frayne. The house was my father's."

"I've heard tell of him. Tory, eh? You fancy his politics, do you?"

"I don't fancy politics at all." Frayne turned back to the counter. "I came here to be shut of them."

The sergeant smiled. "You've taken to roost in a bad spot for neutrality, friend. British fort at one end of the lake, and yourself at the other." He laughed and took another whip of licorice. "No, sir. I wouldn't be in your shoes when the shooting starts. Not for a whole mine of gold."

"Old Red's gone, Dada. He went through the ice. The cart's gone, too. Topas says you must ask Mr. Aldrich for help."

The boy has found Benet trudging back through the woods, a small, dark, gnomish figure clothed in a leather jerkin and a short cloak that wraps him so close he seems headless, a body that moves in abrupt, instinctive jerks, thrusting blindly forward through the ice-crusted snow, dragging the light slavers' net behind it. Jacob goes nowhere without it now. When his nerves can no longer resist the temptation to sleep, the net lies over him like a blanket.

"How did you find me?" he says, his eyes peering out of the cloak hood. The boy's voice has not reached him; he has not really heard the news about Topas Logan's capture, about the soldiers, about the death of the ox, about Aldrich. Alone in the woods, Jacob lives on another plane, beyond history or geography or loss or gain; the boy has come to claim him back, and for a moment, Catcher resents it. "Why the hell did you come?" he growls. "How did you know where I was?"

"I can find anything in the woods," Tim tells him. "I came out here before. To watch my— To watch Frayne."

To remember, he means. Till the day John came to the coopering shop to buy the churn, Timothy had kept the past like a dark planet in his mind, in his muscles and his senses of taste and touch and smell and sound. Now it has sights, fragrances, flavors, all intensely specific. He picks bits of it like ripe currants from a bush, letting the juice stain his fingertips. Putting the tiny fruits one at a time onto his tongue and smashing them carefully against the roof of his mouth, till the flavor is clear and precise and makes his jaw ache with its tartness.

How he showed me the stars through his surveyor's lens, and

I cried when I found I couldn't touch them. How he came and bent over me in the dark and the smell of the candle came with him, and the smell of the cold night. The stars are cold, Tim, and cold has a fragrance. Take a deep breath of it. Let it into your bones. When he kissed me, his mouth left a flavor of ripe grain, like new bread on my skin.

The boy shakes himself, spitting out the memory. "I hate Frayne," he says all of a sudden, trying hard to believe it.

"Frayne," Jacob echoes, as though the name means nothing to him.

His musket beside him, he sinks down onto the trunk of a fallen sycamore. It is not a tree that is native here; someone planted it, a whole grove of which this is the last survivor. Beyond is the lopsided ruin of a cabin, a small field once cleared for its garden now grown up in clumps of yellow birch and scrubby pines and one or two hickory trees. The snow drapes them, lies in cone-shaped caps on the old stumps, as though it is drawing them upward. Molded by fingers of wind, it forms turrets and dungeons in the hollows, and the ice hangs in prisms from the weighted boughs of the half-grown pines, making a faint music in the currents of air.

In a strange way, his quest for Frayne's soul has freed Catcher Benet. There are no wives here, and no contracts for barrels. Nothing to covet or to despair of, no rich and no poor, no hope and no expectations, no pride to be swallowed again and again till it chokes him. Here America is pure and unpossessable. Here there is only the cumbersome track of a quail through the snow. The long knife-slash of an opossum's tail, the small leaps of a weasel. The rap of a redheaded woodpecker on a hickory branch. The nervous scolding of chickadees. The cold music of ice to grace the ear.

All this, in Jacob's mind, is summed up in the wild girl, Jennet Sparrow. She is the continent that flows west with the rivers, and it is her purity that keeps him in the woods now. If I could see her and touch her, he thinks, I could bear anything. I could learn to love Hester. I could live, and do good in the world.

Benet suddenly draws a deep breath and seizes the boy in his arms, holding him so tight his ribs ache. "Christ," he says. "Christ."

"Dada?" Timothy says, pushing away from him, frightened. He scuffs at a sycamore leaf in the snow and Frayne's voice finds his secret ear. Say it, son. Say sycamore. Again he shakes it off, the sweet-sour flavor of currants. "Did you hear me? The cart's gone in the lake."

Catcher drags himself back. "Never mind. I can put us new wheels on the old one."

"But the ox, Dada. Old Red. He's drownded."

The boy's eyes are full of tears. Oxen are kind, warm-hearted, brave, enduring. When they are young, they are awkward and fumbling as puppies, and they live many years, If you are caught out in a blizzard, they will lie down beside you and the heat of their bodies will keep you living. If you die, they will pine for the sound of your voice.

Flakes of memory leaf up around Tim like a flight of crows from a cornfield. A big, deep-jowled black dog dead in Frayne's arms, the dog's head sagging backwards and his huge paws splayed out, the man sobbing without shame, so loud someone comes out with a lantern. What's the use of bawling so for a dog? Hester leans in the doorway, the boy clinging onto her skirt. Frayne's knees buckle and his face buries itself in the thick fur of the dog's belly, his hands stroking and stroking it, red with its blood. They shot him, he says in his soft, careful, hypnotic voice. Because he was better than any of them.

"We'll bury the ox decent," Jacob says gently, his arm around Timothy.

"We can't! Don't you hear me? He's drownded! He's sunk in the lake!" The boy's fists pound on a tree trunk till a shower of snow falls down on them. "Don't you see, it was Frayne's doing! It must've been, Topas said so! Frayne caught him out one night in the woods and got it out of him about the bordering. Asked him all kind of questions. It was Frayne told the army on you and the rest of the smugglers, and now they're taking Topas to Cayuna to prison!"

Jacob sits very still, his eyes on the snow. "I didn't want you to know, Tim. How I'd shamed you. I did wrong to get mixed up in it, damn fool business. But we needed the money, and your mother promised she wouldn't say—"

"Lots of men smuggle! Smuggling's better than spying. Frayne's a damn spy, he must be! Who else would've told the army on you?"

"Now, now. They been after us these six months, Tim. Long before he came back here."

"But they never caught you till now!"

For a long time Jacob sits silent and Tim tries not to look at him.

"So then," Benet says at last. "What should I do?" In this place, with the boy before him, he is without will. Frayne's guilt or innocence is nothing, his own tangled heart is nothing. Only Timothy matters. What he wants. What he loves. "Am I bound to kill him, do you think?" he says vaguely.

"I hate him!" The boy's voice is a scream, so high and shrill it brings down more snow from the branches. There is a breaking sound, so deep in Tim's chest it is not possible at first to recognize where it comes from. He stares down at his fists as though they are clubs. "I hate you all!" he cries. "I don't care what you do!"

He seizes Benet's second-best musket and runs, a senseless zig-zag among the trees, dodging the memory of John Frayne sitting crosslegged in front of a fire, his black hair falling over his forehead and his voice just beginning a story.

Once upon a time there lived a young prince whom the gods made invisible. He could see and know others, but being invisible, he himself was forever unknown.

Sergeant Ferris marched his prisoners away to the town jail and the boy Sam loaded Frayne's packages onto Pewter. In front of the Dog and Lantern, the sleigh-coach from Cayuna drew up, and young Lawyer Slocum made his way out at the shop door. But John blocked his path.

"A minute of your time, sir," he said. "Step into the inn with me, and take a glass of hot punch before your coach goes. I have some business that wants lawyering."

The young man looked nervously over his shoulder at Hetty Fanning, whose bright little shrew's eyes missed nothing. Then he grinned. "Devil take all dragonesses! Lead away, sir! Lead away!"

The Dog and Lantern was a coaching inn of Captain Sandy's time, built broad and sturdy, with an upper story that stuck out partway over the street. On the east side there were commodious pens in which drovers might keep their herds of cattle and swine and geese and turkeys. Until late October, even the best of the roads was a sea of mud in which wagons and coaches foundered and overturned, and cattle got stuck to their haunches. But once the roads froze hard, those with goods for sale or visits to pay or business to transact hurried to do so before the worst of the winter snows set in, which was usually just after Christmas.

Still, there were always some latecomers; even now, a woman was driving twelve or fifteen racketing geese down Broad Street, and a half-dozen cows lowed mournfully in the pen. A freight wagon was being hitched in the stableyard too, the little old driver swearing and spitting and stamping at his four great draft horses.

"That's old Doxy Floyd," said Will Slocum with a chuckle. "Comes in every week at half-past twelve on the Thursday with

Aldrich's trade goods, and out again on the Friday. Good as an eight-day clock."

The old teamster crossed the yard to a rope ladder that hung down from a small landing on the uppermost floor of the inn. He tucked up the long skirt of his double-caped oilskin, gripped the ropes on each side, and scrambled up like a monkey, to disappear through a window.

"Way things work in King Herod's domain," Slocum said, giving a nod to old Doxy Floyd's curious exit. "Front door for ladies and gents. Ladder for drovers. Strong language. Aroma of horses. Hard on genteel business. What the eye don't see, the pocketbook don't grieve for. Ah, this is more like it!"

They entered the Dog and Lantern to discover a fine bar-parlor of the old-fashioned kind, with a serving wicket and three huge, high-backed settles drawn up in a circle before a great fieldstone fireplace. No Franklin stoves for Peter Underwell. His inn was a haven of tradition, and serving girls in white caps and aprons trotted in and out of the kitchen with mugs of hot punch and plates of ham and warm brown bread and Mrs. Underwell's famous pickle relish and cranberry jelly.

"Now then," said the young lawyer, settling down with a sigh to a pewter mug of rum punch that still steamed from the landlord's hot poker. "What can I do for you—Mr. John Frayne, ain't it? Bad habit, eavesdropping. But it's useful, in my business."

"You know my story, do you?"

"Seized property. Squatter. Wife with two husbands. How can I help you?"

"I want my father's land back from Aldrich—enough of it to live on. I want to be free of my wife and I want my son back. And I want it done legally. Will you help me?"

Young Slocum gulped, burned his throat on the hot punch, coughed, and poured down a glass of cold water to put the fire out. He looked around to see if anyone had noticed. The Federalist Club was having luncheon at the Dog today, and a number of well-dressed gentlemen were putting their heads together over the New York City papers the sleigh-coach had brought in from across the Divide. The lawyer craned his neck, taking count of them. Zadoc Beale. Reverend Mitchell. Dr. Hallam. Ah, Herod Aldrich was missing, thank God.

Will Slocum cleared his throat. "As for the lady, I'll file the bill of divorcement tomorrow, and once you sign it, she's the legal wife of old Catcher, till death do 'em part. And the boy—if you're determined, I think I can compass that too." He looked sidewise at Frayne. "*Are* you determined?"

"Yes, of course. But— Well, I'm still a stranger to him. I need time."

"Once you give up your claim to his mother, the longer you wait, the harder it'll be. Not mistreated, is he?"

"Not so far as I know."

"How old?"

"Ten."

"Go for a cabin boy or an infantry drummer at that age. Almost a man." The lawyer shook his head and the stovepipe hat he had forgotten to remove tipped foolishly sidewise. "It ain't custody you want, Mr. Frayne, sir. It's his heart. And I can't get you that by law."

John did not protest. His pierced hands lay flat on the table and he felt Will Slocum's clear-eyed gaze on them, but he did not try to disguise them nor defend them. He turned them palm-upward, like an empty cup. "What about my father's house?" he said quietly.

Slocum gave a soft whistle. "Win back the Frayne patent? Me? My old Governor was in on that business at the very beginning. Finest young law-dogs in the country came up for it—Aaron Burr, Mr. Hamilton."

"Perhaps, then, if Mr. Hamilton is still at practice, he might have some information concerning the status of—"

Slocum stared. "Why, Hamilton's dead, sir! Burr killed him in a duel some five years back!"

"Ah." Frayne bowed slightly. "I had forgot. If you ever go west, you will find that it cleanses the memory of trivial details."

"Trivial? Jefferson's government all but fell from the shock of it! Hamilton was a great man and Burr is ruined forever!"

"I have known but two great men in my life, Lawyer. One was an Indian wise man who died in a fight over who owned a beaver skin. The other hanged himself when I was four."

Slocum nodded. "Ah, yes. Your honored papa. But as to his patent, it was contested in court for some fifteen years on your mother's behalf, before it was sold off to Herod Aldrich."

"I've offered to buy a modest parcel of land, that's all, including Bay House, at more than double the going price, but Aldrich will do no more than rent it to me. Why? Is he so rich?"

"Too pig-headed to be properly rich. He's a miser for acreage, sir, he covets the owning of land as some men covet treasure. Men want homes of their own, they want to buy, not rent from a landlord. But King Herod won't sell, he'd rather have land than money. Might cut the timber for boards, but you can't ship 'em overland and we're too far from a river to float 'em. Some profit in potash."

"And more in smuggling?"

The lawyer laughed. "I'll say nothing to that, sir, and you couldn't expect it."

"He can smuggle the whole state of New York up to Canada, so far as I'm concerned. But that sergeant may have other ideas, and surely the sale of a useless parcel of land is better than the risk of bordering, if he's in need of cash money." Frayne sipped at his punch without enjoying it. "There are—others involved, to whom I have promised a secure place to settle. At the moment I'm a squatter, but that cannot go on, and if I am to make Bay House my home, I won't do so at the whim of a landlord."

"Oh, Herod don't have whims." Slocum looked Frayne up and down, and the boyish grin broke over his even features again. "Even if your name wasn't Frayne, he wouldn't be able to stick you, you know."

"Why not?"

"Because, sir, in despite of your somewhat eccentric attire, you're a gentleman, ain't you? Talk like one. Move like one. Got the carriage and the confidence and the education. King Herod ain't got 'em. Tries like sixty, decks out his house like a circus wagon. But he can't come up to it. Besides land, he had only two things that ever brought him to anybody's notice, and those were his wife—she was a Smails, of the Philadelphia Smailses, you know. And his daughter. The fair Susanna." Here young Slocum took off the hat and held it against his bosom. "A pearl, sir. A pearl. We were to marry, bless her memory."

"You have my condolences, Mr. Slocum. How did she die?"

"Confounded buggy turned over. Wheel struck a rut. Broke her neck."

"I won't take up any more of your time, then." Frayne finished his mug of punch and stood up. "To act against the father of a woman he has loved would be too much to ask of any man."

"Didn't love her, sir. Not really up to it. Fine girl. But too far above me to love."

"But you say you meant to wed her."

"Oh, my old Governor chose her. Sake of future ambitions— his, not mine. Pa's running for Congress in two years' time, and he needs the Smailses behind him. Old Aldrich means to stand for the Senate and his Federalist cronies wanted somebody to tell him when to make a leg in company, all that sort of thing. Yours Truly elected. He can't stick me, either, but he gives me a bit of pin money now and then, like a kept woman, and that helps me go down."

Frayne smiled his crooked smile. "So Squire Aldrich is a Federalist, is he?"

Slocum laughed. "A piss-pot Tory, yes. Ain't that what they call 'em in England? All the failings of a regular king-loving Tory, but none of the virtues." His smile faded. He stared into his hat again, then glanced over at Frayne, suddenly serious. "I must warn you. You know better than most, Mr. Frayne, that it was a bitter war up here in the mountains. I doubt if any court in these parts would give you back your father's patent—unless you gave 'em no choice under law."

"And how would I do that?"

"Well, they do say there are parcels still open to question. They come up in court now and then. But—"

"What kind of question?"

"Boundaries overstepped. Titles unclear at the time of seizure. Oath never refused."

"Explain, if you please. Oath?"

"It—uh—seems the Committee of Public Safety got somewhat above itself, seized land from some who had never been offered the Oath of Allegiance. Wasn't offered, couldn't refuse. Couldn't refuse, couldn't be stamped as a Tory. Couldn't be stamped, couldn't be seized upon, not legally. But plenty were, all the same. Cases tied up in the courts these thirty years on that question. Plaintiffs get old and die, children take over. Papers dusty. People dusty. Future dusty. Property dust."

"If these oaths were administered, where are they written down?"

"Why, in Albany. The ones this side of the mountains, anyway. Every Committee had a Secretary, and when they examined a Tory, they kept a transcript-of-record. At least that was the rule."

"And if the rule was not kept? If there's no record of the oath?"

"Then the seizure ain't *necessarily* legal, sir. It can be filed against and reversed. But almost none ever have been, and in your case, with such a large parcel—"

"I want you to look out that transcript for me, Mr. Slocum. The record of inquiry into my father's politics. The record of deed to the parcel upon which Bay House stands. I'll pay you well, but I must know where *I* stand."

"Oh, I'll do that for you, and glad to. But what then?"

"I mean Aldrich no harm. I only want to make him see reason."

Will Slocum smiled and shook his head. "Herod Aldrich and reason? Oil and vinegar, sir. Take my advice, Mr. Frayne. Don't set your heart on it. There's other land and other lakes."

★   ★   ★

John's blue eyes took in a wave of commotion among the gentlemen reading their papers. "Who the devil are that lot?" he said,
irritated.

"Them? That's the Federalist Club." Slocum laughed.

But Frayne's features grew more and more intent. "What are
they saying?" he asked, his hands gripping the edge of the table.
"What are they talking of?"

The men by the fire were becoming agitated, even disorderly.
A pasty-faced old man with powdered hair in a queue stood up
and shook his fist at the ceiling, and a bespectacled young man in
the long black coat of a parson helped him back to his chair and
called for brandy. Snatches of conversation rose now and then
above the clatter of dishes and the rattle of knives and forks.

War. Invasion. Missouri. Teach them a lesson. Indians. British.
Four hundred of their lives for the four hundred dead.

"Four hundred dead?" John Frayne whispered. "So many. So
many."

He seemed to be speaking to himself, and Lawyer Slocum
stared at him, puzzled. But the serving maid who came to refill
their mugs with punch took the words for a direct question, and
not a rhetorical one.

"Aye, sir, four hundred, ain't it dreadful? The British sent their
Red Indians down on the fort and they killed them all, settlers
and Continentals and all that was living, so they did."

"Whereabouts?" Frayne whispered. "What fort was it? When?"

"Oh, it's some months ago now, sir. Papers is always as slow
as molasses coming up from York City and Philadelphia. But they
say there was a big fight at a place they call Fort McKittrick. There
was a company of Yorkers there, got up two year since right here
in—"

"McKittrick? In the Missouri country, above St. Louis? But
there aren't four hundred whites in the whole of that country, nor
a hundred miles around."

The maid sniffed. "Oh well, the newspapers know, I expect. Maybe it's a different place, but it's out west, anyhow. Indiana maybe. The territories, I don't know one from another." She smiled and blushed prettily. "I never was one for geography and maps."

We regret to inform our readers of shameful news from the West—of which we might not even now be informed, were it not for the impending departure from office of Mr. Jefferson and his band of Republican poltroons, to whom no insult by King or Emperor seems too dreadful or costly for this nation to endure! On the morning of 22 September 1808, more than a thousand armed and mounted savages of the Sauk, Fox, and other tribes surrounded the gallant garrison at Ft. McKittrick on the Blind River in the Missouri Territory some two hundred miles above St. Louis. Settlers from the surrounding country had been harried by these ravaging brutes for many weeks, and a number of women and children had fled to the Fort for protection. Bearing guns and brandishing sabres of British manufacture, the alliance of savages drew up to the gates and their leader, one Firewalker, demanded the return to the tribes of all settlers' lands, which they claimed with great impertinence to be rightfully their own. Captain Divis Taylor, after talks with the Chieftain, was unable to restrain him, and the garrison proved insufficient to resist. All within the gates of Ft. McKittrick were slaughtered, near four hundred civilians and brave Continentals betrayed by a spy in the pay of the British and their Indian Cohorts, who provided maps and details of the fort and its garrison! How long shall we meekly succumb to such treacherous incitement of murder and rapine in our Western lands? Let us avenge Ft. McKittrick! Drive out the Union Jack and its Traitorous Spies

from the continent of North America and bring peace to
the West and fair trade to the Seas!

Known Dead, Company C, New York Rifles, New Forge,
Talbot County
George Floyd, Sergeant
Patrick Lampson, Private Soldier
Pierre Labiche, Corporal
Charles Hall, Private Soldier
Robert Josselyn, Corporal

VII

the city of larks

It was spring in the City of Larks when they brought the guns to me, and the old, rusted sabres, Frayne tells them. When they wanted my maps.

He makes his confession two days after the news of the massacre at Fort McKittrick, sitting crosslegged at the feet of the others. The wine bottle stands on the table, but nobody drinks from it, not even the Frenchman. John's voice is level and quiet and from time to time he pauses, his head bowed very low. As he speaks, his hand cups the instep of the girl's boot, as though he can sense her capacity for forgiveness from the very shape of her, whether she draws away from him or not.

Jennet hears his breath with the planes of her face, with her fingertips that lie flat on her lap, reaching towards him. When he is like this, she does not need his words, they are no use to her. His eyes are like the light at the ends of two long tunnels that begin somewhere under the earth, under the white, frozen lake on which snow has begun to fall again.

What will reach him? she wonders. What turns a ghost back into a man? In spite of his guilt and his anger, there is a long-punished sweetness about Frayne, riper and wiser than the Frenchman's blundering innocence. Jennet puts out her hand and lays it on his bent head to make him know her without words. Leclerc's eyes never leave her and the old man sits silent beside her, the fragrant smoke of his pipe rising into the dark rafters.

John Frayne wants to live backwards, to become what his father expected, what his son needed in his absence, what he himself might have been if there had been no war, no exile, no disinheritance, no Herod Aldrich, no west. The girl Jennet wants to keep the past that was Hannah's, but even more, she has begun to want her own future, to explore all possibilities at random. The Frenchman stumbles between past, present, and future, and is abashed by all three.

Only Gabriel, who is old, is completely at home in the present. He lives from moment to moment, does not think too deeply, does not bother to fear the future nor presume to judge the past.

My people had a word that meant city, Frayne tells them, lifting his face so the girl may read him if she chooses. Towotho, they called it.

There was another word in their language for the way they lived now. Zikaha, they called their little circles of mud houses. Village. When I asked them, they had never heard of St. Louis or New Orleans or Washington. Yet the concept of a city, of a hive of men building and working and dependent upon one another, was not alien to them. It seemed innate, something passed on in their blood.

Had they long ago travelled from China or India, perhaps even from Africa? The sound of such places was there, in their music and their poems. Who knows? In some distant prehistory, their fathers might have built great roads and aqueducts and temples, formulated philosophies and the principles of pure science, devised great fictions and epic poems, and invented clocks and fine coaches. Then it was gone. Taken. The wave of decline crested and broke over them, as it will break—perhaps has already broken—over us.

What brought on their darkness, I was soon to discover. But

they still remembered the light and worshipped it. The City of Larks. Towotho hushi.

I had no calendars, but it was the month we called Big Spring Moon. We had been married two winters, and Tacha was heavy with our child then. We had lost one already, a son, to miscarriage. Take me to the City of Larks, she said. Take me where light is, so the child may be safe.

It was a holy place, a place of pilgrimage in the spring. A wide meadow skirted with willows, where hundreds, perhaps thousands of birds swooped and dived in the first light of morning. As the sun rose higher and the light grew flatter and more abundant, they spread out across the prairies looking for food, or perched in the shade of the willow trees. But at twilight they came back again, soaring high over the meadow, then swooping down, pairs playing tag with each other, small flocks weaving in and out of one another's flyways, tempting the gods of collision.

And always the birdsong. In the morning, it was very loud and shrill and manic, and children sometimes grew afraid of it, so intense was it, so hysterical, like a birth-cry that never stops and cannot be soothed or explained. It was said among my people that if you heard it as the sun rose, you would be granted great wisdom and long life. Some universal force seemed to live in those wild cries, something threatened everywhere else, but here dominant and prevailing, unquenchable. In the autumn, we worshipped the snow geese. In the spring, there were larks.

The evening was different. The birds' demons had been exorcised then and their music was liquid and pure, almost like the notes of the cedarwood flutes with which the men declared their love. The evening light struck a high sandstone butte to the west of the meadow and bathed the place in rich reddish-gold, so that by contrast the yellow breasts of the swooping birds seemed to turn white at the crest of the evening. Wherever you saw them— on the wing, nesting thick in the willow boughs—you saw glimmers of moving light.

It was an ancient place, possessed by the natural world and yet resonant with humanity. The hearth circles of many long-destroyed lodges could be seen, slight round depressions in the grass, and by night many dead seemed to draw near in benevolence. I had seen the pre-Roman hill forts in England and the great standing stones. I had slept on Hadrian's Wall and heard battle cries rise in the night and the ghostly legions marching, inexorable, their swords crashing. But these ghosts were otherwise. No battle had ever been fought here, and even death seemed kind and approachable. No treachery tainted the place, and no despair.

Now you know why I wanted her born here, Tacha said to me. She was convinced it would be a girl-child. My wife had seen our daughter in a dream, with larks soaring about her. She will be safely born if we stay here, she told me. The bird-music must be the first thing she hears.

Tacha was afraid of the birth that was coming, and it soothed her if I lay with my hand on her belly where the child was. I felt it move inside my girl-wife's body, and that night for the first time I was whole and sufficient as I had never been with Hester, not even—much as I had always adored him—when our son Timothy was born. Anger and bitterness and the loneness of exile fell away from me that night in the City of Larks. For that brief space, I was no longer depleted by the debt I had always believed that I owed to my father, by my boyish guilt for his dying. It would come back again later, and stronger than ever, but that night I was myself at last, and I felt capable of greatness in my own right. I believed I would never go back and live among white men again. I had found my people at last, and come home.

But it didn't last long. New guilt came to find me. I was exiled again.

The band we belonged to had drawn up their summer lodges on a rise to the south of the City of Larks, where there was good water and grass, and small game in the thickets. One old woman came down into the meadow with Tacha, a granny who had delivered many babies and was skillful, and we arranged to summon my wife's mother and aunts when the time came.

As for myself, I was never permitted to go anywhere alone. The old wise man, the Prophet, came with us as always, and the young boy who still spoke for me when my grasp of their language proved insufficient. I was used to them, and their presence did not alarm me.

But there were others this time. Almost a dozen of the young fighting men brought their blankets and robes and made rough camp at the edges of the meadow. Those to the south were all Foxes, the same clan as my wife, and they bore the same small teardrop tattoo on their foreheads that she did—the symbol of their *gens*. But the braves to the east were Raven-people, troublemakers and bullies seldom friendly to any of the other clans, and archenemies of the Foxes.

The Prophet was practicing some of his magic just then by our fire; the boy had bound him hand and foot with rawhide thongs, and one by one he worked at escaping them. It was morning, and the birds were screaming like mad things.

Who are those men by the willows? I asked him. They're Ravens, aren't they? What do they want here?

One was a thick-headed fellow called Firewalker who had a grudge against me. He had wanted Tacha for a second wife, and if that had not been enough, I had also done him out of a buffalo tongue—a great delicacy indeed among a people so short of food by the end of the winter that they caught mice and roasted them.

What does Firewalker want here? I asked.

He and his friends were playing at hot-ball with a stone from the fire and seemed peaceful enough. But the sight of him made my nerves prickle.

He will do nothing now, said the Prophet. He is waiting for the birth, to see if the child is healthy.

And if it is not?

He will cause it to die. His spells have some power, but he wants even more. My friend shrugged his shoulders and a thong slipped away from his wrists and lay like a dead snake on the grass. If the baby should die, he will kill you, he said, and take your woman for a slave-wife. He will kill me, too, to take my power to himself.

It was a revelation. I sank down by the fire. Why? I whispered. What's my child got to do with you, or with him, or with power?

Everything in the world is power or no-power, Saku. The Prophet's legs gave a nervous jerk and the last thong fell away. He stood up easily, his body still as supple as my own, though he must have been seventy. The Ravens say I have betrayed them. That my counsel is no longer good.

He had been for many years a kind of saint among the people. It was said he had brought wounded men back from the dead, that he himself had once died and awakened. My people believed there were seven deaths for every man, with a life between each death that could not be perceived by the others, like two men walking parallel lines with a wall of mirrors between them, each seeing only himself though either might have reached out a hand and touched the other. The Prophet had left his eyes, so the boy had told me, in the land of the seventh dead, the perfected dead, and they had given him the secret eyes of wisdom that could see through the walls of perception.

If the child should die, or if the woman dies in childbirth, they will say it is proof that you are evil, Saku. My magician laughed softly. They do not think you are really a god.

They are right, I said.

We had long ago dispensed with any deceptions between us. I was his puppet, a political instrument he had used with success to keep at bay the clans who favored war and conquest. When the Ravens began to feud over broken taboos or charges of disrespect or which brave owned a pony, when they beat their war drums for a raid to take slaves from the Maha or the Assiniboin or the Otoe, then he would bring the leaders before me. Saku finds no good in these war drums. Saku is angered. Let Saku decide.

So I had taken the buffalo tongue from Firewalker. So I had taken my Tacha.

Panic clawed at me now, and terrible anger. I could almost have killed the old magus myself. I am no god, I said. Christ. Let me just take the woman and go.

He smiled. Gods do not always know themselves. Some are

blind to their natures. Besides, where would you go where the Ravens could not find you? Hear that? It's too late now, in any case.

There was a great cry from inside our lodge, louder than all the mad shrieking of the circling larks. As though the Prophet had willed it, Tacha's labor had begun.

The child's birth took all day and most of that night. The birds came back in the evening, but they kept to the farther willows, disturbed by the woman's cries. For a man to enter a birth lodge was taboo, and Frayne sat outside with the old magician. In the darkness beyond the firelight, he could hear the Raven-men and the Foxes who were Tacha's relations drawing nearer.

Then it was quiet. No more screams came from the lodge. The granny began to sing, a low, monotonous chanting.

What is it?

A girl-child. Dying. Perhaps dead.

Frayne could bear it no longer, he burst into the lodge through the low door of painted skins. Blood and afterbirth were everywhere, and the old woman was washing Tacha and singing a death chant under her breath. He pushed her outside and began to wash his wife's limp, slender body himself. There was a heavy, sweet smell of burnt sawgrass in the lodge, the herb that caused visions and killed pain when you breathed in its smoke. Tacha had been bled in the Indian fashion, two small slits cut in her forehead just above her brows, to let out the evil spirits.

She was very weak, but when she opened her eyes and saw John there, she was terrified. You must go out, Saku! Do not touch me, I am not clean!

Tacha struggled in his arms and he stroked her and held cool water to her lips to make her drink. She was shaking and he lifted her up to him, held her body against him, rocking her back and forth. No one can keep you from me. You take me apart and

keep pieces of me with you, inside you. Wherever you are, if you
live or die, I will walk there.

I can't hear the birds, she said.

It's night, my soul. They are sleeping.

Is the baby dead?

Frayne looked down at their girl in her small basket-cradle.
She was purplish-blue, barely breathing, and one leg was twisted.
Not dead, he said.

Let me feed her.

It's too soon. She's still sleeping.

Like the other birds, Tacha said, and fell back on the robes.

In the kitchen of Bay House, the candle is guttering. It goes out
and they sit in the firelight, shadows flickering on their faces.

"After Hester, I had not thought that any living thing in the
world could love me," Frayne says. "Never hoped for it. Never
thought of it. I drifted. Worked. Wandered from place to place.
Then Tacha was there."

His pale, fathomless eyes rest on Jennet and the eyelids flicker
shut, so that he sits there as though he is sleeping. The girl has
slipped down from the bench and her body leans against his left
side, a slight pressure that seems to make the story come easier
from him. The kitten lies at her feet sound asleep, its white chin
in the air and one paw over its eyes.

Behind his spectacles, Leclerc's eyes are streaming. I had not
thought that any living thing in the world could love me. Could
it be true, he thinks, that I am not, after all, unique in my solitude?
This handsome fellow—for indeed, even scarred as he was, Frayne
was handsome— Could he have wandered as I have, doubting his
right to be taken for human? Scouring the universe for love?

The Frenchman takes off his spectacles and cleans them absent-
mindedly on the end of his necktie, then wipes his eyes with it.
Marius is not yet whole in himself, and hope always eludes an
unfinished creation. When he is with the others, here in Bay

House, he aligns himself by them, collecting them like pieces that will put him together, hiding behind their community. But alone— walking the lakeshore, making the chairs, eating dumplings with the apprentices—he drifts nearer and nearer to the chasm he has always dodged away from. The terrible gulf that is love.

But for whom? For whom?

As for Gabriel, he sits very still tonight, scarcely seeming to breathe, with Frayne's buffalo robe pulled close around him, and when he speaks it is a matter of great moment to them all, as though a tide has come in or a quiet rain begun to fall.

"How long did your little one live?" he says at last.

"Four days."

"Mother and me lost three after we had our Ned. Youngest lived but an hour." The old man gets up and puts another log on the fire. "I thought I was young enough till then, plenty of life in me. But after them deaths, I begun to be old. I trusted God no more, nor my own poor bones neither. I still loved Mother, indeed I did. But living had a different taste to it. I blamed myself, that I must have done some terrible wrong them three babes paid for."

"Light the candle again," John tells the Frenchman softly. "Please, Marius. I want Jennet to see me. To hear what I say."

The rest comes from Frayne like slivers of glass being drawn from a wound. Leclerc is the surgeon, the voice of the priest in this confessional semidarkness. His questions are clear and steady, but he turns his eyes away, watching only the girl.

How long did they wait? When did they come for you?

Firewalker waited five days, until after Uma's burial. Tacha was still shrieking with the women of the Fox clan by the grave when he and the others came to confront me. You must understand. They were bully-boys, a gang of toughs far more alien to my people than I had ever been, for all my white skin. They had no people, thugs never have. As human things, they had never been finished, they were lacking some crucial cog, some balance-wheel.

They cared nothing for the City of Larks and all its gentle ghosts. Firewalker's thugs saw a crack in the fabric of things-as-they-were, and they plunged their fists into it and into Tacha and into me. From being a god, I went to being a devil in the space of an hour. I was my father's son at last, living all his torments over again.

What did they say you had done? Of what did they accuse you?

You stole the child's soul, they said. You are a witch, not a god. We have heard from the Assiniboins of others with white skin like yours, men with red coats to the northward, and they are not gods. Besides, you saw the woman with her birth blood still upon her, and you touched her uncleanness. The child Uma died for it, and you must die, too.

Where was the old man, the magician? Could he not help you, monsieur?

I hadn't seen him all that day, he had not offered prayers at the burial. They had taken him away, and the boy with him, so I had no one to speak for me. I could not be certain the thugs understood what I said, and I fell back on hand signs.

The child was my own, I told them. Half my heart has gone with her. Look! Do I not grieve for her?

I had slit the skin of my upper arm and put through it a small twig of willow leaves, as was the custom. It was the hour when the birds were out feeding, and from the main camp to the south, I could hear many grief-cries, far more than for Uma, far wilder and more fearful.

Where is the Prophet? I asked them. What have you done with him?

Firewalker stamped his foot in the sand by the campfire. Pah, he is dead, and his catamite too, and good riddance! He was an old fool. He said the beaver I killed was the property of that thief Brown Horse of the Foxes! He belied me and he is dead.

A great man does not die for a beaver skin, I said.

They had formed a tight circle around me and I could see that, like all thugs, they hated one another far more than any of them hated me, or even feared me. If Firewalker failed in his ploy to seize power, if he weakened or showed any sign of confusion, one of the others would take him down in his turn, and the next would take him, and on and on.

What had they done with your wife, Monsieur Jean? With Tacha?

She is shamed, Firewalker said. She has gone back to her father's lodge. The women have taken her to purify her. When you are dead, I will take her for a servant-wife.

My mind was reeling. I had only one thing to give them that might save us. At the end of the winter, I had begun to paint the maps.

You said they had guns and sabres. Tell about the guns.

Firewalker threw down a bundle wrapped in greased deerskin and tied with thongs, and one of his bully-boys cut it open. There were five rifles—very old, but good Lancaster guns with walnut stocks, and the barrels not rusted. American guns. Beside them was a handgun, an old duelling pistol with silver chasings. Two sabres lay with them, the tips blunted and the edges long since worn away from misuse.

There had been only bows and arrows and spears in the camp since I had been with them, and my own gun had been stolen by the men who tortured me and threw me away. I myself was not allowed weapons; gods did not need them, so the Prophet had told me. The boy had hunted our game for us and ate at our fire, or if I caught a rabbit for the cooking-pot, I did it with snares. Now I stared down at these good Yankee guns and felt the universe tremble.

Where did you get them? I said.

Parties of feuding American trappers worked the Missouri country, scrambling to stake their claims to trade with the Indians, and many used such rifles. But the pistol and the sabres—they were gentlemen's weapons, officers' weapons.

Spies' weapons?

At the Spaniard's post by the Council Bluffs of the Maha, I had seen men up from St. Louis who wore such fine swords. They wore no uniforms, they did not dare. But they could not give up their elegant weapons.

What manner of men were they, monsieur? British? French?

Let me try to explain. After Napoleon sold us the west, only Americans went there. Whatever language they spoke, whatever shreds of private loyalty they possessed to other nations, whomever they spied for and killed for, they were all Americans. All equal, with the same right to carve up the pickings. The Creoles hated the British, the British hated the French, the Kentuckians hated the Yankees, the Yankees hated them all.

But surely they knew they could not claim the west as their private preserve. What did they want, monsieur? What was the truth of them?

Power, my friend. Alliances. A grip on the balls of the future.

And the spies? Were there no patriots among them, no idealists?

A few, perhaps, and they were the greatest danger. Most were no different than Firewalker's thugs.

And you? Which were you?

I? I was— I was Iko. The toad.

Tell the rest of the story. Tell about this Iko, the toad.

One of the thugs struck me down, and Firewalker put his foot on the back of my head so that my face was ground into the cold ashes of our fire. A lodge in mourning kept no fires, and I had been fasting for days. Besides, I had lost blood from the mourning-cuts and the sight of the guns made me dizzy and sick. The cold click of the metal, the invisible mechanism with a will of its own— even for food, guns have no other purpose but taking. I had seen men shot to death, but I myself had never turned a gun upon anything human. I have not, to this day.

Where did you get these guns? I said to them. Who killed the men that owned them? You? The Spaniard from the Council Bluffs? The Redcoats?

It is not up to toads and slaves to ask questions, Firewalker told me. That is your name now. You are not Saku. You are Iko. Toad.

He laughed and the others laughed after him, like a pack of lackeys to a lord. Then he let me up and one of the others threw me down beside the skin of weapons.

Tell of this, Firewalker said. What are they good for?

I tossed the sabres aside. These? I said. Nothing. They need to be mended. Heated on a forge and pounded straight. Sharpened.

His eyes narrowed; to be cheated would make him lose face in front of his bullies. We will fix them, Iko, he said, puffing out his chest like a bullfrog. *I* will fix them. You are a fool.

I knew he was bluffing for the sake of the thugs, of course. My people could sharpen a blade with a flat stone to a keen edge, but they had no forge hot enough to mend steel, and no proper anvil. Firewalker changed the subject; he nudged the guns with a gingerly toe.

What are the sticks for? Those dogs the Assiniboins said they made fire and killed many enemies. But no fire comes out of them.

I examined the wrappings and found there were no powder horns nor bags of shot in the parcel. I looked up at him. What I must tell is great medicine, I said. It is only for chiefs. I will tell no one but the one who is chief among you.

I let Firewalker look into my eyes, that it would mean danger if the bully-boys heard. Come, Iko, he said, and shoved me into the lodge that had been ours.

I could see Tacha everywhere inside. On the bedplace where we had lain together. On the hard earth by the dead fire, where she had knelt to make corn cakes. On the pile of hides where she sat to do beadwork. I could see all the colors of her body, the soft fawn of her belly and the small of her back where the skin was almost as white as my own.

Gone. Gone.

I had no more hope and I fell back upon stubbornness. I stood gripping a lodgepole and Firewalker struck at the scar on my face with his fist. Tell me this great medicine of the firesticks, you insolent toad.

I was bleeding, but I did not let go of the lodgepole to stanch it. Did they give nothing else? I asked him. No horn bottles? No leather pouch?

Hah, he snorted. Horn bottles? What good are they for killing?

What did you give for the firesticks?

Six horses.

You were cheated.

He struck me again, and my body swayed with his blow, but did not stagger or fall or bend.

These guns will not fire without powder and shot and lint, I said. You need round lead balls, heavy, a whole sackful. Black powder that explodes with a spark from this piece of metal. I showed him how the gun worked. To my shame. Christ help me. To my shame.

You must go on, Monsieur Jean. You must tell it all.

When there is no powder, I said, there is no fire. If there are no lead balls, even the fire will kill nothing. The Assiniboins have made a fool of you.

I could read Firewalker's fear, how it came from his tensed limbs and the muscles of his neck, how his brown toes curled under, trying to grip the earth that was slipping beneath him. On the strength of these few ancient and useless guns, he had rallied the thugs to his cause. He had killed my old friend the magician on the strength of them, on the promise of power they bought him. Now he saw it all crumbling, power yielding to power, and I did not ease the pressure I had put on him.

If I say to your friends that you were cheated, they will replace you, I told him. They will kill you to be free of you. Which will it be? Grey Squirrel? Fast Rabbit? He-Who-Walks? Which hates you most?

I will make this powder myself, he boasted. I have great medicine.

You cannot make it. I paused for a moment. Only white men have the medicine. But I know where you can get it.

You will tell!

You can trade for it. At the Redcoat fort to the north.

I could not tell him to take me back to the Spaniard's post. If I did so, I knew Manuel Falla would surely kill me, and I could do nothing for Tacha if I was dead. The British were my only hope, and I could not think of them as my enemies, nor the place called America as my country. My country was Tacha, and I would have sung for the Devil to keep her from harm. We were then

five days' travel south and west of the Mandan villages. There was
a border with Canada according to Jay's treaty, but nobody knew
exactly where it was this far to the west, and the British had a
garrison from which scouting and spying parties ranged south,
sometimes as far as the Pawnee and Otoe country along the Missouri—as our own men ranged well to the north.

I know their tongue. I will take you to the Redcoats, I said.

I had no idea if I could find the place. It didn't matter. Moving
mattered. Space mattered, the maps of my mind. They were my
only chance, and my wife's, and I cared nothing for consequences.
What have you to trade with them? I asked him.

Horses. Squaws.

They need no horses. They have many, and many squaws. But
one thing they do not have. They will trade for it gladly.

Tell it, he demanded, and I could not help smiling. Tell what
they will trade for.

Me, I said, and I showed him the maps.

"Iko the Toad was five months drawing maps for the British,"
Frayne tells them. "He was marched north on a rawhide leash tied
to Firewalker's pony, a journey that took a further month. He
begged to see his wife before they left, but they would not allow
it. Toads, he was told, have no wives."

John needs no more questions from the Frenchman. He gets
up and begins to pace, now, his moccasins scraping the floor Jennet
has carefully scoured and sanded. She takes the kitten in her lap,
her fingers stroking and stroking it. How fragile she looks, he
thinks, looking down at her. As though the candlelight passes
through her breast and her thin shoulders, through the bones of
her hands.

The girl's eyes do not leave him. Who is he now? Who is Iko
the Toad? Who is speaking? He has surrendered his personhood
to shame.

"Iko was traded for two dozen or so British rifles and the

powder and shot to supply them," he says. "Firewalker became
their ally, and his power seemed to have no limit. He brought
other bands into the British command. As I came east, I began to
hear of their ravages."

"So it was them paid you all that gold, then." Gabriel's voice
is sad. He is thinking of his lost son, Ned.

"No. Iko took his life from the British, but he took no
money."

"Then where . . . ?"

"From a madman. Mad Carrington, everybody called him, but
the toad had liked him. I suppose he made Iko think of his father,
who had known him long ago in England. Carrington had built
himself a castle on an island in the Mississippi, just above New
Orleans, and he wanted maps of the west to mount an invasion
and conquer all the land west of St. Louis, all the way to the
western ocean. He was mad as an owl, they had locked him away
by the time the toad got back from the west. But in his way,
Carrington was honest. The money he had promised to pay Iko
was waiting in a bank in St. Louis. It made him a very rich toad
indeed."

"Damn you! Stop that!"

All the evening, Jennet has said nothing and her speech has
lost most of the ease it has gained these past weeks. Tam oo. Top
dat. Frayne looks down at her, surprised. Wherever he has been,
she has reached him.

"Come back," she says. "Be here. Be with me."

With what terrible anguish she loves him, thinks Marius
Leclerc, as though she is doing a violence to herself—cutting the
veins of her wrists or smashing her bones with a hammer. It frightens him to think of it, makes him feel sore and angry at himself.
Such passion as hers is beyond me. I was born without it, as some
men are born with a finger joint missing.

"She is right, monsieur," he tells Frayne quietly. "Do not call
yourself a toad. You must not punish yourself with this terrible
name. It hurts her to hear it."

Frayne turns on him, his eyes cold. "You poor decent fool.

Don't you understand? The killing began even before I had finished the maps. Settlers. Small garrisons. Parties of trappers and peddlers. South into the Otoe country, east toward the Lakes. They allied with the Sauks and plunged down the Ohio, and along the Missouri almost to St. Louis. Thugs gathered other thugs to them. Those who were struck, struck back at the Indian villages, they didn't know the peaceful from the bully-boys and they didn't care. Whites, Indians, British, Americans. New thugs gained power, and some wore uniforms, some sat in the Senate and scoffed at the President. Lies grew, new horrors were invented to stain the dead. It was my father's time come back again, and just as before, I had caused it. I had fed them my maps."

"I'd almost begun to believe it couldn't find me here. That you—
That this place would make me clean of it somehow. Of course I
was wrong."

Frayne reached into the breast of his shirt and took out the
folded page of the New York City newspaper with the story of
the massacre at Fort McKittrick. He laid it on Jennet's lap where
the kitten was sleeping.

"Your brother is dead," he told her. "When you have read
that, remember the guilt of Iko the Toad. There's a gun in that
corner, and powder and shot on the mantel. I can't stay here with
you tonight, but I won't go so far you can't find me."

He bent and let his mouth brush her hair and linger there for
a moment. Leclerc could not bear to watch it. He stood up and
drew off into the darkness.

"Come and kill me," Frayne said to the girl, "if you think it
will help you. I'll be out on the ice."

He picked up his pack and went into the garden. It had snowed
an inch or two since dark and the two men could not hear his
footsteps as he left them. There was a sense of collapse in the
kitchen, an airless contraction, as though the walls might cave in.

Through his badly-smeared spectacles, Marius looked down at
the newspaper. He had heard the apprentices talking of something,
some terrible story that seemed to delight them because it made
war almost certain. Already a battalion was forming at Cayuna, to
march up to the border and challenge the British.

"Shall I read the paper aloud to you, *ma* Fauvette?" he said in
his soft, uncertain voice. I will protect you. I will lie. I will invent

a universe in which there is no pain, and build it like one of Zimmer's chairs.

Jennet put the kitten down and stood up, the folded sheet of newsprint clutched tight in her hand. "God damn you!" she said. Od am nu.

These exposed vowels were terrible to Marius, they were the beating of wings against walls. She had lived all her life in the cage of her imperfect body and she could not escape it. Whatever she did, whatever she thought in the lonely cave of her mind, whatever of talent or brilliance or sweetness she contained, it would, in the end, go to waste, and the world would reject her. She was like Frayne, they were two halves of the same doom, they imprisoned themselves.

And I, too, Leclerc thought. I am the cage in which I flounder. Christ Jesus, Mary, Mother of God. Give me a reason. Give me a purpose. Give me a rock on which to break.

"I don't want you here," the girl said. She wanted to be cruel, to hurt the old man and the Frenchman. "This place was mine and my mother's, and you all came and took it. I don't want any of you! Can't you leave me in peace?"

She took up the candle, and soon they could hear her boots overhead, marching back and forth, back and forth across the schoolroom floor.

Alone in the cold upstairs room, Jennet unfolds the page of newsprint and lets the light find it. The words there are not clean and simple like her mother's, they are puffed up like a boil full of pus and only a few of them reach her. Four hundred civilians and brave Continentals. Treacherous incitement. Thousand savages. Known dead, Robert Josselyn. My brother. My Robbie.

What is love? If it is honest, then it alters like Frayne's self, from minute to minute, and just now it is rage in the girl. Her fists pound down onto the old school desk until the discarded globes in the corners roll sidewise from the vibrations, turning continents on edge, setting at naught the orbits of planets.

"Annhhh-ahhh," she moans. "Annnhhhh-ahhhh."

They are the first sounds she can remember making, the most primitive part of her, where all fears live, and all passions. They were her first awkward attempt at the name of her mother.

Jennet stumbles up from the desk again, throws her body against the wall, crashes down, crawls into the corner, gets up and launches herself again and again and again. Downstairs, the two men can hear her, but they dare not intrude upon her now. The old man is silent, pretending sleep, and Leclerc slips outside and stands looking up at the faint light of her candle in the window, at her moving shadow where it smashes the bitter arrogance of God.

One last time she crashes against the wall, one last time slides down it, hands clawing the ruined wallpaper, the wainscotting. She crouches there on the icy floor, her head between her bony knees and her thin body huddled into something stunted and broken, almost beyond recognition.

"Annhhh-ahhhh."

The cry echoes out past the walls of the ruin, resounding on ice and snow and sky. All night, all through John's confession, she has been feeling the net on her body again, weighing down on her, smashing her breath before it can leave her. God has trapped her again, He has put love before her and snatched it away for a joke. If she mourns for her brother, if she is true to him, then must she not drive John Frayne away from her? What does it matter what caused him to spy for the British? He is guilty. His maps. His indelible memory. His love of his ghosts.

Nothing else matters. Because of him, Robbie is dead.

And yet she is not sure. Rage is spent now and something else takes its place. Her mind begins to examine possibilities, cutting the threads of John's story and weaving them in other directions to see if they make a better pattern. If he had not used the maps to save himself and Tacha, what would he be then? If he had traded them instead to the Spaniard or to some American? Would they have been gentler? Would their greed have resulted in kinder crimes?

Each time the threads break. She remembers his words that first night in the balsam grove. *I want you to know we are equals. That not only women are used.* If he is guilty, Jennet thinks, then I am guilty, too. To become an instrument of those who have glimpsed the ape with the eye of gold, to be used by the greedy and the mindless, against will, against pride, against honor—what else is a rape? She might have fought them till she died that cold day on the ice, but they were too many and too drunk, and the net was upon her.

Was it not upon Frayne in the City of Larks?

Jennet bends double, remembering the grinding ache of Caleb's sex inside her, worse than painful because it was meaningless, because it made a joke of her. "I want to die," she says. "Annnnhhh-ahhh. I want to die."

A shudder passes over her, so that she clutches herself to keep from flying to pieces. Then for a long time she sits hunched on the floor, barely conscious.

At last she drags herself up the wall and balances there till her legs will support her. She takes Hannah's box from the hiding place and lays out the old journal, looking for some wisdom, needing to see her mother's handwriting, to smell the scent of her that lies crushed in the pages.

God pardon the torn Heart, says a blotted line in red-brown ink. *In what mists do we stumble. God pardon the torn Heart.*

Jennet lays her cheek on these words for a long time, while the candle in Daniel's blue-and-white cup burns lower and lower. "I love you," she says. "Please. Please. My heart."

Does she speak to her mother, who is now only words on a page in the squiggles of a badly-sharpened pen? To her father, who is candlelight? To John Frayne, the traitor? To Saku, the god? To Iko, the toad?

Robert, she says. It is her mind speaking this time, the articulation perfect. *My Robbie. Little brother.* When the answer comes, it is his voice she imagines, though she has never before heard it clear.

What the devil's got into you, Jen? Don't take on so. You know I don't like it.

It's true. You never fussed, not even when you were little and I used to sit and rock you for Hannah.

Or if I did fuss, you didn't hear it. What you didn't hear, you either ignored or made up as you liked it. No more sense than a beanstalk, you had, and not near as wide! Why, look at you, you're skin and bones! I always said you'd be a skinny old maid.

Lump! That's right, tease me!

Beanstalk! Beanstalk! Skinny little beanstalk!

Charlie never teased, he was born angry and I never could love him, even handsome as he is. He hurt me too much and too often. But you never did.

He didn't mean to hurt. He was only sixteen when we left for the army. All boys are damn fools at sixteen.

Bosh. Most are still sixteen when they're eighty. Did you really love me, Rob? Was I truly your sister? Or did you only pretend it? Was it just kindness, as some men are kind to stray dogs and saddlesore horses?

Love is always part kindness. Especially to sisters.

I remember the first time I saw you, when I helped Hannah bear you. How you slipped out from between her legs like a little wet red seal, your eyes already fighting to open. I was eight years old, but I went often to birthings with her and I knew what to do.

I know you. You watch everything. Everything stays in your mind.

Daniel was gone that day, I don't know where. Hunting. Wandering. He was like me, he thought too much even then, and did not always know where his feet took him. Do you remember that day, Rob? Some children carry memories of their bornings, that's what Hannah said once. Like a caul you come into the world with, that never quite will come off you. We were in a far place then, driven away from our own.

I know. Nova Scotia.

There were no women with us, not even Aunt Julia. Only Hannah. Only me, the bastard daughter who could not be adopted even after they married. Bastard bitch. Charlie called me that once, and you knocked him down. Is he dead, too? My Robbie. Why didn't you come back for us? Where did you die? Did any woman come to wash your long body that was so like my father's? Did she close your eyes with her palm and stroke the leftover fear from your muscles and lay your arms straight by your sides?

There are no more answers. Robbie is gone now, and the schoolroom is bitter cold, the only warmth the small glow of the candle. The old boards crack and moan, crucified on their nails, as Jennet picks up the stub of pencil and writes on her page of the journal. *Dearest Robert. I hope you are peaceful. I knew you would never come home.*

She does not cry. All her tears for her brother were spent long ago, in the months of hopeless searching. She stands dry-eyed by the high windows, feeling the draft where Frayne has boarded up the broken pane that set the trapped bird free. The snow has stopped and the lake is quiet, only a dark hunched shape near the hole in the ice where she let Hannah's body slip down to find Daniel.

It is John Frayne, keeping watch for his ghosts. Waiting for her to come and kill him. To set him free of all the dead he takes so greedily upon his soul.

"Pardon torn hearts," Jennet says to the cold darkness. Then she goes downstairs and begins to work the almost-mended loom.

Come inside, she says. Don't be stupid. You'll freeze to death here.

It is almost moonset when she comes out to him at last. Frayne does not hear her footsteps on the lake-ice behind him, nor notice the light of her lantern. He has taken something out of his pack and he cradles it in his arms, rocking back and forth, keening softly. It is a strange song, and like all music, it reaches the dulled tympanum of Jennet's hearing as an irresistible, rhythmical energy. Wind on her face reaches her the same way, and the sharp scent of the trees in the balsam grove.

Where is her mouth that once brought me sweetness?
Where is her heart that bestowed understanding?
Where are her small feet that were bright in the morning?
Where are her hands that wove the light of the stars?

His voice rises and falls and rises again, the ancient mourning song of his dead wife's people. Jennet crouches down beside him, but he is gone from here. He is back in the City of Larks.

She lays a hand on his arm and he stops singing and looks at her, his blue eyes as pale as the fresh snow he has brushed away from the hole in the ice. Everything he is and has been can be read in those eyes, shifting layers of sweetness and fury and suspicion and pain and shame and indecision. They are like the light at Breakers Island that her father turned by hand with a wheel like a turnspit, the beam always turning away, glancing off the faces and shadows of other waves, other rocks.

Where is Tacha? she asks him. Where did you leave her?

You didn't bring the gun, he says.

I can always go get it. Answer me.

He looks down at the bundle on his knees. She's here, Jenny. Some of her small bones. A lock of her hair. I couldn't leave her.

Jennet nods. It seems perfectly proper to her. How did she die?

Slowly. He looks up at her, fixes her luminous face in his mind. Then his eyes close. When the British had finished with me, I went back to the City of Larks, the last place I had seen her. It took a long time. I couldn't remember the country anymore. I suppose my mind had been too long filled with other maps. I stumbled on the place very early one morning in late autumn, when there was fog rising from the ground.

Was she living?

No.

And you dug up her bones?

They hadn't buried her, they had put her body on a high wooden platform to let her be cleaned by the wind and the rain and the birds, the holy larks. It was a kind of honor. They said she had chosen it, so her spirit could keep watch for me. So I could find her.

You told me once she died singing.

I didn't think you heard me.

I heard. Just now I heard buzzing. Were you singing?

Yes.

Was it what she sang?

Something like it.

Say it again. Say what it means.

Where is his mouth that once brought me sweetness. He tells her the words as his wife would have sung them, and Jennet slips her hand through the crook of his arm so that it lies on the skin pouch of relics. Where are his hands that wove the light of the stars.

Where was her mother? Where was the granny, the midwife?

Gone away.

Everything goes away. My father had a house like Bay House, it was very fine. My mother and I lived in another house, but it had a loom and a spinning wheel and a frame to make quilts. We had aunts and cousins. We laughed together, and sometimes we danced. She bends to lay her face against his arm. In the end, everything goes away.

Yes.

Hannah said it was God's will. I hate that god.

Oh. Yes.

Do you think there are others? Gods that are kind?

I hope so. You make me want to hope.

Frayne?

Dearest Jenny.

They said my father was a traitor, too. Always, to one side or the other. All his life.

Why?

Because he had no side. He was like you, he didn't care about politics. Governments. Only people. Who was hurt. Who was hungry. Who could be saved. He fought for that and they punished him for it. In the end, he believed he deserved it. That he had done something terribly wrong to the world without meaning it. You would have been friends, I think. One by one, she lifts John's hands to her mouth and kisses the nail holes. He saved me. Hannah taught me to work and to fight. He taught me to live.

Teach me. Christ, Jennet. Teach me.

For a long while, they are silent. Tell how you found Tacha, she says at last. Where were the others? Had they all gone?

Some of the clans had resisted Firewalker. Many of the Fox-people had died in the fighting, and the rest went away to the south, to the winter camp. They had left an old couple behind to guard Tacha, to see that her bones were not stolen or disturbed. They would die there, they were too old to keep up with the tribesmen. This was their last home, and she was their companion. They told me how it had been with her. How she could no longer believe in the living.

Where is his mouth, Jennet murmurs. That once brought me sweetness.

To tell it now sounds unnatural, but I have no shame for what I did then. Except for my son, except for the ghost of my father, Tacha was all I had ever truly loved. I climbed up onto the burial platform with her that night and laid myself down beside her. It was odd, but she didn't lie as the dead are laid out. She lay on her side as she had always done, almost as though she had turned herself in her sleep as she used to when she heard me come into the lodge, to welcome me to her. Almost seven months of weather had changed her. I drew her against me—very light, very clean and dry—and put my hand where her belly had been, where the child had grown in her when we were happy. I slept with her bones all that night. I lay naked beside her, to be with her, to make her feel my love where she was. To put no barrier between us.

Did she come to you? Did you dream her? My mother dreamed my father the night he was drowned. Maybe tonight I'll dream Robbie.

I saw his name and I remembered your wish when we opened the treasure, Frayne says. I knew it must be your brother. You loved him very much, I could hear it in the way you spoke of him.

Jennet shakes her head. What difference does my loving anyone make? Robbie used to joke me and call me a skinny old maid, and he was right, I'll never have a husband, I'll never have anything other women have. I'm not a woman at all. I'm a freak. I'm a thing that can't hear.

She speaks too fast and the words tangle into nonsense; Frayne catches only a few of them. Old maid. Never. Husband. Gone. Freak. He has begun to hear with her ears and think with her body.

Don't say such things, he tells her softly. She can sense the tone of his voice by the way his eyes look, how the focus shifts and the pale color grows darker. Old maid? Why, look at you. You're only a girl.

I'm nine-and-twenty. Jennet glances at him. Robert would have been two-and-twenty in May, in the spring.

Frayne looks down at the bones in his lap. Christ. How you must hate me. You must.

Yes. She looks out across the empty lake. You didn't answer. Did you dream Tacha? That night you lay with her bones?

I—I saw nothing. Only the fog. Towards morning, I fancied

I heard the larks, but it was only illusion. They were all gone, too, they had flown away south.

And then you took the bones.

I stole a few of them. These few. It was a great sin. He takes her cold hand in his own, lifts it up to his mouth to warm it. But you must understand. If you don't, no one in this world ever will. How— How she came upon me and made me live for a while. As you have. I had no right to ask more than that. But I did ask. I do ask. I had to keep her. I think she helped me to find you.

He bends low over all that is left of his wife, of the last of his youth. The girl waits, silent beside him, the frail light of the lantern touching his dark hair that is frosted with fine, glittering snow.

Snow has a character, a kind of personhood. When you have lived all your life with it as Jennet has, it conveys an intent. Some is harsh and driving, accusing and angry and punishing. Some is soft, wet, fertile, binding gouged earth and burnt, broken trees like a promising bandage.

But tonight the snow that falls on the Bay of Spirits is dry and perfect, self-sufficient. It promises nothing and denies nothing, as impartial as the gaze of God. Adrift in this luminous indifference, all the dead, all the living are equally innocent, equally guilty. Equally in need.

Now you can let her go, the girl says.

Frayne studies her, his eyes warmed by the lantern light, by the aureole of falling snow. I am yours now. Whatever you say, I will do.

From the stone bench in the garden, Marius Leclerc sits watching them, two dark spirits scarcely moving on the white breast of the lake. The sky is pewter-grey with the reflection of the snow and it is very quiet, the quince bushes enchanted with snowfall, every twig glittering, every dead leaf turned to silver. A raccoon, looking for food, catches the Frenchman's scent and scuttles up the papery trunk of a birch tree, sending a sheer veil of snow down onto him.

At last Leclerc sees Frayne's long body unfold itself, and the girl's slight shape twine close against him. He hands her something, an awkward dark shape like a package, like one of the old Tory's treasure-hoards. Jennet kneels down and holds it in her arms for a moment, rocking it back and forth. Then she lets it go through the hole in the ice.

So, he thinks. She has absolved him.

On the bench in the garden, the little Frenchman sits sobbing, but the two on the ice do not hear him. There is another watcher in the garden, too, a goblin-shape that moves without sound but with unshakable purpose from pear tree to quince bush, from springhouse to privy, from shadow to shadow, always nearer to the voices and the shapes of these aliens.

Jacob Benet, Catcher Benet, has been here all night, as he is most nights. Watching. Listening. Grasping at shadows. Sometimes he slips into the house through one of the broken-out windows or a wall burned away in the fire, and watches the girl at her loom or hears Frayne's hypnotic voice as he reads to her.

Wind-driven and sea-worn, we reached this kind island,
Long past midnight, the stars all gone out and our arms weary of
  rowing,
We stumbled ashore and fell onto this jagged shoreline,
Glad of any harbor and aching for nothing but rest.

John?

Hush, dear. I'm blowing the candle out.

I want to know why you told me about the maps. You didn't have to.

Some things have to be spoken.

But I'd never have known about the British or anything. I might never have known about Robbie being dead.

I wanted you to see me as I am. Jenny?

Don't talk anymore. Blow out the candle now.

If you change your mind, if you want me to leave you, I'll go. I'll be gone in the morning, you won't ever have to see me again.

Don't be stupid. I wouldn't be here now, would I? Besides, the workroom isn't finished. And Gabriel can't bring the beds down those stairs by himself. Anyway, I need help with the stable if we're going to have a cow. We are, aren't we?

But I might bring you danger. Men might come looking someday. The army might even arrest me and put me on trial.

Pooh. Men always think they're so important. Anyway, the roof might fall in first. Or I might break my neck on the stairs. I don't believe in someday. Lie down, Frayne. I want to sleep now.

He pinches the candle out and stretches himself on the few cold, polished boards of the library floor, the shelf of books a small, precise shadow in the light of the moon that has come out to explore the newfallen snow in the garden. Slowly, in these weeks, the house has begun to heal itself around them, within them. In the spring, he thinks, I'll plant rosebushes and lavender, for the fragrance.

Empty of secrets, he draws a deep breath and lies watching it drift and disperse in the cold.

Frayne turns on his side, the position in which she prefers him to sleep so that she may lean against him without being embraced or entangled. But Jennet is still by the mantelpiece, the fading moon turning her slender body fishlike, quicksilver. Except for that day by the lake he has never seen any part of her naked, and when she comes to him now, she seems almost to swim through the darkness, her skin sheer as frost in the cold.

He sits up, kneels on the floor and waits as she puts down the old quilts she still sleeps on. She is shaking, her whole body trembling. But not from the cold. I don't want you to fuck me. Promise it won't be like fucking.

It won't. I want more than that.

Are you talking? I can't see you.

Never mind. Never mind.

His hands find the backs of her knees and slowly climb the terrain of her body, the rising curve of her buttocks and the slight valley that is the small of her back. The bones of her spine are like the ridges of White Lady and Old Dog and all the mountains that pile one onto another into the pale, haunted mist of the west. The Shining Mountains. The promised land of second chance. His face is pressed against her flat belly and he thinks as his scarred cheek touches it that he will not bleed anymore now, that after this night, whatever may come to him, he will die whole and unbroken, all his seams mended at last.

Thank you for buying me the bonnet, she whispers with his mouth on her nipple. Thank you for the bolt of cloth.

VIII
king herod

In the middle of February, two days before the Federal Ball, John Frayne's wife Hester Benet sat, flushed and ill-at-ease, in the west-facing winter parlor of Herod Aldrich's grand brick house in the center of town. Dissatisfied with the dull red-brown of the local bricks, he had had the house painted a gleaming cardinal red, and then had each brick outlined with white where the mortar secured it. To the festive visitors who had already begun to fill the town in anticipation of the ball, the house in its wooded grounds stood out like a gaudy, ungainly palace among the blocks of squat frame houses.

Hester had not sat for some time in this parlor. She had forgotten how small and awkward it had always made her feel, how like an inept and unfaithful servant. Though it was large and high-ceilinged, the west parlor had Franklin stoves set into the fireplaces at either end and it was warm enough to keep pot plants alive in the mountain winter. They crowded against the bow windows—boxwood and ivy and potted roses and orange trees and rosemary clipped to the shape of a swan. Herod's late wife Eleanor had loved them and he kept them for her sake, out of gratitude for all that her family connections had brought him. The Smailses were strong Federalists and had influence in every state north of Virginia; without them, he would never have won a clear claim to the Frayne patent.

But like Hester, Aldrich himself felt uncertain here, among these reminders of his dead wife. He had known very little of Eleanor and had made a virtue of telling her next to nothing about his own early life. It had always seemed better that way, as though too great an intimacy might somehow despoil the smoothly-functioning machine he required of marriage.

Now that she was dead, this virtual anonymity allowed him complete freedom to worship the woman to whom he had never given more than a shadow of himself while she lived. For eleven years now, ever since Eleanor's death, he had kept the house exactly as he thought she would have wished, had he known her. He made a passive dream-wife of her, a dream-mother to their daughter Susanna, and he tried always to live so as to please this imaginary dead woman. He chose furniture and ornaments to suit his idea of Eleanor. When her plants grew sickly, he had others shipped out from Philadelphia to take their place.

But since his daughter's sudden death in the summer, this west parlor oppressed him, the huge mahogany pianoforte that had been hers seemed to gobble up all the air, as though it had some strange life of its own that defied him. With Frayne's wife here, Herod's sense of oppression in the room was even worse than usual; Hester's very existence was a reproach, and he was certain that somehow, Eleanor must know of it.

"What shall I do now?" Hester asked him. "What will the law do with me?"

"I can't spare you much time today," he said brusquely. He hated that whining tone of hers, as though he had struck her. Herod did not hold himself responsible for what had become of her. Whatever she had come for, he would not be wheedled into spending himself on her behalf. "It's late, and I've a large party expected any minute now," he told her. "Friends come up for the doings."

The countrified word was typical of him; Aldrich was never comfortable with formal social events, and it was easier to endure them if he reduced them to the level of a quilting party or a cornhusking. Still, he knew that the supper after the Federal Ball might prove crucial if he was to call in his favors and lay claim to a nomination for the Senate in two more years. He had invited a few of the most influential party faithful to come up early and spend an extra evening or two in the hope of forging strategic alliances, now that the Federalists had the upper hand in the Congress again.

Perhaps tonight, when Judge Phillotson and Bart Hargrave from Cayuna and high-and-mighty Senator Cyrus Shackleton from Albany had taken enough of his port and Madeira to make them grow mellow . . . Herod Aldrich himself was teetotal, but he could not afford to be too finicking where his friends were concerned. Politics was business, after all. It was how things were done.

Webs of influence tangled his mind, the possible repercussions of each action setting up crosswinds and downdrafts, spinning and whirling like the snow-devils out on the lake. He scarcely remembered that Hester was in the room at all as he paced the expensive French carpet, his hands clasped at his back, fingers fiddling nervously with his coattails.

One of the house-slaves, a woman his wife had named Phillis, came padding in with an armload of firewood and he scowled at her, embarrassed. Aldrich felt he was weak to keep slaves, that he ought to be rid of them. But it was not a matter of principle. There was an intimacy about their silent presence in the house that his womenfolk had found homelike and comforting, but to Herod it seemed preternatural. He might almost have believed they read his dreams, so silently and calmly did Phillis and her husband, Cato, anticipate his needs and keep his house in order. Now that Susanna was dead, they had little to do and were idle and gossipy. They knew too much and talked too much, and he might have sold them at a good price.

But Aldrich had not had the nerve for it. Change frightened him, even the slightest alteration of his accustomed circumstances.

Suppose he should rise of a morning and find his favorite lolling chair to the left of the library hearth instead of to the right, where the light was best? How if he found the keys of Susanna's pianoforte undusted, or the song sheet she had played from on the very morning of her death no longer spread out upon the curved music rack as though she might somehow come back to it, as though he might hear her high, sweet voice again?

> *I sowed the seeds of love,*
> *And I sowed them in the spring.*
> *I gathered them up in the morning so soon,*
> *While the small birds so sweetly do sing.*

Suddenly, without conscious intention, his own voice went off like a firecracker in the tense quiet of the parlor. "What are you doing there?" he snapped at the slave woman. "Who the hell told you to play that piano?"

There was a stunned silence, and Phillis looked up at him, wide-eyed. She was nowhere near the pianoforte. She stared vaguely up at the plasterwork festoons on the ceiling and scuffed her boots on the rug. "Mr. Herod? Mrs. Fanning says to ask if you want Sam to bring up that there barrel of oysters for supper?"

"Yes. Yes, certainly," he said more evenly. "By all means." But Phillis didn't go, and he could feel his anger rising again. "Well," he growled. "What else? Be quick, can't you?"

"Beg pardon, Mr. Herod. Lawyer want you, that's all. Mr. Willie."

Ah. Will Slocum, back from Albany for the ball. A year ago, he had danced all night long with Susanna. Graceful as a swan, she had been, like the shape of the rosemary plant on the windowsill. *I valued her,* Aldrich was accustomed to say to the sympathetic wives of his political cronies, and beneath the careful layers of old-fashioned gabardine, something ached in him like a heart.

On his daughter's tombstone, Herod Aldrich had had carved the words *Not Mine for Now, But Mine in Heaven.* It was how he conceived of eternity—a place where all property rights were at last perfected. Including the elusive right to Bay House.

For if truth had been told—which it seldom was—Aldrich's claim to the famous Frayne patent was not entirely clear. He lay awake in the long nights of the northern winter, planning out lawsuits to squelch those who quibbled over disputed titles within the huge tract, and paid countless surveyors for inconclusive maps of his uncertain boundaries. *MINE,* he wrote upon them in thick carpenter's pencil. But he knew that the right challenge to his claim might cast him into sudden disaster; that was why he had not yet dared send the bailiffs to evict the three squatters from Bay House—the fear of a possible counter-claim, of a public embarrassment at just the wrong moment. Litigation had cost him, in the long run, almost more than the patent had brought him in rents.

Well, well, he thought, grasping for comfort. Young Will Slocum had been useful a time or two in looking out records to defeat angry claimants, and in bribing them if he could not. Perhaps it might be the same with Frayne.

"Tell Lawyer Slocum to wait," Aldrich told Phillis. "And never mind the stove wood. I'll attend to it myself."

The slave woman glanced curiously at him, then at Hester, who sat forlornly on the long silk-covered settee that stretched the length of one wall, and Aldrich had once more that odd *frisson* of foreboding, as though he had given himself away. Phillis was visibly pregnant, and that, too, made him shudder and wish to be rid of her. Something secret and sly about a woman with a child in her body. Something knowing and ruthless and out of control.

Yes, he must sell them, and waste no more time about it. Phillis and Cato must go.

The black woman padded quietly out and Aldrich went to sit beside Hester. "You should not have come here alone, my dear," he said curtly. "Where is Jacob? You should have come both together, to put a bold face on this business. I have not seen you at Sunday service for more than a month. You must let people see you are husband and wife still."

"I don't know where Jacob is," she said. "He's gone out again."

"He has no intent to confront Frayne with any violent purpose, I hope?"

"I don't know what he means to do. He waits and waits. He's gone most every night now, and half the day, too."

"Gone? Where?"

"I don't know. I thought at first it was the smuggling. But if you know nothing of it—"

This open confirmation of what everyone knew was more than he could bear. "There is no smuggling in New Forge!" he said angrily. "*My* town is law-abiding!" In the afterpresence of Phillis, in the nearness of his daughter's piano, Herod Aldrich had almost lost control. He was clumsy in manner at best, but he struggled to regain a superficial composure. "Jacob has been wise to wait," he went on more calmly. "Law is law, but it can always be turned to a purpose, if one is patient enough." He saw no equivocation in this remark, and went quietly on. "Has Frayne not come to visit you and the boy? Has he made any move, filed any papers with the court?"

"Tim spoke to him once at the shop. The fool boy says he'll kill John before he'll go to live with him."

"You must talk some sense into him, then! For the love of heaven, Hester, can you not even manage a boy of ten?" Again he fought for control, tried to speak with some patience. "But you yourself have seen nothing of Frayne? He has not told you his intentions regarding the marriage?"

"Nothing. No word at all. Why doesn't he come, Herod? What's he waiting for? It's been more than a month since he came from the west."

"He's a blackguard." Aldrich waved a hand in front of his face. "He has some foolish delusion of reclaiming his father's house."

Will Slocum had written and told him—out of habit, as he told Aldrich everything—about his encounter with Frayne at the Dog and Lantern, and Herod could only grit his teeth at the thought of what the news from Albany might be. If the search for title to that crucial parcel at Bay House should uncover some uncertainty, it could call all the rest into question, and Frayne was not a poor dirt-farmer with no money. He would not settle so easily as the others for a sensible bribe.

But it was more than the risk to Aldrich's property that unsettled him. In the years since the patent came into his hands, he had taken a secret delight in watching the old house fall slowly to ruin. On summer afternoons, he would ride out alone to the place where the shore of Lake Paschal curved southward and take inventory of the mansion's decline as it came into view—how many panes were left in the windows, which of the orchard trees had toppled in storms, how many shutters were missing. As Bay House slipped down into hopeless decay, Herod's own fortunes had begun to rise towards an eminence he could as yet only dream of, and it seemed he drew power from this inexorable depletion of the past, from making the old house a mere trivial relic.

Now that Frayne had come back, it galled Aldrich bitterly to hear every day of some new repair, some restoration of the old place. Every shingle replaced, every new piece of glass or brushful of whitewash diminished him, until he almost began to imagine himself sinking and growing trivial in his turn.

And these foolish stories of treasure, too, were a constant thorn in his flesh. Aldrich did not quite believe them, of course. A twilight tale, like the stories of Indian ghosts. Like the strange life of Susanna's piano. Still, perhaps he could make use of it. What would he not use, to be rid of John Frayne?

"No doubt he hopes to secure his property before he takes action in the matter of your—er—marriage," he told Hester, putting a brave face on it. "But there is no chance, I assure you. My claim to Bay House is rock-solid."

She laid a hand on his arm. "I'm afraid, Herod. You must help me."

"I?" He stood up and began to pace again, carefully skirting the piano. "What have I to do with it?"

"What does the law say? Will they put me in prison for having two husbands?"

He wanted to laugh at her innocence, but he did not. Her fear gave him control of her. "They might," he said. "You're guilty of bigamy, you and Benet. A woman is her husband's legal property, and under the law Frayne has been robbed by this ill-considered marriage of yours."

"Ill-considered?" Hester looked up at him and her eyes struck sparks. "Oh, aye. And who was it brought Jacob to my door and told me I must court him and marry him and ask no more return of you, once you'd done with bedding me? Robbed, indeed! If Jack Frayne's been robbed by anybody, it's you!"

"Be quiet, for the love of God!" Herod could feel the room draining his life from him. The plants were all bent with grief and the piano was weeping great tears. "What happened between us was—a mischance, nothing more." He fumbled, seeking a word that would silence her. "I had been near three years widowed, and I— No, I shall make no excuses. It was a madness, and I take full blame for it. But I have tried to make amends since, you know that. I gave you money, a fair settlement."

"It wasn't enough!"

"It was ample for any careful housewife! You have no sense of economy, madam!"

"Maybe. I was never careful, God help me." Hester stared at the scuffed toes of her boots. "But after you said we must end it, I waited two years and more for Jack to come back from the west, and grew poorer and poorer. I could scarcely buy enough firewood to keep warm through a winter, and the boy was always hungry."

Aldrich shook himself like a wet dog, trying to throw off his anguish. He felt his dead daughter was listening, that his wife's eyes were fixed upon him, sorrowing and reproachful, the bones of her hands folded carefully in prayer.

"Two years is not long enough to prove death under the law," he said, hardening his heart to Hester. It was true he had rushed her into marriage to keep things quiet. There had been gossip among the slaves, and he had wanted a seat on the County Electoral Commission that year; he could not afford any shadow to be placed on his character.

But he could not let the past weigh with him now. He was guilty of nothing; no man of the world would ever have faulted him, surely. "You— You should have waited longer before you married," he stammered.

"Two years is long enough to starve! I knew nothing of law but what you told me, and I knew Jacob wouldn't wait forever for a woman to wife him." Hester's voice was full of tears, but there were none in her eyes. They were blank and still and empty. "I don't love him, but I've been an honest wife to him, Herod. Jacob doesn't believe so. But I have."

Aldrich felt a dangerous warmth on the back of his neck, the onslaught of compassion. "Now, now. Frayne may do nothing at all," he said kindly. "If he sees that the boy doesn't want him, he may go straight back where he came from."

"Why have you not driven him away for a squatter?" she cried. "Why have you not acted against him?"

He could not let her know that he dared not. "It— It isn't advisable yet," he told her. "There are reasons— You don't comprehend these matters of property. Leave them to men."

Hester was silent, studying the turn of his countenance, the beads of sweat on his forehead. A fever seemed to have struck him, and he mopped at his face with his blue-spotted kerchief. She watched him, wondering how far she might push him.

"If Frayne comes for the boy," he told her, "Jacob dare do nothing to prevent him. You must see he does not."

"How can I? I cannot answer for Jacob. But—what if John *should* be prevented?"

"Then—" He sought for a word that would ensure him her silence. "Then," he said, "Frayne may choose to prosecute your bigamous union. Your crime."

Hester stood up and went to where he was pacing and snatched up his hand to stop him short, eye to eye with her. "And what of your crime, sir? How if he should prosecute that?"

He stared. "Mine? I have done no crime against John Frayne. Except with you, and that was as much your doing as—"

"You have taken what should have been his and mine and my

son's, all the land that should have come to us, you and your fine friends in Albany that your wife's father bought you! You have taken his father's house—my house!—and let it fall to ruin, just as you ruined me and left me empty!''

"You ruined yourself, madam!" He backed away from her, as frightened as though she had pointed a gun at him. "I took nothing, I bought the land and the house fairly, the patent was not Frayne's to keep!"

"But you didn't buy me, did you, Herod?" She stared down at his hand, which was outstretched before him to fend off her imaginary blows. "When John began to suspect me a faithless, foolish creature, he asked me but one time who I'd been with, but I never said it was you. He caught a glimpse of you once, when you left it too late and would not go from me till near morning. He saw you, I know he did."

Aldrich could scarcely breathe, there seemed to be a great weight on his chest. I must sell the slaves, he thought. I must burn the piano. I must poison the plants.

An adulterous wife could be prosecuted, and if the name of her lover were known, he could be hauled into public court and fined. But it was an old law, and no one paid heed to it these days. Besides, after nine years, who would believe it? He had been careful, careful. Even Susanna had no suspicion of it. And there was no one else in the house but the slaves.

"You say he caught sight of me. Does Frayne know it was— that it was I?" The words almost choked Herod Aldrich, and the sense of being sucked slowly downward made him give at the knees. "Did he see me clear? Did you tell him my name?"

Hester laughed. "He never asked but the one time. I thought he would ask again, I held it out like a carrot before him. But he never asked the name again."

"So he doesn't know me."

She could hear the breath come out of Aldrich, the release of his fear. He stood with his hand braced against the piano. "But you must help me, Herod," she demanded. "Else I will tell John

the truth of it now. I will tell Jacob, too. I'll tell him you and I
are lovers yet. That I sleep with you every night he's from home."

He took another step backward and stumbled against the piano.
"Tell away! No one will believe you. You will ruin yourself."
Under his fist, the keys struck a discord.

"I care nothing for that. I am lost."

Hester was still for a moment, her fingertips brushing the silk
of the sofa. "Once you made me believe that you might even love
me," she said softly. "I used to want that, for a time I thought I
would die without it. Perhaps I did." She turned to him, and he
felt something cold enter him, the knife-blade of her hate. "What
did you want with me, Herod? All those years ago, when I was
only Mrs. Sheldon the surveyor's wife and meant nothing to you—
why did you take me then?"

Aldrich's pasty face was as flushed as Hester's, but he felt strong
now, seeing her so despondent. "I knew you were not Mrs. Sheldon," he said with a faint ring of triumph. "I knew it from the
first."

"But how? John and I were careful! We told no one!"

"Frayne's father's old steward, a man called Blunt, had come
into my household. He caught sight of your husband and knew
him at once—the eyes, the voice, the stature, they are all like his
father. I said nothing in the town—old Blunt's wild stories were
a byword. But I believed him, and I was right."

"So when you began to pay court to me, and when you came
to desire me . . ." she whispered. "When you lay moaning in my
arms, it was nothing to do with me? It was only because I was
Frayne's? Like the patent. Like the house."

He did not contradict her and she said nothing more, only
went to stand by the windows, looking out through the leaves of
Eleanor's plants, looking up at the blank grey sky of which her
own eyes might have been shattered fragments.

"What do you want of me?" Herod Aldrich said at last, his
voice a hoarse whisper. "More money?"

"I?" Hester laughed softly, and the laughter fell like stinging
mist. "I want to eat your heart."

Herod makes sure Hester is gone before he tugs on the crewel-work bellpull to summon back Phillis, the house-slave. "Show Lawyer Slocum in now," he says.

"I know my way, sir! No need of showing!"

Will Slocum bounds in, dressed to the nines in a peacock-blue serge spencer jacket that just brushes his corsetted waistline, a white satin waistcoat embroidered in silver and blue, and snowy-white stockinet breeches cut short over the ankles. A white shirt of fine muslin with a collar so high it almost grazes his cheekbones, a pleated chitterling frill down the front, and a white silk cravat. Grey kid gloves and black slippers polished to gleaming with glycerin. And the hat. Such a hat. A brushed beaver top hat so tall it overbalances him and all but knocks the candles sidewise in Eleanor's chandelier.

The young man sweeps it off with a flourish and treats Aldrich to a graceful bow. "Ain't I a blade, Mr. Aldrich, sir?" he chirrups. "Phillis, what do you say? Am I fit for a grand duke's birthday party, or am I not?"

The slave woman giggles. "I say you handsome as a cock-turkey in the last half of October, Mister Willie!"

Aldrich scarcely sees the gaudy costume. His mind is still with Hester, with the threat she poses. With Frayne, and the house at the Bay. No one knows what it means to him. He has told no one and now that old Blunt is dead, no one remembers the whole of it, how it began.

"That will be all, Phillis," he says sharply.

She tugs on the strings of her cap and bobs him a curtsy. "Got to water Miss Eleanor's plants yet, Mr. Herod."

He knows she will listen to whatever they say. But in the matter of Eleanor's plants, he can deny nothing. "Very well, then," he tells her. "Get on with it. But keep quiet."

Phillis goes into the passage and returns with a bucket and dipper. She begins to move about among the rosemary and ivy and geranium, trimming a spent leaf or a blossom here and there and ladling water onto each potful, turning each plant so as to catch the light, rearranging the pots into different configurations.

Aldrich sits down at the end of the long striped settee, his fingers gripping the padded mahogany armrest. "What says Albany about this latest outrage in the territories, Fort McKittrick and these savages in the pay of the British?" he says, skirting the subject that most concerns him. "Have you war news, Willie?"

"I have news, sir. But not about war." The young lawyer's eyes register a mild amusement, but suddenly he hesitates. "If I was at all up-and-coming in the lawyer business, I ought not have told you I'd promised to do that job of work for Mr. John Frayne. Deed to the patent, and so on." Slocum takes a folded sheet of paper from his pocket. "But I couldn't see it would harm him if you did know, and as it happens, I was right."

Herod braces himself, one eye on the slave woman. "Well, then. What is it? Let's have it out."

The lawyer's smile has disappeared now. "I'm afraid," he says, "that Bay House is John Frayne's for the taking, Mr. Aldrich. Or anyone else's who cares to go and squat there. But it ain't yours to rent and it ain't yours to sell. Oh, you can claim it, but you won't keep it, not with a Republican sitting on the Bench of Claims now. They don't like you, sir. They want you down, and as for those Federalist friends of yours, I'd as soon trust a weasel."

"Lower your voice, for God's sake!"

Willie Slocum stares. Herod is shaking with a chill that seems to come from the window full of plants, where Phillis is still poking about. He can sit still no longer, he gets up and strides to the wing-rocker where the lawyer is lounging and snatches the paper from his hand.

"Pure nonsense!" Aldrich says, having read it. "I own that house and land! I have owned it since—since—" He tosses the paper onto a leather-topped writing desk of polished rosewood. "I refuse to believe it. This cannot be true!"

" 'Fraid it is, sir." Will Slocum rocks back in the chair and stares coolly up at him. "Look at the list of parcels. Not there at all. Not part of the rest of your patent. Deed and title to Bay House, wherever they are, ain't filed in Albany in your name, nor in anyone else's."

"Then where the devil are they?"

Slocum shrugs, a silken rustle of his waistcoat. "Might be down in York City. Might be lost. Might be in the hands of a trustee. Might be buried out at Bay House."

"But surely— Deed or no deed. There is no question of—"

There is a soft knock on the door, and Cato, Phillis's husband, comes on quiet cat feet into the room, wearing the bright red-and-blue livery and the horsehair peruke he always sports on special occasions. "Pardon, Mr. Herod, sir," he says, "but Judge Phillotson and Mr. Hargrave and Mr. Shackleton is here. And their ladies."

Aldrich stares at the paper in his hand as though it has spoken. "What?" he whispers. "What?"

"Judge Phillotson and his lady, sir, and Mr. Bartram Hargrave from Cayuna, and Mr. Senator Cyrus Shackleton from over to Albany," Cato repeats. "Shall I put 'em in the back parlor, Mr. Herod?"

Cato glances at his wife, who is still dipping water onto Eleanor's orange trees. Phillis's eyes grow somewhat larger, her brows arch, and she bites her lower lip to keep from laughing—always a sign of fresh gossip she is itching to tell him. Through the open door come the sounds of trunks and hatboxes being dragged upstairs, the chatter of ladies' maids and the jovial banter of gentlemen, and the heavy, dark smell of Judge Phillotson's Spanish segars.

But still Aldrich says nothing; he stands as if he has been bewitched, and it is Will Slocum who nods at the servant. "Back parlor for the gents, Cato. Upstairs sitting room for the ladies, that'll do nicely. Better bring 'em tea and a muffin or two, keep 'em busy."

Cato goes out, and in a few minutes more, Phillis trails after him with the bucket and dipper, leaving the door ajar after her. Talk and laughter drift in from the farther rooms, but Herod Aldrich gives no sign that he hears it. He stands very still, with his hand on the breast of his daughter's piano.

"How are you, sir?" the young lawyer asks.

Willie Slocum is sorry. He had thought it a good joke at first to spring this trick on the old boy. At his age, Slocum takes few things seriously, and besides, in a patent of thousands of acres, what can a few overgrown gardens and an old ruin of a house matter? But this is some deep wound in Aldrich, and Willie is not a cruel boy.

"Let me get you some spirits," he says. "You are ill, sir."

Herod shakes his head. "Have you told this to Frayne yet?" he says at last.

"Ain't had the time, only got to the Dog an hour ago myself."

"You will not tell him. You will say nothing to anyone. Especially to Judge Phillotson and Senator Shackleton and the others."

"But I must tell Mr. Frayne, I can't fail to apprise a client of—"

Aldrich's voice is hard and cold. "You have already broken his confidence in telling me. Has he paid you anything? Has he retained you with tender?"

"There's been no money changed hands as yet, sir, but—"

"Then your duty is clear. I make no claim upon your loyalty as my poor daughter's suitor. As one who has enjoyed the intimacy of my family circle and the freedom of this house. Who has used me. Used. Me. Who— Who has taken my money and spent it on trifles. On ruffled shirts and— Trifles. I say only that I was your client before this ruffian Frayne was ever known to you. I have retained you and paid you. Your prior obligation is to *my* interests, not his."

"Why, if you put it like that—"

"I do. I *do* put it like that. You will say nothing to John Frayne. As for this paper— Many errors are made by copying clerks in these bureaus of government. I *own* Bay House! All the Frayne property was awarded me, the whole of the patent, regardless of individual parcels. It was all perfectly legal. It was voted upon by the Court of Claims. It was signed by President Adams. As for you, you will do as you're told."

Lawyer Slocum stands up. He is angry now, a boy's anger that wants only to hurt. "I'll tell Mr. Frayne whatever I wish, sir! You may choose to own slaves, but *I* am not one of them! And if you want my advice, you'll take whatever price John Frayne's offering for that land, and be damned glad to get it. If he takes you to court for Bay House, you could lose every square mile of your precious patent."

"Let it go then! Let all the rest go! I must *keep* Bay House! I *will* keep it!"

Slocum shakes his well-groomed head. "*Why,* in the name of God? Place can't be properly rebuilt, there's more mice than sound timbers. If lightning strikes it again—"

Aldrich's round face is very pale and his hands clutch at the slivers of air. It is almost gone now. The plants have almost devoured it. The piano has gobbled it up. "Lightning did not strike Bay House," he says.

"But of course it did! Susanna told me."

"I did. *I* struck it. I burnt it."

"Sir?"

"It was mine. I burnt it."

"But—why?"

"To watch it go down at my will. To put an end to it, once and for all."

The man is mad as a hatter, and Will Slocum can only stare, openmouthed, his hands bracing themselves on the edge of the rosewood desk. "I don't—understand you, sir. Why should you—"

"Because! They shut me out, they locked the door on me! I was a boy then, not much older than you are. It was beautiful there, the gardens all blooming. I dreamed it for weeks before I dared go and ask them for work. And they turned me away, they laughed at my poor clothes and my heavy boots and—"

"Captain Frayne? Why, he hadn't the reputation for such high-handed—"

"Not him. His servants. A man *is* his servants. That old bastard Blunt, the old steward, *he* locked the door upon me, and he laughed. Clodpole, he said. Awkward booby. As though I was deaf and could not hear them. As though I was dead. But I can hear it yet, the last whisper. How the key ground the lock shut. How they laughed in the parlor, and the deep voice that sang. *His* voice. Captain Frayne's voice. How someone, some woman, played upon a piano. His wife. His daughter."

Herod sways where he stands, and young Slocum reaches out to steady him. "Sit down, sir! You will fall! Let me call a physician!"

Aldrich turns and stares at him, blank-eyed. "All these years, it has urged me, up and up. I bid for old Blunt from the poormaster when he was doddering and put him to serve in my kitchen. I own Bay House now, Jack Frayne will *not* take it from me! I own it all, and him with it! *I* am his father now, not that Tory. Let him do as *I* say!"

Will shakes his head, his hand still gripping Aldrich's shoulder. The young man speaks softly, like a guide in a country of avalanche. "Tory he may have been, but Alexander Frayne was never put the oath, sir. I could find no record of it."

"Oath?"

"The Loyalty oath, sir. It's true that the Committee of Public Safety of Talbot County had charged him. The Bill of Charge was the point on which Hamilton won the case. But there was no formal hearing, only a few months of hectoring and a mess of assumptions. He was a clever old fox, I'll say that for old Sandy Frayne. Saw what was coming, and before they could put him the oath, he up and hanged himself."

Head bent, the young man looks out from half-closed eyes at the almost-old man who will surely topple to the floor if he lets go his grip.

"I daresay he cared more for owning than for living by that time," Will Slocum mutters.

Herod Aldrich breaks free of him and once again his fist crashes down on the keys of his daughter's piano. "I want to sell those goddamn slaves!" he cries.

Though she was a slave, the woman Phillis was far from helpless. She had been born a possession, but only as some are born backwards, or with big ears; it had nothing to do with her mind—which was keen, though without education—nor with her sense of survival.

"Old bastard," she whispered, having overheard her master's anguished cry.

The small world of a household is like an ocean, full of weathers and portents. Tempests raise monstrous waves among the prosaic tides of daily living, but they happen only rarely, building slowly to climax over months, sometimes years. The secret currents that feed them flow warm and cold day after day, making the atmosphere wholesome or bitterly poisonous by turns. Stagnant latitudes are sometimes reached in which no healthful winds blow at all, and human creatures slip over the side into madness and tear at each other, or worse still, at themselves.

Herod Aldrich's house had sailed into such a latitude now. And Phillis—it was not her real name, but she wore it as Cato wore his powdered wig and his fancy-dress livery—could read the weather with the skill of a seasoned helmsman. Even before Frayne's return, before Miss Susanna's death, she had begun to sense danger, as birds sense a storm rising. King Herod—so the servants and slaves all called him—had been too long becalmed here since the passing of his wife. He paced the halls at night, wandering in and out of the changeless rooms, touching the furniture, staring up at the portraits on the walls of the upstairs gallery. No one knew who they were—fine ladies with children at their feet, reverend gentlemen in powdered wigs and silk breeches. He had bought them in much the same way as his slaves, in a job-lot from an estate auction in Philadelphia, and Doxy Floyd the old teamster hauled them up with the trade goods they took every Thursday for the smugglers' barrels.

Like the parlor piano, the portraits had taken on some meaning to her master that Phillis did not comprehend, and Aldrich stood staring up at them sometimes with glazed eyes, almost as though he might weep with shame.

"Going down," she murmured to Cato. "Better watch out, we go with him."

Her husband's brown eyes seemed to darken. "Down where, girl?"

"Just down."

That morning she had felt it beginning to happen, as soon as Catcher Benet's wife knocked on the side door and came in as she used to. Phillis was the only one of the household who had been here then, almost nine years ago when Miss Susanna was away at school and King Herod began to grow restless. "Leave the side door unlatched tonight, Phillis," he would say. "I fancy a walk in the garden."

Then, just after midnight, the woman would come through the box hedge and up by the back staircase, bringing a smell of plain cooking on her gown, of onions and cabbage and boiled mutton. Phillis made it her business to know her by name—Mrs. Sheldon, the surveyor's wife, who lived with her baby at the end of Mull Lane.

"Balderdash," grumbled old Haymon Blunt, Captain Frayne's long-ago steward, who was on the poor-rolls now, and too old to do much but stir pots by the fire and gossip. "Sheldon, indeed! I saw her husband. I knew him by those eyes, like a dose of cold water. Jackie Frayne, he is, the old pirate's son come back for his gold, or I'm a monkey's grandsire! I know, I was there when they hid it. Boxes and boxes! Trunks and kegs of it! Mrs. Sheldon, my arse! Mrs. Frayne, that's who *she* is! Mrs. Jack Frayne."

Phillis waited and watched, thinking it had only been another of Blunt's tall stories. Then suddenly Sheldon the surveyor was gone, and the side door to the garden was kept locked again. A year went by, and another. Now and then Hester came to the back door and was given work on washdays or when the feather-beds wanted airing. She brought her child with her, a little boy with strange blue eyes who seemed too old for his age and never cried or fussed. His father had gone west to find work, Hester told them, and one day she came with a letter, asking to have Mr. Aldrich advise her. They were shut up a long time in the second-best parlor, and not long after, Hester Sheldon turned back into Hester Frayne, and was married to Catcher Benet.

All these scraps were to Phillis like cloud-shapes and the flight of birds at sea, like the gathering of ice on the spars. They were her only defenses and she kept them and added them together and laid them end-to-end and side-to-side, feeling them grow greater and more worrisome. When it was known that John Frayne was back, she knew something would come of it. Now at last it had.

"Got to water them plants," she said, knowing her master could not refuse her; she needed to hear more, to make better sense of the pieces. King Herod's face was grey with shame and fear, and the woman Hester was blank, used, left over. It was how you felt on the auction block, and the slave woman felt sick, remembering. When she showed her to the door, Phillis could feel Hester's body drift beside her, as though it could no longer resist even so much as the pressure of air.

As soon as she was gone, the young lawyer, Mister Willie, went into the parlor with Herod. When he came to announce the arrival of Judge Phillotson and Mr. Hargrave and the others, even Cato could see there was something the matter between them. Phillis left the room as she was bid, but she didn't follow the guests to their rooms; instead, she came back to the hallway outside the west parlor and began to polish the mirrors, making certain the door was still ajar.

"I want to sell those goddamn slaves!" she heard Aldrich say. He might have been talking of old clothes he had no more use for.

Phillis had been sold twice before. If you'd given good service, some owners let their friends know you were for sale, and it wasn't so bad if you got bought up by somebody who knew you, somebody you'd waited on and opened the door for already. Otherwise you were advertised to the dealers who came through twice a year in their wagons. They looked you up and down and pulled open your mouth to see if your teeth were sound, and some made the young ones peel down for the fun of it, poking and pinching and squeezing. If the dealers bought you, they tied your hands up together in a long line, sometimes twenty or thirty together, and chained the two at the ends to an iron ring set into the wagon bed. If you fought or tried to run, they put a rope net over you like the ones Catcher carried. Hauled you over the mountain to Albany, maybe down to York City. Big sale barns there, they could put thirty or forty on the block together. *The slave Phillis, about thirty-two years, household servant, full-bodied and of good behavior, strong enough for field work, presently with child.*

"I want to sell those goddamn slaves!" she heard Herod cry out.

Being pregnant made you worth more, because once you dropped it, they could sell off the baby away from you. Phillis lurched forward, her palms flat on the polished glass of the mirror. The block was already there, in King Herod's voice. The ropes, she could feel them. The hands that tore the child out of her. The iron ring. The net.

"Hush, girl, they'll hear you," said Cato's voice in her ear. She had begun to weep without knowing it, deep sobs that shook her and rattled the mirror. "What they saying? What trouble?" he murmured.

When they owned your body and all the work of your days, you grew a secret voice for your soul to talk with and even to think with. Poor women had it, if they were owned by bad husbands, and most children had it. Slaves had it, too. It was why Phillis had loved Cato and married him, because his secret voice was sweet and proud and strong.

"Meaning to sell us," she told him, her fist in her mouth to stifle the sobs. "I heared him."

Cato pulled her close with his arm and she could feel him

shaking. "Dealer won't keep us together," he said. "Not likely."
Even if their marriage had been legal, few masters would buy a
couple together, and both of them house-slaves. "I expect we got
to run, then," he said, and she could feel the fear in his bones.

"No, sir!" Phillis's mind danced and whirled. To dodge catch-
ers and dealers with a child in her belly? It couldn't be thought
of. "Got to be another way. Got to give somebody a reason to
take us both," she said. "Got to have something besides our own
selves to sell 'em."

"Sell? What you mean, girl?"

Phillis detached herself from her husband and wiped her eyes
on her white apron and straightened her cap. "Never you mind,"
she said. "I'll fix it." And as she went up the back stair to carry a
pot of tea to Mrs. Hargrave's room, the scraps and signs of nine
years' watching came together and found their use at last.

Phillis dropped Celia Hargrave a curtsy and began to lay out the
tea things in silence. *He* was there in the room, too, the one she
had come for—Bartram Hargrave, who stood a better chance than
King Herod to be senator next election. Bartram Hargrave, who
had power Herod Aldrich could only dream of, and kept many
slaves.

His wife had been a beauty. She was fading some now, and
people said he had fancy women when he felt so inclined. But he
still kept his wife like a princess. Phillis took stock of her out of
half-closed eyes—a rose-colored silk gown with triple sleeves and
a drape of Irish lace on the shoulder, and a garnet necklace that
sparkled at her long, slender throat. Pride bought that necklace,
thought the slave woman, smiling to herself and laying the palm
of her hand on the child in her belly. Pride bought them laces,
and when a man is wife-proud, you can get at him that way.

"My dear," Bartram Hargrave was saying, "this man Aldrich
is utterly impossible! There was a time when land and property
ruled in this country and if you had enough of it, you could share

out the future over a civilized game of bezique in some parlor in
Philadelphia with half a dozen others just like you. But the old
days are done. Jefferson and his Republicans have changed everything. The poor have a vote now, property or not."

"You mean poor *men,* do you not, dearest?" His wife sipped
her tea and smiled at Phillis.

"Now, Celia. The point is that the poor have votes, but not
enough education to know what is good for them. They have to
be cajoled, coaxed, wheedled into being governed by the right
men, men who know what's best for the country. Otherwise we'll
have some backwoods monkey in the White House before long,
and spittoons in the best drawing room, and the Devil's own time
to get rid of them both!"

"My dear Bartram, you're an excellent rhetorician, all you need
do is speak to them simply. I'm sure that even the poor will know
your value."

"That's all very well, but when you get up to speak, it doesn't
matter if they understand you or not, you can't convince them
with logic. You have to make them love you, you have to buy
out the newspapers to sing your praises, and court them with
parades, rumbustious speeches, fireworks, music."

"And whisky?"

"Oh, barrels of whisky. And all that takes hard cash, Celia.
Ready money, not great tracts of unsettled land like this patent of
Herod's. I tell you, he's got a great name in these parts, but he's
a relic, a dead weight to Federalism. And he's all but bankrupt, so
young Will Slocum was telling me."

"But, dearest, even General Washington was not a rich man
by those standards. He had little cash and great property."

"Yes, and let me tell you, if Washington were still alive, he'd
be as much of an albatross to the party as Aldrich."

Celia smiled. "Well, then, perhaps poor Herod should become
a Republican."

"What difference would that make? They don't want him
either. These old fellows have no sense of the times, Celia, no
more than Jefferson has. The poor want a war with England, and

we must give them one, and soon, too, or we'll all find ourselves going begging next election."

Phillis offered a tiered silver dish of elegant little sweetmeats and Celia Hargrave selected a Shrewsbury cake. "And Aldrich doesn't want war?" she said.

"God knows why not. It's the only salvation of business in this part of the country, just like everywhere else. But he's pigheaded. Won't be told. And Talbot County still votes as he tells it, and carries most of the other upstate counties with it."

"But it won't vote for you?"

"Not as a war-hawk." Hargrave kissed his wife on the forehead and laughed. "I could stand them to rum punch till Doomsday, and they'd never vote for me, not so long as King Herod's name is untarnished and I can't find anything to smear him with. I tell you, my love, I'd be putty in the hands of anybody who'd give me a nice bit of sin, you know! Something just venal enough to bring the fellow down and put his votes in my pocket."

Phillis offered him the tray of cakes and a purposeful sob escaped her. "Beg pardon, sir," she said, and dropped him a deep curtsy, so that she staggered and almost fell. "I don't mean no harm, only—"

"Why, Phillis!" cried Mrs. Hargrave. "Steady her, dearest!"

Hargrave caught the slave woman by the arm, and Celia poured her out a cup of tea. "Now, then, Phillis. Tell us what is the trouble."

"Thank you, ma'am," Phillis said through a sniffle. "I don't mean to cause you no trouble. Only I got me a child comin', and Master meaning to sell us, ma'am." She glanced slyly at Celia, who was childless. "Sell me and Cato both. Ain't nobody to buy two house-slaves together. I don't know what become of this little child. . . ." She was sobbing openly now, her apron over her head.

"Sell you? But whatever for? You are excellent servants, I'd buy you myself in a minute!" Hargrave frowned, puzzled.

"For true, Mister Hargrave?" The apron was lowered and Phillis's red, watery eyes studied his arrogant, composed features. She judged him as though he stood on a block with a shackle around his neck. No better than Aldrich. But sleeker. Stronger. Likely to last a good long time, and no sign in the eyes of that terrible future contained in the piano, in the plants, in the job-lot portraits. No fear of going down. "Be your slave, sir?" She allowed her sorrowing features to light up with joy. "Oh, I'd like that just fine!"

"But *why* does your master mean to sell you?" Celia persisted.

" 'Feared we'll tell on him, ma'am, that's how I reckon." The slave woman wiped her eyes. " 'Feared what we know, I expect."

"And what *do* you know?" Hargrave's black eyes were unreadable; he knew the offer of a deal when he heard one, but he was not inclined to accept any kind of merchandise untried.

"Can't say it out loud, sir. Weighs heavy on my soul, but he's still my master." Phillis looked up at him; she was no more a novice at trading than he was. " 'Less you willing to offer for us now, me and Cato both? Then I be free to tell you whatever you wanting to know, sir."

Bartram Hargrave smiled to himself. Then he glanced at his wife, and she nodded. Celia Hargrave's beauty was not her only credential, and she had not been a politician's wife for twenty years and learned nothing.

"Sit down, Phillis," Hargrave said kindly. "Drink that tea and compose yourself. And then lighten your soul of Mr. Aldrich's secrets. King Herod's not your master anymore."

IX

drawing in

At Bay House, the day before the Federal Ball is a festival morning. They have finished the loom, and it is time for drawing in.

Dressing the loom, some women call it, and others say bedding, as though the thread and the loom were man and wife. For many years of her childhood, Jennet had no name for the process at all. It was a thing you did, like eating or walking, and the name of it lived in your fingers. When at last she was forced to consider abstractions, she learned to call it drawing in.

Aunt Hope is a frequent visitor to the house now, and she has come today to help them. There is no walking wheel yet in the workroom and the yarn is her spinning—a dark-blue wool, fine but resilient, to make a new cloak for Jennet. The old woman is a skilled and practiced dyer and she knows what will set each color. For indigo, she saves up fermented urine in buckets and tubs to set a perfect cobalt blue.

When the hanks are lifted out with the paddle, they are unpromising, a greenish color like half-dormant grass at the end of summer. It is only when the air completely envelops and marries the wool that it turns color. Blue is like no other shade; it refuses control. It is like the ice, like the crystals that form and connect and release one another, setting free in the world an electrical charge, the energy of pure art.

You can darken it, muddy it, leave it too long or not long enough in the dye kettle. If you do it by rule, it will always escape you. Blue cannot be created on purpose. Like the ice, like the unspoken marriage between Frayne and Jennet, it simply happens, the discipline of chance that must be submitted to.

There is glass in the workroom windows again, looking out towards White Lady, and a fire crackles in the great hearth. There is a rough worktable and benches and joint stools—all made quickly by Gabriel and Leclerc—and Jennet has hung up her bunches of herbs from the rafters, and some of Hannah's quilts to insulate the walls. They have been kept many years, but they are still bright, the patterns still clear. Red Roses. Northumberland Star. Bridges Burning. Burgoyne Surrounded. Hearts and Bones.

Gabriel is hard at work building shelves and store-cupboards and a real, old-fashioned settle, and Frayne has brought down the ancient bedframes from upstairs. He has set one in the kitchen for the old man and the other one here, for Jennet, with a mattress full of Zimmer's cornhusks supplied by Leclerc. It is her place, to which John comes only by invitation. He assumes nothing and demands nothing that is not of her giving. There are locks on both the doors.

"What are you doing?" he says one day, peering in through the door to the old kitchen garden. He has been burrowing about there all week, digging away the snow at the roots of a hedge of currant bushes to look for something, some spot on his mind-map. He wants to find everything his father has hidden, replace everything, give the world back to Jennet as it might have been.

"What the deuce is it?" he says. "What're you up to?"

The girl is balanced on a bench in the rectangle of the hallway doorframe, the old black woman on tiptoe beneath her. She does not turn to him, does not need to know what he says. She has begun to hear him as she used to hear Hannah, with the secret resonance of mind.

Frayne comes in to stand near her, to see how her thin body curves and reaches, how her brow is bright with confidence; this work seems to define her. "What is it she's doing?" he asks Aunt Hope softly.

"See them there pegs?" she replies.

At intervals of the uprights and the lintel, someone has bored holes and inserted round wooden pegs the width of a broomstick and about eight inches long. "Oh, those," he says. "I meant to saw them off level, but I haven't got to it yet."

The old lady cackles, and fragrant smoke rises from the pipe she keeps tucked in the corner of her mouth. "Saw 'em off? Ain't nobody but a damn fool man go and saw off a good set of warping pegs."

Aunt Hope studies him, as she has done for a long while now, since the morning after Frayne's confession when Jennet first brought him to her door. She has noticed that he does not look unconsciously away from her black skin as most white men do. That he takes her hand in greeting, and does not hesitate. That when he wants something, he gets it himself and does not give orders, nor assume over anyone the right of a master. She has noticed, too, that when she teases him, his eyes crinkle with laughter.

A good enough man, the old woman thinks, for a white man. She has not called him by name yet, but when the time comes, she will know it.

"Weaver-woman put them pegs in," she says, taking pity on his abysmal ignorance. "If you ain't got you a board nor a warping-reel, you most always got you a doorway. See there? Watch her hands."

The girl is winding the wool back and forth around the pegs, making a complex skein that, once it is finished, will pull free as the loom takes up yardage. Frayne watches her skilled fingers move with simple pride from one peg to the other, carrying the yarn like a spider casting out delicate filament, till the ancient doorway is almost filled with blue strands. Where they meet at the top, they cross over. The porrey-cross, Aunt Hope says it is called. The lease. This the two women tie loosely with twine, and then section off the rest of the yarn into two-foot lengths, all tied in the same way. Finally, using her hand like the bone crochet hook Frayne remembers seeing his mother use to make lace, Jennet loops the sections together into a long, many-stranded chain of cobalt blue.

He watches over them all that day as they finish the warping, lounging in and out from his treasure hunt in the garden. Aunt Hope stays the night, using Jennet's old pallet by the kitchen fire, with Frayne on the floor nearby and Gabriel in his stately new bed. Long after midnight, the old lady hears footsteps, sharp little tapping steps that come down the hall. Then the light of a candle, and the girl's soft, sandy night-voice.

John?

He has been waiting, wide awake. He says nothing, gets up from the pallet with almost no sound and goes to where she is standing. Lays her narrow palm lightly above his mouth to give her his answers.

My soul, he says.

I can't sleep. Boots can't sleep, either.

He's not supposed to. Cats catch mice at night. They sleep in the daytime.

I'm not a cat. I can't sleep.

What frights you?

The loom. The drawing in. If I spoil it.

It has a meaning to her he cannot yet put into words. There is some spirit in it, like the white stones of the old magician. Perhaps it is her mother she is afraid of failing, perhaps Hannah comes to her through the loom, through the quilts on the walls.

He goes to his pack and takes out the wise man's holy stones cast aside by the thugs at City of Larks, and presses them to her lips. Kiss them, he says. They are prayer stones. They will keep your hand true.

You believe that?

I think so.

To focus the nerves on something clean and neutral, something innocent—it is how they have all come together here. An outcast, a deserter, a blind man, a witch, and a mad girl. They are all flawed, all lamed by living. But together they are perfect and possible. Together, they are the color of blue.

Jennet kisses the stones one by one. Then she leans her forehead against him. The Frenchman. Marius. He worries me.

Why? He seems all right.

No. He's slipping away. He's like you were, he never forgives himself for living. You're not still like that, are you?

Frayne's head droops. Sometimes, he mumbles. When my father is near me. When I think of him.

He hasn't forgiven you yet?

I don't know, he says. How can I know? Then he takes her hand with the prayer stones still in it. Shall I talk to the Frenchman?

Let me think first, she says. Come and read to me now. Make me sleep.

They disappear into the dark of the passage and Aunt Hope can hear the girl's feet tapping away toward the workroom. The old woman waits for a while, perhaps ten minutes. Then she creeps down the hall towards the wedge of candlelight that falls through the open door. The end of the long chain of warp thread is already tied to the back beam of the loom, ready for morning, and the loops lie piled onto a three-legged joint stool. The candlelight falls upon the blue strands, turning them purple and green and black, disclosing infinite possibilities.

The holy oil Love took to hand, and washed the woman's face, the
    daughter of princes,
Bathed her clear brow and her bright eyes and her lips with ambrosia,
The immortal dew of gods that made her seem taller, younger,
Full-breasted and rich with milk, her skin like carved ivory,
And all done as she slept.

John? Have you seen Timothy? Have you talked to him?

Yes.

Is he kind? Would he like me?

I think so. I hope so. He doesn't like me, though.

You have to win him, the way you did me.

I don't know where to start, Jen.

My father used to come and play with me sometimes, before anyone knew he was really my father. Before I knew there were such things as fathers. We used to make snow angels, and once we went coasting down the hill. He was my friend. I was happy then. I like coasting.

I know. I've seen you.

Have you talked to Hester yet? To her husband?

I'm her husband.

No, you aren't. You're mine.

For a time Frayne is silent, absorbing this gift she has suddenly given him.

Let's go coasting together, he tells her at last. I can build us a sled.

He snuffs out the candle. In the liquid dark of firelight, he sits on the edge of Jennet's bed, his back propped on the cold wall, reciting from his mind-book. If the words are merely his own, if the story drifts away into new paths, he follows them, true only to the shape of the tale, his voice riding the dark like a boat on the tide. In this house of spirits, no book is ever finished. No story ever comes to an end.

The girl is against him, wrapped in a quilt, her arms around his neck, and Frayne holds her like an instrument, like a harp or a cello. Fingers barely touching her, cupped to fit the curve of her cheek.

Ah, what a gentle sleep, she murmured, waking.
How it folds away anguish,
And the storm-tossed disquiet of earthly dreams.

Jennet's breathing changes, deepens. On the braided rag hearthrug, Boots the cat, too, is sleeping, and even Frayne is fast asleep. But Aunt Hope, their *voyeur*, their guardian, is suddenly more than awake, her eyes fixed not on the chaste pair in the bed but on the window that looks out to the garden. There are shadows moving about there, near the bushes where Frayne has been digging.

Hope's breath comes in quick stabs. She has not always been free, and she has never lost the fear of it, nor the prison-rage that sleeps under even the most docile of slaves. On tiptoe, she crosses the room, waking only the kitten, and rubs off the frost from the windowpane.

It is Guido and Caleb and Royall. She knows them by their sizes, by the way they slouch and slap one another, as though they are coy, teasing lovers. Once they came drunk to her house and took three of her cats and hung them up by their necks from the stable rafters, where they knew she would find them. They hid away in the straw and when she cried out in her grief, they began to laugh and came out to torment her. She took up a pitchfork and a sickle and went after them, and caught the littlest one with a tine in the buttocks.

"Scum," she murmurs soundlessly, her mouth kissing the window glass. She lifts the latch of the outer door softly. It will not do to wake Frayne and the girl. The loom is waiting, and it matters more than these goblins. Sleep matters, and morning, and the drawing in of blue.

Besides, Aunt Hope knows how to hate, she is good at it and she is selfish about it, too. For the moment she wants it all for herself.

"Ain't nothing in them goddamn bushes," says Royall. "I'm freezing my dick off."

"Shut up and quit your whining!" Caleb orders. "I gotta get further in."

He sprawls out on the ground, pawing under the bushes where Frayne's pickax has gouged out a pathway of holes. "There's been treasure hid here, all right. Lookit!" Caleb scuttles out from under the bush and holds up a ragged scrap of leather. "Froze down, likely, and this here come away when he pulled it out. I seen him. He found something, whatever it was. Took it inside. And it ain't the first, neither. I bet he's got a whole roomful in there. Gold. Silver. Maybe jewelry, Sandy's old woman had it in buckets, that's what old Blunt used to say."

"Do we go in after it, Cab?" says Guido. "Or what?"

"You want to take him on barehanded? We ain't got no rifles with us."

"Could slit his throat, if he's sleeping."

But Royall has had enough. "You're full of shit, Cab. I ain't slitting nobody's throat, and neither are you! Anyhow, I'm freezing, I can't feel my toes no more."

"I'll fix Frayne, don't you worry." Because of his failure with the girl on the ice, Caleb's greed is fueled by resentment and jealousy. "I'll bring him down."

But not tonight. They set off across the lake, hobnails crunching the snow, and Aunt Hope's fingernails drag down the glass of the window like furious claws. Her wide eyes close for a moment, curtains drawn over her anger. Then they open again, calm and absorbed.

Another shape has appeared, stepping out of the balsam grove onto the shore. It is thick and muscular and hunched a bit at the shoulders. A small man, but strong, a rower or a wielder of axes. "Ha," she whispers. "Catcher." It is what the poor always call him, what they frighten their children with. Jake the Catcher. Catcher Benet.

He stands very still in the bright windless darkness, watching the disappearing shapes of the three rootless men, like flotsam on the breast of the lake. He drags something behind him, thrown over his shoulder like a cape, and when he moves, the old woman can see in the bright spill of moonlight the interstices of tarred and knotted rope.

The drawing in takes all the next day. It is a delicate business, each step precise and expertly ordered: the tying of warp to the back beam, the easing of strands at perfect tension through the heddles, the winding of the warp beam, the final tying-off to the cloth beam. Each strand must remain firm enough to be useful, but not tight enough to stretch or break.

A piece of cloth is a living thing, Jennet's mother once told her. If you draw in correctly, every thread has a life of its own. When you weave it, it answers the pattern. When you touch it, it sings.

This thread-song the girl hears now with her fingers. As they did over Frayne's wounds, they drift over the taut strands to try their resilience, to feel the slight energy that comes from them, that they are smooth and ready and alive. The men gather to watch her weave the first row of the piece—Gabriel from his workshop in the old servants' quarters; Frayne and Leclerc from the library, where they are doing something in secret they will not let anyone see.

The Frenchman comes almost every day now, once his work at Zimmer's factory is finished. Aunt Hope cannot quite make him out, whether he loves Frayne or hates him, and Leclerc seems just as uncertain of his own feelings, his position here. Still, the old black woman can't help but like him. Madame Pomfrey, he calls her, and she trots away like a pleased little pony, cackling behind her hand.

Jennet picks up the shuttle, and her foot is already on the treadle that opens the shed when she remembers something, a part of the ceremony she has almost overlooked. She slips down from the weaver's bench, and produces from somewhere the cracked amethyst goblet. "Wine," she says, and pours out for each of them in turn the cheap red wine Frayne bought at the Dog and Lantern.

"Don't recall I ever tasted wine before this," says Gabriel, trying not to make a face. "Odd stuff, ain't it? Neither sour nor sweet."

"My, that's fine," Aunt Hope murmurs, smacking her lips. "I got me a regular tooth for grape juice."

Frayne takes the goblet and holds it up to the light, turns it round and round. "Your mother's, Jen? Hannah's?"

"My father bought them. There were eight, but the rest are all broken."

He sips the wine very slowly, his eyes lowered, feeling Leclerc's gaze upon him and the old lady's stinging glance, like the edge of a whip.

"Where are the white stones?" Jennet says, once he has finished. "Let me touch them again."

As the others watch, Frayne finds the holy pebbles in his breeches pocket and holds them to his own lips, then to hers. Voha, he whispers. E-hani, our father in heaven. Bring grace to her hands.

Gabriel cannot make out what is happening. "What's she doing, John?"

"Praying."

Jennet slides onto the bench again and her left foot bears down on the treadle, raising the heddle to open the shed. Her right hand takes up the shuttle with the bobbin inside it and moves it through the lifted threads. Pulls down the beater stick to keep the weave even. Pedals again. Thump, replies the loom. Thump-ump. It is a solid sound now, and full of promise. But no more beautiful to Frayne than when she wove only ice.

"John," says Aunt Hope softly.

He looks down at her and smiles. It is the first time she has called him by name, and it means they are friends at last. "Mother?" he says.

This mild filial endearment may be going too far, but she permits it. "I seen them scum in the yard last night," she tells him.

"While you sleeping. Royall Watts and Caleb Beck, and that other one, that weasel Guido Hubbard."

"I know. Hobnails. I found their tracks this morning when I went out to milk."

"Catcher there, too. Had his net with him. I seen."

"He's been watching since I got here," Frayne says. "But he's a decent man. If he meant harm, he'd have done it by now."

"Maybe so. Maybe just waiting. Mendin' his nets." She studies him with narrowed eyes. "Scum poking around them black currant hedge. Why you dig up under there? You find them treasure they talk about?"

"Not treasure. Come and see. We've been fixing it up, the Frenchman and I. It's a present for Jennet."

The thump of the weaving stops all of a sudden. Somehow her name always reaches the girl, even when she cannot read lips. It is like thunder or the raucous cries of jays, or Frayne's voice when he reads in the darkness.

"What?" She looks around at them, tongue between teeth.

John laughs. "There now. I thought the word 'present' would fetch you."

"Pooh," she replies, and goes with them to see.

He has gathered all the treasure here, in the library, spread out on Leclerc's perfect floorboards where the rebirth of Bay House began. There is pewter, and most of a set of porcelain plates, and five cups and saucers, a brown-and-cream pattern. When you hold one of the cups by its handle, light streams through the fine-ground bone beneath the glaze, and if you put it over your ear like a seashell you can hear a distant roaring, the sound the speaking world makes to Jennet, like the drawing in of the tide.

There is an old clock without a case, its tiny wheels and gears locked in position at the hour of half-past five. A small pewter nursing bottle with a silver nipple on the end. A cracked mirror, peeling foil from its back. An oil painting, cut out of its frame and rolled up in a hollow tube of oak all these years, and hidden behind a piece of wainscoting. The portrait is that of a woman Frayne cannot identify—some cousin, perhaps, or one of his father's many mistresses. She is dressed in the fashion of the 1750s, her face long and chalk-white and patrician, her hair dressed very high and powdered to a faint blue. Her eyes glazed, absent, disturbingly wild.

There are toys and amusements. A cracked chessboard and four pieces, carved out of black walnut and pale beechwood. A knight, a bishop, and two pawns. A hobbyhorse, its braided mane nibbled by mice and its bells rusted. Two pair of ice skates, one smaller than the other, the largest big enough for a man, the smallest almost the right size for Tim.

There are more books, dozens of them, so carefully wrapped and sealed in leather and wax that the pages crumble away only at the corners. There is Fielding, John Donne, Aristotle, Erasmus, Shakespeare, Smollett, Sophocles, Plato, Dante. There are dictionaries—of languages, of plants, of rocks, of stars, of fishes, of medicines, of ships, of kites. Most of all there are maps, atlases of desert countries whose names change as fast as the sands that drift over them, maps of the oceans, explorers' maps, and the speculative maps of old philosophers who drew out the countries of amazons and dragons and men who wore their heads beneath their ribs.

All these the girl touches and admires, her brandy-colored eyes wide and her lips slightly parted. At the heart of every human fragment there is a hidden purity, a virtue that heals if you let it, and she moves among these things of Frayne's reverently, turning the pages of old books, bending over to take in the scent of them, feeling the shape of the ink with her fingertips.

But in the end, she has eyes for only one of Frayne's treasures. It stands in the center of the room where the light from the newly-glazed window falls onto it—the spinning wheel Jennet has wanted, a huge old walking wheel of the kind used for wool. Its diameter is more than five feet, much too big for tiny Aunt Hope, who would have to trot back and forth at a fast clip to work the wool evenly. But the girl is tall, she takes after her father. For her, it will be just right.

"It must've belonged to Mrs. Datchet, my mother's house-keeper," Frayne tells them. "The wheel was plastered up in the south attic wall, God knows how the fire missed it. The small pieces were under the bushes, half-rotten. Marius took them back to Zimmer's and used them as patterns." He glances over at the Frenchman, who stands apart from the rest, in a shadowy corner. "He did a good job, did he not?"

"Lord be praised," Aunt Hope murmurs. "Ain't that fine? Ain't that a miracle?"

Leclerc has sanded each piece and rubbed it by hand—with no drop of oil that might soil the wool during spinning—until the carefully-turned legs and the long, low bed and even the spindle gleam in the cold afternoon light. Gabriel, who knows woodwork-ing better than the others, feels over the pieces with his long, heavy fingers. "Birch, is it?" he asks Leclerc.

"*Oui,* monsieur." Slowly, with tentative steps, the Frenchman limps out of the dim corner. It is his habit among them to distance himself now, as though they are steam, and he has been scalded and fears to come too close.

And yet he cannot stay away from them. When he is whole, when he is able to manage the heart of himself and take purpose from it, he will no longer need them. But for now, they still nourish him, he feeds from them as he did from the ripe pears in the garden.

"Before you could talk, *ma petite,* did you miss words?" he had asked Jennet one day as he fitted in the new cloth beam. "Did you know what they were?"

They had just whitewashed the walls and she was scouring the floor with clean sand and a brush, her skirts tied up and an old pair of Gabriel's breeches underneath them. But she had a habit of looking up now, whenever she knew someone else was in the room, of scanning faces to see if anyone might be speaking.

"I think I always knew there were such things as words," she said. "I could see the lips move, how they were different when people laughed or were angry."

Leclerc's balding head was bent very low. "But your brothers," he said. "They could hear and speak?"

"Robbie and Charlie were lucky. In the school in Scotland I had a friend—Jane, her name was. She had three sisters and two brothers, and all six of them were like me. Deaf and dumb."

She used the phrase casually, but with too much bravado, firing it off like a gun.

"Did you like the school?" Marius limped out from behind the loom and sat down at the worktable Gabriel had built her. "Were they kind there?"

"Not kind. Not unkind. They had too many rules, and most of them were the wrong rules. Except for the matron, they were all men, even the pupils. Only Jane and me. Not many people think girls are worth teaching. But my aunt paid them enough to make them try. Jane loved it, she liked rules. She was happy there, but she was always afraid of other people. Outside people, you know. When they said she had to leave, that it was time she must live in the world, she killed herself."

"But you did not."

"I wanted to, for a long time. Frayne says everybody wants to sometimes." Jennet scrubbed her way along the floor to Leclerc's feet and began to unlace his boot. "Hold still. I want to see," she said.

She studied his clear, restless eyes behind the spectacles. If human flesh and blood did not exist, he would be happier in the world. With wood, with hammers and saws, with fire and water and fruit, even with animals, he is easy and comfortable. But with people, he is disconcerted by his belief in his own incomplete incarnation. Finding himself unlike the brash and the easy, he believes he is nothing, and this scorn of himself is like an old path that is safe to walk, though it leads nowhere.

When his lame foot and ankle were bared, Jennet sat cross-legged on the clean floor, examining, smoothing the tendon and bone and the hard knot of scar tissue where the grapeshot had caught him. Leclerc looked down at her, oddly unabashed by this intimate touching.

"I made you an ointment," she said at last. "Frayne bought me the medicine."

She got up and went to a shelf above the newly-restored hearth and brought back a small earthenware pot with a cork in it. Then she knelt down again and began to smooth this preparation over the scar and the spur of crooked bone. When she was finished, she looked up at him.

"Are you afraid of me?" she said. Except now and then with Frayne, her words did not vary in tone or expression, they were all equally loud, equally matter-of-fact. Are. You. Afraid. But just now, as she spoke to the Frenchman, they were soft, almost whispered.

Marius glanced away, he had not yet been able to meet her steady gaze for long. "Yes," he said.

"Why? Do *you* think I'm mad, too, like those people in town?"

"No, no. Of course not. But—you see me as nobody else does. What I might be. How far I fall short."

"I don't understand that. Might be. I never did. I didn't see anything wrong with what I was, even when I didn't know words or signs or anything people were saying. I was myself. I was alive, I had colors and shapes and smells, and softness and cold and warm, and they made me happy. But it seemed to matter so much to everybody else, and I began to think something was missing in me. My father knew more words than anyone, and he was missing two fingers, and I thought the words must live there, in that empty space on his hand. So I tried to cut two of my fingers off, just in case it would help."

Suddenly she reached up with her ancient, faintly-webbed hands and drew his face down to her and kissed him. His eyes closed, Leclerc was amazed by the cool strength of her lips on his own, how they drew him towards her without arousal, without pity, without scorn of his clumsiness. He felt the warmth of her salve on his ankle.

"You and Monsieur Jean," he asked her when they parted. "Are—are you lovers now?"

Jennet got up from the floor and put the pot of ointment back onto the mantel shelf. "Don't cut off any fingers, Marius," she said. "Let yourself be."

"Good solid grain," says old Gabriel. "Not too much weight, but enough to be steady." He nods his approval of the spinning wheel. "I couldn't have done better myself."

Marius draws closer, a smile on his face and his spectacles shining. "I used birch for the bed-piece," he tells the old man. "But the legs and the spindle are cherry. To match the spokes of the old wheel."

"I have a treasure for *you,* too, Frenchman. Or I should say, my father has." Frayne drags a battered old tin trunk from under the library window. "Open it. I only found it yesterday. I've been saving it for last."

Awkwardly, Marius goes down on his knees, his lame foot sticking out at an angle behind him. The latches are rusted and stubborn, but he pulls them up from the hasps. For a moment he hesitates, as though a thousand troubles will fly out if he opens it. But at last he lifts the leather-covered lid.

Inside the trunk is a violin. God knows who last played it, but it appears very old—perhaps a century—and it lies on a bed of cedar shavings to keep insects away. Someone has removed the strings, which would only have rotted, and the bow is not strung, either. Marius lifts the instrument up carefully, certain it will spring apart in his hands. But a miracle occurs, and it does not. He tucks it under his double chin and takes up the empty bow. His fingers make the shape of a chord on the stringless neck and the bow hovers above the breast of the instrument. Moves back and forth to some inaudible melody.

Make me a hero, his bones are praying to the tune of a Bach Adagio. Use me. Repair me. Make me an instrument of life.

The deaf girl is watching him, an absurd, stubby figure sawing a useless bow across a voiceless fiddle. But from somewhere in the sway of his body, an ache that is music reaches her, takes her. "Beautiful," she says in her awkward, grating singsong. Bu. Tea. Full.

Frayne leaves them together, feeling the need of the ordinary. It is late now, the February sun almost ready to drop behind White Lady, as he trudges outside in a wind-driven squall of snow to see to the hens and the horses and the small milk cow he has brought from the pens at the Dog.

He takes his Lancaster rifle with him, primed and loaded. Since he came here, he has not touched it, not even to hunt game for the table, and when he carries it now for fear of Royall and Caleb and the others, a wave of nausea floods over him. The innocence of the shy little Frenchman, the hard purity of the girl, the bluff kindness of Gabriel—they belong to each other. Jennet is almost herself again; for four days, she has not chopped open the hole in the ice where her mother is. Frayne himself is the only corruption, with his ghosts and his guns and his scars.

John?

The voice is clear and high, almost sweet in the gloom of the stable, very different from Jennet's. Even after nine years, he knows it at once.

Hester, he says. So you've come.

She steps out from the cow's stall to let him see her. You've changed, she says sharply. You're not handsome anymore.

Frayne smiles, a brief glimmer. You'll have to find some other way to hurt me.

No, she replies, her voice softer. You never were vain.

He takes stock of her blackened teeth and the grey in her hair where her cloak falls back. You're well? he says.

I am as you see me. Hester is shivering, the wind cutting into her through the open door of the stable. He tastes it, smells it. It has the fragrance of snow.

Come inside by the fire, he urges. Warm yourself.

No! I won't go into that house. I don't want your kindness, it's too late. She sinks down in the straw, the cow's hooves almost upon her. Bends her head down to her lap, her arms hugging her body. Rocking herself like a child. Christ, I hate you. Why didn't you come back sooner? Why are you here now? Why do you torment me? Why in God's name are you here?

Till he came back, Hester had felt she could endure what had become of her. The pointless work. The cold bedroom. The vomit. The hard, pewter-colored sky that was the bitter mask of God. But now her girlhood stared back at her, passing judgment. It scolded her every night in the dark as she lay praying for sleep to erase her.

What have I done? Frayne thinks as he looks at her, feeling once more the old temptation to turn the random collision of atoms to personal guilt. He fights off the urge to enfold her, to lift her up. I haven't come back here to harm you, he says softly. I had to know you and Timothy were safe, that you wanted for nothing.

Safe? Hester echoes, as though she is no longer sure what the word means. She feels she is standing on a thin crust of ice, on the lip of a volcano. You deserted me, you left me with the boy. I had to marry. I had nothing, no money.

Come, Hester, I sent you five hundred dollars. A bank draft, a name where you could write for more when it was needed. From New Orleans, did you never get the letter?

She stares. Five hundred is almost a fortune, the interest will bring you enough in a month to live in comfort even in Boston or Philadelphia. Glittering chances she has never imagined present themselves to her and are smashed before her eyes.

What's a bank draft? she says. I got a letter. But you know I can't read.

He stares at her. Surely someone read it out to you, then. A travelling letter-writer? A schoolmaster?

She drags herself up from the straw by the frame of the stall. Remembering the day in Herod Aldrich's chilly library, how his daughter had been playing her piano and singing in the parlor beyond the closed door. *I sowed the seeds of love, and I sowed them in the spring.* How Aldrich glanced at the letter and threw something into the fire and then turned to stare at his leftover lover. Divorcing himself from the spoor of his flesh on her body, the seed he had left in her that she had carefully killed.

You'll get no help from John Frayne, he had told her. Jacob Benet is a good steady man, you must marry him. Catcher Benet.

So he was rid of me, she whispers. She takes a step or two into the stall and her body leans toward the warmth of the docile little brown-and-white cow. So I was caught and he was free.

Hester? Frayne says.

He cannot hear her, she is talking to herself, to the woman she might have been with the five hundred dollars Herod Aldrich threw onto the fire to keep his control of her.

You're Jacob's wife now, John says gently. Let it be so. I've filed the papers already to let the court know it. I won't interfere in your life.

Will you take back the boy? she says.

Tim hates me, he loves Benet.

Do you want him? Do you want your son back?

Christ. Yes.

Then you must take him. Don't give him up to Jacob.

The love Hester has never been able to feel for the boy Tim overwhelms her, it sends a sharp birth-spasm through her belly and loins that doubles her over, her face against the warm back of the cow. But it is also her vengeance on Jacob.

When I am dead, you must take Timothy. You must promise. Frayne can no longer bear it, he steps into the stall and holds her against him. The feel of her is a shock to him; she is light and dry, like Tacha's bones. Take me back, John, she whispers. Christ. Keep me. I love you.

Now, now. You don't, you know. You never did. You can't

help it. His hand strokes back her hair and his lips brush her eyelids. Hush, he says. Hush. You're not going to die.

I love you now! Let's go away from here. Take me with you!

You haven't changed, he says, remembering the high meadow in Devon that looked down at the sea. *There's a ship far out. I wish I was aboard it. I wonder where it's bound.* Is Jacob such a bad man? he asks her. Does he hurt you?

He smothers me! Smashes me down. I shall die if I am not free of him!

Hester, dear. Hester. Don't you remember? Before I left you, when you told me you had taken a lover?

What? What should I remember?

You said those same words of me then. You smash me, you and your father. I'll die if I cannot be free of you.

That was different! I was different then!

Were you? Can you tell me that if I took you from Benet tomorrow, you would not say those same words to me again the day after, or the day after that, and drive me away again? You must settle somewhere, Hester. So must I.

You love *her,* then? she murmurs. The old midwife's daughter, the mad girl?

I'm not sure anybody knows what love is, it's like believing in God. Smug people boast of it, and call the rest heathens. I need to be with her. I guess that's enough.

So. You will send me to ruin for her sake?

He hesitates for a long moment. The familiar temptation of endless guilt stretches in front of him, unmapped and huge, like the sky above the plum thicket where the Spaniard's men discarded him. He remembers the words of the old Indian magus. *The gods are wise to be jealous of the granting of freedom. No god is strong enough to take it back again.*

I was never your enemy, he says slowly, not even when we caused each other pain. If you are ruined, I will be sorry to know it. But it is not of my doing, and I will not carry it. Whatever was between us is long over, and I didn't grudge you the freedom you wanted. Now you must not grudge me mine.

You won't have me for your wife, then? she says. You won't take me back?

You must pick up your choices and carry them, Hester, he tells her in the low voice she has dreamed of. Even if they crush you, you must bear them, and so must I. It's what freedom costs.

He lets her go and moves away, gets the wooden milking pail and the three-legged stool and sits down to his work. But she can't let him go yet, she must punish him first.

I never told you the name of my lover. Don't you want to know? The sour tone has come back to her voice, the old hateful taunting he remembers. Do you sleep with the mad girl? Is she better than me?

That's no business of yours. Go home to your husband. He's a decent man. Take some comfort of him and try to love him. You and I were done before we started.

No! Don't you want to know who I slept with? Who you saw that night, who made you a cuckold?

I already know who it was. His voice is turned inward, the words as measured and mechanical as Jennet's. I remembered him almost the first time I saw him again. I think I always knew.

No, you didn't! How could you? It was Aldrich. Herod Aldrich. He took your father's house and his land, and he took me!

Frayne is silent, his hand working the teat of Boss, the little cow. A stream of creamy yellow milk shoots into the bucket, freezing almost as soon as it hits the scoured oak. He looks up at Hester, his blue eyes like ice in the darkness.

I'm so sorry, he says gently. You can't hurt me anymore.

It was dark and the windows of Herod Aldrich's gaudy brick house were blazing with lights when Hester reached it. She came like a shadow through the gap in the box hedge and up the brick steps to the side door to which she had once had a key.

There was a hallway with a tall case clock in the curve of the staircase, and above the stair she could see long, white, sober faces, the false portraits he had bought to give himself stature with his powerful friends. In the west parlor beyond, there were many candles burning and she could glimpse the silken skirts of women, the polished boots of fine gentlemen. Someone was playing Susanna's piano. Ah, she thought with secret pleasure, that will give Herod pain.

A servant went gliding down the hall with a tray at his shoulder. She knew him, it was Cato the slave, Phillis's husband. "Let me in, Cato," she cried, and banged on the door with both fists. But he did not seem to hear her.

Next Hester went round to the front door and the carriage entrance, a long, treacherous path through a small orchard of plum trees whose sharp, spiny boughs caught at her cloak. Once she fell and had to drag herself up, and the spiky shoots tore her hands and made them bleed. The front door was painted red like the bricks and it had a big brass knocker in the shape of a pineapple. Hester rapped with it loudly, and once more she pounded on the door with her fists. "Phillis!" she cried. "Cato! Let me in to your master! He owes me a debt!"

At last the door opened. There stood a man she had never seen before, a fine gentleman in a lavender silk frock coat with gold lace facings. "Please, sir," she said, "I must see Herod Aldrich. Is he at home?"

"Wait here," he said gruffly. Then he called over his shoulder. "Here, Aldrich! There's a beggar woman at the door wanting to see you! An old gypsy or some such. Ha, ha! I'll have her into the parlor, shall I, to tell us our fortunes?" Then he turned back to Hester and handed her a penny. "You're a bold baggage, I'll give you that. Go off now, and don't bother us again."

"I'm no beggar woman, sir. I must see Herod. He has a debt to me."

For as long as she could remember, Hester had resented her life and believed she could not be to blame for it. She could let go of John Frayne without much regret, as she could let go of any man. But she could not forget the five hundred dollars he had sent her, the money that Aldrich had burned in the fire. It was the price of her life, and he had bought it with a lie.

That she had chosen to trust him instead of Frayne, she did not consider. She did not remember her rapture when Herod gave her the key to the side door, how she had moved through the shadowy house touching the brocaded chairs and the marquetry tables and the heavy velvet door curtains as though she possessed them. "He owes me five hundred dollars, and I will have it," she told the dandified fellow, and tried to slip past him into the hall. "I will have justice," she said.

But he shoved her aside with a ringed hand. "Take yourself off, you impertinent hussy, before I call the law on you! You've had what you came for, and a penny is more than you're worth!"

He slammed the door and Hester stood there for a moment, listening to the laughter beyond her, where there were lights. She could not have said whether it was ten minutes or two hours later when she tramped around through the snow to the kitchen. This time it was Mrs. Harriet Fanning, the clerk from the mercantile store, who answered her knock. On special occasions like this, Hetty Fanning was entrusted by Aldrich with the supervision of all the arrangements; she was proud of this power, and she deluded herself that she might one day be mistress here, now that Miss Susanna was dead.

She tugged her ruffled cap straight, the pink ribbons dancing. "Oh, it's you, is it?" she said, peering jealously out into the darkness at Hester. "Well, and what do you want? We're busy here, we have no time for impudent sluts!"

"Let me in," Hester murmured. "I am cold. Let me sit by your fire. I must see your master, I must talk to him. But they have shut the door on me."

"And quite right, too. Go and tend your own house and whichever husband will have you, and do not trouble your betters again!"

So once more Hester is shut out, and the house has no more doors to knock upon. She trudges down the long path through the garden, and at the end of it, she turns to look back at the lighted house that seems to ride like a child's gaudy kite upon the darkness. The air is heavy and wet and cold and it smashes her, like Frayne's love, like Jacob's. I must go to the high meadow, she thinks. I must go where I can look out to the sea, where the sea-wind is.

The streets are empty, only the taverns still lighted. But lone women are not allowed into them, and besides, she has only the penny the fop at Herod's door thrust upon her.

Home. I must go home.

But she cannot remember where it might be, nor how she has come so far away from it, to this dark place where nobody knows her. There have been voyages and long journeys on foot and on horseback, hopeless travels that began years ago, long before she met Frayne on the hilltop. Her mother and the aunts—have they not travelled with her, looking over her shoulder, scoffing and scolding? From the day of her birth, perhaps even before it, she has beaten her young wings against that iron insistence, until now they are mere featherless appendages that flap and flap and will not lift her up.

*   *   *

Up one lane and down another Hester wanders, coming at last to the end of Green Street where the cooper's shop stands, and the little squat house with the great lightning-struck maple beside it. Someone she knows lives there, she is certain of it. She can scarcely think who it might be, but perhaps they will let her in.

When she knocks at the door of her own house, no one answers, and when she tries the latch, it is locked, like all the other doors of her life. This is my place, she thinks, recognizing it suddenly, as though she is blind and knows it only by the touch of her fingers.

My place, where they must let me in.

"Jacob," she cries, the name coming from some place in her mind she can no longer reach by will or by logic. "Timothy! Open the door! Let me in!"

But the boy has gone out early and has not yet come back, and Jacob is off in the woods, as he is every night and most days. He comes in only after she and Tim have eaten supper, to make certain she is safely in bed, and then to lock her in like a prisoner.

Tonight, though, not knowing when she might return from seeing Frayne, Hester has laid pieces of firewood in her side of the featherbed to make it sink down, and then pulled the quilt over it to fool Catcher, to make him believe she is safely asleep and locked in as always. But now her own trick has fallen like his net upon her, and the door is still locked tight.

"Jacob!" she cries again. "Let me come in, my dear!"

Suddenly she is drowning in love of him, of somebody, some memory of a hard, warm human body, some dream of one. Whose body it is does not matter, perhaps it has never mattered, never even existed. Her senses of time and place are washed away, and she calls to the dream again, by a different name this time.

"John! Let me come in to you! John!"

But no answer comes. If I climb up high, to the high ridge, she thinks, he will see me and know me. If I take off my bonnet so my hair blows free and the sun catches it. Then surely he will not resist me, he will know me and love me. Up. I must climb up.

*   *   *

It is important to die in a clean, high place. There is a ladder nailed to the trunk of the maple tree, and Hester drags herself up it, catching her gown and leaving a scrap of purplish-red behind on a branch, her fingers almost too cold to hold on till she reaches the hexagonal platform above. Timothy's treehouse is a stronghold from which she can see out very far to the west, where White Lady rises above the black shapes of the spruces and firs, above the pewter gleam of the lake. There is a fog rising, and the strange rumble of February thunder, the kind of winter tempest that rains ice if it breaks.

But Hester does not hear it. She is suddenly at peace and does not resent dying as much as the prospect of any more living. It is good to be cut free of the world, of the need to blame and be blamed.

She lies down to wait, her head pillowed on her arm and her body curled like a child's under the cloak. When the winter rain breaks against her, it is not cruel. Death touches her as delicately as snow, like her long dream of Frayne's fingertips, soothing the pain and the fear from her.

In the morning, Jacob will find her there in the treehouse, enclosed in a sheer jacket of ice under which she is young again and more perfect than he has ever imagined, and when his tears fall upon her, they, too, turn to ice.

A deep fog over the Bay of Spirits that long night, and the flicker of lightning from beyond White Lady. Aunt Hope has returned to her cabin and the Frenchman to his quilts in Zimmer's attic—or so he has told them. There are smugglers on the lakeshore again, they have not been stopped by the arrest of Topas Logan and the loss of Jacob's ox. You can see their torches break through the fog halfway up to the border, and hear the wolf-calls that follow them, wailing like men.

It is very late and the girl is still weaving. She has squandered almost a dozen of Frayne's candles, they are burning in every corner of the workroom, stuck in old saucers and jam pots and bits of broken crockery. She wants Hannah to see the color blue.

They are together tonight, and at peace with each other. In the far corner, the spinning wheel seems to turn of itself in the shadows, and the quilts on the walls are very bright. The hole in the ice is healed shut now, you can hardly make out where it was. If there is a storm tonight, it will be gone for good, but Jennet does not need to see it. She is like Frayne, she carries the map in her mind.

She has woven almost four yards since the drawing in. Not yet enough for a cloak, but enough to wind in a deep, rich cocoon round the cloth beam tomorrow. Where the candlelight strikes it, the blue turns dark green, like the spruce trees in Captain Sandy's grove. Like the forests of Maine she still wanders through in her sleep, as she did in her childhood. Until Frayne came to her, it was all that kept her from dying—the thought that, once dead, she might never again smell the fragrance of pine.

I missed you so, she says to Hannah, and lifts her foot from the treadle. The wheel ceases to spin in the shadows. The quilts whisper on the walls in the chimney-draft. Thank you for bringing John to me. For coming back to watch me weave.

She slides down from the bench and turns to find Frayne with her now, standing silent in the midst of the room. Who were you talking to? he says.

My mother.

Did you see her?

I don't need to. I hear her.

Like the Frenchman's fiddle?

Yes.

The weaving is fine, Jen. In the west, you could make a good living at it.

If anything happens to you?

What do you mean, happens?

If you go away with your wife and your son. If you leave me.

You shouldn't spy on me. If you'd asked, I'd have told you that Hester was here. It's all finished with her. I sent her back to Benet.

He puts a hand on Jennet's shoulder and feels the concentrated energy of her, the thing people call pride inside her. She is tensile, like a piece of fine wire, supple and hard at the same time.

It's what my mother always said, she tells him. If anything happens to me, you'll survive.

In the bright dance of light, she begins to undress him. Unlaces his shirt and pulls it over his head, unfastens his breeches. He is dressed like an ordinary farmer now, a leather jerkin over plain homespun. His gentleman's clothes await grander occasions, she has seen them laid out in one of the upstairs rooms, like a man's body to which the soul has not yet returned. As for the buckskins, the clothing of his western self, they seem to have melted into thin air.

Jennet has been cutting and sewing with Aunt Hope, but she still wears the old faded gown she had on when he met her. She waits while he takes it off for her, and the heavy quilted petticoats, too, and the shift.

I belong to you now, she says in her soft-rough voice. I don't mean like the treasures, like something you can steal or sell. More like an arm or a leg. Is there a word for that kind of owning each other?

Frayne smiles. Weaving?

Don't leave me for my own good, she tells him, her hands gripping his wrists as though she is drowning. If you run away, take me with you.

You make me proud, he says. You make me clean.

She has only her stockings left, and, bum-naked and freezing and half-ashamed in the brilliant candlelight, he kneels down to remove them. Puts his face in the precious hollow of her hipbone, his mouth moving across her, inside her, her hands clutching his hair. He has forgotten the light, the cold, the gun he has left in the kitchen. Forgotten himself.

On the bed, she says, like married people, and he tips her up into his arms and carries her to the crackling mattress of cornhusks.

I'll put out these candles, he says, remembering. It's too bright.

But she is already lost, she cannot let go of him. Her legs lock around him and he bends above her, all but broken, feeling her fingers at the base of his spine, walking back and forth across him like the light feet of a mouse in the snow. It is an exquisite pleasure she seems to know by some instinct will release him to her, make him leave the others behind, the living and the dead.

Hold still, she says. Don't go so fast.

You're smiling. I like to see you smile. I like the sounds you make.

If you're still talking, I can't hear you. Don't let go yet. I want it to last.

He laughs, unable to hold himself in her much longer unreleased. Is your mother still watching? What will she say, do you think?

She'll be happy. She is happy. Yes. Now.

His body is lost in her, all his geographies surrendered. If he still has a soul, it lives in her fingers, in the sharp crook of her elbow, in the slight, soft swell of her boyish breasts, in the fine blue veins that run like map-lines beneath the skin of her thigh. Together, they are solvent and whole.

They say, he whispers, his lips making the word-shapes on her shoulder, there is a river that heals all wounds. It is pure white, like snow or the blossoms of prairie-cotton. You are my white river. If I die, I will come back to wash my heart in you.

The girl lies very still in his arms beneath the quilts, letting his voice flow over her, not bothering to work for the words. They are inside her, they seem to come as much from her own body and mind as from Frayne's. Perhaps it is the nearness of her mother's bold spirit that leads her to keep nothing back from him tonight, to urge him to enter her from many doors and fill her, so that she cannot tell where she ends and he begins.

Give me a name in your other language, she says at last, when he lies drowsy and spent beside her. A name for the west.

Frayne lies thinking for a moment. Kanawin, he says. Will that suit you?

Kanawin. Did I say it right? What does it mean? And don't say mule!

It means Iceweaver, he tells her. Girl who weaves the ice.

She considers for a time. It's a good name, she says slowly. But I like Jennet better.

Yes, he says. So do I.

The storm is closer now, shafts of lightning coming down just beyond the spruce grove, on the face of the lake. If there is snow, there will be twice as much as usual. Thunder snow, they call it, heavy wet snow that breaks down trees and buries sinkholes and snares, hiding footpaths and roads and making the world seem newborn.

The thunder rumbles like Benet's empty barrels, the torches of smugglers and soldiers both lost in the fog. If anything moves in the garden, Frayne and Jennet, absorbed in their weaving, do not notice it. They know nothing of Hester, and they do not see the Frenchman, Leclerc, look in at the brightly-lit window and watch them, his tears making a veil of ice on his spectacles like the cataracts on old Gabriel's eyes.

Nor do they see until morning that someone has painted in bright blue letters on the side of the springhouse two simple words that can tear into pieces the painstaking weft that is Bay House.

Traytor! shouts the future from the wall of the present. Spy! echoes the past.

X
the map of true north

Papa, where is America? the man/child Frayne asks his father. Can you find it on maps?

Early next morning, while the others still sleep, John has struggled out through the deep new snow to milk the cow and gather the eggs, and has seen the words painted in an awkward scrawl on the wall of the springhouse, with the fearful imperative of an ignorance that cannot even spell its delusions.

Traytor!!! it screams at him. Spy!!!

Now he sits crosslegged on the reborn floor of the library, one of his father's old atlases open before him for comfort, the deep voice of Captain Sandy wrapping him in memory—which, as always, lives in the present tense.

Some people say you can find anything on a map, Jackie.

Then show me America, Papa.

All right. You see here? This green space? And here. Read what it says there.

The boy was taught his letters at three, but he is still shy of attempting this magic trick in front of his father. North. America. North America?

Yes. Alexander Frayne shifts his six feet five inches and three hundred fifty pounds in the library chair. For a moment his blue eyes—Frayne's eyes—glaze over, and he stares out the high windows at the northward sprawl of the lake. Then at last he takes a fresh sheet of paper from his desk drawer, dips his quill, and begins to draw. With a few quick lines and a circle, a stick-man emerges. Underneath it, he writes his son's name, *Jackie*.

It's me! cries the boy Frayne, delighted. A map of me!

Then his father's huge laugh roars out, echoing off the high walls of books on their careful shelves. Why is it you? Because it says so?

Well, no. But— Yes, I guess so. It says my name. It must be me.

He pushes the boy's finger down onto the stick-man. Has it a heart? Can you feel it pounding?

Of course not! It's not *really* me. I'm here.

Are you sure?

You're teasing, Pa. I'm sitting on your knee. Of course I'm here!

The broad hand strokes the boy's thick black cap of hair. And if I called you Frederick, say? Or Samuel? If I made you wear an old suit full of holes and serve Blunt in the kitchen and turn the meat on the spit and sleep with the black beetles, and called you nothing but Boy? Who would you be then?

Jackie thinks for a moment. I would be—me.

Would you, indeed? The same arms and legs? The same mind, with the same scanty furniture in it, that can't do its sums without counting its fingers?

The boy laughs. Yes, Pa.

And how if I write this instead? Alexander Frayne crosses out the boy's name and writes *Turtle* under the stick-man. Does it make you feel different?

Of course not. I'm not a turtle!

And this? He crosses out *Turtle* and writes *Tory*. Is it still a map of you?

Yes. No. The shape is a little like a boy, but it isn't me.

And this? The father writes *Traitor*. Is that you?

Of course not. I don't even know what it means.

Nor do I, Jack. So then. The map is only a scribble, and the words mean nothing. But now where is Jackie?

The boy giggles. I'm still here, Papa.

And where is America?

The four-year-old John Frayne runs to the library window. It's out there, Pa!

You're trying to fool me. I see trees and a lake. A few birds. Old Blunt puttering round in the garden, raking up leaves. I don't see America.

But what is it, if it isn't America?

It's a fairy tale, Jackie. A trick of the light.

Who owns it? Does King George? Do you, Pa? Does George Washington?

Anyone may claim it, but no one can own it. I claim you as my son, and I may corrupt you and bring you up badly, teach you nothing but curses and greed, keep you from all learning and conscience and religion. But if at last, after many stumblings, you discover yourself and are true to what you know, you will always confound me. You will come through in spite of me. This country—any country—will always be more than the petty pirates who stake claims upon her, as the bone of a poet, long dead and rotten, is still more than the dogs who chew on it. Look at the map again, Jackie. Read what it says there. Not America. The other word.

North, says the boy Frayne. He studies the map, puzzled. Where is true north, Pa? Is it a trick, too?

His father does not answer. Come with me, Jack, he says. Let's go out on the lake.

It is late autumn, almost the end of November, the quince bushes bare of all but a few saffron-colored leaves and the wild geese gone away to the south. They take a small boat, a fishing dory so light

the big man's weight nearly capsizes it. But Sandy Frayne is lithe
for his size and at ease in his body, and he handles the boat with
practiced skill. He rows out into the middle of the lake and then
ships the oars and lets the dory drift on the lake-tide.

Now then, Jackie. Put your hand over the side, into the water.
How does it feel?

Cold! The boy snatches his hand out. It is so cold it frightens him.

Feel again. What besides cold?

There is a strange thickness, a density that was not there in
summer. Within the liquid, ice is already inherent, demanding its
genesis. The water is very dark, every atom concentrated into this
great, inexorable transition. If you are caught in a boat during
freeze-up, when the molecules of water connect into crystals and
the crystals connect again into ice, the new element will reject you
as an irrelevance in the universe, it will freeze you in solid, unable
to move till the ice is thick enough to walk upon. So entrapped,
heedless fishermen have frozen to death, their oars useless, their
tiny boats crushed by the moment of process.

Feel how strong it is? says the father. There is north on the
map, like the boy in the picture. But beyond it, inside it, there is
absolute north. True and hard and unbreakable. A true definition.
Feel how it drags at you in the cold of the water, like a magnet
at a pin?

True north, the boy whispers. Am I unbreakable, Pa? Are you?

Sandy Frayne lifts him up and buries the small, cold hand inside
his own waistcoat to warm it. Everything living has a true north
inside it, Jackie, he says. Like a compass. When it seizes you and
drags you true with yourself, it can't be predicted and it can't be
resisted. Some do break from the force of it. The best, I think, do
not, but none can refuse to be tested, and my turn is coming, as
yours will. Can the lake resist freezing?

No, of course not.

Submission is what it demands, Jack. A trust in becoming. The
pure submission of water to the discipline of ice.

North, the boy murmurs.

Christ Jackie. Alexander Frayne buries his great shaggy head in the boy's small arms. Don't forget me. I love this lake, and this steel-colored sky. I leave them to you and your sons. Remember me. Remember the map of true north.

When he first saw the words painted on the wall of the spring-house, John Frayne knew for the first time how the girl had felt under the net. He sank down on the broken bench in the garden, unable to think or to act. At the times in his life when he has been least free—in his uncle's household in London, under the Spaniard's torture, at the end of Firewalker's rawhide leash—he has always conceived of freedom as a singular thing, an escape from connection. A man walking alone through a clean, unbetrayed place, or a thin stalk, a hollow reed in the water. Now the stalk has grown visible roots, it has human branches. If one of them snaps off and is lost, all the others will suffer. Freedom is Jennet. Tim. Gabriel. It is even the gentle Frenchman, Leclerc.

Half-blind in the brilliant new light, John stares at the writing on the springhouse, trying to reason who has done this. The broad printed strokes have been made with a paintbrush, in the same bright blue paint with which Dutch Schiller had been painting his Conestoga wagon at the smithy next door to Jacob's shop.

But it is not like Benet to do such a thing, and besides, he has had a dozen chances to take such petty vengeances and has always forborne. As for Aldrich, he need not vilify Frayne, he has only to sign a complaint for trespass to get him driven out as a squatter. And as the guilt-borne panic drains away from him, Frayne is certain the words have nothing to do with the massacre at Fort McKittrick, either, nor with the maps. Fear is usually greater than fact, and if the army were hunting him as a British spy, that little bulldog Sergeant Ferris would have had him in shackles by now. No, only his friends know his history and he trusts them completely; they will never betray him. Jennet, Gabe, the sweet-tempered Frenchman—they will never say a word out of turn.

So then. The words on the wall are no organized persecution, they are a stab in the dark, a blind, boyish taunt. Whoever wrote them has spelt the word "traytor," like the banner at the Young Men's Academy where the cadets drill every afternoon on the sidewalk. Boys of sixteen and eighteen are signing up as recruits now in droves, most of Zimmer's apprentices gone and the war fever mounting. Perhaps some of them have decided to punish the old Tory's son in order to prove themselves. Or perhaps it is Caleb and his friends, come spying out treasure, the pot calling the kettle black.

Frayne collects himself, moving past personalities, considering time, place, the compass points of geography. The message must have been painted after dark, sometime after the Frenchman left Bay House and before the storm broke, at near three in the morning. The cold has kept the blue paint from drying and the rain has made some of the letters weep and run down the wall. When he scrapes away the light, new snow at the foot of the springhouse, there are slobberings of blue paint there, spilled while the work was done.

Think, Jackie, don't assume, his father's voice cautions him. See with the eyes of snow, Saku, the Prophet advises.

Their voices have become one in Frayne's mind, and he turns to the east, where the pale sun is just breaking through the last of the snow clouds, to let it find his face. Takes up handfuls of clean white snow and holds it to his left breast, his forehead, his lips. E-hani. Walk with me, my two fathers. Make my mind white with wisdom.

Crouching down, he puts his face to the packed snow at the foot of the springhouse wall, where he has uncovered the spill of blue paint. Eye to eye with it, he can make out the recent impression of a bootheel, a hollow flooded with the heavy rain that fell before the new snow, and then quick-frozen to solid ice. On the other side of the paint blobs, there is the ice-shape of a narrow toe. Right foot, left foot. They are small feet, even smaller than Jennet's, planted not very far apart and the toes sunk much deeper in than the heel.

A boy, not tall enough for eighteen nor even for sixteen. He cannot spell; his mother cannot read or write and he has been thrown out of school for striking the master. He paints with the wide brush and the bucket of blue paint taken on the sly, when his neighbor wasn't looking. He has had to stand tiptoe to reach halfway up on the wall, to paint the hard words he has heard spoken all his life of his father, of his grandfather. Traitor. Spy. Tory. He has tried to shake them off, to deny their existence. He has taken a new father and loved him. But Frayne and his ghosts will not leave him alone, they come back and back, and this is his weapon against them—the most terrible words he can think of, a blindfold against any glimpse of forgiveness.

"Oh Tim." Frayne says it aloud, and watches his breath leave him in a word-shape that, after today, he may never claim back again. "My son."

In the Indian villages, nothing was done without ceremony. When a man went to meet his fortune, his true north, in war or in hunting or in trading with unknown tribes, he washed his body and painted it in the color of his hope. Black for the death of an enemy. Red for life. Blue for wealth and success. Yellow for victory. White for peace, for perfect healing.

Upstairs in the cold bedroom from which part of one wall is still missing, John Frayne strips naked and washes himself in a bucket of snow. On his chest he paints two zigzagging white lines with some of the whitewash they have used in the workroom, one for peace of the soul and the other for peace of the body. A fingertip of white on each eyelid, to make the vision clear. He dresses in the fine new clothes that make him look like his father, but he cannot pray anymore to his father's English god. Instead, he sings in his mind-voice the Prophet's medicine-prayer.

If my enemy is a bear, make me a hawk to fly from him. If he is a hawk, make me a fish to swim from him. If he is a fish, make me a

beaver to live with him in peace. If he will have no peace, make me a
rock, for rocks are broken only by the anger of gods.

When he is finished, he goes into the schoolroom where Jennet
keeps her own treasures and her few simple ornaments. A sort of
book lies there, what looks like an old diary of some kind, and he
folds a note into it, between the stitched pages of gnarled, old-
fashioned writing, where he thinks she must surely find it.

Wait for me, he writes with her thick, stolen pencil. Trust me.

Then, cloaked and hatted and wearing—absurdly—the moccasins he still refuses to surrender, he pads downstairs to the workroom. The girl is still sleeping, her hair swirled on the pillow and
one arm thrown up above her head, as though she is waving. He
bends over her and waits a moment, letting the damp warmth of
her breath mix with his own. Slipping his hand under the quilt,
he lays his fingers on her left breast, then on his own.

But he must do more, in case he should be wrong and can
never come back to her, in case more than an injured, angry boy
is accusing him.

The girl has left her sewing on the table overnight and there
are pins in it. Frayne takes one and drags its point across his wrist
where the vein is; when the heartblood comes, he squeezes out a
drop of it and touches Jennet's lips in her sleep, to leave her the
taste of him. It is how he married Tacha. It means he will find
her and walk with her through seven deaths, if she remains in the
world and he leaves it.

I will come to you in the grey afternoons, I will come courting,
and my voice in the air will be love.

"Frayne! John Frayne!"

Jennet plunges dangerously down the back stairs and through kitchen and passageway, her eyes wide and her mouth gaping open as it used to before she remembered what words were. Gabriel is at work under the boarded-up dome in the front hallway, repairing the wainscoting in the hope of discouraging rats and raccoons. At the sound of the girl's boots, he looks up and grins.

"Ah, Sparrow my dear, I'm glad you've come. I can manage the nailing well enough by feel, but I need another pair of hands to—"

She careens into him, almost knocking him over. "Where?" she cries, regressing to monosyllables.

"Slow down now." Gabe lays down his hammer. "Where's what?"

"John. Where John? Can't find!"

"Why, he's about the place somewhere, he must be."

"Bas. Tard," she says in her rough, grating voice, like a machine with a gear gone wrong. "Liar."

She slams into the library and out again, then runs up the main stair and kicks open the door of Frayne's room. Finds a bucket with some water in it. A wet flannel, half-frozen already. His old homespuns folded neatly in a pile on the floor, his flop-brimmed hat set on top of them. But the suit of gentleman's clothes that has been laid out here like a second self for more than a fortnight is gone. Only the high, cuffed riding boots are still there, as if he has just stepped out of them.

She goes into the schoolroom, but she does not even glance at Hannah's journal, does not see the note he has left her. She takes her father's broken sword from the nail where she has hung it, and slings it over her shoulder again. Then she rushes downstairs and puts on Hannah's old cloak and grabs Gabe by the arm, dragging him into the kitchen. "Gun," she says. "Where gun? Where sack?"

Frayne's rifle and pack are nowhere in sight, they are gone like the dress suit.

"Slow down, girl, I tell you!" The old man catches her frantic body in his arms and holds her hard, till at last she stops fighting and is still, her head drooping and her shoulders hunched. "Say what the trouble is. Clear as you can, so I can make out what you want."

She draws a deep breath to collect herself, then another. "Come-one-two. With-one-two. Me."

The snow has stopped now. There has been no wind and it has not drifted, but it is very deep, fifteen or eighteen inches at least, deep enough to have melted the ice underneath it. Where John has trodden it down on his way to the milking, it has made a treacherous packing of slush that is already refrozen, but they flounder through till they stand facing the wall of the springhouse.

"See?" the girl says.

"Nay, lass." Gabriel squints, shakes his head, squints harder. "I can't, you know. What is it?" He moves closer, till his nose is almost brushing the wall, and traces the shapes of the bright blue letters with his long forefinger, spelling out the words as he goes. "Traytor. Spy." When he has finished, he looks back at her. "So you think he's cleared out, then? Gone on the run?"

"Army?" she says, her eyes wide with fear.

"Nay. Army don't trifle with such-like."

"Where then?" Jennet's fists pound down on the wall. "Damn. His. Soul."

"Now, now, my dear. If he was taking out from you, would he have stopped to milk the cow and gather the eggs? Didn't you see them there, in the kitchen?"

This halts her, and she breathes in the cold air, seeking balance.

In her pocket, the three white stones rattle. "Fancy clothes," she says. "Gone. Horse. Gone."

"See there, that proves it!" Gabe is triumphant. "If a man's on the run, he don't need to dress like a gent, now does he?"

But Jennet has been too often abandoned, and there is no convincing her. "Damn him," she growls, her fists clenched. "God damn him." She would say the same if she had found Frayne dead.

Wild-eyed and furious, she rushes into the stable and snatches up the adze from its corner and begins to push her way through the deep snow of the garden, down toward the lake.

"Where you going, lass? All that rain, and the snow on the ice—there'll be rotten patches! You stay off it, you hear me?" But all Gabe can see is a huge blur of white that swallows Jennet's slight figure before he can stop her. "Sparrow!" he cries. "Come back here!"

But of course she cannot hear him. The old man plows blindly after her through the snow as far as the balsam grove, but there he catches his foot on a root and falls flat, helpless, snow in his mouth and eyes and ears, and the terrible truth of old age pegging him down like a snared rabbit. That he can no longer reach what needs rescuing. That he can only listen and wait.

From the face of the lake to the northeast, he can hear Jennet crying, "Annnnhhhh-ahhhhh," intermixed with the blows of the adze chopping down and down at the closed-up hole in the ice.

She is hacking at random, stumbling here and there and pawing out new spots from the deep snow, but no matter how hard she smashes down with the adze, it chips away only superficial shards. She is shut out, alone in a huge blankness in which even her senses desert her. Her eyes water in the cold and she can see only a few inches before her. The sharp scent of the pines is too far off to smell, and there is no wind to carry it to her. The only thing left to touch is the coldness of snow.

She does not hear Gabriel calling out to her from the fir grove.

She does not hear, either, the footsteps behind her, like the thick paws of a badger. Does not feel the air buckle in upon itself and the wind rise, knife-edged and unbroken as a wind in the desert, while Catcher Benet spreads the net that sifts down on her like sand.

There is no lust in him, she thinks, looking out through the ropes at Catcher's face. Not even the lust she had seen in Frayne's eyes when he first brought her to Bay House, that had made her sleep with the sword beside her—a lust for her spirit, for something that will save him.

Jacob Benet does not want to be saved, yet he does not *not* want it. He is an animal in winter sleep, the life in him sunk deep and silent, with a will of its own. There is a gulf between him and the world, and whenever sleep approaches him, his body struggles back from the edge of it, terrified of the endless fall, of the jolt of letting go.

He has been out all night in the storm, huddled under makeshift shelters and outcroppings of granite and the shells of old cabins. Near morning he made his way to the cave where the last of the girl's things were, with her scent still upon them. Without lighting the fire, he moved through the place looking for her, his fingers clawing at the ledges, at the few bunches of herbs that still hung there. Finding once more the ice-blue gown and the mended lace and the petticoat, he unwrapped them and laid them carefully about him, his hooded black eyes seeking them out now and then, as though they were candles in the cave.

Then, when the snow stopped at morning, Jacob went home and—seeing the scrap of her gown caught on the treehouse ladder—climbed up to find Hester frozen to death there, perfected by the new skin of ice around her. She had never before seemed so beautiful to him, so tender and needful and unselfish, and it did not seem possible to him that God was so cruel as to transform her only when it was too late. Surely she was *not* dead. Surely some drug, some spell, could still waken her.

You love me now, he said to her, pawing away the snow to kiss her forehead. I can see that you love me. I will give you a child now, as you wanted. I promise you. I promise.

He lay down beside her there in the high cold for a long time, and took her in his arms and held her against him. I will take you where the wild girl is, he whispered to her lifeless body. Surely she will do you some good.

And so Jacob Benet had lifted his wife up onto his back and carried her to the stoneboat he used to haul firewood and, wearing the old yoke of the drowned red ox on his own shoulders, he had dragged Hester up the wooded slopes to Jennet's cave.

Now I will bring her to you, he told his wife in the deep, hollow darkness, and he kissed her lips where the ice made them shine.

Don't fight, Jacob tells the girl Jennet when the net comes down over her. He pulls the sword from its belt on her shoulder and throws it away. It's no use fighting, he says, and stuffs his kerchief into her mouth to keep her from howling. After that, speech leaves him, as though he, too, were born mute.

When they reach the cave, his face is bleeding where her fingernails have clawed him and his hand where her teeth have sunk into it, but Jacob does not seem to feel it or resent it. Most of the way is uphill, along the rocky bank of the little stream, and the girl cannot walk in the deep snow with the net lashed tight around her. She falls again and again, her hands and face bleeding and her ribs bruised by rocks and tree stumps hidden under the snow. The last part of the way he carries her as he had carried Hester down from the treehouse, like a burdensome sack on his back. As they pass it, Jennet sees a kind of sledge outside the cave, made of barrel staves lashed together like an Indian travois, a strange contraption attached by a rope to an ox-yoke that lies beside it, though there is no ox in sight.

Her eyes observe it, but she is too spent and too cold to pay it much heed now. She is covered with snow that is turning to ice, her gown and petticoat soaked and the wet wool weighing three times as much as it should. The hood of the old cloak has fallen back and her hair is snow-crusted, tiny droplets of ice hanging from it around her face and neck.

Once inside, she lies in a sodden heap where he drops her, motionless and shaking with cold and anger and the knowledge that she is alone here, that Frayne will not come for her, that she dare not need him, that not even Hannah can help her. If she has become a new self, something truer and stronger than before, then this is its baptism.

Jacob, too, falls down exhausted in the doorway, but the girl is so still that he thinks he has killed her, and he gets up at last to see. When he turns her over, still trapped by the net, her red-brown eyes stare up at him, wide open. The blue silk gown and the lace and the embroidered petticoat and stays are laid out on the stone ledges of the cave, watching like revenants. He makes a fire and lights the candle stubs she has set here and there, but Jennet hunches away from them, wild in the shadows.

Benet will not have it though, he drags her into the light again. I want to see you, he says. That's all. He cuts loose the rawhide thongs from her feet and arms. Then he lifts the net from her.

Besides stealing, Jennet's best weapon has always been watching, studying faces and the movements of bodies and the language of eyes and hands. Catcher Benet's hands are thick and hard and might be cruel if he wished it, but even when she clawed him and bit him, he didn't use his fists on her. When he lifts away the net and gazes down at her, there is an odd look of amazement on his blunt features, the mortal wonder of a man who has gone out fishing and come back with a mermaid. He pulls the kerchief out of her mouth.

You can talk now, I've heard you. Talk to me. Help me.

The boy has taken his second-best gun, but Benet has a fine

old musket with him, the one his father used in the war—his treasure. Are you going to shoot me? she says.

No. He stares down at the gun as though he has almost forgotten it. Maybe him. When he comes for you. I don't care anymore, but the boy wants him dead.

Jacob glances away into the shadows, at something that lies there, a dark shape tied up in an old striped blanket. But the girl's eyes are only on him and she shakes her head in frustration.

Don't turn your face away. I can't hear you if I can't see your mouth move.

He turns back to her, obedient. When Frayne comes for you, I must kill him. I mean you no harm.

He won't come. He's run away.

I don't believe you. He's not the kind to run.

I know what I know. I don't lie. She shudders and moves a few inches nearer the fire, shaking the water from her hair. Drops strike the coals and hiss faintly, making small puffs of ash. Men always run away, she says. They say they want love, but they don't, or if they do they squander it. Mostly they just want to own things. If you love them, they feel rich and prideful, they strut and boast with their bodies. Have you ever seen the laugh rich men have around women?

You can't see laughing.

I can. How they throw back their heads and let their eyelids go almost shut, looking down at the world as though they were standing on somebody's bent back. How they never hurry, like a mill wheel just beginning to grind.

He is caught in some wheel, she thinks. Some subtle thing that drags him so slowly he has been caught all his life and not noticed till now. A delusion, a dream he took in like a fragment of bone in a mouthful of soup. All things come to him who waits. Hope for the best. Life, liberty, and the pursuit of happiness. Early to bed and early to rise makes a man healthy, wealthy, and wise. At nineteen, at thirty, he might have spat out the rubbish and been free and built a clean, simple life for himself. But not now. It is too late now.

Do you love her? she asks him. Do you love Hester? Did you ever?

You can't love what you don't know. You can't know women, they don't want it.

Of course we do. Don't be stupid.

He bends his head again, then lifts it. In the lochs in Scotland, it was said there were ancient sea monsters living, that now and then they came to the surface and looked around, trying to take in the world as it was now, trying to absorb everything in a blink, before they went under again. Jacob's movements are like that, his rhythm viscous and ancient, like the slow pouring of oil into water, his mouth opening now and then to suck in the cold present tense.

Why did you let that man take me? she asks him. That day on the lake, when Frayne first came home. You didn't want me yourself, but you turned your back and let them fuck me, as if I was nothing.

I thought you were mad. I didn't know you would mind.

Jesus Christ, do you think it doesn't hurt if you're mad? If I was a horse or a dog, you'd have stopped them.

He crouches, clutching his musket. I know better now, he says carefully. I am sorry.

The devil with sorry. Jennet feels an odd power over him, and a control of herself, of her new voice in the world, one that does not define itself by anyone. How long will you keep me here? she asks him.

Till Frayne comes.

And if he doesn't?

Put on the silk dress now, Benet tells her. Put on the cream-colored lace.

As she takes off the sodden homespun gown and the quilted petti-coat and the wet shift underneath, he sits hunched by the fire, watching with his ancient black eyes. When she is naked, shaking with cold, Jennet turns and makes him look at her.

There, she says. Is that what you wanted?

No! Ashamed, he puts his hands over his eyes to hide from her.

Look at me, damn you! Why else did you drag me here? She snatches up a burning stick from the fire. God damn you! I'm not nothing! If you don't look at me, I'll set you on fire!

Jacob takes away his hands from his face and for a moment the fire she holds dazzles him so that he thinks her whole body is burning. She is very fair, very slight, the buttocks cupped outward only vaguely, the long plane of her back so frail he is sure he can see firelight through her skin. Her breasts are not rich like Hester's, they are small and flat and boyish, the nipples rose-brown and hard in the cold, drooping faintly downward. Below them, her ribs are bruised and scraped raw and there is a smear of blood on her belly where a tree branch caught her.

He feels an ache that has nothing to do with desire. It is the sadness in her that moves him, a remnant of pain that will always live in her, like the healed-over nail holes in Frayne's hands, that makes her exist on a level Jacob Benet can glimpse but will never be able to reach. As a boy, he could not shoot deer for the table because of their watchful, sorrowing eyes, but his father made him go hungry until he had learned to kill without feeling, to kill feeling itself.

For God's sake, cover yourself, he says angrily, as he always did to Hester when the sight of her moved him. You look like a whore.

Indeed? Jennet sniffs, and her chin lifts a little. I've never seen one. What do whores look like, pray?

They sell their bodies! All women do!

You think Hester does. That's what you really mean.

He looks away, at the shape in the corner that is his wife's blanket-wrapped body, and the girl's eyes follow him there.

Well, *I'm* not for sale, she says, if that's what's bothering you. Go outside now. Get some snow in the kettle and put it on the fire for me so I can wash. I don't want to get blood on this gown.

*　　*　　*

While he is gone, Jennet goes to the shape in the corner, already certain of *what* she will find, but not of whom. John, she thinks. John Frayne. Did the net take you, too?

Hands shaking, she folds back the blanket, and relief drowns her for a moment. It is not Frayne, it is the woman she saw with him in the stable—the wife with two husbands. Pulling a quilt around her, the shivering girl kneels down beside Hester, fingertips touching her. Most of the ice is gone now, but it still lies in the hollows of the dead woman's eyes, in the cleft of her chin, in the curve at the base of her neck. There is no wound, no blood except where the trees in Herod's orchard scratched her hands.

Benet brings in the kettle of snow and the girl stares at him, cold and furious. Did you do this? she says, her hand on the musket.

He stares down at Hester's face. I—locked the door, that's all. I thought she was in her bed, I locked her in as I always did, and the boy, too. Only—

Damn you! Who made you her jailer instead of her husband?

I wanted to keep her, that's all. I thought— Great—great possibilities. Jacob stumbles, connects with the cave wall, almost falls in the fire. She wanted everything all at once, but it took too long. I believed. I trusted him. I'd have done anything.

Who? Who made you a catcher? Why?

Trust nothing but money, he said. Jacob staggers back again in a circle, like a gnat at a candle flame. King Herod. He said I must wed her. He gave me money to start up the shop with. Thirty shillings. He made me Catcher. It wants a steady man, he said. A foot up on the ladder. I loved the boy. I loved Tim.

Aldrich paid you? Look at me! I must see when you answer!

Jacob sinks down by the body. I began to love Hester. Only the whole town talked of us after, how I'd wed myself to some other man's whore, and I couldn't—I couldn't—love her whole after that. How could I? They laughed, the servants, the men at the inn. . . .

Dear Christ. And did you never wonder why Aldrich was so keen to get rid of her? Why he paid you to wed her?

Who? Aldrich? he mumbles.

Jennet is too quick for him, her mind leaping beyond him. They were lovers, she says. They must have been. Hester and Aldrich.

His blunt, stubby hands hover like mittened paws above his wife's body. Thirty shillings, he says softly. Trust nothing.

What have you done with John Frayne? The girl's words are blank and measured as always, but her thin body shakes with emotion. Have you killed him already?

She has picked up the musket. He is too near mad to be certain, but if his answer is yes, she will shoot him. It is one of the skills Hannah taught her, like weaving and the baking of bread.

No, he whispers. I locked the door, is all.

He stumbles into the fire, kicking up a shower of sparks, voiceless, his mind trying to grasp it. I saw Hester there in the bed, but outside there was another Hester. Pulling her cloak round her. Walking. Climbing the ladder. Perhaps there are two of everyone. More than two, that come and go without warning.

But can you not help her? he says at last. The ice. She's so cold.

Jennet lays down the musket. Benet is no danger now. Her eyes search him, trying to find what year he thinks it is, what century. She's dead, the girl says.

No! You can help her, I know you can! That's why I brought her. You must try!

I'm not a doctoring-woman, I'm a weaver.

I know. When I saw your hands move, I knew you would do me good somehow. You must help her now.

You can't weave the dead back together, she says softly. You have to let them go.

On the night of drawing in, Marius Leclerc had left Bay House just after eleven o'clock, as the thunder began to rumble in earnest. But he did not go home to Germantown as he told the three friends he meant to. He went to Schoolcraft's tavern and got drunk for the first time in his fifty-two years.

It was a long, low structure built in a hurry, of split logs set upright and chinked with mud that dried and fell out every summer and was seldom completely replaced. Someone had cut all but the topmost branches off a fir tree that grew in the yard, and two men were throwing knives at it by the light of an open fire.

The place had a broad porch with an overhanging roof that sagged in the middle, and under this a half-dozen more men and three boys, too full of liquor to feel cold, were passing a jug amongst them. Inside, a smoky fire burned in a hearth of crumbling, brownish bricks from which wisps of straw stuck out here and there. Four long plank tables with benches around them filled the shadowy room, and a tall, lank-haired girl with a swollen belly moved awkwardly back and forth from the serving bar—a blackened pine plank laid across two hogsheads—as she brought ale and whisky and rum punch and occasional plates of undercooked bacon and fried potatoes to the customers.

"Here, Nancy!" cried a big man in a long drover's coat. "Where's Caleb? Does he claim it? Or ain't you sure whose it is till you see the color of its hair?"

There was a general round of laughter, but the serving girl paid it no heed, only wiped the grease from her hands on her skirt and eased her girth between the crush of customers.

"If Caleb won't have it, best try Crazy Alvis," hooted a man with an eyepatch. "He'll have most anythin'. Won't you, Alvis, old fellow?"

Alvis Coy was the town simpleton, an innocent of near forty, thickset and cumbersome, who did odd jobs for Tucker School-craft. At the sound of his name, he gaped round the place, and when he caught sight of Leclerc in the doorway with Frayne's violin under his arm, the look of sober concentration Alvis customarily wore became one of wild delight.

"Fiddle!" he cried, pointing his finger at the Frenchman and stamping about and waving his arms. "Alvis dance!"

"He's right, by God!" cried the Eyepatch. He got up and walked over to Leclerc. "It *is* a fiddle! Say, ain't you the Frenchman from Zimmer's?"

"*Oui,* monsieur. But I— I only came in because—"

Marius could not say why he had come. He had meant to go home to his bed like a sensible creature, but he could not. Music filled his mind, and the precise movements of the bodies he had seen through the window as he watched over Jennet and Frayne. Theirs was nothing like the wild, bankrupt lovemaking he had witnessed between the soldiers and their women. It was still and complete, like the making of some beautiful object. Some simple, perfected form that was true and absolute.

All night the words Sparrow had said kept coming back and back to him. *Don't cut off any fingers, Marius. Let yourself be.* Perhaps, after all, I am not a fool, he thought. Perhaps I need not be like the soldiers, nor even like the foolish apprentices. Yes! Yes! I shall be as I am. I shall be whole.

Without realizing it, as the lake fog thickened, he had begun to walk toward the town, following no special path, dragging his lame foot like an old bear dragging a trap. When he saw the lights of Schoolcraft's tavern and heard singing, he thought at first he had stumbled upon a church holding mass.

"Get him a drink, Tuck!" somebody called to the landlord, and Leclerc blushed. "But I have no money with me."

"Never mind, Frenchie! You play us a tune and take a mug

or two of Kill-Devil on me! We'll have us a Federal Ball of our own!"

"That's right! Who's for a dance?" hollered one of the young boys just come in from the porch, and some of the rest followed him, stumbling and reeling with drink. "We're joining up with the brigade from Cayuna the day after tomorrow!"

"Avenge Fort McKittrick!" somebody hollered. "Hooray for the Stars and Stripes!"

"Yessir! Let's have us a dance!"

The inns in town were the territory of the Masons and the Federalist Club and the Philosophical Society—the nobs, the poor called them. But even had they been welcome in such high-toned places, laboring men would still have come out to Schoolcraft's because, in a world in which responsibility was heavy and even small things were often of deadly importance, nothing much mattered here, and nobody cared what they did. The floor was littered with slippery wads of tobacco juice spittle, the tables were soaked an inch deep in grease and spilt whisky and candle drippings, and the smell of unwashed bodies mixed with the strong perfume of whisky and rum and ale could almost make you drunk before you put a mug to your lips. You could throw knives, shoot bottles off the fireplace shelf, carve your name in the tabletops, pick fights for the fun of it. The jokes were broad, and the funniest joke of all was the unwitting stranger who stumbled into Tucker Schoolcraft's without knowing the rules of the game.

"Here, Frenchie, here's a mug for you!" With a wink at the others, the drover in the long coat steered Marius deeper into the room.

"Leave him be, Micah," said the girl Nancy. "Have some pity. He's a decent gentleman, he ain't used to Kill-Devil."

But the drover paid her no heed. "Drink deep, Napoleon! Down the hatch!" he cried.

"*Merci,* monsieur," Leclerc said out of habit. and they laughed at the words, not unkindly. Mercy. Mercy, monsewer.

Somebody put the simpleton Alvis up on one of the tables and he began to turn round and round with his arms outspread—his idea of dancing. Now and then he got dizzy and stepped off into thin air, and fell with a crash. But they laughed and picked him up and put him to turning again. They lighted more candles and gathered around Leclerc, a ring of drunken, grinning, half-shaven acolytes. He blinked, and somebody took off his glasses and threw them into the fire. He did not mind; if he could not see, it was easier not to think.

Somebody patted him on the shoulder. "Don't mind 'em, friend. It'd be a rare treat to hear a tune from that fiddle."

"But monsieur," Marius protested. "I cannot. You see? It has no strings."

Tucker Schoolcraft stepped out from behind his counter, a great lumbering hulk of a man with long grey hair tied back at his nape and an apron that didn't half stretch around him. He went to the mantel and took down an instrument far more properly called a fiddle than the fine old violin Frayne had found. The shape was boxy, the neck was awkwardly curved, and the wood thick and lifeless. But there were strings, and the bow was set and rosined.

"Damn peddler couldn't pay up his tab," said the innkeeper, "and I took his fiddle instead. But none of these monkeys around here can play it. Go on, Frenchman. Give us a tune, give us Kemp's Jig, now, that's a fine one!"

"Or Bobby Shaftoe!"

"No, no. Speed the Plough!"

Leclerc put the blackjack of punch to his lips and sipped at it gingerly. It made his tongue burn and he disliked the flavor, which was very sweet and cloying. He was used to potent cider and Zimmer's beer, but this was nothing like either of them.

"Don't sip like Aunt Tessie at tea, man! You'll never feel the good of it that way!"

Marius grinned sheepishly and drank it down in a single gulp, and the men cheered. There was a fierce burning in his chest and another even worse in his throat and the mask of his face. But he laughed aloud and stamped his foot on the floor. The girl Nancy brought him a dipper of cold water and he drained it, feeling her eyes on him. "You are kind, *ma chérie*," he murmured.

"I like them words," she said softly. "I like how they sound."

"Be a good fella now," they told him. "Give old Nan a nice kiss!"

The girl drew away from them. "Don't make him," she said. "Can't you see he's bashful? What's he want with the likes of me?"

But they pushed her towards Leclerc, her great belly almost bumping into him. He stared down at it, uncertain what to do, whether he was obliged to make it some reverence. Her eyes were blank and did not seem to see him, but Marius laid his fingertips gently on the swelling shape where the child lay inside her.

He had never done such a bold thing before, and by some instinct the men seemed to know it. They fell silent, and he could hear the girl's breathing, which was measured and low, a kind of wordless language that spoke to him. I am like you. I am not whole yet.

He took up her hand and bent very low over it, his lips brushing her knuckles. For a moment he let his hot cheek rest on the back of her hand, which was cool and oddly soft, though her fingers were calloused with work.

The girl Nancy stared down at the top of his head where the hair was thinnest, and something about it made her secretly glad, as though she had seen a fine branch of bittersweet in the woods, or heard a loon's cry on the lake in summer.

Leclerc's sober gentleness took the men by surprise. In spite of their teasing and their use of the girl, they were fond of her, and it made them glad to see her kindly treated. None of them sniggered, and several clapped him on the back or took his arm.

"Friend," one or two of them called him. "Fiddler," said another. "How do you say 'friend' where you come from? What's it like there in France? Is it anything like here?"

They stand Marius up on the bar counter and he begins to play—not the jigs and reels they all know, but old songs from his Norman childhood he thought he had long since forgotten.

Au clair de la lune, mon ami Pierrot,
Prête-moi ta plume pour écrire un mot
Ma chandelle est morte, je n'ai plus de feu
Ouvre-moi ta porte pour l'amour de Dieu.

More and more he plays, faster and faster, the simpleton Alvis stamping back and forth on the long table and the men dancing arm in arm with each other, making long lines and crossing, whirling each other around, crowing like roosters, laughing, falling down. Someone brings more rum and Leclerc drinks it and goes back to playing. *Il était une bergère. Sur le pont d'Avignon. C'est la mère Michel.* There is a noise of horses in the yard, but he scarcely notices it. They bring him whisky next, the kind Schoolcraft's is famous for, made in a still on the slope of Old Dog, and he drinks that, too, and goes on playing, happy and sweating, stamping his foot to the rhythm.

Then some men burst in, a young boy or two with them. There is a stink of burnt powder from their muskets and they are all winded, wild-eyed, some bleeding from slight wounds. "Bring us a jug!" one of them shouts, and the dancing stops.

Marius cannot make his eyes focus, they are too full of music, and besides, someone has taken his spectacles. Somebody pulls Alvis down off the table and he whimpers a little. Something clatters to the floor and one of the new men, a small fellow with a red knitted cap, kicks it into a corner. It is Frayne's precious violin, upon which Alvis has danced until its breast is shattered to slivers.

"What happened?" says a voice. "You look like the Devil was after you, Guido! Where's Royall and Cy? Where's old Farley?"

"Cy took one in the head. Army patrol got Royall and Farley, goddamn 'em." Caleb spits into the fire. "Put a bullet in Farley's leg, too. He was driving Vince Dale's old sledge and they seized all we was carrying."

"King Herod ain't going to like it," somebody mutters. "That's two shipments lost in just over a fortnight."

"Fuck Herod! He won't sit in jail for it. He just cops in the goddamn money, and lets us take the hindmost." Caleb downs a mug of ale and chases it with whisky. "Well, I'll get my own back, if I get my hands on the bastard who blabbed on us. Just you see if I don't."

"What cargo tonight?" asks Tucker, looking worried.

Caleb downs another whisky. "Lancasters," he growls.

The men are silent. Running rifles is treason, it means hanging, and they all know Royall and old Washington Farley, who farms a tree-choked patch on the slope of Lion's Tooth. In small groups of three or four, those who want nothing to do with the business clear out, until only the drunken recruits and a handful of the roughest-hewn remain. The young boy who came in with Caleb and his friends makes no move to go, only sits very still by the fire—a handsome, brown-haired little boy of nine or ten, with strange light-blue eyes that cannot be mistaken.

Ah, thinks the Frenchman, rubbing his eyes to clear them. His son, it must be. John Timothy Frayne.

"Didn't need nobody blabbing, Caleb," Schoolcraft says as Nancy refills the men's mugs. "If you ask me, you was damn fools to try making a run, after what happened to Topas but a fortnight ago."

Guido hunches over his hot rum, waiting the right moment. It is always his function to needle and prod and urge the others in deeper, but in a real fight, he is the first to cut and run. "Oh, somebody blabbed to the army, all right," he says, his voice like the stinging of a fly. "We know well enough who, don't we, Caleb?"

The two men with knives have come in and are throwing now at a picture of Jefferson somebody has tacked to the wall. "Aye," growls one of them, "that Tory bastard up at Bay House. I warrant he's been spyin' on us ever since he come back here."

"Feedin' his pa's grudge, most likely," says another. "God-damn traitor."

Guido stings again. "It was Frayne set the army onto us a fortnight back. Topas says so for sure, ain't that right, Tim?"

"Ask him yourself," says the boy, his voice sounding oddly like Benet's, turned inward, a hammer that pounds and pounds against his brain. He had not been able to face another night locked inside the cottage with his mother, and just before dusk he slipped away into the woods, where the torches were beckoning. When he fell in with the men, he knew them only as friends of Jacob's. He knows them better now.

Somebody has given Tim hot rum, but he doesn't drink it. He cradles the mug in his two hands, savoring the warmth, the smooth, animal hardness of the boiled leather blackjack. Beside him, the simpleton Alvis rocks himself back and forth by the fire and whimpers like a puppy.

"Where's your pa, Timothy?" Schoolcraft asks him. "He know you're out with these rounders?"

One of the knife-throwers laughs. "Which pa you mean, Tuck?"

"Go to hell." Tim picks up Jacob's second-best musket from where he has laid it, and stamps angrily out, into the lightning-haunted dark.

There is a crash and a squawk of the fiddle, and Marius tumbles off the bar counter onto the floor and lies still, feeling seasick. The men's talk reaches him in a jumble, creeping into his mind to lie dormant there. He stares foolishly up at the serving girl, Nancy. "*Pardon,* mademoiselle," he says. "What ship is this? To what place is it sailing?"

"Be still," she tells him, with a glance at the men. "Don't let them notice you. Be quiet."

But it is already too late. "Who the Devil's that?" Caleb Beck gets up and comes over to peer at Leclerc, shoving Nancy out of the way with his boot. "Ain't that the gimp Frenchman that goes back and forth to Frayne's place? Guido! Luther! Bring him over here."

"Ease up, Cab," says Tuck Schoolcraft. "He's a decent fella."

"Shut your trap!" barks Caleb. "Sit him down there. Give him another whisky."

They sit Marius down on a bench and Caleb stands beside him

and pulls his head back, till his own face is no more than an inch away. Leclerc can smell his sour breath and the anger that sweats out of him. "Listen here, Frenchie. You're in tight with that fellow Frayne, ain't you?"

"Look out!" cries Guido. "He'll spew in a minute!"

Leclerc gets up and stumbles to the door, but he doesn't reach it. Doubled up with pain and nausea, he crouches there in the corner and retches over and over, until he is empty and his ribs ache so that he thinks they will surely cave in with shame. Nan's arm is around him, her cool palm on his forehead.

But once more Caleb pushes her away. She doesn't go far, only stands in the shadows, her body braced against the wall. "You know Frayne or not?" Caleb demands.

"I— I— I do." Leclerc looks up at him, gasping for breath.

"And you know what's been going on there, at the house? You're friends?"

"Friends." Marius says the word, and his voice drifts away into nothing. The nausea has gone now, but he is still dizzy and confused, no longer sure where he is. "Yes. He is my friend," he says. "But, monsieur—"

Caleb helps him up and leads him back to the bench and sits down beside him. "Well, then. You'll be glad to know I'm a friend of his, too. Old friend. So's Guido here. And Eli, and Teague over there. And Luther, too."

"Oh, hell," says Guido with a snigger. "We been friends since the first day Frayne come back here. Ain't we, Cab? Out on the lake?"

He has struck the sore spot. If Caleb needed a reason for vengeance, it is his memory of failure with Jennet in front of the others, and even worse, of running away from the apparition that came at them swinging the ice-pole. Guido runs away, and Royall, and even Teague and Luther. But not Caleb.

"Last we seen Frayne," he says to the Frenchman, "he was lookin' out all that treasure his pa hid away for him up at the old house. Never heard if he found it, though."

Leclerc's eyes close. "He has indeed found a treasure." He is thinking of Sparrow, of her face when she saw the spinning wheel. It swims before his eyes, and certain of its features are like those of the girl Nancy. "Many treasures, but one great one," he says softly. "Worth far more than gold."

"I knew it!" Guido begins to dance around. "I told old man Aldrich I seen him dig up something big and heavy out there in the meadow! Under that rock, it was! I told you! Gold!"

"No, no, monsieur," Leclerc says with infinite patience, "You don't understand."

But they don't listen. Caleb's appetite for gold is as keen as his lust for women. "Frayne came here with money, too," he says. "Where'd he get it?"

"I cannot say. I—"

"Nobody comes by that much aboveboard. Somebody owns him, and he ain't King Herod's, I know that for a fact. So whose is he? Excise? Army?"

"British!" cries one of the recruits. "Them British spies are all the hell over!"

"He's a traitor, by God, just like his pa!"

The room is swirling around Leclerc, but he cannot keep silent. "No, no," he says. "Monsieur Jean would have nothing to do with any army! Since the newspaper. Four hundred. . . ." His voice drifts, grows distant. "Sparrow's brother. A nugget of pure gold. A god told me. Set up a loom." All John's stories seem to swirl in the Frenchman's head, but which are true and which are fables? The voyages of Odysseus or the cottonwood boat in the rivers to the westward? The spinning wheel in the attic or the ape with the eye of pure gold?

"Maps," Leclerc murmurs. "The maps."

"Maps?" Caleb catches this dangerous word and his eyes are like rifle-shot, small and round and leaden. "Aye, so that's how they got us! We had all our trails set out careful, and till Frayne come back here, they was safe as houses! Now all of a sudden them patrols're waiting for us behind every tree between here and the border, places nobody knows about but us! It all adds up, by Jesus! He's a surveyor, that's what Jacob said. So that's where his money come from! Frayne tracked us and made maps for the army, and made himself rich by selling our necks to a noose!"

The fact that patrols have been doubled for three months before John's return; that trodden paths are easy for anyone to spot in the winter, when the undergrowth is bare of leaves; that pure mathematics long ago dictated that they would one day be taken, with maps or without them; that they are small fish and no reward has ever been offered for their capture, nor ever will be; that no officer in his senses would pay more than a few shillings for any of them or all of them together, now that the embargo is about to end—none of this enters Caleb's head. Or if it does, his vanity discards it. Where proof is wanted, it can always be found, that is the first rule of justice.

The past is the present. All truth is invented. All falsehoods are true.

Besides, now that Catcher is gone, Caleb Beck is King Herod here, and Firewalker, and Napoleon. But he must prove himself by flexing the muscles of power. If he does not, he will not keep it long.

"I don't give a shit *who* Frayne's spied for!" cries Caleb. "A spy's a spy, ain't it?"

"They shoot spies, don't they?" says Guido, uncertain.

"*I* do, by God," says Caleb. "But I'll have his treasure first, and I'll teach him a lesson. And that wild bitch of his, too!"

"We're with you, Cab," mumbles the oldest recruit, who is barely sixteen.

"Down with tyrants," says another, and slumps down in a drunken heap before the fire. "We'll take him, all right."

"Take him?" Leclerc, confused, dizzy, sick, and ashamed, drags himself from the bench. "Take whom?"

"Napoleon," somebody says, and they all laugh. "We'll take old Boney! The Duke of Wellington. Lord Nelson. The fucking Prince of Wales!"

The room reels around Marius, the men's faces crack apart and spin away into the distance, to come flying back suddenly—noses, ears, eyes, lips, like projectiles fired from cannons. The last face is John Frayne's.

Leclerc turns to Nancy, his hands clutching her forearms. "What have I done?" he asks, desperate. "What have I told them?"

He falls and they lift him up by the arms and lug him into the corner where the smashed violin lies discarded. He remembers the sensation of being dragged so before—the way his head bobbed up and down and the painful curvature of his back, the terrible pull on his shoulder sockets. Where has he known it before? Ah, to be sure. After the Emperor's visit, when the orderlies dragged him to the dead cart.

Life is the print of the same hoof on different ground.

I desire my son to walk many days upon deep grass, over the four hills of living. I desire him to be content with the white light of many mornings. I breathe the south wind upon him for sweetness. I set his feet upon fire and turn him to the east wind for courage. I set his feet upon water and turn him to the west wind for mercy. I set his feet upon stone that the north wind may breathe truth upon his soul and make him free.

—*The Sacrament they call Turning the Child*. The Mind-Book of John Stephen Frayne, in the Moon of Ripe Strawberries, the year 18—

When he leaves Bay House, Frayne goes straight to the cooper's shop to look for the boy. He sees the marks of Jacob's stoneboat that cut a broad chasm in the deep snow, and the floundering bootprints of the one who has dragged it. The house door is open and he steps inside without knocking, not needing to be told, *they have all gone, it is finished here.* As though he is mapping it, he wanders from one small, cold room to another, parting door curtains, executing slight changes in the placement of chairs to make travel easier, to relieve the pressure of atmosphere. The personless rooms make him think of the compartmented pods of certain poisonous plants, each section containing a precise number of seeds which spill out measured doses of potential damage as the tough, fibrous walls that surround them are broken one after another, opening door after door after door of secret harm.

It is a roof and four walls and a chimney, but no ghosts will ever bother to haunt it; things have collected in the rooms, but they seem to have no connections one to another. The kitchen fire has gone out in the night and no one has kindled it. A bowl of milk with chunks of bread broken up in it stands on the table, the milk frozen around the edge into thick, bluish crystals of differing shapes. In the bedroom, the quilt has been turned back and three pieces of cordwood lie along one side of the feather tick, a fourth placed crosswise on the pillow, a wooden head on a wooden body.

John climbs up to the loft and finds the boy's pallet there, still made up in a corner, beside it his treasures: a hoop made of hickory splits and an ash stick for rolling it, a fragment of broken deer's antler, a homespun bag of marbles, a red-and-yellow top someone has whittled, a paper boat, a bronze-shelled turtle in a brownish glass bottle. Tacked to the slanting, unplastered boards overhead is a map, printed long ago in faded brown ink on crumbling paper worn out along its folds. To the right, a space marked *Ocean,* dotted here and there with small islands and continents pared away to show only a jagged shoreline. *England. Europe. Sweden. Russia. The Indies.* In the center a narrow strip pocked with tent shapes to represent trees and mountains, with dragon-tailed lakes and rivers that eat one another like avaricious snakes. *American States,* the map says, and beyond it, in the huge blank space that fills the left half of the page and wanders past it, past the tack in the wood and past the roof and past the dooryard and past the torches that sail like small boats against his private dark, the boy has traced in thick, greasy pencil a route to St. Louis and then to New Orleans, and has written there the words that are all he has ever known of his father.

John Stephen Frayne, it says. *West.*

Frayne touches the map and the colored top and the paper boat, and puts his lips to the holy piece of antler. Then he climbs down from the loft and the boy is suddenly there in the open door to the shopyard, with Benet's musket held to his shoulder and aimed straight at Frayne. His pale eyes are huge and liquid and for an instant he and John enter each other, diving into the sea of their mutual nescience. Who are you? If I once let the knowledge of you inside me, shall I ever be able to scour you out?

John Frayne's hands lift, his palms facing the boy, the scars of the nail holes puckered like burn marks and faded to a strange, textureless white, like the frozen milk in the bowl. He takes a single step forward and there is a sound like gears grinding, the drop of the hammer, the slight snap and flare of the spark. When Tim fires, the old gun makes the hollow, mushy noise of an ax in rotted wood, and Frayne feels the collision of air against his face and the bitter scorch of burnt powder in the bridge of his nose.

He staggers back a step and rights himself, and the musket ball smashes into the clock shelf behind him, the clock falling down with a dissonant chime. The recoil knocks Tim backwards, into the snowy dooryard beyond, but he picks himself up, rams home another ball, and raises the gun again.

It tracks upwards and to the left, Frayne says quietly, instructing him. He steps into the center of the room, where the boy can take aim at him from outside. You have to compensate. Keep the shot true.

What? Tim's head jerks up. What did you say?

Another step, an inch nearer. If you want to tame a wild dog, bear the skin of a dog on your body. Think the thoughts of a dog. Dream his dreams. If you want to hit me this near, he says to the boy, brace yourself on the wash-bench there and go down on one knee. Time yourself by my breathing. Then fire.

The hell with you!

Tim is thinking of summer, of Frayne's long body circling and diving in the dooryard, catching lightning bugs in a bottle made of cheap, cloudy glass. Me! cries the two-year-old Timothy, and John lifts him up, up, lets him soar through the humming June twilight, with the tiny lights all around him like ripe fruits on the tree of the dark and his father's laugh warm inside him. If you want to catch fireflies, don't attack them. Make a cup of your hands and wait for the light to fly into them. Light. Say it with me, son. Light.

Again the gritting of gears. The pendulum drop of the hammer. Frayne is utterly still.

If you're old enough to kill me, you're old enough to listen. You don't know me. You don't know who I am.

I know what you've done, it's the same thing!

No, you don't know. Besides, I've dragged that trap with me all my life, and it's too goddamn easy. Once in the west, when I was starving, I ate roasted mice. Did it make me a cat?

Why did you go? Why did you run out on us?

I didn't run. Your mother had a lover. She preferred him to me. She begged me to go, and I did as she asked me.

Liar!

Think. Does your mother love Jacob? Does she love you?

The boy's face turns aside for a moment, as though Frayne has struck him. Then he turns back and fires.

Again the snap and flare of the powder, the bitter taste that grates in the nose. The hollow noise that bends the air backwards and thumps it against John's ears. At the last second, Timothy jerks the barrel upward and the ball buries itself in the ceiling beams, sending down a rain of the dried onions and apples that hang there.

Frayne comes out into the yard where the boy lies—sprawled in the snow again from the recoil, struggling to reload the musket, pouring in powder and wrapping the ball in greased lint. Eyes peer out the window of the blacksmith shop.

John glances towards it. See there? Old Schiller wants his blue paint and his brush back. Now you're done tarring my springhouse wall with them. It was you, was it?

Yes, damn you, and I don't care! Tim scrubs at his eyes with his fist. I hate you! You set the army on Topas and the others, you're in their pay! If it wasn't for you, we'd still have Old Red!

He is sobbing now, half-choking on grief, and for a moment Frayne stands there dazed. Truth has spun in a circle and arrived at absurdity. His treason is not maps nor lies nor the massacre of innocents. It is the death of an ox.

I told no one about the smuggling, Tim, he says. The army was on them already. I'm in nobody's pay.

But the boy doesn't stop to reply, only fires. This time the ball dives into the breast of the fine new greatcoat and John feels a dull thump against his rib cage. Then a bright, searing pain in his left side, curving like a burning arm around him as the deflected ball plows a deep graze in his flesh. He lurches sideways, steadies himself against the wild-eyed mare Pewter with the Lancaster rifle still tied across her saddlebow.

Why don't you get your gun? Timothy gasps as he reloads the musket. Coward! Why don't you shoot me back? I want you to! Damn you, why don't you shoot back?

He is at the deep downward curve of his life when childhood still fights to survive in him, defending itself *in extremis* with bad language, bad company, guns, knives, anger, disregard. Now and then a man comes to life in his eyes—sober, innocent, clean-hearted, coming and going like a shadow.

Suddenly Frayne drops to his knees in the snow at the end of the loaded musket, the gaping mouth of the barrel smashed against the breast of his coat. Shoot me, he commands the boy. I'm worthless. I'm a liar and a villain.

No! I—

I ran out on you, didn't I? Go on. If you're out of shot, there's some on my saddle.

You— You're crazy! You're a spy and a traitor! You are!

Then execute me. Call it justice. Maybe it will be.

Yes. Tim stares at him, at the dark blood that is soaking through the fancy coat below the left sleeve. Yes. All right. He holds the musket with both hands and John can feel its pressure on his chest waver from moment to moment. Tim's small index finger on the trigger trembles so wildly that accident may at any moment remove the possibility of moral choice. This is true north, the inevitable moment of ice that must be submitted to, if they are to live in the world.

Suddenly there is a sound like the rattle of death in the boy's chest; he gasps for air, but there is no more air in the universe. He drops the musket and the powder flares, sending a ball into the wall of the cooper's shop; Timothy sits down hard in the snow, sobbing, taking in shallow, painful gulps of cold air with the north wind behind it.

What shall I do? he says. I don't know what to do. He is innocent now, all his toughness burned away into childhood. His arms are around Frayne's neck and his face is buried in the collar of the blood-soaked gentleman's coat. I shot you. Jesus, I shot you. Dada, help me. What do you want me to do?

*   *   *

Remember the North Star, Tim? Frayne whispers, lifting him up like the treasure from under the Ship Rock. Remember the time I rode you on my shoulder, and we skated all night in the dark?

XI
coming through

There is a moment in the weaving of a piece when the warp threads are all filled and the bed of the loom contains no more space for working. The treadle falls silent and the sheds cease to lift and drop, and the made-up fabric must be wound onto the cloth beam. If it is sound cloth with a true grain, the work will go on and more yards will be woven. But if the grain is drawn false, the threads too loose or the selvage edge ravelled, then the piece must be cut out and given up.

Coming through, her mother always called it, and so Jennet will remember that last night of her girlhood. The night of the Federal Ball. The night we came through.

All that day, she has been with the dead. She and Jacob have brought Hester's body to Aunt Hope's cabin to be laid out and tended, but now Benet has gone off somewhere, the stoneboat and the empty ox-yoke lying like the shed skin of a snake in the dooryard. "Go and look for the boy," Jennet told him, but he did not seem able to hear her. Jacob was no longer with her, he is no longer anywhere—not even with Tim.

With the old black doctress to help her, Jennet has washed Hester's body and scrubbed her soiled clothes with strong lye soap, as she did her own mother's. When the petticoats and the old gown and the worn shift have dried by the fire, the girl dresses the dead woman and smooths life from the limbs as Hannah showed her.

Throughout this labor, something in her seems suspended, as though she is unwilling to return to Bay House now that Frayne is gone. But it is not merely his disappearance that holds Jennet in abeyance. It is the truth that came to her in the cave, as she stood there, stripped bare before Jacob's antediluvian gaze. That no life is only a love story that ends well or badly or does not end at all. That with John Frayne or without him, she is a woman of honor and intelligence and tenderness, and she is only just learning how not to be always at the mercy of these dangerous qualities.

Now I can live, she thinks, and all day long she has been wondering upon what terms this new life must be claimed. Her long neutrality ended, Jennet requires continuance, the assurance of gardens in summer, of an earth she cannot be driven away from, once she has dug it and pulled out its weeds.

What she wants is Bay House. If Frayne is really gone for good, she must manage to keep it on her own terms. But how?

As it happens, there is another visitor at Aunt Hope's today, a most fortuitous visitor for Jennet's purposes. The slave woman Phillis, not responsible anymore for the fancy midnight supper at Aldrich's house tonight, has left it all to the others to manage and has come to drink rose-hip tea with the doctoring-woman.

"That old King Herod," Phillis crows, "he get his lickin' this night, that's for sure! Think he so smart, gonna sell me and Cato off! Guess we showed him, all right! Got us a fine new master now! Call him *Senator* Hargrave pretty soon."

As they sit by the fire, the cats prowl around them in twos and threes, sniffing the dead woman's body as they did Hannah's when she lay at this same hearth. Because they themselves have not brought it about, death in humans always disconcerts them;

they grow fearful and snappish and launch themselves without warning at the living women's ankles, claws out and ears laid back.

"Get away, cat, you spoil me this dress!" Phillis fusses. "Miz Hargrave, she give me this here." She holds up the skirt for Aunt Hope to feel. "Ain't that fine, now?"

"Hunh!" snorts the old doctress. "Too tight over your belly, girl. Ain't no good for that babe you got in you."

Phillis laughs. "You got any more tea, Miz Hope? I sure do fancy this rose-tea you got here."

Jennet does not bother to read what the others say, and only sips now and then at the tin mug of tea. She sits very still and prim on a bench by the fire, the dress of ice-blue silk smoothed carefully over her lap and the lace round her shoulders. She is waiting for something to end and something else to begin, for a path to open and claim her. The cats seem to feel a sympathy with this and they do not attack her as they do the other two women; the big striped tomcat called Joshua jumps up to the table beside her and rubs against her arm and trills in his secret cat language, deep in his silver-pink throat.

For the rest of her life, she will remember that warm, insistent, animal pressure that vibrates on her skin. Will recall in vivid detail that there were five butter biscuits left on the plate that afternoon, and the broken half of a sixth. That at the hour of dusk in which everything began to change, Aunt Hope's homespun skirt was the color of butternut shells, with a greyish-white thumbprint of biscuit dough dried on the belly.

The talk drones on, a low buzzing in the distance, but all of a sudden something reaches Jennet—a draft from the fire, an urgent glint from the eyes of one of the cats, the sharp edge of the slave woman's laughter. It snaps her to attention. What is changing? What chance is passing? The girl's head turns sharply, her eyes fixed on the self-satisfied mouth from which words are still coming.

"Wisht I had me that old piece of paper Mister Willie brought," Phillis says with a chuckle. "I'd fix that King Herod then, all right." She smacks her lips over one of the biscuits. Now there are only four. "Yes, ma'am, he be so poor then, old Catcher

Benet go out with his net and catch him up for the Poor Sale! Ha, ha!"

Paper. King. Net.

Jennet's head lifts. "Paper?"

Hope nudges the slave woman. "Say that word out for her again, girl. My lamb, she don't hear good."

Phillis giggles. "Paypur," she says in a condescending baby-voice, and Aunt Hope swats her, disgusted.

But Jennet has no time to be offended. She stands up abruptly and the Joshua-cat hisses and dives away to his corner. "What kind of paper?" she demands, looking down at Phillis. "What did it say?"

The slave woman shrugs. "How I know? Can't read no paper."

"Blast you. You were listening. Tell what you heard."

Jennet's eyes are cool and wild and dangerous. Phillis, looking up at her, pulls back a little. "Law paper. Mister Willie Slocum, that lawyer-man, he brought it back from Albany. Says that old spook-house at the lake ain't no more King Herod's than nothin'! Anybody claim it, if-an' they care to."

House. Lake. Claim. Anybody.

The girl's hands clasp together in a motion of prayer. "Me?"

"Sure enough you. Why, even me and Cato, we could claim it ourselfs and prove it up, if so be we was free folks, and earnt regular money." Phillis clicks her tongue and shakes her head, and her starched white cap crackles. "That ol' King Herod, he riding down for a fall, though, you mark my words. My new master, I heard him say so to my lady, as how Herod ain't half so rich as he thinks he is. Why, most all this country round here, all been took wrong from them Tory-folks."

"Hunh! Everybody knows that!" Aunt Hope boots a marmalade kitten halfway across the room. "Somebody take, somebody took from. Somebody got the chain on 'em, somebody else jerkin' it. When my old master died, they read me his testament. You free now, they said, so I gone out and walk me down the road—full of sass, you know, free and easy and breathin' in air that was mine by right. After while, though, there come up a rider alongside

me. What you doin' loose on a work day, Miss Nigger? he says.
I'm free, I says back, I got me a paper to prove it. Well, he looks
me up and he looks me down. I don't care for no paper, he says.
Paper don't mean nothin'. You don't look free to me. He turns
his horse on me and rides me into the ditch by the road, and
when he's done with usin' me, he gets up off me. I guess you
know now who's free and who ain't, he says."

Jennet's dark amber eyes watch like the cat's. "What did you
do to him?" she says. What. Do.

"Killt him, my lamb. Yes, I surely did. I dogged him four days
and I waited my time till I got him to himself and I stuck a corn
knife clean through him." Hope takes up a lump of cone sugar
and dunks it in her tea and sucks the sweetness down. "You got
to kill what wants killing, else the snakes own the world."

Phillis chuckles. "More than one way to kill a snake, Miss
Hope-honey. Yes, ma'am! You just wait till tonight! King Herod
go down, all right. I seen to that."

She reaches for another biscuit and the girl knocks it out of
her hand. "Damn you!" Jennet explodes. "I can't hear you with
food in your mouth. Tell how the land was took wrong from
the Tories!"

"I don't know! Wrong, that's all I hear. Not rightful." Pouting
and sour, the slave woman brushes crumbs from her lap. "Looky
there, now. You gone spoilt my clean apron, girl!"

In all Jennet's life, she has learned to do two things better than
any others: to weave and to steal. As a child, she would slip in
and out of her great-aunt's fine bedchamber and take a ring or a
pair of eardrops from her dressing table. For a time, she would
carry them about in her pocket, slipping her hand now and then
into the dark, warm place to visit them, learning the sensation of
richness, of fineness that came from the smooth metal, the odd
earth-warmth of the amber and emeralds and amethysts. She did
not need to possess them. When she had learned them, fed from

them, she would put them back again, so precisely that they were only seldom missed.

Now there is something more important to learn, something that may give her Bay House.

"Where is paper?" she says, reverting again to the old aborted sentences. She catches herself, takes a deep, restorative breath. "Where is this paper? Where does Herod keep it?"

Phillis shrugs. "How I know that? Mighta throwed it in the fire by this time."

But Jennet is not to be deflected. "You saw! Where put?" she demands, and begins to shake Phillis till her bones rattle.

"The piano room!" cries the slave woman. "The table he got there for writing on! Let go my arm, you gone break me!"

Jennet drops her like a sack of coals and snatches up Hannah's old cloak from the bench by the fire, wrapping it round her, pulling on a pair of Hope's mittens.

"Where you going, my lamb?" Aunt Hope's eyes are narrowed to slits in her burnt-paper countenance. "What you want with that paper? What you thinkin'? You tell Aunt Hope where you bound for!"

The girl glances back at the small, dark, smoky room and the prowling cats and the dead woman lying as though she is asleep. A phrase of Hannah's comes back to her. *A woman's light is a dark lantern that burneth underground.*

Aunt Hope tugs at her. "Tell me now, where you going to?"

"Up," Jennet says, and is gone in the gathering dark.

The Federal Ball has begun at last, the greatest event of the winter. By nine o'clock in the evening, all the candles are blazing in the assembly room above Tom Lashaway's inn, and the fiddle and the flute and the cello are playing Sellinger's Round beneath a huge cascade of red-white-and-blue bunting. The young country girls in their white muslin and homemade lace and the rawboned sons of farmers and small tradesmen move shyly, as though they do not recognize one another in these dress-up clothes, tracing the figures they have learned from the travelling dancing master, Mr. Kennicott, who stands proudly on the platform calling out to them now and then in a spirit of helpfulness. "To your left, Miss Eliza! Capital! Excellent! Now, then, Mr. Jefferson Edwards, a little less prancing and a little more dancing, if you please!"

In an ell near the punch bowl, Cyrus Shackleton, the new senator from Albany, lays out a pinch of snuff on his white glove and takes it delicately into one nostril at a time. He wears gold-buckled dancing slippers and a blue sateen coat faced with broad bands of silver Brussels lace, and all the while he talks politics, his small yellowish eyes take disdainful account of Herod Aldrich's dull brown frock coat and his ill-cut waistcoat of Quakerish grey. The old fellow has been of use for a time, thinks the elegant senator, but his power is waning along with his money. You have to know when to discard these big frogs in their puddles of horse-piss, and move on to bigger frogs and bigger puddles.

To discard the past because it is past, the old because they are old, the used because you have used them—that is how you make liberty serve you.

The air by the punch bowl is oily with cunning. Over Herod Aldrich's slightly bent head, his friends glance at each other like hangmen awaiting the daylight, consulting pocket watches and the nearness of wives and acquaintances, making sure of their own reputations before they proceed. It has all been agreed between them; Judge Phillotson gives a slight nod of permission, and Bartram Hargrave consults a few notes he has made from what Phillis has told him, the catalogue of King Herod's sins.

"My dear Aldrich," Shackleton begins, "you really must see sense in this business of the old Frayne property. Nobody in Washington City gives a fart who's a returned Tory and who's not anymore." He pulls the lace handkerchief from his sleeve and sneezes into it with the greatest delicacy. "You must sell him the place and be done with it."

Herod Aldrich looks from one complacent, well-fed face to another, stupefied and furious. "Give Bay House back to John Frayne? But you cannot be serious! The land is mine and the house is mine, and I shall keep them!"

Hargrave smiles and lays a hand on the storekeeper's shoulder. "Indeed, sir, I think you have no choice in the matter."

With Herod Aldrich out of his way for good and the vote not split between them, a seat in the Senate will be Hargrave's for the taking, and once his power is consolidated with lucrative favors, it is unlikely he will ever be turned out. The House of Cronies, the British lords call it, and they are not far from wrong.

And a man with the money this Frayne is said to possess may be useful, if he is indebted for just the right favors. "We do not say you need *give* your property away, old fellow," Bartram Hargrave continues, adding a soft sleeve of kindness to his delivery. "Only sell it to him for a fair price, before the—er—state of your affairs becomes known."

"Affairs?" Aldrich's head jerks sharply. "What affairs? I have nothing to hide."

"Come now, Herod." Judge Phillotson draws a step closer. "We are not fools, man. We hear a new rumor about you every day, and if these land titles are seriously disputed— Why, you could lose everything."

And so could they all. They have all bought up Tory seizures that will be called into question if Aldrich's vast holdings are found illegal. "No, no. You must sell John Frayne the bit of land he wants and consider it the price of salvaging your other holdings. It's a small enough thing, after all." The judge pauses, bites his lip. "And then—"

"What do you know of my titles?" Herod snaps. "Who says they are disputed? Who told you? Will Slocum? Mrs. Fanning? What spy has been telling you lies?"

"Why— Why, no one needed to tell us anything! You're forever having surveys made and paying off contested claims! It must have you near bankrupt, sir, how could it not?"

Phillotson glances at Hargrave and Shackleton, and then at the newspaper editor, Zadoc Beale, who has joined them. "And once Frayne's claim is settled, Herod, you really must agree to give up all ambitions in politics."

Bartram Hargrave looks sober. "The land claims, I'm afraid, are not the only rumors that are current about you, Mr. Aldrich."

Shackleton takes out a silver toothpick and picks at a fragment of honeyed walnut that is stuck on his tooth. "If you do not forswear public life, sir," he says in his bored, lazy voice, "you will surely be published an adulterer and a villain, and utterly ruined."

Herod is dumbfounded. "Published? Who will publish me?"

"Why, I will," says Zadoc Beale with a smile.

"You! But I brought you here, sir! I gave you a house at half-rent, and a printing office! I sponsored your son at his baptism! You owe me a duty! Have I not been your benefactor and your friend?"

Friend. Duty. If he means to save himself, Aldrich has used the wrong words.

Beale glances at the others, and the look is tossed back and forth amongst them. *The game is beyond him,* it says. All the rest is an irritating irrelevance. Madmen, lunatics, debauchers may come to power and keep it forever, so long as the game has been properly played. *He is no longer a thing we can use,* Bartram Hargrave's look tells them. *Bring him down,* say Judge Phillotson's eyes.

Until the ball began, Herod Aldrich had had no reason to suspect that such an ambush was being readied for him. Dinner last night had gone well enough—oyster pie, smoked pike, calf's head, roast wild duck with cranberry chutney, Dutch cabbage and gingered carrots, and a cream almond pudding to finish. The ladies had adjourned to the drawing room for a table of whist, while the men lounged over brandy and segars in the dining room, There was a knock at the door, some old gypsy woman looking in for a hand-out. But Herod scarcely heeded the business. Hargrave's wife Celia had begun to play upon Susanna's pianoforte, one of the stylish new parlor songs that were all the fashion now. It troubled Aldrich deeply, he despised such music, all those pining gentlemen and fainting damsels. He had felt certain the piano would refuse them for his daughter's sake. But it did not, and that, too, troubled him.

As was his custom, he had walked the whole house after all his guests and the servants had gone to bed, taking his candle and stopping under each of the portraits in the stairway to study the faces of the nameless forebears he had purchased by lot. One by one, he had begun to reinvent them—a woman with a chalk-white bosom and a scowl like a stormcloud, an old man with a bagwig and a face like suet pudding. My aunt Russell, ma'am, he had told Mrs. Hargrave. Five thousand a year and a great estate outside Hartford. My great-grandfather's brother. My uncle Nathaniel. My wife's Boston cousin, Mrs. Emily Smails, a great lady.

The portraits exacted no tribute and they played no games of shifting influence. They kept their distance and served their pur-pose, the button eyes flat and dead behind a veil of crazed varnish. Their reputations were spotless, their influence vast and mysterious, their wealth beyond imagination. The plants and the piano might accuse him, but these bland faces supported Herod Aldrich in everything and their wisdom was unfailing. "Need I ask these fool guests of mine, these tame herd-dogs, what to do about Frayne?" he had inquired of Uncle Nathaniel's portrait. "No, sir! Thank you, no, sir! I need not!"

But Aldrich had only just gone satisfied to bed when Cato came with a candle and roused him. "Gentlemen at the door, sir. Looking somewhat discomposed, Mr. Herod. 'Fraid you best come."

He had found them waiting in the hall—Caleb Beck, that gadfly Guido Hubbard, and another they called Teague. Chiming in like three badly-set clocks, they told him the story of that night's run to the border. How the soldiers had fired warning shots at the sledge driving headlong over the frozen lake and Cy Waterston had taken a musket ball in his temple. How Royall and old Wash Farley were taken to prison and likely to hang.

At first, Aldrich could not take it in. He blinked and closed his eyes for a moment, adjusting his focus until the wheels of self-interest began to turn and the gears to click and grind again by long habit.

"Well then," he told the men, "you must sort the business out for yourselves. It is no concern of mine. *I* am no borderer."

Guido sniggered and Caleb rubbed his sleeve across his mouth. "They're your trade goods, sir," he insisted. "Doxy brings 'em in on your wagons."

"Aye," said Teague. "If it wasn't for you, we'd never have done more than trade a little moonshine and a few hundred-weight of potash. Call it your concern or not, you get your share of the profit, don't you, just like Jacob for them barrels of his? Better price than you could sell them Pennsylvania rifles for, legal, that's for sure. And we take all the risks."

The storekeeper straightened his back and his face grew flushed. "I *do* sell my goods legally, sir! I sell them to *you* on fair terms of credit."

"Oh aye," Teague snarled. "Knowing we'll pay double once we've got 'em across for you."

The gears clicked and the wheels spun faster. Aldrich glanced up at the portraits for strength. "Where you come by the money to pay for my goods is your own concern, and so is what you do with the merchandise once you have got it. That is business, Mr. Teague, it is the way of things in the marketplace, and my price must reflect it. Supply and demand. If you choose to risk the law's retribution, you can scarcely expect me to share it."

The smugglers looked from one to the other. *My men,* he had always called them. *My good fellows.* Teague and Guido stared down at their boots, and Caleb's eyes grew piggy and blank. When a man has been used and cannot deceive himself otherwise, he must either batter himself down for a fool or take it out on someone else.

But they dared not aim so high as King Herod. Not so long as there was another target to hand.

"We ain't come begging you, sir," said Caleb dully. "We hold Frayne to account for what happened to Cy and the others."

"Aye, it's him told the army on us," cried Guido. "You must help us to fix him!"

"Keep your voice down!" Aldrich felt cold, and pulled his dressing gown closer around him.

"Only give us your say-so to drive him off that place of yours, like the squatter he is," said Caleb. "That's all we want, is to do things legal. That way, if he fights us, we've the law on our own side. We been watching him long enough, and it's time we done something."

Herod's blank eyes brightened. "And what have you seen in your watching?"

"Oh, there's treasure, all right." Guido jittered from one foot to the other. It was what Aldrich wanted to hear, so he said it again, embroidering freely. "Gold, by God. He poured it out on the ground and I seen it glitter!"

Teague was silent and angry and said nothing. He had already decided he would not follow Caleb's lead much longer, but this was not the time to say so. Let him fall on his face, and there would be power going begging. Then move, and step into the breach.

"The land and house are mine," Aldrich was telling them. "I

have clear title to all that is found there of value. If there is treasure, it's mine, too." His cheeks were flushed and there was a bead of sweat on his forehead.

The men looked at each other again. A deal must be struck now, otherwise they would see no profit from all this business of Frayne's downfall.

"Well, sir," said Caleb tentatively. "If we was to go in and get that Tory gold for you, and drive Frayne and that woman of his out for good and all—"

Herod began to see the solution to his troubles with John Frayne, even to his dwindling Philadelphia bank accounts. If what these men said was true and he used them skillfully, it could all be done at arm's length, like the smuggling, like the marriage he had arranged for Hester. Nothing need touch him. Nothing ever had.

"Whatever the treasure may be," he told them, "I will give you a third of it to share amongst you. That is fair reward, is it not? Indeed, my good fellows, I cannot do better."

In the shadows above the staircase, the portraits seemed to smile. Herod went into the parlor and bent over his desk for a moment, writing out a few words on the back of a bill-of-sale for salt herring. Then he returned to the hallway and handed the paper to Caleb.

To Whom It May Concern. Be it known that I, Herod Buchan Aldrich, Legal Proprietor of the Patent of Talbot County, do Depute unto the Bearers in the Absence of other Legal Authority, the Right and Duty of Carrying Out an Eviction upon the Persons and Property of any now dwelling unlawfully and without Lease or License upon or within the Parcel called Bay House, Borough of Lake Paschal, New Forge, York State, Made this Twenty-First Day of February, 1809.

"Supposing he fights back and takes after us," said Caleb, "and supposing we kill him?"

"You do not understand these little matters of business," Aldrich said, with a kindly hand on Guido's shoulder. "That is none of my concern."

★   ★   ★

It is growing late now, and the Federal Ball is reaching the high point of excitement. *"Drummond Castle!"* Mr. Kennicott calls out to the fiddler, as one set of dancers makes their reverences and leaves the floor to the next. Will Slocum, who has been flirting full-tilt with the elegant Celia Hargrave, leaves her to a young officer of the Cayuna regiment and retires, hot and exhausted, in the direction of the punch bowl, where the plot against Herod Aldrich is rising to a frenzy of its own.

"Come now, sir," Will hears old Horatio Phillotson say, "We've been told about some of your private doings, don't think we haven't! You wouldn't want them all in print, I think? All published in Mr. Beale's paper to be read in Cayuna and Albany and Philadelphia?"

"My personal life, sir, is without blemish!" Aldrich sets down his cut-glass cup of punch so near to the edge of the table that it totters and smashes to slivers of ice on the polished oak floor. "I am a father to all these people here, I am much loved by them as a moral example! I defy you, Phillotson, I defy you all to—"

"Do you, indeed?" Hargrave's eyes glitter like the glass. "A man who has committed adultery? I forbear to mention the lady's name—especially now she is dead—but we all know of it."

"Dead?" Aldrich staggers, supporting himself on the table. "Who is dead? But you cannot mean Hester is . . ."

Again the damning glance is exchanged. He has just admitted to the first of his sins. Beale makes a note in his pocket-book. *Down.*

"Did you not know?" Hargrave cannot help feeling a little sorry for the old boy. "Frozen to death in the storm. Her—er—husband came to arrange for her burial with Reverend Mitchell just as he and his lady were leaving to come here, he told me of it himself. Jacob Benet—is that the fellow's name?"

"Dead? She is . . ."

There is some barrier between Herod and the rest of the room. It muffles the music and the sounds of the dancers' feet, and makes the candlelight withdraw into a huge distance. Heat and cold do not reach him. The positions of things are all wrong, the pieces of his own body in all the wrong places. When he moves his hand, his feet take a step instead.

Cyrus Shackleton feels almost sorry for him. Glancing over at Hargrave, he selects a bunch of black grapes from the *épergne* in the center of the table and adjusts the pleated frill on his cuff. "Stap me, Bart, but I think we may leave tumbling the ladies to the preachers to punish. None among us is lily-white in that regard, eh?"

Hargrave, who is well known for his incessant *amours,* flushes scarlet. His own power is being tested against Shackleton's, and Herod Aldrich is an irrelevant abstraction now, a blunt weapon. Until now, Hargrave has not quite realized his true opponent, but once it comes home to him, fear makes him even more determined. "And shall we leave smuggling aside, too?" he snaps at the Senator. "I received word today from the militia at Cayuna that a party of borderers was apprehended with three crates of Lancaster rifles last night. The same rifles that came in on your freight wagon last Thursday, Mr. Aldrich, the crates signed with your clerk's receipt mark." He sneers in Shackleton's direction. "Lily-white, sir? It is hardly a term *I* should use!" A point scored, he turns full-force upon the dazed storekeeper. "No wonder you are set against war with the British, it would put paid to your smuggling. Well, Mr. Aldrich? Do you deny it?"

Herod stammers. "I have no—need to—to— The rifles were sold. I— I have bills-of-sale for them! All perfectly legal. Perfectly—"

He is adrift now, the tide of battle pulling him from one to the other of his tormentors, then tossing him back again. He turns in a circle, his feet shuffling in an odd little dance and his white hands flapping like birds' wings. His face has a strange, bruised look and his eyes do not seem to focus except on the fruit in

Shackleton's hand, on the grape pips that are now and then spat onto the floor.

Will Slocum cannot bear it. "Come, sir," he says. "Let me see you home, you are not well."

But Herod's fist strikes out suddenly, as though it is worked by wires, and the young man falls almost under the feet of the dancers.

"You!" Aldrich says, staring down at him. "You betrayed me! You are all traitors and spies. Hester is not dead, you are liars! Get out! Get out of my sight!"

His voice is low and hoarse and when he looks out across the room, he is certain he sees a great net stretched above him, almost invisible, fine as a spider's web and glittering warmly, like gold. All his knotted fabric of greed and possession is still spun, like Benet's, from the innocent faith that life is a ladder of infinite possibility. That whatever ruin you wreak to achieve, it will not count against you in the tallyings of God.

Herod shakes his head like an animal, and rubs his eyes with his fists to erase the huge and growing net, but it will not disappear. When he moves, it moves with him.

Will Slocum picks himself up from the floor. "I have not betrayed you, sir," he says quietly, "whatever these jackals have told you. I spoke to Mr. Frayne this morning as I told you I meant to, but to no one else, I swear it. Come, now, let me help you from the room."

But Aldrich no longer seems to see him. "They— They will nominate me for the Senate," he says vaguely. "The Party will not overlook me. And after that, I shall seek an ambassador's post. Perhaps even stand for President. My people know my value to them and they will reward me. I am loved hereabouts. I am. . . ."

Judge Phillotson glances at the others and gives his head a slight shake. The fellow is lost. Perhaps this man Frayne will at least be a sensible chap, a little more tractable, a little more free with his cash and cynical enough to take some pleasure in his sins.

"I don't doubt your people love you, Herod," the judge says, "but they don't put up the primary candidates. *We* do."

"Whole thing's a myth, my dear fellow." Shackleton nibbles on a piece of shortbread, feeling oddly sorry. "Nature of democracy. Will of the people. Like the virgin birth, or the three wise men, ain't it? I ask you, sir, three men together, and all three of 'em wise?"

Herod Aldrich will not permit the young lawyer to help him home. Shaking off Slocum's offers of aid, he stumbles from the inn and enters the grateful silence of his own snowy park. The gaudy brick house has always been a beacon for him, something to move towards, but now he loses his way on the path between the plum trees, not certain whether he is coming home or going away, whether the place is his own or whether he is only a squatter there.

When he enters the hall, someone is playing Susanna's piano.

It is strange music, unworldly, the rhythm slightly displaced and the notes now and then slurred a half-tone up or down, slipping into modality. Susanna is playing, Aldrich thinks, and stands still with his hand on the door to the west parlor, certain that if he opens it, the crowded dead will come pouring out and overwhelm him.

But John Frayne knows well enough who is playing. He hears her as he runs like a shadow through the cold white dark of King Herod's garden, and draws a deep breath for the first time since he returned with his son to Bay House and discovered her gone. Jennet plays as she speaks and as she dances and as she makes love, each note picked carefully out of her memory and placed precisely beside all the others, rising without warning into passionate and fortuitous art, like the making of blue in the air.

My lamb, she gone after that land paper, Aunt Hope had told him, trotting out breathless to meet him, with Gabriel hard at her heels. Ought to skin me that fool girl, that Phillis! The west parlor, she say. The piano room.

He skirts round the house to the west, and the sound of the

music grows louder. The French windows are open to the cold air, the white lawn curtains drifting out as though it is summer, and the forest of orange trees and geraniums and roses shivering in their pots.

Jennet is there, Frayne can see her. She has pushed the mahogany bench back, away from the great black instrument, so that her body balances on the edge of the needlepoint cushion, her forearms extended and her fingertips flat on the keys. Music reaches her. Not the sound—which is little more than an urgent vibration against her inner ear—but the beauty of making it, of making anything. She touches the keys precisely, very lightly, her face rapt with abstract devotion. It is like her to do such a thing, to come stealing and stay to play the piano; John has never seen her so elegant, so much in control of herself, so regardless of harm.

He is about to step into the room, but it is already too late to snatch her away with him to the safe dark garden. The door to the inner hall opens and Aldrich is there, he is in the room with her now, his body seeming to sway as the candlelight flickers.

Susanna? he says. Dearest girl. Are you come back to me?

Do the dead hear? Jennet Sparrow does not, and she does not look up. Herod rubs his eyes with his fists, trying to see her more clearly, trying to erase the cruel, glittering net that has followed him here from the ballroom, through the darkness of the garden and into the hallway. It is here now, hovering over him, over the girl at the keyboard. But Susanna will free him, she will lift it from him.

Yes, surely his daughter is here again, she has come back to him. The fine silk of the handsome gown that rustles faintly when she moves her hands along the keys. The living skin, pale cream where the low-cut gown bares it, with a light touch of shadow at the base of her ear, along the curve of her cheek, in the scarcely-glimpsed cleft of her boyish breasts. The living hair that glints red in the light of the candles. The living hands that touch and do not touch, that hold sound in a glass cup as though she might spill it.

My dear, he whispers.

And then, as Frayne watches, the door opens again. She's dead, says Benet's heavy voice, and Aldrich gives a great groan.

Susannaaaaaaaaaaaaaaa.

Jacob glances at Jennet and something in her graceful distance makes him angrier at Herod. Catcher jerks him around, and his eyes cut like a knife. Fool! he cries. It's Hester I mean! *Hester* is dead! See! We have killed her, between us. She is dead!

The mathematical sequences of the music reach a fermata, and the dull grumble of Jacob's voice enters Jennet in some deep place, so that she glances up at last and sees them. The men the gun the dead woman. For Hester is here, too, a terrible rider on her husband's back, her arms tied around his neck and the weight of her death like stones piled on top of him and smashing him down. She is the net now. Perhaps she has always been.

Jacob's musket is slung over his shoulder and it slams into him at every step, but his endurance is endless. He is ground into pure bone, into rock.

Look at her, he tells Herod. She is beautiful. You can love her now. Open your eyes and touch her! Touch her now! Say, I love you. You are beautiful.

Benet slips out of the noose of the dead arms and puts Hester down gently on the long, silken sofa, but Aldrich merely stands there, his empty hands outstretched above her, still not quite touching. Still not letting her in.

Hester need not have died, of course. At Bay House or at Aunt Hope's cottage, they would have taken her in by the fire, or even at Schoolcraft's. The treehouse was her choice, and the long snow, and the ice, but the dead are never quite guilty of their own dying, no matter how much they desire it, no matter by what course they arrive at it. That great weight is left to the living, and Jacob carries it now, all turned into rage.

Suddenly Jennet's mechanical voice breaks in upon him. We had washed her, she says angrily, getting up from the piano. Could you not let her rest?

I must do something for him, she thinks, and the thin blade

of the word pounds at her like the ax on the ice. *I* must do it. I. I.

Benet shakes himself. He is down on one knee now, his back braced on the door frame, his musket aimed at Aldrich's belly. How could I leave her? he says. How *could* she rest with him yet alive and telling his lies in the world, as though she was nothing? He must tell her the truth, that he loved her! *I* must make him tell her!

Dazed and distant, Herod stares at the old gun, at Jennet, at Benet. What do you want here? he says vaguely to the Catcher. Who are you? Can't you see that my daughter is playing? Go back to your music, my dearest. Think nothing of him.

Jacob's whole body is shuddering, as though a current passed through him, as though he stood on an earthquake. Christ how I hate you. You takers and breakers. You stealers and dealers. You secret laughers. You door-closers. Hester told me about you, she warned me not to believe you. You don't eat food, you eat silk sofas and marble-topped tables. You shit grand pianos and pictures.

The room is growing cold and the candles dance and flicker in the draft, as Frayne steps unnoticed through the French windows behind them. I was so easy, Jacob is saying. I believed all your promises. Christ, you might as well kill me and eat me as use me like dirt.

Suddenly he pivots sideways and fires into the row of pot plants and the window explodes in a shower of glass that spits out at the girl and throws leaves and blossoms into Aldrich's face. Frayne has left his rifle with Aunt Hope, but it does not matter; he could not have used it on Jacob. He dives into the room like a heedless swimmer and grabs for Jennet, pulls her down to the floor and smashes her to him, and they lie there together, cocooned in one another against the flood of harm.

Don't move, Jacob says and fires into the piano, a terrible cacophony like the end of the world.

The girl shrinks against Frayne's body, her hands over her ears. Her pain is physical, he can feel it in all her muscles, feel the nerves jump against him. She lays her face flat against his chest to feel that his heart beats, that whatever the gun does, they are still inside one another, the same two people as before.

There is a clatter in the hall, and in a minute young Slocum stands open-mouthed in the doorway. For God's sake, man, he says to Jacob.

He takes another step and is swatted away with the barrel of the musket. Lie where you are, Benet says. Be quiet and don't move again. I have nothing against you. It's him.

Jesus save me, the boy mumbles, only half-conscious. His ribs are broken and his mouth is full of blood where he fell against the hall table. There is a loaded pistol on it, kept there in case of marauders.

But the Catcher does not see it. He does not see anything, now, but the lies. And Jennet.

Jacob, she says. She gets up from Frayne's side and moves toward Benet an inch at a time. Look at me, Jacob! Damn you, look!

She is alone now, and utterly free. John could force his care on her, dive for her again and smash her down, but the Catcher's gun has a life of its own, and any sudden movement may cause it to fire. Jennet steps lightly through the rubble of flowerpots and piano keys, the pellucid silk of her gown clinging against her like smoke. Her hands feeling the air in front of her, fingers spread open and faintly cupped.

Jacob, he's using you again. Don't lie down like a whore to him.

Whore? he growls and the trigger clicks. Frayne is not breathing, he has forgotten what it feels like.

Jennet is very near the Catcher now. You're worth more than he is, more than the whole pack of them, she says. Don't throw yourself away.

I don't care! Benet cries out. He must say it! I killed her, he must say that! I loved her and I killed her!

The musket explodes again, and the desk erupts into splinters of guilt, but Jennet does not flinch. She pulls away the lace at the throat of her gown so that her long, fragile throat is bared, and the swell of her small breasts. Touch me, Jacob, she commands him. Put the damn gun away. Give me your hand.

Catcher lifts his broad, pawlike hand from the musket, and the girl takes it up and lays it flat on her breast. This is life, she says. Here's what it feels like.

The gun is still in Benet's other arm and for a moment John Frayne thinks it is over, as the barrel slips downward, aimed harmlessly at the floor.

But Herod Aldrich sees nothing. He hardly seems aware of what is going on around him, of the choking stink of gunpowder and the rain of plaster and glass. He takes a step, then another, his feet moving him into the hall, the net still spread above him, above them all.

No! cries Benet. You will not walk away from me! He thrusts Jennet aside, tossing her light body like a dry branch. She crashes against the wall and slips down it, but Frayne dares not go to her now. The Catcher's gun is wild, it fires at the chandelier, at the Franklin stove, at the floorboards.

Say it! Say, I used you to death! Jacob moves slowly, keeping Aldrich's pace as though they are shackled together, and they step carefully over young Slocum, who still sprawls unconscious. Past the pistol on the hall table. Up the stair, marching up and up, till the portraits of mythical ancestors look down at them, bemused and aloof.

Say it, goddamn you! Jacob fires into the face of a sullen dowager in a silk gown, and the old canvas cracks with a sound like a stick in a fire. Then he turns the gun on Aldrich again.

But Herod scarcely seems to have noticed the barrage of musket fire. I don't know you, he says vaguely, looking down from the landing above as though he himself is painted on canvas. I must see to my guests now. If you care to stay to dinner, ask my daughter to have a place set for you in the kitchen.

The gun in Jacob's hand is invisible to him. Frayne and the half-conscious girl are only shadows at the foot of the stair. Aldrich goes up another step, and Benet sights the musket at the small of his back.

Let me help you, Jacob. Frayne runs soft-footed up the stair, till his mouth is almost in Benet's ear. Let me tell you a story.

The Catcher growls softly, his thick shoulders shaking. Christ. Why was I put in the world?

John Frayne seems to be calling him from a great distance. Jacob. Jacob. Listen. The boy loves you. Tim loves you.

One word has reached Benet, the only one that may save him. The boy, he whispers. He's a good boy.

The gun lowers as though of itself. It is over, Jennet thinks, and Frayne draws a breath so deep that his whole body shudders with it.

But it is too late. The front door creaks open and Hargrave and his lady and Judge Phillotson come in. "What's this!" cries the judge, almost tripping over the bloodied, moaning form of young Will Slocum. "What the devil?"

Then Celia Hargrave glances up at the hallway where Jacob still stands beneath the shattered portrait, his face turned to Aldrich and the gun dangling from his arm. She screams, and Hargrave dives past the judge to snatch up the pistol from the table.

Annnhhh-ahhhh! Jennet cries, the wordless birth-cry of instinct. John is between Jacob and the pistol, but Hargrave only cocks it and fires into the fancy plaster ceiling. Frayne's hand is almost there, almost grasping the butt of the musket to take it from Jacob, but geography prevents him. There are still three steps between himself and Benet. Eighteen inches due east. A half-turn to the southward.

The coefficients of time and space are too much for him. Hargrave has just enough time to fire into the ceiling again, and by instinct, by the will of his muscles and the nerves of his fingers, Jacob lifts the old musket and fires.

* ★ * ★ * ★ *

After that, it is a strangely slow and quiet, even calculated, business. The musket ball takes Herod Aldrich with a dull thump and very little blood, hitting him full in the chest and making only a small, almost imperceptible hole in his waistcoat. For a split second he peers down at it, puzzled. Something seems to be leaving him through it, but he cannot imagine that it might be a soul.

I am tired now, he says, and turns slightly away from them. I think I will not wait to dine.

John wrests the musket away and for a moment Catcher Benet wavers in the air, his feet scarcely touching the stair step. Frayne turns round to the others, to the girl who still waits open-mouthed at the foot of the staircase. It is over, he would have said. He has no other weapons.

But there is no time to speak. Bartram Hargrave glances at Phillotson, who blinks once or twice, taking time to unravel the message. Then he nods, and the invisible net that has hovered all the evening over Herod Aldrich comes down upon Jacob. There is a click and a flash from Hargrave's pistol, and Benet's animal body blooms red in the candlelight, his eyes taking in every fragment of life that remains to him. His dull black eyes fix last upon the girl Jennet, the sweet hollow of her throat.

But no words come from him. No cry escapes him. Jacob slumps down against Frayne and for a long moment the two men embrace, heads on one another's shoulders, sharing the wound between them. Then the weight is too much. They crash down together, tumbling head over heels to the bottom of the staircase. Like stricken lovers, they lie tangled together there, the one dead and the other unconscious, the silken body of the girl thrown across them both.

Hannah, Jennet thinks as she lies there, her mouth gaping soundlessly and the stolen paper scraping the soft skin of her breast. *How did you grow so pure from your anger? You who were sudden and wild and wise only in spite of yourself. How did you bloom and grow roots in this dark?*

*　　*　　*

In Bartram Hargrave's eye, something glitters like a nugget of gold, and on the upstairs landing, Herod Aldrich lies dead in the net of his power.

Under Sparrow's cheek, Frayne's heartbeat is steady and clean.

The Frenchman Leclerc has slept all that day in the back room of Schoolcraft's tavern, and when he wakes it is dark again. A single candle burns by the bedside, and in its glow he can see the swollen shape of the girl Nancy moving among the shadows. For a moment he feigns sleep, observing her cautious movements, how she picks up a white pitcher with a cracked lip and pours out water into a tin basin. How she sets the pitcher down again, wiping the lip with a cloth as though she were stanching a wound.

What room is this? he says.

Mine. She sits beside him on the narrow bed and begins to wash his face with the cloth.

Where are the others, the men and the young soldier-boys? Have they all gone?

Yes, Nancy tells him. Long ago. When she has said it, her small white teeth bite down on her cracked lower lip and she looks away from him. They're having the fancy ball in town tonight. You've slept the clock round, or nearly.

Her hand moves the cold wet cloth in a circle, letting it lie for a moment on his parched lips so that he can suck the water out. He has learned something now; he knows that liquor dehydrates and a drunk is a desert. Leclerc lies with his eyes closed and she wrings out the rag again and puts it across them.

I've never drunk so much before, he mumbles. My head aches.

Tell me your name like you did last night, she says, and lifts his hand to her lips. I like to hear it. I wasn't always this kind of a woman. I had a home once, and a chair with pieced cushions. A featherbed we would air in the springtime.

Last night, he says. Marius cannot remember much more than

this girl and a clutter of music, but there is something, something. I don't remember. Where have the men gone, Nancy?

She lies down beside him, her body cupped in the curve of his own. Don't think of it now, she tells him. I want to love you, I wanted you all night when you were sleeping. You're so kind, and it wasn't your fault.

Fault? He tries to sit up and his head seems to explode. He half-expects to see it drop off and roll away, like the head of a Russian soldier he saw beheaded by a cannonball. What have I done? What have I said? You must tell me, I went mad last night and I cannot remember! Where have the men gone? What are they doing?

They mean to kill your friend Frayne, she says. To take his gold.

But there *is* no gold!

She sits up on the edge of the bed. They think there is. When they asked you, you said there was treasure.

I? But I only meant— Marius stands up and almost falls, the room swirling around him. His bad ankle will not support him and he sits down hard on the floor. Fool, he says. Fool. I must stop them! I cannot betray him so, I must make things right!

Did you hear me? she says quietly. What I said before. I love you. Let me come with you. I can't stay in the world by myself anymore.

Marius has no horse and no mule and his foot is bad and she is heavy with the child and the snow is still deep on the forest trails where no one has ridden or walked. It is not far to Bay House by the main road, but they go by a roundabout way—a slow progress that takes more than an hour—in case Caleb and the others are watching them from the darkness.

They are barely in sight of the black hulk of Bay House when Nancy cries out. See? They are waiting for him! There, the light!

Cursing the loss of his spectacles, Leclerc can just glimpse a torch flare in the woods above the meadow at the back of the house. In a moment another answers it, off to the left. They haven't gone in for the gold yet, Nancy tells him. Caleb's waiting for something, he wants to hurt them, he likes it. Her hand reaches for Leclerc's. Jesus I hate him, she says.

They plod on through the snow, and when they are close enough to catch sight of the candlelight in the kitchen window of Bay House, the pregnant girl stops to rest on a tree stump, easing herself awkwardly down and wincing as the child kicks inside her. She looks up at Marius, the moon washing her face. You haven't asked whose it is.

Leclerc takes off her mitten and chafes her cold fingers and kisses them. *Je le sais, ma chérie,* he whispers. It is yours.

"Frayne ain't home. Ain't nobody in there but the blind man and the boy and the old black witch." Guido scuttled back to the foot of a big maple in the sugar bush beyond the meadow and stuck his torch in the snow. "I looked in the window and they never seen me. We could go in and get that gold and be gone 'fore Frayne ever gets wind of it."

"No. I want him. I want that bitch-girl of his."

"Aw, Cab, now. You got old Nancy, ain't you? Nancy's a sensible girl."

"Shut your jabber." From the branch where he sat, Caleb Beck could see the road from the town and the snowy face of the lake and the narrow track that led round it to Bay House. All night he had seen nothing but a doe and a family of possums, but now all at once another kind of shadow moved. "See there!" he said with the arrogance of a major general. "I told you they'd come."

Two shapes made their way through the deep snow, a woman in a long cloak and a man in a heavy, dark overcoat, their faces muffled in hoods and scarves. "That's the crazy woman, all right," Guido said. "I know that old raggedy cape she wears." He squinted into the luminous, snowy darkness. "But that ain't Frayne. Ain't wearing that old skin cloak of his. Looks like some nob or other, come out from the town."

The figures—Leclerc and the tavern girl—disappeared into the dark spruce woods; from there on, they would not be seen clearly again till the house door opened to them and the candlelight showed up their outlines. Caleb dropped down from the branch and picked up his musket. "Get Teague down here," he commanded, and Guido moved into the open and waved the torch up and down, up and down.

No torchlight answered. Guido signalled again, but there was still no reply. "Reckon he ain't there, Cab," he said, with the whine in his voice that meant he himself was weighing the virtues of a hasty retreat. "Reckon he weaseled out on us, and two of us ain't enough to take Frayne. Not with the old man and the boy to help him. And that old witch, she ain't nothin' to joke about, neither. I guess Aldrich'll wait for his gold."

They had not been in the town, they knew nothing of the fall of King Herod. "Goddammit, Guy." Caleb spat brown tobacco juice into the snow. "You want that gold, or don't you?"

Guido jittered. "Sure I do, Cab. You bet your life I do."

The two travellers reach Bay House and Leclerc raps on the kitchen window; old Gabriel unlatches it, letting it swing open to release the fragrance of pipe smoke and venison stew. That you, Frenchman? Gabe says in his deep voice. What's up? Is that my lass there with you? Where's Jack?

Je vous en prie, monsieur! I beg you, put out the candle and let us come in! There are men in the woods!

The boy Timothy smashes the wick with his thumb as Benet has taught him, and the Frenchman and Nancy slip into the dark room. It is not very warm, the fire is banked and it is cold enough to freeze coffee in a cup five feet away from the hearth. But to the tavern girl, it feels like a warm place.

The five of them huddle close to the embers and patch their

stories together, the boy's eyes wide and Aunt Hope clutching
Frayne's rifle and murmuring, I knowed it, or growling under her
breath, Them scum. When they have finished, she gets up and
puts on her old black cloak and pulls the stocking-toe cap down
tight on her ears with a muffler on top of it. Gonna get me a
chopping-ax, she says. Chop off that scum's head like a chicken,
if I get me the chance.

No! Nancy cries. Caleb will hurt you! He's a bastard, you don't
know him, he hurts everything!

Aunt Hope looks her up and down, turned aside from her
purpose. You not far from your time, honey. You gone big as a
punkin. You stay still and don't fret, now.

Leclerc is silent, staring into the fire. Through no will of his
own, he has betrayed more than John Frayne and the others, and
he knows it. Something has grown up in this ruin that matters in
the world, that has stature and gravity and honor, and he carries
it now on his shoulders. The loom with the blue cloth upon it.
The spinning wheel. The books. The polished boards. If Guido
and Caleb and the others break in and tear at it with greed-
poisoned fangs, what was made here will sicken and crumble and
never come back again, it will never again dare to exist in the
world. What name can he give it? Something to rest in. Something
to die for. A clean place in the heart.

And to the girl Nancy, too, he owes a debt. I love you, she
said to him. Surely such a gift requires recompense.

I must cleanse myself for her, he thinks, and be whole. I must
lead the wolves away.

It is then that Marius remembers what he has labored so long
to forget—the bitter cold morning at Austerlitz, how the Russians
were led onto the ice in pursuit of a decoy detachment, how the
bugles had blown and more and more had followed, thousands of
men and horses and carts and dogs strangely no longer running
toward war, but away from it. I must trick them, he says aloud. I
must make a delusion that will lead them out onto the ice.

It is why he was saved with this knowledge inside him, why
he limped away into the dead cart and escaped, why he was drawn

to the Bay of Spirits. To use this terrible trick in the service not of death nor of conquest, but of life.

Frayne's buffalo robe is lying by the hearth and Leclerc picks it up and throws it around his shoulders, tying the rawhide thongs across his chest. Seeing him, Nancy gets up from the fire. What are you doing? They'll take you for John Frayne and they'll shoot you!

He lays a hand on her hair. They must catch me first, *ma belle*.

But your leg is bad, you can't run from them! And you haven't even got a gun!

I can shoot, Tim tells them quietly. And my—my father left us his rifle.

Everything about Timothy is quiet. Like the girl before Frayne's return, he is half in one familiar world and half in another he may never wish to explore any further. Gabriel has shown him the treasure and Aunt Hope has told him about Hester, and for a long while the boy sat alone with a candle in the half-restored library, tearless and voiceless, poring silently over the Captain's old books, the sea charts and maps. Perhaps it was their crumbling paper that broke him at last, their sense of huge unmeasured distances like the one between himself and Hester, both dead and living. Gabe and Aunt Hope heard his sobs in the kitchen, in the stable, in the workroom. There was no place to escape them.

When he came out, Tim was quiet again, a little boy who at ten years old has forgotten forever what it is to be young.

I'll go with you, he tells Leclerc. I'll go out in the grove and keep watch with the Lancaster, and if they come, I'll fire off a warning. Then you go out of the front door, like you're my— Like you're Frayne, on the run from them. The snow's deep there, they won't be expecting it if you take that way, it'll buy you some time. You can be near out of their range on the lake before they even spot you.

It is a good enough plan, and the only one they have. Give

me a torch, says the Frenchman, and Aunt Hope binds a rag around the end of the poker, soaks it with tallow, and sets it alight.

Take this, says Nancy, and she gives him Frayne's long ice-pole. Hold it in the middle. If you fall through, don't let go of it, let it catch on the hole. You can pull yourself up, if you just don't let go.

Frayne and Jennet are on their way home.

It is a strange sensation, this knowledge of owning a place in the world, and although they both have desired it, it frightens them both. When they reach the last curve of the shore before the path to Bay House, they pause in the darkness, she on the mare's broad back and he on foot, leading her. Keeping a last fragment of distance between them. Must we own one another now, become one another's possessions? If we grow too many roots here, will we girdle and die?

I thought you had left me, Jennet says, and slides down from the mare's back to stand beside John in the darkness, where she can hold up her palm to his mouth and catch his words in her fist.

I know you did, he says. Gabriel told me, when I took the boy home. I'm sorry.

She laughs in the darkness. When I thought so, I was angry at first, and then I was hurt, and then scared. And then something else came. I can live without you now, if I have to. Without anybody.

Years later, when they have travelled away from each other in different directions and returned and travelled again, at times when they are both far from the Bay of Spirits, he will keep an inventory of everything he should have said in reply to these words of hers, on this night, in this place. But for now he can only be silent, feeling the ache of the simple truth that sparrows, unbroken, will fly away.

Did you read the paper I stole for us? she asks him.

Stole for *you*, you mean.

For me, yes. For me.

You didn't have to steal it, he says sharply. You could have been killed.

His body resists her when she touches him, even his flesh is angry, afraid of losing her. Will they give you back all the land now? she says. Will you be richer than Aldrich? Will you be squire?

Who, me? Now it is Frayne's turn to laugh. Not likely. I still don't have the deed, and besides, I don't want a court battle. God knows what might happen.

The west, you mean. Fort McKittrick.

The army may still come for me, Jennet. You must never forget that.

But we can stay for a while, though. For now?

Yes. They'll sell me back the house, that's all I want. Tim will have it when he grows up. I don't care about anything else.

Me neither, she says, letting her free hand drift down onto his chest. Why did that man have to shoot Jacob?

If Benet had come to trial, it would all have come out. What dirtied Aldrich would have dirtied them. They had used him too long, he was one of them.

And Jacob wasn't. He wasn't anyone's.

Her face is wet with tears when he touches it. How could you risk yourself for his sake as you did tonight? he whispers, and buries his face in her shoulder. After what he did to you. After the net. The ice. How can you mourn him so?

I don't mourn him, she says. I just mourn.

A gunshot. To Jennet, it is like the stamp of a foot on an attic floor, but Frayne recognizes the sound of his Lancaster rifle.

He stares into the dark and she feels his body grow tense again, but this time not from anger. He says nothing, only grips her hard by the hand and begins to run, pulling her after him, leaving the horse behind.

What is it, what's that smell?

There is smoke in the air, and Jennet can see a strange flickering light on the lake. The thatched roof of the stable is burning, the flames racing into the clump of yellow birch that grows beside it, making a huge finger of light in the darkness.

Get the mule out! Frayne hears Gabe's deep voice bellow. The frightened lowing of the little cow and the honking bray of the pack mule, the skittering cackle of chickens.

Look! the girl cries, and they stop dead still.

On the lake-ice, a dark figure is running, floundering through twenty inches of snow, the long ice-pole balanced in one hand like a tightrope walker's staff. By the light of the torch he carries above his head, they can see the buffalo robe around him, and the gleam of his balding head where his hair no longer covers it.

It's the Frenchman, Frayne murmurs. See how he drags that foot? What's he doing out there?

Look at me! Jennet tugs at him. Look at me when you talk! I can't hear you!

The Frenchman, Frayne says into her hand, and points at the lake.

Two more torches bob and stumble behind Leclerc, moving farther and farther out onto the lake-ice. It's Frayne, all right! cries Caleb's voice. See that buff hide? We smoked him out with the fire! Circle around, now! Cut him off!

Jennet and Frayne start to run again, out onto the ice in the wake of the torches, pine smoke filling their noses, their lungs. Frayne's legs are longer, and he has learned in the west how to wade through deep snow in moccasins, curling his toes under like claws. But Jennet fights her way gamely after him, silently following the moving torches, keeping back just enough to be hidden by the darkness, scarcely seeing the bodies of the Frenchman's pursuers, who do not know they are secretly his quarry.

Then suddenly Frayne sees them clearly—three men and three torches, not more than fifty yards ahead. Leclerc bobs and circles, waving the light like a beacon. Come, he cries out to the darkness. Come for me!

The unbroken snow is too deep for Guido, he is scrawny and short-legged, and when Caleb stops running and braces his musket, the little man falls face down and lies there, spent and useless.

Frayne! Caleb shouts at the Frenchman. We come for the gold! We got Aldrich's warrant to throw you out! If you give us the gold, we won't hurt you!

Leclerc is still moving, the long pole bobbing up and down in his hands like a well-sweep. When it strikes the ice to his right, he feels an odd pulpy resilience, like knocking your fist on a melon. He veers to the left, putting the patch of rotten ice directly between them.

Come for me! he shouts again, the words broken apart by the cold and his accent, so that they sound almost like Jennet's. Come. For. Me.

Caleb fires his musket into the ice at the Frenchman's heels. Frayne, goddammit! he squawks.

Go back! John Frayne orders Jennet. Firing into the ice can take them all down. Even now, cracks are spreading out from the hole Caleb's bullet has made, and he must be stopped before he fires again.

Aldrich is dead! John calls out to him. He can't give any more orders.

What the devil? Caleb whips around, staring, but all he sees is a man in a gentleman's double-caped greatcoat. It isn't Frayne, it can't be. Frayne wears a buffalo robe.

Christ Joseph, Guido moans. It's them spooks.

Here! cries Leclerc, still inching to the left. Without his spectacles, he cannot see Frayne, with Jennet still coming on through the snow behind him. They are dark blurs on the shadowed ice beyond Caleb's torchlight. I am here, Marius calls again. Come and get me!

Caleb Beck! Frayne moves closer, counting on confusion to protect him. Didn't you hear me? Herod Aldrich is dead, shot to death in his own house.

Caleb's mind is thick and dark with fear for a moment, and then, slowly, inevitably, the wheels of greed begin to turn in him, and the golden gears to grind. Aldrich is dead now. Two-thirds of the treasure was to be his, but now it is all mine. The Tory gold is mine.

He begins to run again. Here I am, shouts the Frenchman. No, here! Frayne echoes. Confused, Caleb dashes first in one direction, then in the other, tossed back and forth by their voices. He snatches up Guido's rifle and fires into the patch of rotten ice a few yards from Frayne and Jennet, and no more than two feet from Leclerc.

John feels the ice tremble and heave under him, then slip side-wise. Jennet is motionless beside him, her eyes fixed on Caleb, and Frayne drags her away a split second before the mouth of the world opens below them. Get back! he shouts.

But Caleb has no time for more than a strangled shout as he goes down. Then there is a slight cracking noise, the sound ice making a fault line from the rotten patch that has caved away with the impact of gunshot. Beneath the snow, the cracks are invisible, there is no knowing which way they have travelled.

Guido scuttles away on all fours, making for the eastern bank, and the three friends are alone on the ice now, the torches all quenched. Despite the danger, there is a sense of relief among them, that they are alone now and clean. Leclerc stands motionless, not even breathing, as he stares at the gaping black hole in the snow-covered ice. It is man-shaped, the size of a grave, the water almost as dense as fresh-dug earth.

I want to live now, Marius whispers. Mary Mother of God let me live.

Frenchman! John calls to him. Keep hold of the pole and walk backward. Straight back. Don't turn around, and try to keep your weight even. The crack hasn't run that far or you'd be down by now.

Marius takes one step back, but with the second, his bad ankle twists sidewise, strained beyond endurance. He topples forward and there is a terrible smashing sound as the faulted ice splits apart. Jennet gives a terrible howl and Frayne grips her hard by the hand to keep her from running. They can do no more than watch as Leclerc goes straight down into the crevice that grows broader and broader, the thick black water irresistible. For a split second the two ends of the pole catch on the sound ice to both sides of the crack, and Marius hangs from one hand there.

I betrayed you! he says to Frayne. I was drunk. I was mad. I told them about the gold.

To hell with gold. Hold on. John's voice urges him, probes

his mind as it rises and falls. Your hand is your soul, it has a grain like fine wood. Hold on with your fine soul, Marius. Be wood now. Be a floorboard. A bookshelf. You don't belong on a pile of corpses. Hold on till I come. Be a chair. Be a loom.

Lying full length on the ice, Frayne inches himself almost to the edge of the dark water where Leclerc dangles, holding out Guido's musket for the Frenchman to catch hold of. I am gone! Marius cries out, as the ice under one end of the pole breaks away and sends him down.

One minute, perhaps two, a man can keep breathing in such cold. There is no time to fetch ropes and pulleys, no time to be sensible. John takes off his greatcoat and jacket and slips into the water, and the last thing he hears is Jennet's wail.

They are long minutes, longer than centuries, and it is darker under the ice than any death he has ever imagined, and so cold that his body curls itself in a circle, like a landed fish in a bucket. The weight of the water is brutal, so bitterly heavy that he cannot swim in it, cannot make his arms and legs move because the brain can no longer send signals through the smashed nerves and muscles. Objects bump against him now and then, but he cannot see what they are. Perhaps they are tree branches, or boxes of treasure. Perhaps they are Tacha's small bones, or Hannah's. Sounds, though, seem to be magnified, the bash of the dense water against his ears like cannonfire.

Then there is a suction, the water pulling him sideways toward some object, a fallen tree or a submerged rock. He drags himself, gauging the shape of it in case it is Leclerc. But it is too small. The body of Caleb, already frozen solid, curled like a shellfish and sinking down slowly to rest on the lake bottom. By sheer will, he eases himself away from it; if it freezes onto him, it will drag him down like an anchor.

Frayne leaves Caleb behind him, fights upward, the water bearing down on him. Past, present, future tangle together, all the tenses battling in the slam of his heartbeat.

One minute is gone now. My father is richer than yours is, he's got a whole barrel of gold. A lie lives in the world till the teller is dead. I am dead now. Iko the Toad is dead. If I come through into the air, I will be somebody new. Do the dead think? Do they hope for the living? I fear the wild beasts. I fear the wild winds. I kiss the green earth of my fathers. Forgive me the first lie now, Papa, the most terrible. Let me die clean, let me be clear like the ice.

Something kicks him full in the face and he tastes blood in his mouth. I am dead. Do the dead bleed? A pair of boots that do not seem to have legs attached to them dangles in front of him and Frayne digs his fingers into the sodden leather, claws his way inch by inch. The Frenchman's legs, they are stiff with cold.

Later in his life, when he is an old man struggling to pick up a baby's rattle from the floor, Frayne will remember the mysterious strength of his own arms that pushes Leclerc's inert body upwards, till they break through together into the air with the torchlight above them and the faces of the boy Tim and of Aunt Hope and Jennet, and the strange tear-stained face of Nancy, and Gabriel's huge hands waiting to catch them and pull them in like a pair of gaffed salmon from the cold breast of Spirit Bay.

Saku? Do the white gods believe in salvation?

Not without dying.

Ha-no-nah. There is nothing to dying. It is living that turns fools into gods.

Exhausted, not able to stop shivering no matter how many quilts Jennet piles over him, John Frayne lies flat on his back by the workroom hearth that night, with his head in her lap and the Frenchman murmuring to Nancy in their bed in the corner, a soft musical sound like snow-melt slipping down rocks.

In the spring, will you dig me a garden? Jennet asks him. I want to plant carrots for Tim. They make your hair curl, Hannah said so.

He laughs, looking up at her. I didn't know you could play the piano. Who taught you? Your aunt? Do you hear it, or only imagine you hear it?

You ask too many questions. Read to me.

At her command, his voice rises, his fingertips stroking the sainted hollow of her throat.

I have never set eyes on anything like you.
Not man nor woman nor spirit nor god, nor the paragon of animals.
I look at you and the wonder of your wild heart overwhelms me.

They sleep a long time, very deeply, and near morning he wakes to the rise and fall of the treadles and the rough-soft voice of her loving that feeds him like breast-milk.

Thank you for carrots. Thank you for the color of blue.